UN-CIVIL SERVICE

Stephan Michael Loy

MID-WORLD ARTS
Indianapolis, Indiana

For Amy, my First Reader.
Also for the Pen to Paper Writers' Critique Group,
who inspired the germ of this story.

Many thanks to the
Indianapolis Writers' Meetup Group,
without whose help this work
would not shine.

And special thanks to Rich, Belinda, and Linda
my final readers before publication.

Other Books
By Stephan Michael Loy

Nightwatch Series:
Last Days and Times
Shining Star
Fiona Street
Galactic Geographic
Redemption Song
Bad Lands
Uncivil Service
Voice of the City
Transporter

All Novels:
Last Days and Times
Isis Wept
Shining Star
Conqueror's Realm
Fiona Street
Redemption Song
Galactic Geographic
Bad Lands
Uncivil Service
Voice of the City
Transporter

Trade Paperback Editions
Available through **Draft2Digital.com**
Hardcover Editions
Available through **Lulu.com**

ebook Novellas and Long Short Stories
Available through Smashwords.com
Ridealong
Bug Hunt
Blood and Water

Part One: Nightmare

"Hello, hello. Remember me?
I'm everything you can't control."

--*What You Want*, Evanescence

Prologue: Visitation

Lieutenant-colonel Allen Sanders still pulled on the heavy, camouflaged shirt of his ACU fatigues when he marched through the thrown-open doors to the Lawrence-Livermore Trans-Universal Field Generator facility. In his wake tromped three heavily armed soldiers, their Field Officer, and the Officer of the Guard. They met a short, plump woman in jeans, sandals, and a faded t-shirt showing GEEK CRED! in bold lettering, a Star Wars movie poster under the words. Four soldiers, also in armor and weapons, stood gathered in a semi-circle behind her.

"Report!" Sanders called into the gathering.

The soldiers deferred to the t-shirted woman.

"We've experienced an operational anomaly," she said, raking her fingers through her short, unkempt brown hair. Her voice sounded hollow in the canyon of the atrium. Except for the ceiling tiles fifty feet up, all the surfaces were polished terrazzo. "I can't imagine what caused it, but we're efforting that analysis right--"

"Chief Engineer Eglemann." Sanders's tone rumbled. "It's two o'clock in the morning. English, please."

The woman froze. She scrunched up her face as if she smelled something bad. "The generator's active."

"Active? What exactly do you mean?"

"It turned on. We have a trans-universal event forming in the well."

No one spoke for a second. Sanders stared across the wide, empty atrium at the massive double doors to the generator room. "It turned on," he finally said. "I wasn't aware it even worked."

Eglemann winced. "Yes, sir. That's precisely the problem."

The colonel turned to his Field Officer of the Guard, a thin, hard-carved captain with a hatchet-cut frown on his face. "Place a perimeter around this building. No one comes or goes without our knowing." He acknowledged a brief affirmation, then turned a sour eye on the t-shirted woman. "Eglemann, you're with me, and I want your explanations somewhat more lucid." He strode toward the double doors, Eglemann falling in beside him.

"Right now I can't imagine what to tell you," the engineer said. "We were doing dry calibrations, not even a power source engaged, and the thing ... just ... turned ... on."

They reached the doors. Sanders put his hand on the palm reader near the twin latches. "You're an engineer," he said as the reader scanned him. "I shouldn't have to inform you that it can't just turn on. It's connected to two secure nuclear piles and it would take authorization from the Director of National Security or two United States senators--"

"I know that. I also know we have a Category 1 trans-universal event standing beyond these doors and I have no idea how to shut it down."

Frowning at that, Sanders thrust down on the two latches and hauled open the massive doors. The action required effort, but not as much as the size of the doors suggested. Hydraulics hummed in the wall around the entry, assisting in a task no man could manage alone. The atrium filled with a baritone hum, shouts from multiple voices, and the crackle of static discharges.

Sanders and Eglemann pushed into a scene of confused desperation. A dozen or more technicians in white lab coats tore around an expansive circular chamber, a great, towering cavern of man-made space. The curved walls were faced with seven-foot-tall electronic cabinets on two levels, and freestanding control consoles stood positioned just clear of the overhanging upper gallery. The technicians darted from console to console and panel to panel, yelling to their counterparts on either of the levels. They shouted in dry-mouthed urgency, too loud even accounting for the reverberating hum and static chatter. Though Sanders understood none of the technical jargon flying through the air, he had seen enough of war and black hellholes to know the sound of fear.

In the middle of that confusion, ranging between a thirty-meter disk of ceramic hexagons on the floor and an equally yawning parabolic dish fixed to the fifty-foot ceiling, a wavering tendril of orange light twisted, sputtered, and flared. It danced between the two focusing platforms and within the bounds set by four hulking, antennae-peppered pylons arranged around the ceramic circle. The light didn't seem content to stay there. It wanted out, and to grow.

Someone, seeing Eglemann and the colonel from the second-floor gallery, leaned on the safety rail and yelled down to them. "Power throughput's up twenty-seven percent! We're measuring gravimetric distortions at the perimeter!"

One of the white coats ran up to Eglemann, panting and sweaty. He shoved a tablet computer into her hands. "We've confirmed the reactors are offline," he said. "We can't figure out where the lightning post is coming from."

"Are the N-space positioning sensors heated up?" Eglemann asked, glancing at a barrage of readouts on the tablet.

"On standby."

"Activate. We may not have a cause, but we can plot where the thing is coming from."

"Gotcha." The tech ran toward a console across the room.

"Explain." Sanders wanted to castigate someone. It wasn't professional, but there it was.

"It's all bad news, sir. We've got this event, it's barely held in check by the attenuation pylons, it's growing in energy throughput, and we can't bleed it off because the reactors are offline. We can't control what happens here. If the thing balloons up and we're inside its horizon..."

"We'll be transported to who knows where in who knows what universe and we'll arrive as wrong as a three-legged race horse."

"Yes, sir."

"What about the iron?"

"The iron in the attenuation pylons is all that's holding the event in check. If the throughput level increases much more, those countermeasures may fail."

"Increases by how much?"

She winced. "We don't know."

"Eglemann. We've invested two years and four billion dollars in this little science project of yours--"

"Respectfully, we didn't have the slightest inkling of this level of physics *until* two years ago. We're in baby steps, colonel. Don't expect miracles."

Sanders leaned in to within a few inches of Eglemann's face. "Don't expect miracles? When that thing, that Bright Lights Tornado from Hell, is threatening to whisk us all to the Twilight Zone? I think a miracle or two is called for."

Just then, as if it had been listening, the orange pillar of light winked out. An audible snap, then the humming was gone along with the static charge. A strange blue afterglow punctuated the normalized lighting.

Eglemann glanced around, her eyes narrowed.

"Good job," the colonel said. He relaxed -- slightly -- for the first time since the guard shook him awake. "I'll see to making you a saint just as soon as I've had breakfast."

"Uhh, I didn't do that."

Gunfire. Not just a shot, but a long argument between weapons. Egle-mann jumped. The techs taking electronics readings froze in their tracks. Sanders flinched his hand toward a weapon he didn't carry.

The Field Officer of the Guard hurried in past the cracked-open double doors. He was just slapping his pistol back into its holster. "Sir, there's been an incident. With the guard, sir." The captain's eyes shone wide and distant. The man was rattled.

"What do you advise?" Sanders asked. The man had gone four tours in Iraq and Somalia. He could be trusted to keep an even strain.

"Keep the civilians here, escort any others inside the facility to here, and you come with me, sir. I've three men I can trust to guard these folks."

"What's going on?" Eglemann asked.

"Stay here," Sanders told her. "Gather information. I'll be back."

He followed his man to the doors. When they passed through to the atrium, Sanders held a hand out to one of the guards stationed there. "Soldier, your sidearm," he said.

The guard handed over a loaded Beretta and an extra clip.

"This way, sir," the captain urged, and moved to exit the building. He sent two men each in opposite directions through the facility to gather any civilians not already in the generator room. Two more men he left at the doors to the generator, then another prowling the space between the atrium entrance and the generator room's double doors. Each soldier held his assault rifle ready for use.

Outside, only the captain's men occupied the street. No curious onlookers. Of course, there wouldn't be any at that time of morning. The Lawrence-Livermore complex was not a live-in posting. The Officer of the Guard, a wiry first lieutenant, met his captain and colonel with four additional men. The soldiers watched outward against something the officers hadn't disclosed. Still Sanders kept his mouth shut. These were his people; he knew what they were worth. They'd speak when they needed to.

They led him right to the guard shack.

Sanders saw three soldiers posted at good cover outside the low cinder block building. He knew there were others. A secure perimeter had been formed.

"First shift was due to be awakened in four hours," the captain finally said. "Lieutenant, deploy the men to augment security."

"Yes, sir." The Officer of the Guard took his four grunts and tromped into the dark.

"I'm sorry, sir, it's a mess." The captain shook his head. He grabbed at the collar of his armor as if the unit didn't fit properly. "Sixth shift had just come on and fifth was still up and about, so those are the men you see out here."

12

Sanders pricked up his ears. He heard sirens on the horizon, and the phantom drum of helicopter rotors.

Noticing his colonel's interest, the captain made a vague gesture toward those wails in the night. "We had to call them. SOP. And we can't handle the wounded alone."

"The wounded?"

The captain led Sanders up the walk to the guardhouse and through the door. "Cisneros from first shift, he must have gotten up. He came in here, they tell me, and took up one of the weapons fifth was waiting to sign in."

They stalked through the front office, with the counter, the desk, and the two chairs for the Officer and the Sergeant of the Guard. They crossed this to the back room, the common room, where the guard shifts took their orders and stood inspection. The room was an open space with three vinyl couches along one wall and a pool table far to the rear. The door to the arms room carved out a section of wall across from the couches. That door hung open. No armorer guarded the weapons in the space beyond.

He was instead in the common area, ministering to a dozen men in various stages of undress, many of them bloodied, a few of them laid out on the floor. Two uniformed medics moved among the wounded, as did a number of uninjured troops. Except for the bright fluorescent light and the magazines on the tables, it looked like the aftermath of an ambush.

"He ... Cisneros ... said something." The captain paused half way across the room. He looked toward a door at the back wall, at the colonel, then again at the door at the rear of the room. He didn't see the men around him. "He spoke just after taking the weapon, from right there in the door to the bunks. He just took the weapon and went back there."

For a moment it seemed the captain would go no farther. He had taken his commander to the virtual threshold of something terrible and seemed rooted by a crippling internal tumult. Sanders eyed the doorway to the sleeping quarters, stewed on what the captain had said -- *He spoke just after taking the weapon* -- and glanced about the room. Two video cameras nested in the front and back corners. He'd have to get hold of those recordings.

The captain wrestled whatever demon besieged him, then shook his head as if throwing off a punch. "In here, sir," and he walked through the sleeping room doorway.

Sanders followed, fighting an urge to flee the way he had come. The bunk room stank of shit, blood, guts, and cordite, the smells so strong, so intermingled, so thick that they were trapped there. The walls showed spatters in red, white, and gray -- blood, bone, and organ meat. Bodies littered the beds and floor, some of them face down in a viscous fright show of pooling bodily excretions. Sanders wanted to scream. He wanted to rage. These were his soldiers. And if the captain intimated clearly, one of his own had murdered them.

But Sanders did not rage. He kept his commander's face intact. He set his jaw against quivering muscles and scanned the carnage.

One man stood amid that death. The Sergeant of the Guard seemed planted like a statue before a messy stack of two torn bodies on a blood-soaked bunk. One ravaged corpse lay splayed across the remains of a man still tucked beneath sodden Army blankets. The sergeant stared at the dead meat before him and showed no emotion.

"God in Heaven," Sanders muttered, then, more loudly, "How many?"

"Fourteen," the captain said, his voice cracking. "First, second, and third shifts in bed. A few escaped. Fourth shift was still up. They were in the common room."

Sanders steeled himself and cruised slowly up the long center aisle between lined-up bunks. He tried not to get too much muck on his boots. He knew these troops. He had inspected them, counseled them, been privileged to promote them. And they were dead, killed by their own. In peacetime. On home soil. "Cisneros," he said when he came up to the sergeant. They both stared at the almost naked, violated body thrown across another man's bunk.

"Yes, sir," the captain said.

The Sergeant of the Guard just stared at the corpse.

"How..." Sanders's voice fell away from him. He dragged it back to duty. "How did you stop him?"

The captain said nothing, just turned his eyes on the sergeant. The colonel's gaze made it there, too.

"He wasn't right," the sergeant said. His tone held no inflection. "I was with fifth shift, signing in weapons. Durham, that asshole, let Cisneros take his rifle. Cisneros spouted some crazy shit standing in the door, then he came back here, smooth as you please. And started shooting." The sergeant shook himself, but didn't take his eyes off the body. "I didn't know what to think. I was on my way to him before he went through the door. I was gonna chew his ass for shit talk and breaking protocol. Then I heard the bolt go back, and the shooting. Then men were screaming, running, barreling past me. I had trouble getting through the door..."

"It's all right, sarge." The captain's voice sounded as dead as his NCO's. "It couldn't be helped."

The sergeant gave no hint of hearing. "Then I broke through, and he was shooting them in their beds. And I ... put him down."

Sanders stared at the sergeant for what felt like a full minute. In that time, sirens wailed up and landed outside. The definite *WHOP! WHOP! WHOP!* of helicopters reverberated overhead. After a while, Sanders forced his eyes onto Cisneros, or what was left of him. The man's shoulders, head, and one arm hung off the bed. He lay there precariously balanced at the edge of the mattress, nearly upside down. He was naked except for his sand-colored boxers. His torso was almost split in two, but the kind of split you get from a chainsaw or a shark attack. Or an assault rifle held by a brother-in-arms.

Then Sanders recalled the defensive posture of the soldiers outside. "Is everyone accounted for?"

"No, sir," the captain said. "Three missing."

"Which shift?" But Sanders already knew.

"First, sir."

The sergeant tore his eyes away from the almost naked body for the first time. Those eyes were dead. "I didn't move a thing. Because this is, like, a crime scene. Right?"

"Yes, sergeant, and that was forward thinking of you." Sanders gave him one last look, then turned back up the room. He grabbed the captain on his way to the door. "I want every man accounted for. If you trust them, they gear up. If you don't, lock them in detention. Those orders stand until we find those other three."

"Yes, sir. And what do we do when we find them?"

They burst into the common room, which filled with EMTs carrying stretchers and body bags. Two sheriff's deputies interviewed soldiers, and a crewman from air medevac made initial evaluations of the wounded. Only the beginning, Sanders thought. It would get a lot worse, real fast.

"We subdue and capture them. These are our people. Weapons loose but restricted." They dodged through the increasing crowd, the police drawing near to Sanders. The colonel raised a finger to them and leaned close to his captain. "What the hell happened here, Bob? Does it have anything to do with the generator?"

The captain's eyes were clouded. He was still in recovery. "I don't know. To tell the truth, I'm not too clear on what the generator is. But, sir..." and he squeezed his eyes shut for one mental shake of his head. He opened them and locked his newly steadied gaze on his superior, daring the colonel to dismiss what he'd say. "The men told me -- *all* the men told me -- that he had his eyes closed when he did it. Like he was asleep."

Sanders clamped his teeth shut on "You must be crazy!" He'd have to see that security video. "Find those three men. They may be casualties or they may be threats. Either way, they're problems. And check on our civilians. They and the generator are the only thing here worth attacking."

"Wilco, sir." A stronger, oriented captain sent the colonel a perfunctory salute, then pushed his way out of the guard shack.

Sanders stood a little straighter. He breathed a little easier. He had to. The cops waited behind him. They'd want answers to questions. They'd want the run of the barracks, perhaps even the entire base. And they'd want the video. Sanders had to give them nothing. He clasped his hands behind his back, still holding the pistol, and turned.

"I'm sorry, officers," he said evenly. "It's a little crazy around here. How may I help you?"

One of the deputies touched the brim of his Smokey Bear hat by way of greeting. "Sir, I'm Deputy Granger, this here's Deputy Blalock. We were dispatched here on account of reported multiple homicides. We'll need to secure this area and interview all those present--"

"Afraid not."

"Sir?"

"This is a highly classified government facility. You were called as a matter of SOP, but you can't be allowed the run of the land. The Official Secrets Act--"

"Colonel, a number of your men were attacked. Some are dead, from what we can see. There are detectives on the way. Crime lab boys. The coroner. You're not gonna keep us out of here."

"We'll cooperate in all ways possible, but the security of this facility cannot be compromised."

"Colonel--"

"Please withdraw your people and these emergency personnel to the front gate. We'll arrange procedures to satisfy both your jurisdiction and federal requirements as soon as your chief investigators and our public relations specialists arrive."

The cop blinked. His partner glanced around the chaos of the guard shack and thinned his lips.

"Are we clear to go back there?" an EMT called from the door to the bunk room. "Holy shit."

"Clear the crime scene," the spokesman cop, Granger, yelled. "Get all the injured outside and, and..." He gave Sanders a sour look. "Is there someplace we can take the injured, sir? Someplace not classified?"

"The mess hall is across the way. The lieutenant outside can direct you."

"Thank you so much, sir. You've been a great help."

The police didn't bother Sanders after that. The wounded were carried, carted, or steadied on their way across the road. In a few minutes, the guard shack stood silent, at least within. The shouting, vehicle engines, and helicopter turbines stormed beyond the front door.

Sanders stood alone except for the Sergeant of the Guard, who had come to the bunk room threshold.

"What the hell happened, sir?" The sergeant dearly wanted an answer.

Sanders shook his head. "I don't know, sergeant, I just don't know."

They'd need FBI, Sanders thought. They'd need NSA for the stuff too classified even for the FBI. They'd need the Attorney-General to handle the cops--

16

A tromp of boots at the building entrance, then someone crashed through the outer office.

What the hell could get any worse?

A soldier appeared in the common room doorway, panting from lack of breath. "Sir! Captain says you gotta come! The generator building, sir!"

They were off again. Sanders followed the soldier. He heard the Sergeant of the Guard behind him, but did not look back. Out in the open, he caught the lieutenant's worried eye and pointed toward the watching deputies. "Keep those men here!" he yelled, then left the dirty work to his officer.

The generator facility had changed in the last several minutes. When the captain had taken Sanders to the guardhouse, the curb in front of the building had been empty, just a short, dull stretch on an empty road. Three Humvees now parked at odd angles to the curb, one half on the sidewalk. Soldiers crouched in groups of three, using the trucks as shields between them and the facility.

And up the steps at the entry doors stood three men, two in undershorts, one in sweat pants and a sand-colored t-shirt. No shoes, no socks, just sleeping clothes. And each held a Squad Assault Weapon pointed outward from the waist.

The soldier delivered Sanders to his captain, who hunkered down behind the center Humvee. The captain grinned sickly. "Well, sir," he said, "we found them."

"Yes, I see." Sanders peeked over the hood of the truck. "So, can anyone tell me why they're armed? And why they're armed and in their underwear?"

"Sir, I don't pretend--"

"All right. Then here's something I imagine you *can* answer. What are we doing about ... whatever this is?"

"I'll need your go on this, sir." The captain hovered his hand at the radio hung from his field harness. "In case they misbehave." He keyed his mike. "Alpha Team, you have a go."

Watching from defilade behind the truck, Sanders caught a movement far to the left. A soldier had popped up from behind a retaining wall bordering the building's front lawn. He rattled his rifle and dropped back down.

The two near-naked men answered that disturbance with a spray of rifle fire. Bullets thudded into the wall, sparking and blasting out clouds of concrete dust, but the targeted guard was unharmed.

Sanders noticed one other detail that chilled his spine. All three of the gunmen had their eyes closed.

"Jesus, those men are asleep."

"It seems so," the captain said. "There are civilians in that building. High security assets. A situation like this calls for deadly force."

Sanders balked at that. "These are our men. No. Not if we can manage."

"Thank you, sir."

"Have you tried CS?"

"Tear gas does no good, sir. Not so much as a cough."

"Well, they're too well armed to rush, that's for sure."

"On the bright side, they aren't packing more than the mags in their weapons. I mean, where would they hide a reload?"

The colonel shifted his crouch. "You seem to have a plan."

"Yes, sir. With your permission..."

Sanders nodded. The captain clicked on his radio. "All teams, short bursts, overhead, nonlethal. Flank teams stand ready. Engage." He released the mike button and nodded at Sanders. "Let's see if we can get 'em to use up their ammo."

His last few words nearly drowned in a storm of automatic weapons fire. The soldiers behind the trucks, the wall, and at the corners of the buildings across the street threw unaimed bursts into the air while maintaining cover from the generator facility's entrance. The guards at the door answered each burst of gunfire with one of their own. Bullets bit at the street and lawn, some kicking up asphalt around the Humvees, some raining spent back to earth after steep arcs into the night sky.

The racket played out in less than thirty seconds. A thirty-round magazine doesn't last very long.

"Flank teams, go!" the captain snapped into his radio.

Three men rushed in from either side of the building, weapons aimed at their underwear-garbed targets. It took them several seconds to close the gap, but the men at the doors made no move to counter the attack. They just stood there jerking their fingers against unresponsive triggers. The assault crew stripped them of their weapons and bullied them face-down onto the grass. An instant later, the NCO on the scene yelled, "Clear!"

On that word, the entire visible guard force surged at the building. Several took up security positions outside, the now animated Sergeant of the Guard castigating them into a barrier no one could pass. The colonel, his captain, and several rank-and-file flooded through the doors, briefly paused to not shoot the three guards in the atrium, and invaded the generator chamber beyond.

"Thank goodness!" Eglemann cried when she saw who flooded into her space. "The guys out there said we were under some sort of attack!"

"The operative word is 'were,'" Sanders assured her. He watched as the captain dispersed his men throughout the chamber. They made fast work of a search, scoping for any other bizarre dangers that might have been loose that night.

"It's a hack," Eglemann reported. Her crew of engineers huddled close around her at one of the electronics panels along the wall. One of their number cradled a laptop computer trailing a wire plugged into the panel. "As far as we can tell, everything else is a diversion."

"A diversion?" Sanders clamped his mouth shut. She didn't know, of course. "Your theory is incorrect. What we just went through was not a diversion."

"Oh." Thoughts flitted behind Eglemann's eyes, but if she intended to respond, she changed her mind. "But it's a hack. We got a firewall warning, unauthorized outgoing search, so we tagged that and found other internal activity, also unauthorized. Well, it was authorized, but it couldn't have been--"

"It's been a long night. If you could get to the point...."

Eglemann made a strange humming noise, as if hauling words back down her throat. She pointed toward the big double doors for some reason. "All searches were on Doctor Rodriguez's password, but she isn't on site. She's at home. You can't do internal network searches from off site."

Sanders lost all patience. "Eglemann! I don't care!"

The engineer flinched away from him. Her people cowered closer to the wall.

"You don't realize it, but men are dead right now," the colonel barreled on. "Men are dead -- my men -- and my men did the killing! So excuse me if I just don't care about your little computer glitches!"

"It isn't a glitch!" The force of Eglemann's rejoinder deflated Sanders's tirade. He felt immediate shame at his behavior, and a returning heat to his face. He should have apologized. He should have. But Eglemann wasn't done burning him. "It wasn't a glitch, it was an intentional breach of our classified directories. Whoever did this was specific in their targets. They went for everything Nightwatch tagged. Thank goodness most of that's off site and secured only on controlled hard drives. But they went after it nonetheless. We were attacked, colonel!"

Yes, Sanders thought, we were. But not by a hacker sucking down Mountain Dew in some Eastern European stink hole. But then, she still didn't know.

"And one more," Eglemann continued, an index finger stabbing the air. "They were focused on two directories. They wanted everything on Clayton Hostetter but got next to nothing since he's an asset, since his data is hard drive isolated. And they invaded one other directory and got plenty, we're sure of it."

"Which directory?" Sanders asked through clenched teeth. Any number of sensitive files would be disastrous in the wrong hands. The generator. The N-space mathematics sets. The extra-universal address logs and their corresponding connection reports. He discovered he had been pacing before the engineers, and stopped.

"Fiona Street," Eglemann said.

Sanders stood stock still for a moment, then clenched his fists and uttered a single, atmosphere-igniting curse.

"Yes, sir," Eglemann agreed. "I hope we aren't dealing with Snowden."

Street, Sanders thought. Street. How could-- But, yes, that incident two years earlier. She had practically been a celebrity. But no one outside the intelligence community had known the real story. If a hostile power had stolen Street's files... It was like losing the H-bomb to the Soviets all over again.

"I want your data," he said, casting a sharp glance toward Eglemann. "I want it in ten minutes, in your office. Captain!"

"Sir!"

"I want your report, as much as you can muster. Chief Engineer Eglemann's office, ASAP. And I want the video files from the cameras in the guard shack."

"Yes, sir!"

Sanders marched toward the heavy double doors, one fist balled, the other hand gripping his pistol until it trembled. The problem with engineering labs was that they offered so little to kick, and what they gave you tended to be both expensive and delicate.

"What are you gonna do?" Eglemann called after him.

"I plan to find a secure phone. Then I'm calling the NSA, the FBI, and everyone else I know with initials." He pushed open one of the double doors and continued into the atrium. "And when I run out of initials, I'm calling Fiona Street!"

Chapter One

Work, work, work. Equal parts "Hurry Up and Wait" and "Hey, Guys, Watch This." And all of it while traveling coach.

Childress stood outside the doors of the CVS Pharmacy, bored almost to tears. D loitered with him, his eyes always scanning the dumbasses crowding the sidewalk on both sides of the busy street. D wasn't bored. He got *in* to it, he always did. D played the Good Nigger, the straight-and-narrow Captain America federal agent protecting the sweet and innocent taxpayers from blah, blah, blah. He didn't mind dressing like a gangbanger and lurking in doorways, but then, D was a man without standards.

Childress was smarter than that. He stood there at the drugstore's entrance and watched, yes. He shrugged now and then in his oversized hoodie showing its high-contrast black and white silkscreen of a burning American flag. He scowled at the natives, a good hundred protesters, mainly black. They gathered in two tight knots, one in front of the CVS, the other across the street in the Walgreens parking lot. They'd spread into the street soon enough, that's what you did when nobody gave a shit what you thought or even noticed you were protesting. They'd spread into the street to gum up traffic and make the cops act.

Stupid to get the attention of the law. What, they thought they were white college students?

"Linny Ball will never fall!"

"Black lives matter!"

"Welcome to Naptown: one day with no police shootings!"

Right. Nonsense like that. The kind of stuff white folks tolerated only so long as it didn't muck up their plans. These guys were good at it. Now and then they pulled out cigarette lighters they maybe had always owned, had bought at the drug stores, or had taken from a bag passed by the protest organizers. They held those up and flicked them on, yelling, "Can't get whiter, shoot me for a lighter!"

Childress had to admit, that last one had a ring to it.

He looked at D, and grinned. If he had to stand around and watch brothers and sisters make fools of themselves, at least he could have fun with the boys.

"I ain't sayin' they ain't got a point," Childress said. "But it's a fact the dumbass was a black man, in a red state, and harassed by cops. So why'd the stupid-assed muthuhfuckuh pick that time of all times to whip out a lighter and fix himself a Kool? Hell, I woulda shot the stupid nigguh, too."

D huffed. It came off good in his big, zippered hoodie showing a torso-sized portrait of Bob Marley in dreadlocks. D was a big guy, tall and mus-cled like Childress, and a huff from him was like a threat from anybody else. "You talk so much shit, man. I noticed you checking for your agent's ID more than once." He nodded across the street -- north rather than west toward the Walgreens -- at the gaggle of armored policemen at the McDon-ald's. "They make you more nervous than you let on?"

Bullshit. "I said they had a point. Ain't you listenin'? White cop catches a brother walkin' while black, it gonna end in target practice more than the average fuck figures. I ain't immune. Shit, I actually *am* carryin'."

"You're entitled," a breathy female voice said into his ear. "You're a federal agent on duty, cleared by the local jurisdiction."

Childress laughed. "Spoken like the lily-white red-headed Barbie doll you are, Cap. This really ain't your conversation."

"I don't see--" his in-ear radio complained.

"And that's why you white folks need to shut up and listen." Childress looked at D, at the crowd, then over to the upper floor windows of the boarded-up building behind the Walgreens. "You're the only voice that ain't got no point. All that 'All lives matter' bullshit."

"Well ... don't they?" the female voice asked.

"Only to them that ain't got no worries. You don't go down the street with every cop and half the civilians givin' you the hairy eyeball, so you can talk about 'all lives matter' an' shit. My peeps, we hope we don't get shot, beat down, or arrested every time we go buy a quart of milk."

"Oh, come on--"

D shook his head and scratched that thin little Van Dyke beard of his. "Sorry, Captain Street, but I'm with Childress on this one. You can't possibly understand, being white, with white cops, a white army, and white governments. You're always safe, you just don't know it because you don't have to."

"Really. I'm a woman, you know."

"Yeah, we figured that out," Childress said. He gave D a tired look. "She gonna keep this goin', ain't she?"

"Hey, I'm right here," the radio in his ear complained.

"That's kind of the point, ma'am." D never took his eyes from the crowd. "You're 'here' all right, in your ivory tower--"

"Boarded up tenement."

"--boarded up tenement, because you'd look too obvious down here on the street. This isn't your thing. Best you and any white person can do in this mess is shut up and listen for a change."

"I'm feeling an urge to remind you fellas that I am, in fact, your boss."

"Yes, massuh." Childress flashed D an evil grin. "Maybe y'all shoulda thought of that before you hired a bunch of civilians."

"Do we have to fill the net with existential chatter?" A new voice, that one, deep and firm. The ramrod-straight Sergeant Grace.

"Top! Glad you could join us." Childress rolled his shoulders to adjust the hang of his crappy jacket. "So you white folks gonna gang up on us poor, defenseless nigguhs, that it?"

"I'd just like some quiet," the voice answered.

"Yeah, me, too," another put in. "My ear is starting to sweat."

This was getting to be fun. "Who's that?" Childress asked. "Ponce?"

"Tejada."

Childress laughed. "Sorry, man. All y'all Mexicans sound alike."

"Puerto Rican here," another voice put in.

"Mexican, Puerto Rican, what's the difference? At least, that's what the po-po gonna say when they shippin' y'all out." Childress squinted across to the Walgreens parking lot. "So how's about it? Ponce, Tejada. Got your green cards handy? Your papers, they are in order?" He said that last with a cartoonish German accent.

"You always talking shit, Childress," Tejada said through a laugh. "How'd you ever come to work for the government?"

"Ain't you heard, man?" Childress slapped D lightly on the arm and nodded across the street. "I'm a revolutionary. Bringin' change from within the beast."

"Got activity," D said. "Somebody over at the Walgreens is lining up folks on the curb. Looks like they plan to rush into the street."

"Ponce?" the female voice prompted.

"The police over here see it. They're arranging a wedge to clear the intersection, if necessary. Also calling to the traffic control cars up and down both streets. They don't sound very excited."

"Why should they?" Childress snorted. "Bunch a dumbasses jumpin' out in front of cars."

"Keep a close watch," Captain Street said. "We've been tracking this guy for two years. I'd hate to lose him again."

"We cool," Childress said. "That was Chicago. We weren't ready. Now we bringin' the *down*town to *Nap*town."

D groaned.

"Looks like Intel had this one right," Grace said. "We'll see in a few minutes. Stay sharp, people. The window will be short."

"Understood, Sergeant Grace," Tejada's voice answered.

"Ready, top," Ponce added.

"Like I was sayin'," Childress said, "you gotta be careful if you ain't of the white persuasion in this country. Hell, with a name like Tejada, you don't want Uncle even seein' you on Twitter. How you even spell that, man? There an 'H' in there or some other Mexican shit?"

"It's a 'J'."

"A 'J' where it sounds like an 'H', or what?"

"What are you, Human Resources?" Ponce asked.

Across the street, a knot of a dozen or so protesters streamed into traffic, hands up and shouting. Brakes squealed. The street before the CVS became an instant clot of metal. Vehicles jammed in the intersection, too, forcing both streets to a halt.

"Linny Ball will never fall! Black lives matter!"

"It don't take Human Resources," Childress continued. "It's like those poor bastards who buy a ticket to fly, then when they try to board the plane, some prick in a uniform or a starched shirt grabs 'em 'cause their name sounds all ISIS or some shit. He got a funny name, so they figure him for a terrorist, man. Fucker could be a dentist, for all they know."

"Police are moving." Ponce reported. And they were. The cops filed out of the McDonald's parking lot, plastic shields held in front, batons poised before the shields.

"Stand by," Street said. "This isn't our thing."

"Take D here," Childress said. "Our man D DeBoy, a more unlucky son of a bitch you won't find nowhere. What's your first name, D?"

"Man, I don't have time for this."

"You got all the time, nigguh. We ain't got nothin' to do."

"Linny Ball will never fall! Black lives matter!" More protesters poured into the street. They held up lighters, held up hands, and faced the police with attitude and not much else. The cops formed an "L" in the middle of the intersection and banged their batons against their shields. Other policemen not in armor moved into traffic, trying to unknot the snarl of cars. The yelling, horns, and banging were enough to hurt a man's ears.

"Go on, D," Childress insisted. "Tell us. What's your name?"

D sighed. "De'Juajawan."

"De-*who?*"

"You heard me the first time. *Nolan.*"

"Don't change the subject--"

"Oh, please, do change the subject," Captain Street groaned.

"Now, now, I got me a point that needs makin,'" Childress said after a bark of laughter.

"Are you *sure* it needs making?" Tejada asked.

The police pressed the protesters back toward the Walgreens parking lot. The protesters resisted, yelling slogans and insults at the cops and giving ground only grudgingly. Suddenly, they charged the shields, hands up and mad as hell.

"I mean, think about poor De'Jua-- De'ja-- What the fuck was that, man?"

"Fuck you, Childress."

"No, man, I'm serious here, serious as a heart attack. Your momma saddled you with that name. What is it, like, ethnic or somethin'?"

"Maybe we should re-locate." D had his eyes on the dustup in the intersection. It threatened to spread their way, which wasn't much of a distance.

"Re-locate? Why?"

"We're standing in the doorway to a drugstore. Maybe we shouldn't be here when somebody throws in a firebomb. Wasn't there credible intelligence for firebombs?"

"Maintain position," the solid voice of Sergeant Grace said.

"Says you," Childress answered. "You ain't the nigguh down in the riot, man."

"But I am," Street answered.

"Yeah, right. I think I'd see your alabaster ass out here, that's sure."

"Look down."

Childress looked down. For a second all he saw was concrete, asphalt, and other people's shoes. Then a movement to his left caught his eye and he noticed a cat standing a few feet away, next to the wall. A black cat. Like the one his boss always had at her side.

The cat looked up at him, knowledge in its green eyes.

Dimly, a red jewel glowed on its neck.

"Uh, no," Childress said. "I ain't believin' that."

"Close your mouth," the captain said. "You might eat a fly."

For an instant, Childress thought the cat had spoken. He closed his mouth hard and shook his head.

D laughed as if his guts would split.

"Shee-it." Childress waved a hand at the cat to dismiss it. "You white folks full o' tricks."

D's laughter hitched in his throat and came out as high-pitched squeals.

"Yeah, right." Childress sneered. "So let's get back to important shit. Like, we know that De'Juajawan shit, D's fucked up name, is about as cash poor of culture as every faked-up African-soundin' name floatin' through the 'hood. Names like that are enough to make real Africans sprain their eyes rollin' 'em."

"Did I properly express my opinion that you should fuck off?" D asked past sniggers.

"No, you said I should fuck *me*, not fuck *off*, or somebody else should fuck me, like maybe the American jurisprudence system or, you know, somebody. But why would your momma give you a faked-up African-soundin' name, D? It's like paintin' a scarlet letter on your ass. White boys don't even need a picture, man. They see that name, and they go 'Hey there, uh, Winslow, I believe we have us a nigger here.' Resumes, rental contracts, fuckin' Amazon accounts, they got your number good, man, without ever seein' your cocoa-colored face. Your middle name is 'Sorry-assed', that's for sure."

The police pushed against the crowd, forcing them toward the curb. Then car doors opened, drivers climbed out, and some of them yelled at the cops. More cops entered from the McDonald's lot. Someone, a driver, took a swing at a uniform. The cops took him down in a flurry of nightsticks.

"Peel an eye," Street said. "This is about where he's likely to show up. They don't call this guy Voice of the City for nothing."

"De'Juajawan Sorry-assed DeBoy!" Childress roared laughter. He slapped the wall behind him. "That's precious. I'll have to remember that. Hell, I ain't even got *started* on 'DeBoy'!"

Cell phones came out. When the driver went down beneath four cops, nearly everyone in the intersection, police excluded, caught it on video.

Several more of the stalled drivers, about half-and-half white and black, joined in talking trash to the cops.

"This won't end well," Ponce mused. It didn't sound like he knew he had listeners.

"Focus," Street said.

"Just like I been sayin'," Childress continued. "Here we are, Uncle Sugar's finest, and what we doin'? We're *hopin'* things get nasty. That's some whack shit-- Uh, pucker up, kids and kittens. We got action from the west. Up 16th Street. Watch the sky. You dig this?"

A black object, roughly manta ray shaped, rushed in from the west. It approached at roughly twenty feet off the ground, barely below the power lines. It made ground speed at maybe forty miles per hour.

The black cat started purring.

"Got it," Sergeant Grace said. "Can't tag it official. This could be it."

"Talk time's over, brothers and sisters. Gear up." Childress unzipped his jacket to clear access to his holster.

D followed suit and shouldered into the crowd. He and Childress paralleled each other, moving toward the intersection at widely separated points, always glancing toward the approaching aircraft to gauge where it might end up. Around them, protesters screamed at policemen, who ordered them in loud, firm tones to evacuate the street. Childress and D both had their IDs out and opened, flagging them at anyone who paid them any interest, especially the cops.

The cat followed, weaving through the forest of legs as if everyone stood carefully still.

About the time the police alerted on the aircraft, something more immediate tore their attention away.

"Gun!"

The alarm blasted over the net, yelled so loudly that it peaked out in static.

At an old, claptrap Ford, a fat black man, out on the street and shouting at the authorities, raised something nasty in his hand.

Childress's gun hand flinched, but he didn't dare draw, not with all those police around.

Fuck!

The scene froze for a high-res instant. The man gripped the gun, and it *was* a gun. Childress stood helpless, even restricted by his mission. There was Ponce, short, stocky, with his round, dim looking face and stupid three-day beard and his wrinkled salesman's suit. He grasped some bigwig cop by the arm and stabbed a pointing finger toward Childress and D. Tejada approached from far across the intersection, rangy, a freaking basketball player even, in his jeans and Army surplus fatigue jacket. And the cat, the only one reacting with any speed at all, darted toward the gunman like a black blur. Then the moment broke.

"Look! A gun!" some cop yelled, and a dozen pistols and more than one assault rifle swiveled toward the fat man.

"Drop it! Drop it *now!*"

"Fuckin' cops!"

"Drop the god damn *gun!*"

"They gonna shoot him!"

"Drop it or we --"

Somebody screamed.

The crowd lurched like a drunk, first away from the danger, then toward it, then in all directions at once.

"Fuckin' bastard cops!" And the fat man brought up the gun.

Childress flinched at the sound of stringed firecrackers the size of cherry bombs. The cops had fired from all directions.

Not one bullet hit a live target.

Childress saw it, his eyes wide in disbelief. He shook his head and squeezed his eyes closed before opening them again to re-check the impossible.

The bullets, a shitload of them, hung in mid-air, black little hovering bees. Then, with the gracelessness of pebbles, they dropped, clattering to the pavement.

"Shee-it!" Childress hissed.

The goddamnned bullets had stopped in mid-air!

The cat rushed under the fat man's open car door, up his leg, and pounced on his face. The man screeched, dropped his pistol, and fell against his car while beating at his face. He only hit his face, because the cat had jumped to the Ford's rusted top.

Dust, trash, and pebbles burst through the panicked crowd. The jet or drone or whatever it was had halted overhead, fifteen feet off the ground. It looked as wide as a limo is long, with a fanjet under each manta-like wing. A kind of iris opened in its belly and *he* fell out, the guy, the one Street wanted.

There he was, big as life, and in his case life was pretty damned big. He wore a super suit like you'd find at a sports clothing store, one of those form-fitting things only Olympic athletes could really pull off. It was black, matte, minus only an Under Armor logo, and with it he wore combat boots and a weird-assed bicyclist's helmet with a gold visor. Around his tight waist wrapped, umm, a utility belt? Like Batman? Childress paused only a microsecond on that one, then his brain saw the holsters and went red alert.

The brother -- and yes, the mofo was black -- was a walking -- or rather falling -- armory, with big guns strapped to each thigh and a shoulder holster across one pec.

He fell out of the plane, landed on his feet, then slammed himself into two nearby policemen. He hit them like a bag of bricks; they didn't fall down so much as get driven there.

"Federal agents!" Tejada shouted. Childress slipped his weapon from his shoulder holster and aimed it at the ... the ... what the *fuck?*

The man -- *him* -- ignored the announcement. He treated another cop to a one-punch KO then extended both arms and closed his fists. Each forearm wore a bracelet of metal tubes, brassy things, maybe half a dozen tubes to a bracelet, each tube the size of an aerosol can. In the second it took Childress to log that detail, all the tubes spouted smoke and, well, rockets. He had RPGs at his wrists, about a dozen, and they had all gone off at the cops.

Policemen staggered away coughing or sneezing, the luckier ones, that is. The others found the pavement exploding at their feet, sending them reeling backward through the air.

The fat man, the ignorant asshole who'd triggered it all, struggled back to his feet. His face glistened red. The cat crouched on the car, ready to give him some more, but it turned out not to be necessary.

Supernigger snapped a hand to his Batman belt and flung a little something at Mr. Gun For Cops.

And electrocuted the bastard.

Shee-*it!*

Childress snapped out of it. Honestly, the whole thing had spanned no more than two, three seconds. "Stand down!" he called. "Federal agents!"

The man hesitated only a moment, cocking his head as if thinking about it. His back was turned to Childress, and it was a bulging landscape like steel chords and iron plating.

Then the guy slapped at something on his belt and the rules of the world freaked out.

A booming, metallic clang pained Childress's ears, then came back with plenty of reverb. The ammo in his gun cooked off, just exploded in place, whooshing flames through the handgrip. Childress dropped the weapon to save his palms. At the same time, half the cars in the intersection jumped in place as they maybe threw rods, exploded their radiators, or blew up their catalytic converters and therefore half their undercarriages. All the cell phones burst into flames.

"Shit!" Childress roared. "Shit, fuck, and *shit!*" He charged the big man, at the same time willing his numbed hands to close into fists.

Tejada was already there. The big guy in the bike helmet blocked his first and last punch, stepped around behind the agent, and pinched him on one shoulder. Tejada went down quivering.

Well, here goes.

Childress threw himself at the man from behind. He locked one arm about the guy's neck and gave him a coward's rabbit punch in the ribs. It felt like hitting a file cabinet. A file cabinet filled with Donald Trump's tax audits. And poured over with concrete. Childress thought maybe his hand was broken.

Then he thought maybe his arm was broken, too, as Black Batman wrenched that limb from around his neck, twisted it violently, and caused

Childress to flip over it, over *his own arm*, and land on his back in the street. For the cherry on top, the big guy stomped Childress's gut. The air and Childress's will to live wheezed out of him like a squeezed balloon.

He lay there while D took his licking. It didn't take long, Superdude was nothing if not efficient. Happy in his work, the guy was. A fucking artist.

But D lasted long enough for Ponce to make an ass of himself. That Puerto Rican looked dumb, but there were gears behind those dull eyes. He figured out the silliness of toe-to-toeing that big bastard and, while D got his ass whipped, Ponce went for the ship instead. Big Guy wasn't going anywhere if Ponce could fuck up his ride.

So Ponce snatched a flash-bang from the vest of a fallen cop, ran up below the ship, and hurled that bomb right through the iris hole into the cramped cockpit.

Or that's what he might have wished he did. He threw the grenade, yes, but the iris, by some weird and awesomely cool means, snapped shut before the grenade went through. The canister bounced off, fell, blew in a scream of light and sound, and sent Ponce watery-legged and onto his ass.

Then the iris slid open again.

Shee-it!

They were all down, Uncle Sam's finest. Most of the cops were down. The fat gunman was down. About the only one standing was the Big Guy. And the cat.

Childress tried to get up, but barely lifted his shoulders from the pavement before white-hot pain stopped him.

The Big Guy, who hadn't been bothered by the flash-bang, marched to below his ship and reached for his belt. He was getting away. He'd kicked in everyone's heads. Again.

"Yeah," Childress croaked. "Yeah, you better run. 'Cause ... when I get outta the hospital ... I'm gonna take you down." He lay back onto the road. "Motherfucker."

The Big Guy paused at that outburst. He didn't frown. He didn't smile. Probably, he didn't care. He returned his attention to his belt.

He looked like he might tap his buckle -- maybe it doubled as a big button -- but his hand halted short of touching the matte black surface, then jerked sideways in time for a knife to embed itself into one of his brassy rocket launcher tubes.

"No," Captain Street said from thirty feet away. "We need to talk first, buddy."

29

Chapter Two

She knew she didn't look like much, and that was often their undoing. The big, strong, ultimate fighting types usually showed a smirk when faced with a slim little redhead with paper white skin and freckles. Her black leggings emphasized her clearly girly-girl failings, that and her Sketchers, and especially the fuzzy, loose, sky blue pullover sweater. Fuzzy sweaters about never spelled Threat. What could she possibly call fighting? A little tai chi? Some yoga? Miss Minifield's Self-defense Class for Upwardly Mobile Secretaries? Be chivalrous, the big bruisers always thought. Give her a chance to back out. Go easy on her. Spank her bottom and send her home. That's what they thought when they stood like tall rock walls before her. They adopted a different view once they were moaning on the ground, trying to protect their privates.

"You've been a bad boy," Fiona said. She flipped the other knife in her hand and took a few modest steps toward him. "Fifteen assaults in Chicago. Gangbangers, mostly, but a few cops, a taxi driver, and bullies on the L."

The Big Guy yanked the knife from his wrist weapon and dropped it to the pavement. He might have been staring her down, but how could she tell? That helmet and visor covered his eyes. But she could see the lower part of his face. He didn't offer the usual smirk. "I know about you," he said, his voice a booming baritone. "Washington, DC, two years ago. I saw you on television."

"Fifteen minutes of fame." Fiona took another step forward. She glanced at the cat, still on the Ford, and flicked her chin to the right. Oz leaped down from the car and skulked in the indicated direction. That's it. Teamwork. Set 'em up and knock 'em down. Or in this man-mountain's case, plant a flag on top. "So you've beaten up half the police force and nearly all my men. How about you and me talk instead."

"We have nothing to talk about." He looked up at his ship, ready to leave.

"What's your name?" Fiona angled closer in pretended nonchalance. Oz had a good read on the man. The Big Guy wasn't concerned. He was, however, curious. "Come on, if we're gonna talk, it should at least be on a name basis."

"You are Fiona Street," the booming voice said. "You already know me. They call me ... the Voice of the City."

Wow. Nice touch, the pause and all that. "So, umm, Mister City, what's up with the move?"

"Move?" His right hand hovered near his Batman utility belt.

Fiona instructed Oz to watch that hand. It was up to something. "Yeah. You know, you were scaring the crap out of the Windy City, then you turn up in little ol' Indianapolis. Kind of a step down, don't ya think?"

"I'm the Voice of the City. This..." He waved his left hand around. "...is the city."

"I doubt Chicago considers this a city." She wasn't five steps from him. The guy's arms bulged nearly as big around as her waist. And, apparently, he caused firearms to fail. "Okay, I gotta ask. Why haven't you run? It isn't like I can trip up your exit." What could she do with the knife that could make a difference in the next few seconds?

"I am the Voice of the City," the Big Guy rumbled. "And the city wants to know about you."

He was quick, but Oz had a sharp eye, so Fiona saw it coming. He flicked something off his belt. Two somethings. Three, each a flat, star-shaped razor of metal that stank of poison.

Fiona jerked her head to one side to avoid the first projectile. She heard it whistle past her ear. The second whizzed between her chest and upper arm. She was too slow for the third, which embedded in the loose knitting of her top, near her waist.

"Hey!" She flicked the knife at him. It struck between bicep and tricep, making the man grunt. "This sweater cost me fifty bucks!"

He swung at her, a fist like a sledgehammer, but Fiona had done her thing, had lost herself in the mental space part way between her and Oz. She could see the man from two angles, and in that parallax could measure his movements to the millimeter. His attack sailed by within a hair's breadth of her face.

He didn't exactly fall off balance, but he presented his flank as his strike followed through. Fiona hammered his ribs with a scissors kick, then spun on one heel to send her other leg hard into his jewels.

The man didn't even bend over. He grabbed the knife in his arm, threw it to the ground, and jackhammered the sole of one combat boot toward Fiona's face.

Fiona backed out of that one, but she smelled asphalt and rubber from his sole. Then he was after her again, a rapid delivery of driving fists. She dodged them sideways, ducking under the strikes. Then she took the attacking arm in a two-handed grip, changed its momentum, and tossed the man after it into the side of the Ford.

Fiona could have sworn he dented the car, but Oz's angle revealed otherwise. Hitting the car must have winded him, though, for the man paused a second, supporting himself at the doorframe and straddling the unconscious gunman.

Lots of options, Fiona decided, and chose to kick in the Big Guy's head. That was Oz talking, always the pragmatist. Fiona thumped her sneaker into the man's skull before she could stop herself.

The crunching sound against the car's metal both sickened and excited her.

But the guy didn't go down.

"Jesus, you're a brick!" Fiona shouted. "Fall down, why don't you!"

Instead, he stood up. And when he stood up, he gripped something in one hand.

SKUNK! Fiona heard in her head, then Oz was on the man's back, scrabbling over his craggy shoulder to scratch at the exposed bottom half of his face. The Big Guy dropped the contents of his hand, several metallic cylinders that jittered and hummed on the pavement.

Fiona ran at the man. Like the cat, she scrambled up his muscled mass, then rolled across the top of the car. Oz was in her arms -- how he had gotten there, she had no clue -- and they landed as one on the other side of the car.

Then smoke, stink, and watery eyes, but Fiona had tumbled past the worst of it.

The cloud from the exploded grenades dissipated. When it did, and Fiona wiped her eyes enough to see, the man had disappeared. So had his jet.

"Well, shit."

Oz squirmed out of her grip and stalked several feet away. He sneezed, growled, and flicked his ruffled tail.

"Hey!" Fiona huffed. "It wasn't my fault. I wasn't the one who forgot to watch his hands."

Oz had a differing opinion, and it smelled of piss and coppery blood. Sometimes, there just weren't words.

Fiona needed distance when he got in those moods. She climbed to her feet and dragged her mind back into her head. She looked around at the wreckage of the last few minutes, and sighed. She had filtered out all the screaming and running, the sirens and the yelling cops. She had managed to forestall a second wave of police, though her credentials and harsh glares could only go so far. Well, it was over. The locals could have the scene. In a second.

She trudged around the Ford for her knife, the one that had bitten Batman.

The cops the big guy had slapped to the street struggled to sitting positions or coughed and wheezed on their knees. Miraculously, none seemed seriously hurt. Or maybe it wasn't so much a miracle. Perhaps that result had been calculated.

Well, not by her. She'd stabbed the guy, after all.

And tried to kick in his head.

Bad kitty. Bad, *bad* kitty.

An odor of cat box entered her brain. If a shower had been available, Fiona would have stepped right into it. That would teach the little uppity predator.

"Shee-it..." she heard from a few feet away. She stooped to collect the bloody knife, careful to take it by thumb and forefinger as far from the blood--

She found no blood on the blade.

But that was impossible. It had bitten deep in the muscle.

Oh, well, the lab guys could puzzle it. At least they'd coax out some fingerprints. She turned toward Childress and gave him a raised eyebrow.

He didn't manage to sit up, but made it to one elbow, panting.

"You all right, Childress?"

"Somebody drove a fence post through my belly button."

"It happens. You carrying an evidence bag?"

"We didn't come for no evidence."

"Yeah... Hey! Any of you cops have an evidence bag?"

Someone murmured an affirmative, tried to get up to go find the bag, and sat back down. He decided to call on his radio instead.

"You Wonder Woman, or what?" Childress asked.

"Me?" Fiona raised both eyebrows. "Hell, no. Why do you ask?"

He mugged her a look of rank stupefaction, but gave it up with a wince. "Nigguh put down all these cops and all four of us." He gestured to his team members, DeBoy and Ponce of which just then started moving, each rubbing the back of his neck. "But he never touched you."

"I don't know. I thought he was a challenge. The guy's built like a battleship."

"Boss, I was watchin'. He never laid a glove on you."

Fiona offered a grin. "Experience and practice. It happens when you think with your head and not your testosterone."

Tejada, right at Street's ankle, groaned and lifted his head off the asphalt.

Childress raised a skeptical eyebrow. "Now we talkin' boys versus girls? That's bullshit, Cap. You looked like a psychic, is what you looked like. Like you was readin' his mind."

"No, just his angles. Ah, here's my evidence bag."

A patrolman weaved through the unconscious cops, stalled cars, blown-out weapons and fussy civilians to hold out the bag to Fiona. She dropped the knife inside, folded the sack closed, and sealed it with the proffered red tape.

"Thank you," she said. "We'll be signing out this item for rapid processing at the federal labs."

33

"The crime lab boys'll be here in a minute, ma'am. They can handle the paperwork."

"Good. Now, that guy at the car is your gunman. He might need medical aid for electrocution. Some of these officers took shock from RPG explosions. Get the EMTs in here as soon as possible."

"Yes, ma'am, it's being handled. How about your men?"

"Oh, they're all right, I guess. Fellas! You good, or do you need to see the doctor? Hey, somebody nudge Ponce."

By the time they returned to the abandoned office they'd commandeered behind the Walgreens, Sergeant Grace had data. He looked relaxed in his golf shirt and Dockers, even amid his spread of tablets, laptops, and humming printers. The harsh light of an electric camp lantern tried to rob the scene of any sense of ease, but Grace always looked relaxed. It came from fifteen years of NCO training.

The team trundled in holding blue cold packs to various bodily regions, then collapsed onto the chairs and couches scattered about the defunct attorney's waiting room. Of the six, only Grace and Fiona were one hundred percent, and their men were among the best the NSA had to offer.

"Mothuhfuckuh had somethin' under that shit, that's all I got to say," Childress insisted as he stretched out along the length of one ratty couch.

"You *sure* that's all you got to say?" Tejada asked hopefully while pressing his cold pack over half his face. "Because you've been saying an awful lot."

"Fuck you, man. He got some kinda Kevlar, or that shit in the dragon movies, the knight in shinin' armor shit. What they call that shit?"

"Plate mail," Ponce volunteered.

"Yeah, that's the shit. He had that shit on his ribs, man."

"He wasn't wearing plate mail," Fiona said. She helped Ponce into a chair. The man looked zapped, like he didn't know where he was. "I doubt he wore *any* armor, just a compression suit from Dick's Sporting Goods."

"Nah." Childress shook his head. "I punched armor."

"We don't care." Grace stepped to the center of the room, his arms laden with papers and a tablet computer, a Bic pen dangling from his mouth like a cigarette. He commanded attention despite his admin assistant props. Sergeant First Class Alexander Grace stood six-four if an inch, all of it honed muscle, with a chiseled face and ice blue eyes. "I prefer we stick to facts, not conjecture. And the fact is this guy, the Voice of the City, kicked the asses of four NSA special agents."

"And about a thousand cop asses, too!" Childress complained.

"At last official count, it was fifteen." Grace glanced at his watch.

"Then it was fifteen kicked ten times each."

"That would still only be--"

"Nobody cares!" Fiona yelled. Ponce winced and held his head. "Sorry. Grace, continue. Childress, shut up for just one minute, okay?"

"Shuttin' up, Cap."

Grace hunched over his papers and readouts. "He employed some sort of electro-magnetic weapon. That's how he initially stopped all the bullets, then rendered your weapons non-op."

"Non-op?" Childress looked amazed. "Fuckin' gun blew up in my hand!"

"Childress..." Fiona's warning was a low growl. She knew the diode on her neck glowed red, growing more so with each second. She didn't consciously call on Oz, but the cat jumped onto the back of Childress's couch nonetheless. Oz sat there, staring at the agent and growling, his own diode looking like fire. Childress went very still.

"First info from the scene is that your ammo cooked off, lithium-ion batteries caught fire, radiators burst, and catalytic converters exploded." Grace looked at his watch again. Did he have a favorite TV show coming on? "All of these except the radiator fluid contain metallics that can be a combustible hazard in the right circumstances. That's what our tech boys online said. They weren't sure about radiator fluid, but think maybe the device acted on the radiator grid itself?"

"No." Fiona had made a circuit of her men, checking their immediate health. That done, she paced the back of the room. "I didn't notice any other metallic bodies being stressed. It either affected something metallic in the liquid or the liquid itself."

"Lots of rust in radiators,' Tejada muttered, bent over in a chair. "And radiator fluid is flammable."

"Note that," Fiona said. "We need the reports from the crime lab here."

"Already ordered," Grace said. "Then there's the jet. I was able to send the video I took through the agency aircraft recognition database. It came up empty. Our tech support also came up goose eggs. In fact, all the guys said, based on their short observation of its form and obvious power configuration, that the thing shouldn't be able to fly."

"It flew," Tejada said. He rubbed his shoulder.

"Of course," Grace said, "but it *shouldn't* have. We can't know for sure till we get another look."

A round of tired, cynical laughter.

"Send the video to the UFO boys," Fiona said. "They're used to ... nonconventional thinking."

"Wilco," Grace said, and glanced once more at his watch.

"Is there a time-sensitive something going on?" Fiona asked.

"No, ma'am. What about the knife? You said you'd bring back a piece of him."

Fiona gestured toward a coffee table in front of the couch where DeBoy lay, a cold pack between his shoulder blades. "At the time, I meant it somewhat more ... figuratively. But there he is, wrapped up and ready for forensic identification."

"Mind if I peek?" Grace asked.

"You do that, and it's your personal, inseparable baby all the way back to DC. Chain of custody, top." She shrugged. "I wouldn't bother. Weirdly, there's no blood on the blade. I hold out hope for fingerprints, though."

Grace frowned at the bag on the coffee table. "I don't. The way he has these impossible bits of tech, including a plane with questionable aerodynamics that threads over and under and between power lines, and the way he fought you, Captain Street. I think he's one of *them* for sure. One of those improbable beings we've been tasked to assemble, not just an adept vigilante. I wouldn't be surprised if he doesn't have fingerprints."

"If not fingerprints, he at least has DNA."

"Are we sure about that, ma'am?"

"What?" Childress looked askance at Street. "He a fucking ghost or somethin'?"

"You've been briefed," Fiona told him. "If you didn't believe the briefings, I can't help that."

"I don't think this guy has Batman tech," Grace said, straightening. "I also don't think he's absent DNA or dry of blood. I think he has a ... a reality distortion field, or something. That's the only way I know to answer impossible tech that works."

"Maybe we're jumping the gun here," Fiona said, "maybe even the shark. He could just be smarter than us."

"*And* our tech guys back in DC?"

"Well," Tejada mused, "they *do* work for the government."

Grace shook his head. He wasn't giving up that easily. "I'm thinking about Clayton Hostetter," he said.

"Really." Fiona was surprised. "What on earth could that old cowboy have to do with this?"

"Clayton Hostetter ... isn't from around here." Grace put his gear on the coffee table and scratched the back of his head. "Okay, let's say it. He traveled N-space, or whatever it is. He came from another universe. Clayton Hostetter is a nineteenth century cowboy with advanced technology to travel between universes. He's a marshal of some inter-dimensional law enforcement initiative who fights monsters from hell dimensions."

Childress huffed. "Top. You even *look* stupid saying that shit."

Grace threw up his hands. "I'm just trying to think this stuff through. What if this guy is the same? He came from a universe with different physics, so his stuff works."

"Then his stuff *wouldn't* work because he's in *our* universe," Ponce offered, still rubbing his head.

"Stick to spy shit, top," Childress said.

"Table this," Fiona said. "We've worked too long on hope and suppositions. I really want to get something on this guy."

"Well, we have something," Grace said, turning toward the office door. "We have visitors."

Fiona already knew that. Rather, Oz had known it when the newcomers entered the floor. At least three, two of them heavy, none of them smelling like threats. Oz knew some of them.

The door opened and three Army uniforms crossed the threshold.

Fiona and Grace came smoothly to attention. The others gave the arrivals a variety of squints.

"Hiya, colonel," DeBoy said into his couch cushion.

LTC Sanders strode across the room, two others in his wake. One was male, blond, a captain, in the same blue business uniform as his superior. The other was female, African-American, a sergeant, in the corresponding female uniform with skirt and pumps. She gave Fiona a wide, quick grin.

"At ease," the colonel said, and Fiona and Grace relaxed. "Captain Street, you're hell to locate. I've been chasing you down for going on thirteen hours."

Fiona snapped her fingers, calling the cat to her feet. "Field conditions, sir. We've been chasing a prospective. Sergeant Grace thinks we hit pay dirt."

"Yes, I'm sure he's correct. Sergeant First Class Grace is an efficient, effective NCO. Speaking of which, did you get the goods, sergeant?"

"Yes, sir. In fact, I've been carrying them for weeks."

"Carrying what?" Fiona asked. She sensed smells of deception and conspiracy.

"A thing I couldn't get to a uniform store to purchase," Colonel Sanders said vaguely. He glanced around at the civilians. "Any of you men in condition to stand?"

With sideways glances, groans, and winces, all the men found their feet.

Grace rummaged around on the table. "Tejada, you're taking the picture. I only had this." He handed the agent a point-and-shoot camera. "Because all our cell phones burst into flames. This runs on triple-As."

"Guys, what am I missing here?" Fiona asked, but Oz had gone from suspicious to purring.

The colonel looked cross. "Captain Street, front and center!"

Fiona obeyed, snapping to an attitude of attention that felt peculiar in her leggings and sweater.

"Goodknight?" The colonel leaned slightly to his right. The female sergeant stepped into that space, a clipboard held so Sanders could read it.

"Attention to orders!" the colonel boomed. "Headquarters, Department of the Army, and the president of the United States have reposed special trust and confidence in the patriotism, valor, fidelity, and abilities of Fiona Street. In view of these qualities and her demonstrated potential for increased responsibility, Fiona Street is promoted to major with a date of rank of September 28, 2018. Congratulations, major, you're ahead of the curve for detached officers outside their field."

Fiona should have said something. A simple thank you would have sufficed. But, despite her want, no breath escaped her lips. She was like a fish breathing on the floor of a boat.

The Army personnel thought that funny, and laughed.

Oz rolled on the floor, an engine of purrs.

"Straps?" the colonel said, and held out a hand to Grace.

The sergeant handed Sanders two bent shoulder bars embroidered in gold braid and oak leaves. The colonel held these out to Fiona in his left hand. "In my day, these were brass and a friend, loved one, or superior officer would pin them to your shoulder to make it all real. Even if you were in civilian clothes. Well, times and uniforms change, though the sentiment remains. Congratulations, Major Street."

He stuck out his right hand. Fiona took it and shook.

Tejada snapped a picture. The camera flash flooded the room.

"Oww..." Ponce said, and shielded his eyes.

The bars changed hands between colonel and major, then Sanders took a step back. All the military did, Goodknight shuffling her tablet to her left hand.

"Present *arms!*" Sanders intoned, and the four soldiers saluted Fiona. She returned the salute, then quickly wiped tears from her eyes.

Everyone applauded.

Goodknight rushed in to embrace Fiona. The two women hugged and kissed cheeks. "Well done, ma'am," Goodknight said, wiping her own tears. "I'm happy for you. I've known for days, but I couldn't spoil the surprise."

"Thanks, Goodknight, you're a dear." Fiona turned to Grace, her mentor the past six years. She put out her arms. "Well, you old campaigner? Give a girl a hug."

"A superior officer, ma'am. Kind of irregular to hug officers."

Fiona stretched out her arms more and laid on a pouty face.

"Well. Maybe this once." Grace enfolded her in as tight a sibling hug as was proper.

Tejada raised the camera.

"Uh-uh-uh," Grace warned him to laughter all around.

"Well. So much for the good news," Sanders said, glancing about the room. "Street, is there someplace you and I can talk?"

Fiona only had to think for a second. The office proper, the lawyer's space. "Yes, sir, this way." She led him into the back, Oz trailing. This main office glowed brightly thanks to its two large windows. The plywood had been torn down from these to give a clear view past the Walgreens to the street intersection and the CVS drugstore. Two camp chairs flanked a tripod at one of the windows. Atop the tripod perched a set of long-range binoculars. The two officers lowered themselves into the chairs, Oz jumping into Fiona's lap.

Sanders leaned back in his seat, fingers interlaced over his flat stomach. "There's been a security breach at the Lawrence-Livermore facility, the trans-universal generator."

"Sir? I hope--"

"No, not what you're thinking. No terrorists, no covert foreign government exploits. The ... attack ... was two-pronged. What we know so far is that something came through the generator facility via an externally powered trans-universal event. As you know, we've experienced those before." He stopped, then narrowed his eyes. "You vouched for Hostetter. Are you still sure about him?"

"Absolutely. Why? Oh! You don't think he had anything to do--"

"No, I don't. We've sent agents to his place in Wyoming. They've interviewed him and checked around. But the man is who he is. He has a trans-universal attenuation device. He could have whisked from Wyoming to California and back in the time it takes us to get another beer from the fridge."

"But he wouldn't, sir. Hostetter is an honorable man. He's sworn to protect the multiverse."

The colonel's mouth bent up in half an acerbic grin. "Of course he is, Major Street. But do we even know what that means?" He put up a hand when Fiona sat straighter in her chair. "Don't worry. We don't suspect Hostetter. But we had to check him out. Frankly, I don't think he has the wherewithal to do what this entity did."

"What would that have been, sir? If I can know, that is."

"This entity, after entering the facility, sowed confusion by taking over part of our guard force, *Invasion of the Body Snatchers* style." He leaned forward, elbows on knees, and rubbed his hands together. "It somehow got four of our men to wreak havoc, killing thirteen soldiers. While they slept." He watched Fiona, expecting something.

"Umm, killed them while they slept?" Fiona had seen some strange things as chief weirdo wrangler for the US government. "Which were sleeping, sir? The victims or the killers?"

"Both, for the most part. Four men tore our guard force apart with their eyes closed and, we later found out, while in REM sleep. And that was just the start. While this went on, our secure network got hacked, specifically the Nightwatch file system."

Fiona made a pained face. "That's bad. Lot of stuff in those files that would be hard to spin. But not fatal. All the asset files are referenced, but the actual asset data is stored on individual secured hard drives at NSA Headquarters."

"Yes. The asset file hard drives aren't on any network. They have to be signed out and plugged into authorized, controlled laptops on site. But our hacker got hold of more than just the surface data for Nightwatch. They found out about you, major."

The city wants to know about you.

The hairs rose on Fiona's arms. She tried to breathe evenly, to calm her reaction so that it wouldn't affect Oz.

"We think they were looking for Hostetter. Failing in that, they latched onto you. Your signature is all over those asset files."

"They latched onto me? But they're looking for Hostetter?" Fiona felt her brow tighten. "Why Hostetter?"

"We can't say." The colonel leaned an elbow on the flimsy arm of his camp chair. "I imagine it isn't too complicated. The good marshal put a monkey wrench to a bid to destroy eighteen universes. He beat down the bad guy's hand-picked lieutenant and sealed him away from the world with a nuke. I would guess he's made a good many enemies."

"Okay," Fiona said through a rising impression of twitching skin and bent-back ears. "Okay. But me? My file wouldn't do them any good. It's just as secure as the others."

"Yes, it is." Sanders rubbed a curled index finger across his upper lip. His eyes were trained on Fiona's Sketchers. "But you, major, are more public than your assets are. You're an Army officer and you've been in the news. Whoever this exploiter was, he viewed all hierarchical data on you, dropped into the deep web, and touched nearly every professional file that exists on you, including officer evaluation reports and all mission reports, all the way back to your Military Intelligence basic course. Hell, for all we know, he has your West Point records. Then, of course, there's that very public incident in DC…"

"But he couldn't get anything from that, sir. It's locked down."

"Yes, but it doesn't change the fact that this bastard is highly interested in you."

Okay, Fiona thought, so the obvious question was, indeed, the obvious question. "Umm, why me?"

Sanders sat back in the chair. With the worst of it out, he relaxed. He stared out one of the windows. "Well, obviously, there's you and the cat.

That kind of information is bombshell worthy. The Russians have had suspicions regarding you ever since that incident in Washington. They've been struggling with their own awareness-enhancement program." He looked back at her. "But the Russians don't use Doctor Rodriguez's secure log-ins to bypass security. While she's asleep. At home."

"Was--"

"There was no security shortfall on Doctor Rodriguez's end, as far as we can tell just now."

"Then, how did they get her log-ins?"

He stared at her.

Fiona stared back, at least for a few seconds. Then his gaze became too much and she glanced around anywhere but at him. She thought. That's what he wanted, right? She thought about all the peculiar things she had witnessed or recorded in the last few years. Flying mountains, telekinesis, teleportation, prescience, people talking to God and God talking back--

Holy crap, he thinks they read Rodriguez's mind as she slept.

"It's early, major, but we think we've a serious new player. We postulated such mega-players, even superhuman ones, during the Hostetter incident two years back."

He thinks they read her mind? That they took over the minds of his soldiers? Was that possible? Could minds be read?

Dumbass, you're electronically and wirelessly linked to the interpreted mind of a cat.

Sanders made no expression. She wasn't surprising or disappointing him. "Well, consider this a heads up," he said. "We've analysts and agents on every aspect we can think of. It's the ones we can't think of that bother me. You'll be careful?"

"Always am, sir."

He stood and smoothed his uniform coat.

Fiona stood with him.

Sanders cleared his throat. "You're ordered to clean up here and report to head office in DC. I want you close while this is going on. You're as much an asset as those people you bring in."

"Yes, sir."

"There won't be much for you cooped up in the capital. Don't you have some technical refinements and evaluation due? Maybe you should schedule that in."

"Yes, sir." Maybe they could tone down the piss and cat box leavings in Oz's bad moods. And who calls gas grenades skunks?

Fiona opened the door for Sanders, who strode through to the outer office and proceeded to gladhand the nearest agents. He wasn't particularly good at the hail-brother-well-met routine, just as he looked more at home in ACUs than a dress uniform.

"Got one question about this whole officer promotion ceremony thing," Childress called from across the room, where he had sidled up to Goodknight. "So, major, you buyin' the drinks?"

She *did* buy the drinks. She opened a tab that night at a hole-in-the-wall Irish bar in the city center. They called it the Golden Ace or something close to that. On Tuesdays, they have live Irish folk music. But it wasn't Tuesday, it was Friday, and Fiona didn't care. She bought the drinks, the Guinness smooth and the Scotch biting, and once Fiona had a few in her, she sang her own Irish songs. It was a good outing. She only wished that Goodknight had stuck around instead of jetting off with the colonel. Fiona had known the sergeant three times as long as Childress, Tejada, and the others. She had only known Grace longer.

"Come on, you gotta tell us," Childress insisted once Fiona finished leading raucous, atonal harmonies of *Whiskey in the Jar* and *Fields of Athenry*. "I ain't never seen anybody move like that. That superdude couldn't lay a finger on you."

Fiona took a draught from her Guinness. "You never listen, Childress."

"Unless it's to his own voice," DeBoy said.

Everyone took a laugh from that.

"All right, all right, so just figure I don't listen." Childress, who hadn't drunk much, shoved aside his glass and leaned on one elbow. "So, I get they did some magic with you and the cat." That would be the cat in the carry bag on the bench next to Fiona. "The science lab freaks and all that shit. But, that just lets you *talk* to the cat. It don't give you, like, cat reflexes or nothin' like that. Do it?"

Fiona sighed, but with a grin on her lips. She pushed aside the hair from her right ear and showed her neck to the men. "This red jewel behind my ear. It's a diode that shows the works are in order. The works are a load of sensors and chips built into the unit beneath the diode. Surgically implanted. Brain surgery, guys."

"Holy shit, that's fucking amazing," Ponce said. His flash-bang daze had worn off over the day.

"Surprisingly, outpatient stuff," Fiona said. She straightened back up and flipped her hair. "The sensors are connected to the corpus callosum, the part of the brain that handles communication between the left and right hemispheres. It reads, translates, and broadcasts my thoughts, feelings, impressions, what have you. Straight to the unit embedded in Oz's brain. And his broadcasts to mine."

"So you see what he sees and know what he knows," Ponce said. "Like a Google Goggles connection."

42

Fiona waggled her head and enjoyed the sensation of it sloshing back and forth. "No. Way better. Hear, see, smell, touch, taste, whatever sensation either of us sends across the brain's divide, the other experiences to one degree or the other. It can be information or it can be me, all of me, depending on how deep I dive into the connection." She didn't mention what happened if one side of that shared link died. She wasn't one to tell the world her weaknesses.

"That still don't say how you moved like that. Maybe that little kitty could manage it, but you ain't no cat. You don't have them muscles or their reflexes." Childress looked around the bar for the umpteenth time. White people made him nervous, Fiona knew, and there were an awful lot of them crammed into that space. For all his bravado, Childress was not a predator.

"Eh, I don't know," Fiona said. "You'd be surprised how much of what you do is attitude. Oz knew I could do it, so I knew I could do it, so I did it. Not all cushions and chocolate, though. You should have been there early on, with me chasing laser lights and half terrified of showers."

"Glad that isn't now," Ponce said, holding his nose for sniggers. "What about the little guy now? If you share each other's experiences, how's he handle the experience of getting running blind drunk?"

"I am *not* running blind drunk! Tell 'em, top!"

Grace still nursed his original light beer. "Not running blind drunk, gentlemen. I doubt the major *could* run in her condition."

That got bawls of laughter. Fiona grumbled, went to take a snort of her Guinness, and put it back down, frowning.

"So, what about it?" D asked. "Is that cat in your bag ready to phone ex-boyfriends and former bosses?"

"See for yourself," Fiona said, unable to keep irritation from her voice. Was she drunk? She didn't think so. She could quit anytime she wanted to! Of course, any drunk would think that.

D, sitting next to the bag, pulled the top flap, which was only partly zipped. Inside nested a foam rubber pad, a stiff plastic frame that held the sides of the bag apart, and the cat. "Huh. He's, like, passed out."

Fiona grinned. "He never could hold my liquor. Falls asleep almost immediately. It's about the only time I get to be myself these days, this and the periodic upgrades and calibrations. I get a little mental tickle of mice and sunny windowsills, but otherwise it's all me. Huh." She took that taste of her beer. "Don't let them tell you cats don't dream."

"Well," Grace said as he scraped back his chair and stood. "On that note, I think it's time to cash in. They close in fifteen minutes and we deploy back to DC in the morning. Major?"

"Yeah. Right, top. Let's put all these boys to bed."

"I was referring to the tab. It's your promotion party. Pay up." He waved for a waitress. "Childress, it's you and me behind the wheels. Head 'em up, move 'em out. Don't take anything off the commanding officer. She's been incapacitated."

So they paid and wandered out to the parking lot, six special field agents of the NSA crawling into two rental cars. Well, five agents, at first. Ponce was busy throwing up at the curb. Fiona, riding shotgun with Childress, hardly noticed the trip to the airport hotel. Her mind drifted somewhere up and behind her, like a balloon on a string. Her body felt uncoiled and warm. As the street lamps zipped by, she stretched. It had been a good day. She was a major now!

And there was another feeling, something vague, like getting scratched behind the ears.

"You sure about this?" Grace stood at the corner of the car while Fiona loaded the last of her stuff in the trunk. He wore his usual golf shirt and khaki pants. The man practically advertised bachelorhood.

"It's a style choice, more or less," Fiona said. "By driving, I get to see America, understand why we fight, that kind of bullshit, and I get pie from waitresses rather than peanuts from airline attendants."

Grace didn't respond until the roar died away from a departing jet. "Oz doesn't like to fly, does he?"

Fiona grinned. "And there's that." She banged shut the trunk. "It scares him. The result is me gripping the armrests like a passenger in a crash-and-burn, which doesn't help Oz's disposition much, so he gets more nervous, and... Well, you can see the infinite loop there."

"You've taken him on airplanes at least a dozen times. You've *jumped out of* airplanes with him at least a dozen times."

"Yeah, but he still doesn't like it. I think it's a kind of subconscious stand on principle. You know, 'If God had intended cats to fly... And then something clever I can't think of right now."

She leaned against the car and crossed her arms. No leggings and sweater for her that morning. The sweater had found its way to the trash thanks to the ragged hole that throwing star had torn. Fiona felt comfortable that warm, humid morning in a cotton sundress and sandals. "Well, whaddaya think?"

"I think I haven't been prouder of a young lieutenant made good. Major. I imagine you'll be moving on now."

"Huh? What's that supposed to mean?"

"Well, major's a staff ranking. They'll be wanting you to get your admin training in. Maybe War College."

"Uh-uh, not for me. I'm happy where I am, saving the world one South American rebel kidnapper or ISIS terrorist at a time."

"And I've always found that strange about you. You really get a kick out of this work. It's play for you, isn't it, ma'am?"

"Yep. Wildest ride on earth." She thought a moment, looking out across the hotel parking lot. "They take it away from me, I might have to resign, maybe go into private security."

"That would be the Army's loss, major. But I'm not worried. You're addicted."

She grinned, unfolded her arms, and rattled her fingers playfully against the steel hide of her car. "I'm not worried, either. See, this is me not worried. Besides, they'd want to get their money's worth with the brain mod shit and everything." She tapped her temple. "You don't throw millions of dollars at a desk job, top."

"No, ma'am, I suppose you don't."

"Well, gotta get on the road. The boys all in control?"

"They're packing up the last of it, then it's off to the plane."

"And you'll get home a good eight hours before me."

He shrugged. "We have paperwork to do."

She pushed off from the car and made her way to the driver's door. "Oz, we're going. If you'd be so kind..."

Oz appeared seemingly out of nowhere though Fiona knew he had been lounging beneath the car. He circled her ankles and mewled.

"I don't know, guy. It's a Corolla. Doesn't have much of a dash to lie on, but knock yourself out." Fiona pulled open the door and Oz dived inside.

Fiona turned back to her sergeant before she dropped into the car. "I'm not going anywhere, top, except maybe Ohio and Pennsylvania. Want me to pick you up a souvenir?"

"If you're going through Wheeling, a lump of coal."

"That's for bad boys, so, you know, no," and she dropped into her seat and closed the door.

Grace offered her a crisp salute as he stepped away from the vehicle. Not regulation, him in civilian clothes and all, but it was the thought that counted sometimes. Fiona fastened her safety belt, pressed the ignition button, and returned his salute with a casual one of her own.

A few minutes later, Fiona left the airport behind. Half an hour at the most, and she'd do the same for Indianapolis. It wouldn't be the first time. She hadn't told the men, but she had grown up in that small town grown big. Grown up there, but still a stranger. The city never held still; it changed with each breath. And so did she.

Oz had draped himself across the dash in front of her, blocking the speedometer and almost every other indicator. He was there for the sun, not the view. He perched with his head up, eyes closed, purring like a rocket engine. His fur ruffled slightly in the air from the cracked open window.

She was a major, Fiona thought. The Army trusted her, had decided she could do more.

And she *would* do more. If they tried to move her, she'd bargain with the colonel. She had more value where she was, building the trans-universal initiative and recruiting its soldiers. Something was coming, Hostetter had told her, something potentially bad for the survival of mankind. Others had pushed it back, but that victory had been temporary. Earth -- and the universe Earth lived in -- had to be ready when the enemy returned.

It was gonna be a rush, that was sure.

So she hit I-70 and headed east, the sun in her eyes and the breeze whipping her hair. She felt glad for the time, glad for her opportunities in life, glad, for a while at least, to be alone.

Just the two of them.

Chapter Three

Major Raisa Kudashova sat up in bed. It was a true sit-up, a smooth pivot at the hips from fully reclined to fully erect, not the muddled, sloppy, groggy awakening of almost any other person. She sat there, the dark room around her, the sounds of traffic and the morning sun filtered beyond her motel window. Though her blankets had fallen to her waist and she wore only panties, the air-conditioned air failed to raise either shivers or goosebumps across her flesh. She sat there as if listening, her eyes closed, her breathing even.

Then she climbed from her bed.

Major Kudashova was a woman of efficient, considered movement. She stepped briskly across the floor to the bathroom, flicked on the shower, and sloughed off her panties. She stepped under the running water, steam rising to fog the mirror over the vanity, and let the spray needle her clean. She stood there unmoving, her face tilted to prevent water draining into her still-shut eyes. Front soaked, she turned around for the shower to drench her back. Out she stepped, twisting to shut off the spray even as she snagged a towel from the bath rack. For the next several seconds, she toweled herself dry, the surreal pantomime of a robot imitating human movement. She made a cursory pass at her blonde hair, which was so close cut she might have passed for a man if not for her noticeably female figure.

She dropped the towel, left the bathroom, and drew on fresh panties, a pair of linen slacks, a sport bra, and a plain white tank top. Shoes followed, imitation Chucks, no socks.

Then she gathered every possession she had in that room and stuffed them into her single, thin suitcase.

Except for the light-weight Thinsulated jacket that she took in one hand. And the sunglasses. She darted out a hand to the bedside table, took up the Ray-Bans, and slid them onto her nose. A moment later, her suitcase sitting just inside the door, she exited the room and hung the Do Not Disturb card from the doorknob.

She didn't need to switch off the lights; she'd never turned any on.

Major Kudashova knocked on the door across the hall.

"Who is it?" a rough voice asked from within the room.

"Golden frog," Kudashova said in French.

The door opened. She took several strides into the room and heard the latch lock behind her.

"Good morning," the man in front of her said in muddied English. His had been the challenging voice. "You are early. This is commendable."

The man looked to be sixty years old, with graying hair receding above a square but jowly jaw. He stood in the middle of the room in pressed gray slacks and a long-sleeved button-down white shirt with suspenders. The businessman's costume could not hide shoulders as wide as a bridge or the peevish pinch of his face. He held a green paper cup in one hand, a doughnut in the other. He squinted at Kudashova. From the lines around his eyes, he squinted at everything.

Kudashova nodded sharply. She held her hands behind her back.

"Come," the man said, and swung his doughnut toward the room's incidental chair. It stood in the most open section of carpet, facing the wall lamp over the bureau. "Have a doughnut. Or would you rather get straight to work?"

Kudashova tossed the jacket onto the nearest bed. She closed the distance to the chair and dropped into it, her knees spread to a comfortable, self-assured degree. She rested her hands, bunched into loose fists, on her knees.

"Very, very good," the man said, and nodded. "See, Praporshchik Guryev, the major knows well the value of duty. She is early *and* ready, like winter."

"Her example is admirable, Comrade Colonel," the man at the door said. He had stood there like a mouse, unnoticed by Kudashova until he shuffled into the bathroom to wash his hands.

This second man was the antithesis of the first. He was gaunt, hollow-faced, with a large, knobby nose and practically no chin. The hands he bathed in the washbasin looked huge for his slight frame, the knuckles prominent.

The colonel issued a mean chortle and took a sip of his coffee. "No need to be careful, Praporshchik Guryev. You were specially selected for this operation, as was Major Kudashova. Your services, and also your impressions, are valued."

Guryev dried his hands and fiddled about in the back of the bathroom. "My services are freely, faithfully rendered, but I am still confused. It seems strange that you would bring me all the way here from Petrograd when a more obvious, efficient path to success seems apparent."

"Really? And what is this you speak of?"

Guryev came out of the bathroom carrying a huge plastic case. It looked like a toolbox. "Forgive me, Comrade Colonel, I speak out of turn. I haven't access to all parameters of the operation, only those for which I have a need to know." He lugged the box over to the chair and laid it next to Kudashova's feet. "Nor, to be truthful, do I have a desire to know."

"Spoken well, comrade. Operational security. But an unnecessary precaution at this stage. By dinnertime, we'll be on a plane to Russia. The Americans can do nothing to stop us." The colonel stepped to one of the beds, the one jumbled with the doughnut box, several aluminum cases, a huge gun bag, a baseball bat, and newspapers. He plucked up a tablet computer from the mess and handed it to Guryev. The screen showed a face, a 3-D image of a freckled redhead. Fiona Street.

Guryev took the tablet and propped it up in Kudashova's lap. "Very sorry," he said. "You will excuse me?"

Kudashova sat still as a board behind the reflective lenses of her sunglasses.

Guryev glanced from Kudashova's face to that on the tablet. He flicked the face on the screen, rotating it a little to the right. "I'm sure everything's under control, Comrade Colonel. Though I'd be more sure if I knew what to expect between now and my comfortable seat on the plane."

The colonel uttered his dangerous laugh once more. "My, I must be ready for retirement. Even Praporshchiks give me bits of their mind. My good fellow soldier, it's like this." He gestured expansively with his doughnut, as if he prepared to make a speech. "This target, this Major Fiona Street, is a worry to the FSB. As you know, we have nothing in our arsenal like her. To be sure, we have a match, yes. She sits in that chair before you. But still, the ability to blend with the predator, to see what it sees and feel what it feels. This is nothing less than extraordinary."

"Yes, Comrade Colonel, that is clear."

"And so, it is not enough to destroy this weapon, this woman. It is not enough to simply assassinate her. Soon there would be another Fiona Street, another cat or a dog. No, it is necessary to do something more effective than to kill. It is necessary to cast doubt."

Guryev opened the case at Kudashova's feet. It unfolded into multiple trays, each partitioned into discreet little sections filled with colored goop, powders, or tools. He dipped two fingers into one compartment and brought them back slathered in a pale cream. "To cast doubt," he mused. "This is why you brought me?" He rubbed the cream over Kudashova's face and neck.

"It is why I brought you both." The colonel paused in his oratory in order to eat his doughnut. He licked his fingers and took a sip of coffee. "You will use your considerable talents to make our dear Major Kudashova look like Fiona Street. Kudashova will use her considerable talents, plus our technological enhancements, to behave badly thereafter."

"I don't see what that might accomplish," Guryev said. He wiped his fingers on a towel and rummaged in his case. "Please, major," he said without looking at her, "close your eyes and remove the glasses."

She folded the glasses into a fist at her knee.

"Of course you would not understand," the colonel said as he picked another doughnut from the box on the table. "You are the makeup man. As long as you do that job well -- better than I could possibly understand, anyway -- you will do fine. Perhaps you'll wind up a hero of the Russian Republic."

"Aren't those usually dead?" Guryev's hands were loaded with brushes.

The colonel laughed. This time, it was the barrel-chested laugh of a lovable cartoon bear. "I'm going down to the lobby," he said, wiping his fingers with a paper napkin. "They have free coffee down there. Would you like me to bring you some?"

"That would be pleasant, Comrade Colonel."

The colonel was already to the door. "I suppose none for our intrepid major. In makeup, and all that."

"None for her," Guryev said. He dabbed and brushed at Kudashova's face.

Guryev didn't seem to notice the colonel's exit. He focused his attention on the woman in the chair, that unmoving, unresponsive woman who became less a human being and more his personal canvas. He painted her, referring often to the 3-D portrait on the tablet. Zooming in and out of that image, turning that computerized face, he copied every color and blemish from Fiona Street's face to Kudashova's. It wouldn't have held up under close inspection, but close inspection was hardly the point. These were colors for security cameras, details for low-resolution video. Up close, they were too bright, too stark. Kudashova looked like a clown. Still, Guryev might have argued, they would fool even the toughest facial recognition software.

Two hours had passed before the colonel returned from the longest coffee break on record. He entered the room with two Styrofoam cups, careful not to spill them.

"Here you are," he said to Guryev and placed one cup on the table. "Sorry it took so long."

"Hmmm?"

That evil chortle again. "As I imagined. There was a young hostess downstairs, very pretty. She is kind to grandfather types." He sat down on the bed with the doughnuts and sipped his coffee.

Guryev surveyed his work. He held the tablet next to Kudashova's face and, pencil and brush in hand, made a few adjustments.

"Are you aware, Comrade Praporshchik, of the concept of proprioception?" The colonel looked uninterested in his own question. He stared at the wall outside the bathroom.

"I don't believe I've heard that one." Guryev put away his brushes and closed his case lightly. He left Kudashova and entered the bathroom.

"Proprioception," the colonel said. "It's the sense of body awareness, of knowing where you are in space and time. We could not walk without it. I could not hold this coffee in my hand."

"It sounds like a good thing to have," Guryev called from the bathroom.

"Then there's our sense of self, of who we are. These are the things she has in abundance, this Fiona Street. Her sense of self and her physical awareness have been weaponized, you might say."

Guryev reentered the room carrying a red wig. He held it as if it were precious. Across one arm, like a waiter's towel, hung a flesh-colored wig cap.

"That is what fascinates me," the colonel went on. "These concepts, they're all in the brain. Everything we know is but electrical signals interpreted in our heads. How do we know anything is really out there at all? Why, you, Praporshchik Guryev, could easily be a figment of my imagination, not there at all. Who is to say you aren't a cat if your brain receives signals that you are, in fact, a cat?"

"We are not cats, Comrade Colonel." Guryev carefully placed the wig on the bureau beneath the wall light. He spread the cap over Kudashova's short, blonde hair, then arranged the wig atop it. He adjusted it this way and that, making it look natural.

"Of course you are correct," the colonel agreed after a sip from his cup. "But *she* is, in a manner of thinking. A shame to destroy something so incredibly ... unusual."

"She is ready," Guryev said, and stepped away from Kudashova.

The woman didn't move.

"Ah, good." The colonel sat his cup down on the bedside table, then stood. He turned around to lean over the jumble on the bed, pulling over a fat case. "Come, major, for the second phase of your preparation."

Kudashova's head, until then leaned back so that her face pointed toward the ceiling, snapped to the front. She unfurled her fingers about the sunglasses and fit the Ray Bans onto her nose. Then she stood and approached her superior.

"Hands behind your head," the colonel ordered.

She complied. The colonel, without the slightest compunction or show of interest, pulled up her tank top until the rolled-up cloth of it rested atop her breasts. "Batteries," he said, and drew from the case several soft packages. They measured about the dimensions of an ordinary sheet of paper, but maybe an eighth of an inch thick. And they were malleable, like modeling clay wrapped in shrink wrap. He slapped one of the packets against the small of Kudashova's back, and one each at her left and right flanks. They stuck to her. "These will provide eighteen hours of power with constant use. This is good, though you'll need them for less than ten. Better than the last set. Soon, we'll have batteries that are both imperceptible and last for days." He pressed the packets, molding them closer to the major's contours. "There. With your shirt down, no one will notice. Still, wear a jacket."

He stepped back to evaluate his work. "All right. Next, control units." He drew four plastic wafers from the case, all of them flesh colored, about the size of saltine crackers. He slapped these onto Kudashova's back, spreading them between her shoulder blades and to either side of her spine. "You've put up with a lot," he said as he worked. "The Rodina recognizes your sacrifices. Eh, Praporshchik?"

"Of course, Comrade Colonel." Guryev sat in the chair recently vacated by Kudashova. He stared at the redhead on his tablet screen.

"Ha! The Praporshchik is a practical man. He is unlike us, major. He cares only for the precision of work. Patriotism is outmoded to him." The colonel grabbed a harness of spider web thin wires from the case. He threaded the lines between the batteries and the plastic wafers. There was plenty left over. Using surgical tape, he bundled the long leads centered on Kudashova's back and fed them to the base of her neck. "That will do," he said, arranging the single mini-connector that terminated the wires. "You may see to your shirt."

Kudashova, without a trace of self-consciousness, lowered her shirt, unzipped her slacks, stuffed the shirt past her waistband, and did her slacks up again.

The colonel fiddled with what looked like earbuds on white wires. He hung a portion of that contraption in the major's ears, but two other wires, one on each side, connected to just behind her ears via tiny adhesive cups. He snapped the opposite end of this wire harness into the mini-connector at the base of Kudashova's neck. This joined the earbud device to the wafers on her back, almost none of it noticeable to the casual observer. "You look good," the colonel said, and slapped the woman's back. "Look like you're listening to your iTunes. No one notices. Still, remember: jacket. Ready to test?"

Kudashova inclined her head slightly and stepped away from the bed.

"All right," the colonel said, and reached into his case. He drew out a black plastic unit with a touch screen. Frowning at the screen, he tapped several icons, then hovered an index finger over the device. "Energizing units..." He glanced over at Guryev. "Praporshchik."

Guryev looked up from his tablet. "Hmm? Oh." He stood and dragged the chair away from Kudashova, plopping it down at the bathroom door.

"Thank you, comrade." The colonel pressed his touch screen. "Activating."

A sound like erratic puffs of air whispered from within the aluminum case. Moments later, three gray spheres no larger than ping-pong balls elevated out of the box to hover near the ceiling. They remained there for several seconds while the colonel put down his controller, picked up the baseball bat from the bed, and stepped to within a few feet of Kudashova.

"You have control," he said. Then, without warning, he swung the bat at Kudashova's head.

In the next instant, the gray spheres darted to three corners of the room and Kudashova ducked under the colonel's swing, avoiding a bashing from the bat. The colonel, apparently expecting this, corrected mid-swing and turned the bat to crash down upon the major's shoulder. Kudashova leaned backward, letting the weapon pass harmlessly over her front. Then she pivoted and struck an open palm into the colonel's forearm, throwing him off-balance. The colonel recovered with a huff and a chortle, then pistoned the bat toward Kudashova's stomach.

She caught the bat one-handed before it struck. Also one-handed, she wrested it from her larger opponent's grip. She flipped the bat smoothly into a two-handed offensive grip and swung it hard at the colonel's face. It stopped an inch from contact.

The colonel grinned. "Ah, good. Calibrated."

Guryev, who had watched the engagement, shook his head and returned his attention to the tablet.

The colonel took the bat from Kudashova and tossed it onto the bed. He closed the case that had yielded the strange equipment, then pulled a bulging gun bag to the edge of the comforter.

"Choose your weapons," he said as he unzipped the container. Inside lay a 9A91 compact assault rifle. Tokarev and Makarov semi-automatic pistols surrounded it, plus a Beretta M9 and the varied modules of a VSK94 Sniper rifle. Various other deadly goodies filled in the spaces between weapons.

Kudashova lifted out the Beretta, checked that it was empty on safe, and searched around on the bed for ammo.

"Your mission is to attack the FBI field offices in Cleveland and Pittsburgh between the hours of 1300 and 1500, inflicting maximum damage." The colonel took up another doughnut. "Ensure that you are seen on video surveillance and be careful to mask your means of approach and disengagement."

Kudashova loaded a magazine into the pistol. The three spheres drew in from their corners and orbited just above her head.

"When you accomplish your mission, meet us at the escape coordinates without that ungodly makeup. Your flight documents and identity papers will be forthcoming." The colonel bit into his doughnut. He waggled it at Guryev. "You know, these are really quite tasty. What are they called again?"

"They're called Long Doughnuts, Comrade Colonel. They're a delicacy in this region."

Kudashova wrested a shoulder holster from the mess on the bed. She slipped it on and slapped the Beretta into its nylon-and-foam sheath.

"Long Doughnuts? How strange. But they're round, you see, like every other doughnut."

"I believe it's a brand name, Comrade Colonel."

One module at a time, Kudashova liberated the sniper rifle from the bag. It took her only seconds to snap, twist, and plunge the parts together, including the long silencer.

"At any rate, they're quite tasty. So." The doughnut devoured, the colonel sucked his fingers, then gave Kudashova an even squint. "Are you clear on your objective, major? The timing is necessary. The Street woman departed Indianapolis forty minutes ago. The schedule must sync to her travel time."

Kudashova slapped a loaded magazine into the sniper rifle. She chambered a round.

"You understand," the colonel continued, "that delays in her travel time may result in delays to your timetable. Keep close watch on your messages."

Kudashova stood with the rifle, flexing her fingers against its two grips.

"Do you understand, major?" The colonel waited a beat. It had finally occurred to him that something wasn't right.

"Major. Are you all right?"

Kudashova turned the rifle casually on her commander and pulled the trigger twice.

The colonel dived aside. One round thudded into the bathroom wall, but the other blossomed red at his side. He landed with a grunt between the beds.

Guryev was out of his chair, the tablet clattering to the floor. He glanced to the colonel, then back to Kudashova.

She put three rounds through his chest.

By then, the silencer was shot. Any more use and the assault rifle would boom as if its muzzle weren't baffled at all. Kudashova dropped the weapon, grabbed up a pillow from the bed, and angled around to where the colonel lay.

He breathed raggedly, lying on his back, his head propped up against the bedside table. Blood spread at his hip.

Kudashova straddled him. She unholstered the Beretta and bunched the pillow around its barrel.

"Comrade Major," the colonel rasped, then broke into a fit of coughing. "Comrade ... you are an officer ... of the Rodina..."

Kudashova pressed the pillow-buffered pistol against his head and pulled the trigger.

A few minutes passed before the door opened to the motel hall. Kudashova stepped out wearing her jacket. Beneath that hid the Beretta, a Tokarev pistol, and the 9A91 assault rifle. The gun bag full of loaded magazines and grenades hung crossways from one shoulder. She wasn't fooling anyone. Any half-awake passer-by would have noticed the bulges and guessed what they meant. Kudashova didn't seem to care. She locked the door and re-entered her own room to grab the bag and close up again. She switched the Do Not Disturb sign to the door behind which her two partners bled.

Scant minutes later, she tossed her things into the back seat of the colonel's rental car. The assault rifle she slid under the driver's seat before climbing in to switch on the ignition.

Then there was something, a hesitation. After such efficient, non-stop movement, she sat there, looking at nothing, her hands on the steering wheel. She tilted her closed, sunglasses-camouflaged eyes toward the instruments. She touched the gearshift and recoiled from it. She worked the pedals cautiously, causing the car to roar. This went on for a curious length of time before she finally pushed the car into gear and reversed out of her parking spot.

She nearly rammed the vehicle parked behind her, stamping the brake just in time.

Finally, with jerks and chirps of spinning wheels, she edged out of the parking lot, turned toward the interstate, and was gone.

Chapter Four

Fiona pulled into her driveway as dark fell on Alexandria, Virginia. She yawned as she climbed from the car. So did Oz on the pavement beside her. She stretched, on tiptoe with her fists balled. Oz stretched with an arched back and a straightened tail, his claws gripping the rough concrete surface.

"Well, little guy, home at last." Fiona fished in her purse/cat bag and lifted out her house keys and phone. The home security app on her cell showed nothing to report, so she sent the system to standby and plopped the phone back where it came from. "I could use some chow," she told Oz. "I know we had that pit stop at Mickey D's, but I mean real chow, like ice cream, especially after that run-in with Clumsy Girl." She said this as she took the walk to her front door, the cat weaving about her ankles. Anyone else might have tangled in the animal and gone to meet the pavement, but Fiona knew her cat's whereabouts as firmly as she knew her own.

Once in the house, lights on, Fiona dropped her bag in the living room and kept on to the kitchen. She took a can of cat food from the pantry and emptied the contents into Oz's bowl. While he ate, she got herself a bowl from the cupboard and dipped Moose Tracks ice cream from the tub in the freezer. She left the bowl on the dinette table and sat down beside it with the house phone. She couldn't eat ice cream while Oz took his meal. It would taste too much like fish.

She tapped the speed dial for Hostetter and leaned against the table.

"Howdy," came over the line.

"Howdy yourself, cowboy. So you knew it was me?"

"Reckon so. It's this here call I.D. thing."

"Good for you, Clay. You know, you've only had caller I.D. for two years."

"Takes gettin' used to. Like the TV and the computin' machine."

"And running water and electricity?"

"You a cuss, you know that?"

"Story of my life, Clay. Story of my life. Say, everything all right out there in cowboy land? Remember, bud, it's an unsecured line."

The voice on the other end paused, replaced by a sound like the clearing of a throat. "There was somethin' yesterday. Bunch o' boys come over for a talk."

"I heard. They were polite, I hope?"

"If they hadn't been, there woulda been a ruckus." The throat again. "I was concerned. About Sinfonee."

"Yeah, I imagine." Fiona wanted to say something, to assure him Doctor Rodriguez was fine, but she couldn't imagine how to do so in the clear. She settled for, "Don't worry, bud, I take care of you two." It was lame, but he at least knew nothing too bad had gone down. "You know, if you lived in California, you could check on her yourself."

"Ah, well, you know..."

"No, Clay, what do I know?"

"Me and Sinfonee, we got a understandin'..."

"Yeah, you've told me about your understanding. I think you're both loony."

"It works out. I ain't ready for that world and mine is too quiet for her."

"Clayton Hostetter, have you any idea the trouble I went through to find that girl and get you two together? It was, like, real *Fiddler on the Roof* matchmaker stuff."

"Like a what?"

"Sorry. Cultural reference. I just want you two okay, can you understand that?"

"Me and Sinfonee is fine. Don't you fret, though I thank you for the thought. We just need a bit o' time. To adjust."

"Two years? Most people are working on their second crop of kids in that kind of time."

"So, did you call just to whip my hide, or what?"

Fiona held her head in one hand. She felt Oz dismiss his empty bowl; she didn't need to look. He sauntered off to the living room to lick his paws. "I just wanted to hear a friendly voice."

"Well, this here is one, lady. You're a good friend."

"*A* good friend. I'm jealous. You have other good friends?"

"Well, now, I can't rightly say that. There's a few old boys at the bar in town... And, of course, Porthos. Why you always callin' an old cowboy, anyway? Purdy girl like you shouldn't have time for that with all the young bucks courtin'."

"You just said I'm purdy," Fiona said, mimicking his speech.

"Oh. Well, yeah... Sorry, I reckon I was plum out of place. Won't happen again."

"No, you just keep on saying it."

"All right, if you like, long as you know it's meant just friendly-like an' such."

"No, I mean it, Hostetter. Go ahead and tell me I'm purdy again. Right now."

"You're a mighty attractive lady, Miss Fiona Street."

"And purdy?"

"And purdy."

What a dope she was, fishing for compliments from a sixty-year-old spoken-for redneck. Where had that come from? Okay, not where, but why just then? Fiona well knew she was a crazy cat lady. She was the crazy cat lady the cat ladies sidled away from. But she had dealt with that, or so she'd thought... "Hey, good news."

"Go on."

"I got promoted."

Genuine good cheer radiated across the line from Wyoming. "That's mighty fine, Miss Fiona. Ain't no better officer, that's sure, and I've served with some doozies. Congratulations!"

Fiona warmed at his words. Oz peeked in on her from the living room. "Yeah, the colonel read the orders on a stakeout. It was cool. All the fellas were witnesses."

"I'm proud o' you. If it weren't no security violation, I'd brag on you to the boys in town."

"That's okay. I just wanted you to know. Next time we get together, I'll buy you a drink."

"I wager I'll be doin' the buyin'. It's the least I can do in your honor."

"Aww, I bet you say that to all the girls."

"Well, no, I don't speak much o' liquor to the ladies--"

"I was kidding, Clay. Say that to all the girls, it's kind of a meme."

Blank line.

"Anyway, I was just messing with you." She felt a tickle, a familiar tug in her brain. Oz hinted at something, some narcissistic requirement that would build to its usual emergency. Like watching television, or stalking the Roomba. Fiona sat up straighter and kneaded the fingers of her free hand against the tabletop. "Well, it's nice to hear you, Clay. I should take some time off, go out there for a visit."

"You'd be welcome. It's been too long a turn."

"Yeah. When work dies down a bit. Well, I guess I need to go. Oz. I'm his servant, you know."

"You take time for yourself, young lady. That there cat can go catch himself a mouse or somethin'."

"Oh, hell no. It's bad enough keeping the taste of Tender Vittles out of my mouth. But fur! Yeeach!"

An easy, understated laugh. "Yeah, I reckon so. But you take it easy, still. You do so much for ever'body. You need some doin' for yourself."

"Well, thank you, bud. I appreciate the thought."

"You take care now, y'hear?"

"I hear. Bye, Hostetter. You're a champ."

"Ma'am," and Fiona imagined him touching the brim of his hat for her. The phone went dead. It was some seconds before Fiona hung up. The ice cream called to her, but she had lost her enthusiasm for it.

Oh, well, ice cream was good for more than happy treats. It was also good for solace.

The next day was interesting. It started with a knock on the door. Fiona answered in damp sweats with her toothbrush still in her mouth, looking back and forth between the two government agents on her porch. She knew they were government agents. They wore the suits and the rectangular-rimmed sunglasses though the sun hadn't fully risen. Everybody channeled Agent Smith these days, damned *Matrix* movies.

"Yah?" she asked through a mouthful of lather.

"Miss Street, you're to come with us. Colonel Sanders's orders."

"Ah. Uh-kay. Himme a sec."

"Now, Miss Street." The agents separated by a few steps. They unbuttoned their suit jackets as if choreographed to do so.

Fiona raised an eyebrow. Carefully, she leaned out of the house and spat into the bush by the porch. "I'm brushing my teeth, dumbasses. Gimme a sec."

They gave her one. They also invited themselves into the house. They didn't let her go alone to her bedroom to change out of her funky workout clothes. Fiona threatened to strip right in front of them in order to change, but it was an empty threat and they didn't seem to care one way or the other. In the end, she settled for a fresh hoodie and remained stuck in the damp, salty t-shirt and pants.

All the while she wondered what was up. The men were too close, too alert. Their holstered weapons had the thumb breaks down. The man who had promoted her two days earlier had authorized deadly force?

Oz wanted not an ounce of it. He hid behind the couch in the living room, growling and spitting. Fiona couldn't blame him. He'd likely picked up his mood from her. Through the cat, Fiona knew four more men waited outside, and Oz wanted to kill them all.

By extension, so did Fiona.

But she tamped down that urge, focusing instead on dragging a threatening Oz from his barricades and stuffing him into the cat bag. The living room reeked of piss and bile. Fiona hoped it was all in her implant.

Outside, the car in the drive emptied of agents. One at a back door ushered her in then climbed after her. A partner bookended her on the other side. Two more men, the driver and his shotgun, and the originals in a chaser car.

These guys not only had orders, they were scared of her.

The ride into Washington proceeded in strained silence until Fiona noted their likely route into work. "You guys taking the 295?"

The bookends didn't respond in the least, but Shotgun turned his sunglasses at her. "Yes, ma'am."

"The Beltway's quicker this time of day." Fiona was glad of a chance to talk. Oz emanated low growls from his bag. If any hand had reached in there, it would have come out Ginsued to the wrist.

"I don't care for the Beltway," Shotgun said. "The 295 has a better view. You can sometimes see the river."

So, he was the one in charge.

"So, umm, am I in a lot of trouble here?"

"We were just told to pick you up, ma'am."

"Really?" Fiona felt sweat from more than just her recent workout. She strained not to punch in every head she saw. One was driving the car, after all. "Is that all they told you?"

Shotgun watched her before turning back to the front. But he answered her. "Well, that and to watch you like a mouse watches a scorpion."

"Oh." That made Fiona a little less uneasy. "So you see yourselves as mice, eh?"

Shotgun spared her another look. "The grasshopper mouse is one of the most ferocious small rodents alive, ma'am, and a natural predator of the scorpion."

So the guy was an encyclopedia, too?

"Sometimes, when defending its territory, it howls like a wolf."

Fiona's incredulity interrupted Oz's temper fit. She felt an impression of almost vertiginous confusion at her disbelief. "It's all right, honey," she said as she patted the bag. "The nice muscle agent is just talking trash."

Shotgun pointed his sunglasses at her for another long moment, then swiveled back toward the front.

The bookend next to the cat bag edged an inch farther away.

NSA headquarters is a massive, black, rectangular prism in the middle of a sea of parking lot. It dominates Ft. Meade, Maryland and is, in fact, the state's largest employer. LTC Sanders's office hunkered deep within the core of that building, past multiple checkpoints starting with the restricted exit ramp from the highway. Fiona had been through the gauntlet of security enough that she hardly noticed it anymore, but she had never found herself waiting like a fresh lieutenant in the anteroom to the colonel's office. Her status as chief weirdo wrangler and special science project had always gotten her rapid access to her commander. Not anymore, it seemed.

She stood against a wall festooned with framed prints of Special Forces in action, a kind of comic book reality twist of desert chic meets Audie Murphy. She stood to avoid the traffic flowing in and out through the colonel's door, a continual stream of signals officers and dark-suited agents. Then there was her own entourage, her four babysitters from the car.

Needles of fear pricked at Fiona's mind. She knew she was deep in the shithole without a ladder to climb out. She knew it intellectually, a kind of math that came out worse and worse the more she worked the problem. Oz knew they were trapped in a stronger, amygdala-powered way that reinforced the bad math. He cowered in the bag at Fiona's feet. She knew not to let him out. Assuming he'd even poke his head from the bag, he'd likely bolt without plan or destination, and Fiona with him.

Goodknight sat at her desk several feet away, busy as always with paperwork. Every so often, she looked up from her filing or her word processing and offered a sheepish grin of encouragement.

That was the scariest cut of all.

After a wait of one hour and fifty-three minutes, Goodknight put a hand to her phone headset and spoke something quick and muddied. She looked up not at Fiona, but at Shotgun. "The colonel will see you now."

The four guards arrayed themselves to cocoon Fiona in a suggestion. The suggestion was to pick up her bag and march into the office, or be dragged there. Fiona picked up her bag.

The colonel's office wasn't much to brag on, just a desk from Office Depot central casting, two cheap chairs for visitors, and the expected prints of Special Forces glories gone past. The colonel's desktop monitor pointed outward toward the two chairs. Sanders stood facing the back wall, hands clasped behind him.

Fiona snapped to attention before the desk. "Sir, Major Street reports." Sanders didn't turn around. "At ease."

Fiona couldn't manage ease, but she spread her feet and pretended to relax anyway. "Sorry about my appearance, sir. I wasn't given the opportunity to dress appropriately."

That got a tick of his head. He turned far enough to look her up and down with one jaundiced eye. "Have a seat, major."

It was an order, not an invitation. Fiona took one of the two chairs, Oz's bag in her lap.

The colonel nodded to the guards. Three left the office, pulling the door closed. Shotgun remained. He positioned himself at the door and drew his Beretta. He charged it and stood with his hands clasped as casually in front of him as he could while holding a loaded weapon.

The colonel turned full on Fiona. His blues blazed with ribbons and badges, but Fiona noticed most that his jacket hung open, unbuttoned. Years of military service almost made her gasp. Slack privates got vehement dressings-down for lesser offences than sloppy uniforms. Then she noticed the shoulder holster beneath his jacket. So, what position was *his* thumb break in?

"Comfortable, major?"

"No, sir, can't say that I am."

"Have a nice trip?"

"Until now, yes."

"I suppose I wasn't terribly clear when I said I wanted you close, considering the circumstances."

"Umm, I don't know. I thought you were clear."

"And that's why you embarked on a twelve-hour drive, alone, through much of the east-central corridor?"

Fiona blinked. He was pissed over travel arrangements? But they didn't pull loaded guns on you about travel arrangements. Last she heard.

"Major, this is important. Try to concentrate."

"I am, sir."

"Really. You look a bit distracted. Tell me, where were you between the hours of 1300 and 1500 yesterday?"

"Ummm..." Okay, so she had exchanged words with that high school dropout at McDonald's when she didn't like the look of Oz's perfectly legit helper animal papers, but she hadn't been in uniform and why would the Army or the NSA or anybody else care-- But that was earlier, or was it? Had she been on the road, or paying her tab? What the hell did he want? "Sir, I think I was on the road, maybe entering Pennsylvania, maybe still in Ohio. I don't really know..."

Sanders approached his desk. "Maybe this will help your memory." He fiddled with something on the keyboard hidden below his desktop. The computer monitor flared to life with a sullen pop.

Security video. A lot of short, jarring splices, high angle, low, indoor, outdoor, a parade of blurred action showing someone, the same person every time, beating up security guards and a whole lot of guys in suits. The person was a woman. Fiona found it interesting for a moment, then wondered what it had to do with her.

Then the woman, bold as brass, walked up to the camera, stared straight into it, and shot it dead with her pistol.

Fiona squeezed her eyes closed so hard they watered. When she opened them, the video still ran through its horrifying loop. She looked at Sanders's stony face, at Shotgun's statue-like gun stance. She looked back to her boss. "Uh, that," and she pointed at the screen, "that isn't me."

"Do you have a twin sister you'd like to reveal?" The colonel was deadpan.

Sweat stuck to the back of Fiona's shirt. Her palms felt clammy. Oz emitted a low, rumbling yeowl.

"Yesterday afternoon," the colonel said, his tone betraying nothing, "two FBI field offices were invaded by that woman there on the video. She killed four agents and one security guard. She put eight more personnel in the hospital. You see her fighting style. You see the near impossibility of some of her offensive and defensive movements. You see her face. You can see why I'm ... concerned."

"Sir. You know I'd never do ... that."

Sanders came around the desk. "Major Street, if I *wasn't* sure, you wouldn't be sitting in that chair. You'd have other, less comfortable arrangements." He sat down against his desk and folded his arms, the first time he had obstructed the reach for his weapon. "But you have to understand, soldier, I'll need a lot more than faith and assurances before we give you an ounce of leeway."

"Yes, sir. I understand."

Oz didn't. He turned and lashed inside his bag, scratching for escape.

Sanders frowned at the bag, which made the restlessness there get worse. "No," he said, "You apparently *don't* understand. You see, I've been watching you for years. I brought you into the Special Insertions and Extractions team with misgivings. You have no allegiances. You're apolitical, you show no sense of patriotism, no real sense of purpose. I released you to the Internal Security Service with just those traits in mind, and they served you well as you brought those people down. But not so much now. You said you would never attack an FBI field office but, frankly, I've never gotten a feel for what you would or would not do. The only reason you're sitting in that chair and not in a cell is because you've always come through. You've always enthusiastically taken on your mission. You get a rush from it. You live for the excitement, I think."

Fiona gripped the armrests of her chair and wondered desperately why he rehearsed her next officer's evaluation report. She got the gist, but heard only half the words. A full-blown audio-visual fantasy had swamped her senses, one of crippling the colonel, beating down Shotgun, and battling her way through half a dozen security checkpoints to the outside and freedom. Naturally, she'd get stymied by the sheer number of guns between her and the front door. The colonel himself would stop her. If not, Shotgun would stop her dead.

"I know my duty," she said lamely. "That woman on the screen. That isn't me."

"I believe you," Sanders said. He drew himself off the desk and leaned toward her, hands on knees. "Was it Oz?"

Fiona pushed backward into her chair. Heat rose in her face when the damned thing scraped against the carpet. She opened her mouth. An answer was called for. She couldn't give one. It hadn't been Oz. It hadn't been either of them. But could she truthfully claim that the cat was not in charge? She'd been lost in the neural divide before. She knew what the predator felt like. She knew the fog it blew over her mind.

"Hmm," the colonel said, and straightened. That was all. Hmm.

"You're to report downstairs," Sanders finally commanded her. "They're expecting you."

"Yes, sir." Fiona gathered her bag, rose, and saluted. She half expected her boss not to return the gesture, but he did. She headed for the door with as much dignity as she could muster. Shotgun stepped out of her way.

"Major Street."

She stopped at the door and turned back to Sanders.

"We're looking into this," the colonel said, his tone softened. "Facial Recognition is on the video. So is Signal Analysis. Men are on site in Ohio and Pennsylvania, interviewing the surviving FBI agents. We'll get to the bottom of this hole, that's for sure. I deeply hope we don't find you there."

"Yes, sir. Me, too."

"You're dismissed."

Fiona left the office at a fast walk. She avoided Goodknight's pained gaze. Shotgun and his three agents fell in around their prisoner -- and, yes, she was their prisoner -- like a cage. No one spoke all the way to the elevators.

Shotgun claimed one down car, shooing office workers away from it. When he, Fiona, and the other three bricks had arrayed within the car, he pressed the button for the third sub-basement.

The elevator started downward.

"So, what do I call you?" Fiona asked toward the elevator door.

"We don't have names," Shotgun answered.

"We're going to spend some time together. I should know what to call you."

Silence for a while. Nothing broke it but the trundling sound of the elevator box.

"You can call me Mouse," Shotgun finally said.

Fiona didn't feel any better from that.

Chapter Five

Medical Analysis and Augmentation took up 2400 square feet spread among five offices in Sub-level Three. Three nondescript thirty-something ladies ran the front office. They wore .357 Magnums strapped at the armpits of their ordinary green scrubs and kept MP5 sub-machine guns under their desks. They ensured the one doctor, two nurses, three bio-chemists and one engineer were organized, on budget, and safe. Behind the office were two examination rooms and one surgery, both limited spaces appropriate for two or three occupants at a time. The largest spaces housed the lab and the observation room, the latter of which amounted to a small apartment. At the time, it was all deep black, as far from NSA budget lines as a whale is from Death Valley.

And it served one patient.

"Captain Street," called a nurse from the file cabinets behind the security women. "I haven't seen you in months." She stood just over five feet tall and wore baggy scrubs with little pink penguins swarming every inch. Her blazing, kindergarten-teacher smile always struck Fiona as genuine.

"True, Rita," and Fiona tried to force perkiness into her words. "It's major now. They promoted me. Surprise!"

The nurse's face brightened. She weaved past the barrier of desks, ignored by the three gun-toting staff. "That's marvelous! *Major* Street! A grand thing to get used to." She took Fiona by an elbow and led her past the ladies and into the hall to the inner rooms. As they walked, she coaxed the bag from Fiona's shoulder and handed it off to the veterinarian at the Cat Exam doorway. The vet was a plump black woman with short, shiny hair and ordinary green scrubs. She never smiled, and Oz always growled at her.

Shotgun Mouse and his dark-suited bricks reformed around Fiona like a living bubble regardless of circumstance.

"Can't Oz stay with me?" Fiona asked. "Aren't you just examining, you know, me?"

"Oh, honey, there's never just you," Rita laughed. "You two are an item. If you get a checkup, he does, too. Wouldn't want to get out of sync, now would you?"

Nope. Wouldn't want that.

Craning her neck to see the bag disappear into the room behind her, Fiona let the nurse lead her through the next doorway. This room she knew well. She had burned away days of her life within its walls, getting her blood pressure read in that plain upholstered chair, blowing her nose from tissues on that ordinary gray countertop. There were the same stupid posters about nutrition and the evils of smoking, and there was the one with the goat on a fence post, captioned "Go for the heights!" And there, dominating the ten-foot square space, stood the chair that had changed her life, brought from that despicable secret facility where the neural super-spy scheme had hatched. Something like a dentist's chair but wider and with restraints, it looked like what it was, the tool of a mad scientist, a scientist thankfully imprisoned. Fiona really hated that chair. She really hated that room.

She hated Oz's room, too, though she had never set foot within it. He told her all she needed to know, from the metal table to the needles.

"Okay, let's get your vitals and the doctor will be right with you," Nurse Rita gushed. She nudged Fiona into the plain upholstered chair and went to the cabinetry for her torture devices.

"You know why I'm here?" Fiona asked.

Nurse Rita slapped the blood pressure cuff onto Fiona's arm. "You mean, besides your regular biometrics? Some nonsense about assault and breaking and entering, maybe treasonous behavior. But girls will be girls, eh? Nothing like that going to happen here, will it?"

Fiona figured not, especially since Nurse Rita had mastered at least three martial arts and was known as a dirty fighter.

Blood pressure, temperature, heart rate, weight, and body mass later, the nurse left Fiona alone in the exam room. The guards stood outside. They didn't need to stare her down; the room was a box with one exit.

Oz crouched in his cage by then, angry, humiliated, and pressed into a corner. The vet had insisted on an anal gland exam.

The door opened and the doc breezed in. "Good morning, major. Congratulations, by the way."

"Thank you, Doctor Dumas."

Doctor Richard Dumas -- or Dumbass, as Fiona liked to think of him -- was a tall, slim, balding mid-life crisis with a bamboo stick up his ass. His frown was perpetual, even when he smiled. He patted the vinyl cushions of the exam chair and pulled a stool from the counter for himself.

Fiona slogged over to take her medicine. *You volunteered for this,* she thought. And what does Army wisdom always, *always* say about volunteering?

"Your vitals are fine," the doctor said. "Slight weight gain, but I hardly wish to mention it. Maybe one too many pizzas on stakeout?" He hadn't, not once, glanced up from his tablet.

Fiona cringed into the dreaded chair. She kept her hands and ankles away from the restraints.

"I think we'll be taking a blood panel today. Considering your weight gain and other factors, I'm wondering what the analysis might tell us."

Fiona gave him a sidewise stare. "Other factors?"

Finally, he recognized the patient in the room. His eyes wavered, calculating. Fiona hated Doctor Dumbass. But that wasn't fair. She hated all doctors. "Why, yes," he said. "The reason you were so suddenly referred. Apparently, you've gone to beating up government agents for recreation."

"That wasn't me."

He paused a beat before responding. "Really. That's interesting. Because there's compelling evidence that it was, in fact, you."

"Can we just get on with it, doc?"

"We are getting on with it. A blood panel will alert me to hormonal irregularities that could help explain why you did what you did. I'm assuming you *know* you did what you did. If not, a MEG might be called for."

Fiona slapped the armrests. "I didn't do it! I know what I did and where I was and it wasn't anywhere near any FBI offices!"

"Hmm..."

There it was, the infernal Hmm. Doctor Dumbass's patented way to show he thought you were lying. "What?" she growled.

"Hmm?"

"What hmm?"

He punched a few buttons on his tablet. "You know, if we perform a diagnostic on your implant, we could determine if any anomalous activity can be pinpointed within the last few days."

Fiona lay back in the chair and rubbed her eyes with the palms of her hands. "Doc, I do *not* want to let you fiddle inside my brain. It is *not* a fun date."

Dumas frowned, or she thought he did. Since he always frowned, it was hard to tell when he meant it.

He scooted his stool closer to the chair. He gave Fiona his grave look, maybe more grave than usual. "Major. It's not really up to you. You're military. You follow orders. Well, I, too, have orders."

The colonel again. Shit.

"Shall we get started?"

"What about Oz?" Fiona asked.

"He'll get his moment. It's never a complete diagnostic unless both units are analyzed."

"Well, you better warn the vet, because he's waiting for her."

He waggled the tablet. "Already warned. She's a trooper, though. He isn't the first bad attitude she's had to contend with." The doctor coaxed Fiona into a fully reclined position then began to fasten the restraints.

"I'm serious, doc." Fiona lay back and waited for it. "'Cause *I'm* wired and *he's* wired and *mad*. I hope the vet likes cat scratches and anger piss."

She didn't, judging by the commotion next door a few minutes later.

Half an hour later, Fiona drummed her fingers in the horrible chair, waiting for permission to go back to her guards. The doctor hadn't needed to dig into her brain. He had merely opened the implant door at the diode and plugged in some kind of cable. He had strapped Fiona down to minimize twitching once the digital connection was active. Electrical interaction with the brain is a tricky proposition and he didn't want an errant synaptic firing to jerk loose the cable or damage the implant. Taxpayers' dollars, and all that.

It was no picnic for Fiona. She felt the occasional needle prick of released bio-electric data. They came out of nowhere and made her see purple spots. Worse, she felt every terror response Oz projected into the world. Once she thought she might piss herself in sympathy.

Why couldn't they devise an on-off switch?

The doc got what he wanted, though, and left to confer with his veterinarian colleague. He hadn't bothered to release her straps, even the one that immobilized her head.

The door opened and she strained her eyes to see who entered, ready to give their ears a burning.

It wasn't the doctor.

"Sergeant Grace!"

The familiar square-jawed face leaned over her, inspecting her trap with unvarnished curiosity. He looked sharp as well as handsome in his undress blues, his white shirt exploding with campaign ribbons and qualification badges. "So. Somebody finally figured how to keep you out of trouble."

"Get me out of this rig, top. Damned doctors."

Grace shrugged and reached for her head strap. "I suppose it can't do harm, not with all those bricks outside with their thumb breaks loose."

He undid the strap and Fiona shook her head. "Oh, thank God for you. Bastard's forgotten me here." Grace worked on her arm and leg straps. "Hopefully, you're here for a purpose, top. This a jailbreak?"

"Sorry, too close to collecting a pension. I just dropped by. I've got the clearance."

"They think I iced some FBI pukes!"

"I told you to fly with us." He helped her sit up.

"This is no joke. They've got me under guard and the colonel's making veiled threats."

"Sounds bad." Grace noticed the empty stool and decided to make himself comfortable. "Still, consider the pluses."

"There are pluses?"

"Sure. You're still getting paid, aren't you?"

Fiona clambered out of the chair and began pacing the floor. "Please, top. Direct deposit isn't much good if I'm keeled over in an alley with my head blown off."

"That's a bit strident, don't you think?"

She paced a wide circle around the chair. "What, you think they'll send their black budget science experiment to Leavenworth? Not damned likely in *this* world."

"It'll be all right, major. People are looking into it. My people are looking into those people. The right will come out."

"The right, my ass! I want the exoneration!"

"That's kind of what I meant."

Fiona plopped down in the upholstered chair by the door. "I'm sorry. I'm totally bent. They came for me while I was brushing my teeth. I haven't even had a shower."

They ran out of talk. Both stoked their private thoughts, Grace's eyes on the surgery chair, Fiona's mind on her neural link. Oz was quiet. They had drugged him, as usual.

"I gotta get out of here." Fiona was adamant.

"You will. Just relax."

Doctor Dumbass entered the room. He froze for an instant at seeing Grace, then the empty exam chair. The crazy, dangerous patient was loose.

"Over here," Fiona said, gratified to see him flinch.

"Oh. Well." He rubbed his bald head. "Unexpected to see you, Sergeant Grace."

"I've clearance."

"Of course you do. I meant nothing. Major. I must ask a question of you." He seemed relieved to focus on something. "We've by no means begun to analyze your diagnostics returns, but I noticed a spike in neural activity between 3:57pm and 3:59pm yesterday. Offhand, can you account for that signal?"

Fiona just looked at him.

"It may or may not be significant," the doctor said. He had settled on a topic and was putting out claim stakes. "The spike occurred in both units. I'm curious--"

"Oh, yeah." Fiona nodded. "Sorry, doc, it isn't a thing. If I'm right, that would be the infamous spilled milkshake incident."

"Sorry?"

"The spilled milkshake incident. Spell it correctly in the annals of Fiona Street, Government Lab Rat. Some ditz bumped into us at McDonald's. She was carrying the works and it ended up all over the floor. Chicken McNuggets, apple slices, fries, and the shake got me so bad I had to change clothes in their horrible little restroom."

"Oh." He seemed disappointed. "So nothing suspicious there."

Fiona mugged astonishment. "Damned straight it was suspicious. I mean, who goes to Mickey D's for apple slices? And the shake, it was vanilla, man. Vanilla!"

Doctor Dumbass's face contorted. He wasn't repulsed by vanilla shakes. He was just confused.

"She's being a pill, doc." Grace got up from the stool and moved to lean against the door.

The doctor finally caught up. "Oh. Well, just wondering. Anyway, we'll put the full readouts through analysis and see what comes up. The record will contain a full accounting for neural stimuli over the last forty-eight hours, so if there's anything you'd like to tell me up front..."

Fiona showed him a frosty eye. "Can I go now? I have a prisoner role to perform, otherwise those poor boys outside don't get paid."

Dumbass frowned -- maybe -- in harried disappointment. "You may leave. For the lab."

"The blood won't do much good, doc. I haven't fasted. Though I would have if given polite warning of my arrest."

The doctor moved to the door and tapped Grace aside. "To my knowledge, Major Street, you haven't been placed under arrest." He opened the door to reveal Shotgun Mouse blocking the exit. "At the moment, you're a person of interest. And we aren't checking your cholesterol. A fast isn't required."

Trapped. Fiona gave Grace a helpless, hopeful dose of beaten puppy eyes. Grace gave her a noncommittal shrug.

"All right," she said to Shotgun Mouse. "To the lab, Jeeves. Dracula must feed."

"And then the magnetoencephalograph," Doctor Dumbass added while he fiddled on his tablet.

Right.

Fiona trudged into the hall. "I need my cat," she whined.

LTC Allen Sanders slumped in his midrange nylon weave chair behind his ordinary office desk and thumbed aimlessly through the file on his blotter. The room lay in darkness but for the soft oval of light on his desktop. Sanders's command hid deep within the black cube of NSA headquarters. No windows.

The file on his desk was a personnel jacket, its forms and notes spread where Sanders had poured them. Fiona Street, the papers proclaimed. Meritorious Service Medal, twice. Distinguished Service Medal, Defense Distinguished Service Medal, ARCOM. High marks, West Point. Career highlights: rescued the family of the Speaker of the House from FARC terrorists in Colombia. Saved the nation from the dictatorial, fascist plans of an amuck Special Prosecutor. Saved the universe -- Christ, the *universe* -- from incursion by an omnipotent, omniscient entity bent on the eradication of all life, everywhere.

A closer approximation to James Bond didn't live in the natural world.

And Sanders touched his fingertips to the standing plan for her sanction.

That was spy talk, he reminded himself, for murder.

The beeper for his phone sounded. "Sergeant First Class Grace to see you, sir."

"Thank you, Goodknight. Send him in."

Grace entered the office smartly and saluted in front of the desk.

"At ease, sergeant. How's she doing?"

Grace didn't relax by much. He spread his feet and gripped his hands behind his back. "She's worried, sir. She thinks you're out to get her."

"I wonder what gave her that idea." Sanders fingered the sanction order. "Did you tell her we're doing everything possible?"

"Yes, sir. I don't think she heard me, though. She knows how bad it looks. Plus, I think she might be caught in a paranoid feedback loop with the cat."

Sanders chose to ignore that. Fiona Street gave "crazy cat lady" a whole new spin. "She's our girl, Sergeant Grace. We have to do everything possible to help her."

"Yes, sir. I took the liberty of calling in Asset Three. He may be able to cast some light on the situation, assuming it's related to the incursion at Lawrence-Livermore."

"Good thinking. Which is Asset Three?"

"Hostetter, sir."

"Huh."

"Did I do wrong, sir?"

"That guy once thought I was the fried chicken character. You know, Colonel Sanders?"

"He's come a way since then, sir."

"Yes. I imagine so." The colonel couldn't stop fiddling with the sanction document.

"Case Specific," Grace said, his eyes following the colonel's hands. "You aren't seriously considering that, are you?"

Sanders jerked his hand away as if scalded. He thought a while before answering the sergeant.

"You know, back in the bad old days, when this whole augmented human program was under the table even for us and practically run by Nazis, they used political prisoners to test the neural link tech. Captured spies, mostly. Chinese, Korean, Russian. Later, they snatched homeless people off the streets."

"Yes, sir. Major Street brought those practices to an end."

The reminder stung. The colonel passed Grace a warning look that the NCO ignored. "Do you know how many victims they went through before they got the wiring right? Do you, sergeant? Twenty-three. Some died of embolisms, aneurysms, that sort of thing. Most just went bug-brained crazy. They couldn't handle the animal in their head." He straightened in his chair, but couldn't still his hands. They fidgeted on his blotter, avoiding the papers. "We thought there was something special about Street, something that helped her keep it together. Maybe, after all this time, we're getting proven wrong."

"Sir--"

"I won't allow my office to murder federal agents." Sanders spoke with a ferocity that surprised even him. Then he sagged a little into his shoulders, embarrassed. "Case Specific is not off the table, but it isn't my go-to. We'll see what the doctor says."

"I hope not *just* the doctor."

"No. Never just the doctor."

No. They were Special Forces. Family. They kept care of their own.

"Anything else, sergeant?"

"I was wondering about Asset One, the Reiser woman. She's been known to have insight into this stuff."

The colonel grunted. "Not this stuff, her *own* brand of stuff. Her insights are irrational, to say the least. I wouldn't bother. Keep her on the Voice of the City watch."

"Yessir. Wilco."

Sanders waited a beat. Grace gave no hint of wanting to leave. NCOs. "Yes?"

"Nothing else, sir, except I'd like permission to look over the analysts' shoulders. They're good people, but they don't know Major Street. A familiar eye--"

"Yes, yes, I'll have Goodknight arrange clearance. But take a careful tack, sergeant. The analysts need breathing room to properly do their jobs."

"Yes, sir. Sir, if you've no more need..."

"Dismissed."

After Grace left the office, Sanders spent a long time brooding behind his desk. He wasn't a brooder by nature. Normally, he listened, collected data, and acted, and whatever came from his actions was the best outcome from the greatest consideration. He had thirty-eight covert teams in the field. Street's was only one, and still active despite its lead agent. So why did he burn precious time worrying over what would happen to them -- to her? The girl, he was sure. She grew on you. She had a spark outside the usual framework of patriot, Army lifer, or Joined to Earn Money for Dental School. She fought the good fight, saved lives and nations, because, to her, it was fun. That kind of soldier made an old colonel young again.

And yet, he might have to kill her.

He dragged open his keyboard tray and punched up the code to view security video. He moused to the cameras that monitored the observation room down in Medical Analysis and Augmentation. He clicked the feed for Wide Angle, Whole Room and watched as a window opened on his screen.

The video showed Street wandering the room, touching things here and there, the bureau, the television bezel, the bed covers. She paced. The cat hid under a cheap, upholstered chair that looked snagged from a doctor's waiting room. The creature watched the woman with unblinking intensity.

Are you human, Fiona Street? the colonel asked himself. *Are you the same woman I recruited eight years ago?*

He watched her pace the room, and wondered.

Chapter Six

Raisa Kudashova did not wonder anything. She barely had the where-withal to think. She hunkered down in a dark motel room in Annapolis Junction, Maryland listening to Fiona Street via the bug attached to Oz's cat bag. It wasn't your common electronic surveillance tool. Destined as it was for the heart of NSA headquarters, it needed to surmount that building's formidable signals dampening safeguards.

So the bug, slapped into a crevice along the gusset of an outside pocket, used Bluetooth to connect to any computer within a hundred feet, then wormed its way into its host's software to ride signals security checks out into the phone lines and into the wider world. The Russians had not planned this as a timely means of spying within the NSA. The signal delay between picking up sound and delivering it to the receiver would have been no less than twenty minutes. But then, no Russians complained of the delay; the only ones who would have were dead.

Still, the efficiency of throughput had increased almost to real time, for the signal from the bug didn't need to skulk ninja-style through multiple security measures before it escaped to the world. All it needed was to reach the host's network. The network itself listened, and when the network heard, so did Kudashova.

This was not in the bug's design.

Kudashova listened, sitting in the dark while removing makeup with wash cloths and alcohol. As she listened, something spoke to her. It spoke in a soft voice, an understated buzzing, like a swarm of flies on the other side of a wall. The voice repeated what it heard in Street's room, every word, bump, and air conditioning murmur as it happened, faithfully rendered. The voice belonged to the thing in Kudashova's head, the thing that had puppeteered those guards in California, that had fished access codes from Doctor Rodriguez's head while she slept. The voice belonged to a thing that hated, completely and unreservedly, and laughed at Kudashova's silent screams against it. The thing knew. It knew what flowed through whatever it touched, whether that was a computer network it invaded or a human brain it stole. And it knew it hadn't found Hostetter yet.

Hostetter, that hated one, that one who had driven the thing back to its world, had destroyed the thing's most faithful tools, had cleansed creation of avenues of counterattack. The thing wanted Hostetter. It wanted him more than any desire that pumped through its limitless, non-corporeal existence. And there was so much the thing wanted. It wanted fear, jealousy, greed, confusion, death. It wanted nothingness for all minds, dissolution for all bodies. It wanted to be alone.

But mostly, it wanted Hostetter.

Once it got him, it would torture him for eternity. And when eternity was through, it would make him a doll on strings.

And it would *get* Hostetter. It would get him through Fiona Street.

The motel room had gone black. Kudashova didn't mind or notice. She had no idea where or when she was. Maybe the thing would give her back her mind and body once it had what it really wanted. Maybe not. Maybe, to the end, it would make her an instrument of its being and purpose.

It would make her terror.

Nightmare.

"Major, your call has gone through," the thing parroted to Kudashova. It fed her the sounds of footsteps and murmured thank-yous, of the clatter of a phone handset rising from its cradle.

"Clay! Thanks for being home! I need to hear a friendly voice."

"Well, that's me, Miss Fiona. I was plum worried when they said you was in trouble."

Him. Hostetter. Where was he?

"Trouble is an understated word. I wish I could tell you what it is, but they'd just cut us off."

The thing dived through the digital spiderweb that transported Street's voice to the hated enemy. It chased flashing packets of data as if they were real things, like fleeing animals. It stormed from digital switch to digital switch, on-off, charged-rested, one-zero. It stalked Hostetter like a blood beast, closing, closing--

Then nothing. A spray of electric steam, nothing to grasp to follow it. The thing was a predator run off a cliff.

Satellite uplink. Not even nightmare could follow data through space.

The thing roared. It screamed. In the dark motel room, Kudashova groaned, fell from her bed to the worn carpet, and curled into a ball and shuddered. The eyes behind her closed lids bulged and darted. Blood seeped from between her lips where she had bitten through her tongue.

"Maybe you can tell me when I get there. I ain't callin' from the house, y'know. This here's one o' them cell telephones."

"A ... what? Clay! You're freaking me out!"

"I can learn, Miss Fiona. That nice feller you work with, that sergeant, he called me and told me what problems you got. He called me in to help."

"Oh, Clay. I think I just fell a little bit in love with you."

Stephan Michael Loy

"Now, you know that ain't true and no teasin'. I'll be there soon. Gotta stop first in Californie."

Kudashova jerked. She kicked out, crashing a foot into the bedside table. The table thudded against the wall and rattled.

"Hey! Quiet down over there, goddammit! Some of us are trying to sleep!"

She moved like a dazed person, struggling up from the floor, clawing back onto the bed. She lay there a moment, breathing hard, as if she had climbed a mountain.

He was coming. Hostetter was coming. The thing couldn't go to him, so *he* came to *it*.

The multiverse was just.

"When will you be here?"

"Got no way o' knowin'. It'll be on one o' them aeroplanes and I don't rightly judge their speed. But don't you worry. I'll call again when I can. These here phones work ever'place!"

Kudashova growled and bared her teeth, but it wasn't her, she was too busy screaming, pounding to get out. The thing did the growling. The thing hoisted the Russian's body onto its feet. The thing staggered to the guns on the table and almost scattered them to the floor when it snatched up the assault rifle. The thing, not Kudashova, settled into the chair at the table, caressed the weapon as if it were a child, then tore the gun down to clean and inspect it. The thing did that through Kudashova though the major fought it every moment. She had killed her comrades. She would kill again. She would sully her nation and her oath as an officer and there was nothing she could do to stop it.

Because she, Raisa Kudashova, was Nightmare.

"You won't be able to reach me. The building is shielded from electronic communications. We're only talking now through an authorized port."

"I don't rightly know what that means, but I'll be with you soon. I'll get with that sergeant. Come hell or high water, we gonna meet up soon."

Come, hell. *Come*, high water.

Hostetter and Nightmare gonna meet up soon.

Chapter Seven

There is more to reality than reason can gather. Sally Reiser knew this. Reason was not a good friend of hers.

74

"You sure about this?" Gary asked, his tone strained as he put the car in park. "This is not a safe neighborhood and you're way the wrong color to walk in it."

Sally looked at him, her lover and protector. He didn't realize that *he* was the one protected. But Gary loved her, he worried over her, and the streets beyond their windshield were his old stomping grounds. His warnings were not to be lightly dismissed. She looked at him, drinking in his chiseled face, his dark skin in the wan streetlight, the watery reflection of his deep brown eyes. Her mother didn't approve of him. His friends didn't approve of Sally. But Gary didn't care. He was steadfast even when reason deserted Sally altogether. He was the best man she'd ever known.

"I'll be fine," she said, and flashed him a wide, if nervous, smile. "Show me the ticket."

Gary opened his jacket to reveal the end of the blue-and-white envelope peeking from an inside pocket.

"See, babe." Sally tapped an index finger against the stiff paper. "I wouldn't have bought that if I weren't coming back. Too expensive."

Gary didn't even crack a grin. "Can I at least come with you?"

"Not this time, but you're a dear." Impulsively, she leaned across the center armrest and kissed him on the lips.

"I want you safe," Gary said.

"I'm safer than you," Sally answered as she pushed open the door. "I walk with angels, remember?"

She closed the door behind her and, not looking back, started up the empty street. Without prior knowledge, that walk might have been quaint. Old buildings, none more than four stories tall, many showing decorative brick and stone facades laid down back in the 1930s or 40s. Neon signs, LED signs, changeable letter signs, all brightly lit, many buzzing, and all or almost all in Spanish. This was the borderland of Haughville, once the most dangerous neighborhood in the city, still no sparkling Sunday school experience.

The traffic on Washington Street rushed along as if sprinting for safer ground. The cars parked at the crumbling curbs seemed almost to shiver at their prospects for theft or vandalism. Some of them already showed signs of bad luck, several with slashed tires, one with no tires at all.

And Sally wasn't even in the bad part of the neighborhood. The police patrolled Washington Street. It was a city main drag. But the police rarely ventured into the side streets off that thoroughfare, not without backup, or a call, or both.

Knowing this and fearing nothing, Sally, a slight, white blonde, turned off the main road onto an almost unlit street, a dark drop off the face of the earth.

She could hardly see where she walked. This was a problem, as trash, glass, and broken masonry littered the sidewalk along the weedy yards of tired, abused houses. Dogs barked, some of them pounding against the insides of doors. They weren't cuddly pets, those dogs. They heard movement outside and wanted no less than to kill what moved.

"Yea, though I walk through the valley of death..." Sally muttered, but in Hebrew.

Oh, come on. It's just a neighborhood.

"It's the *particular* neighborhood," Sally protested under her breath.

It's a poor neighborhood. It isn't like I sent you into the Nam down a jungle trail lined with land mines and Pungi pits.

"Gee, thanks for the perspective. It'll be a help when they find my body."

You're regrettably full of drama. Look, most of these residents are church-going people, unlike the folks in your neighborhood. Unlike you, as a matter of fact.

"Is there a focus to this, because I would otherwise be focused on what and who is around me."

Got that covered, just keep walking. Sure, we have your crack dealers and your methheads here, even some prostitution entrepreneurs. We got your local gang and their visiting antagonists. And we got your angry sociopaths who would shoot you just to test their latest stolen gun..."

"Making me feel even better."

But they're a distinct minority of the population. Most folks here are just good, God-fearing people. Poor, desperate even, hopeless, and not a lot of legitimate green cards. But good people. Stop being afraid of goodness down on its luck. Okay, stop here.

"Here" was a rundown house like all the other rundown houses. Its porch roof sagged, the long-vanished post that had held up one corner replaced by a two-by-four too short for the job. The window openings showed warped plywood covers. Three junked cars had been slung haphazardly onto the dirt front yard. No light shone from the dilapidated building.

"I hope you don't want me going in there..."

Not just yet. Wait.

She waited. She stood outside the dark house in a cold breeze that whispered of winter. She huddled into her coat and squeezed the cell phone in her coat pocket. A few porch lights cut the dark of that forlorn street, but feebly.

"Okay, so what am I waiting f--"

Gunfire split the somber atmosphere, a continuous chattering of automatic weapons, a great many of them at once. The cracks around the boarded-up windows strobed. Sally started, but didn't run. The maelstrom ended almost before she could blink.

"Holy shit!"

Don't move.

Another blast of gunfire, this time cut off in the first few notes. Then, blaring silence.

All the porch lights went out. Nobody was calling the police about this.

Now. Go in.

"Are you nuts?"

Go. Now!

The voice in her head might as well have kicked her forward. Sally hurried, stumbling, toward the front door. She found the doorknob and turned it. When it didn't work, she didn't think. She leaned back, brought up her foot, and kicked the door as hard as she could. Rotted wood snapped, nailed-in bolts tore loose, and the door swung open until it snagged on interior trash.

No lights inside. Sally didn't have a flashlight. She strode into the house, clenching her fists and teeth.

She hadn't gotten five feet before an obstacle blocked her way. "What do you want?" it asked.

"Uh, uh..."

I will put the words in your mouth.

"Uh, uh..."

The obstacle was a man. He gripped two bodies by their collars, had been dragging the men behind him when he rushed up to Sally. "Who are you? What do you want?"

"I-- I heard-- There were guns..."

You're embarrassing me.

"Leave," the big tank of a man said, his tone non-threatening but deep as a well. "This is not your concern. Go home." He made an end run around her and out the door, dragging the limp forms behind him.

Sally didn't know what to do. She glanced around. She couldn't see much, just a pervading impression of trash piled in corners, of broken, moldy furniture and precious little of that, and of man-sized lumps crumpled against the moldering-carpet floor.

The big man returned, grabbed two more bodies, and exited the house as if Sally didn't exist.

What the hell? Had he *murdered* those people?

She trudged outside where he dropped victims three and four in a neat line with one and two. They lay face down, their wrists bound with zip cords.

So not dead. You didn't tie up dead bodies. At least, *normal* people didn't.

The man bulled past her for the house again. She scrambled aside as he did so.

When he vanished into the house, she looked first from the doorway to the prone men, to the house and back to the men. She stepped over yard garbage until she got to the bound victims, then bent down to probe a neck for a pulse.

Definitely not dead.

She stood, then nearly screamed when she found the man-tank right next to her, glowering down at her through a slit in his helmet visor.

"Why are you here?" he asked, and dropped two more men to the dirt.

Let me talk to this guy.

"I have a message for you, and I plead for your help," Sally said, the words rolling out of her without any effort.

He continued staring at her. His pure, stony strength intimidated. It would have done the same in broad daylight.

"The city needs you," Sally continued. "The world needs you. You are the Voice of the City. Does the city love or loathe the darkness?"

He cocked his head. He might have been curious. "Who are you?"

"I'm a messenger. Come when we call you." And Sally reached into her coat, pulled out the cell phone, and held it out to the man.

He looked at her hand.

"These aren't your enemy," Sally said, pointing at the bodies with her other hand.

"Meth dealers. They're as good an enemy as any."

"You don't need enemies, but purpose." She hefted the phone at him. "Take it. It'll *bring* you purpose."

"Call the police," he said, then snatched the phone from her palm.

Sally flexed the fingers that had held the mobile device. She stared at them, wondering why they were empty. When she looked back up, the man was gone.

She didn't delay. She stumbled out of the yard and quick-marched back up to Washington Street. When she got to the car, she scrabbled at the door latch, unable to make it work. Gary flung the door open from inside and Sally all but fell into her seat. Only then did she realize her cheeks were wet with tears.

"What happened?" Gary asked, grasping her coat, his hand shaking. "I heard gunshots."

"Call the cops." Sally tried to get her heaving breath under control.

"Are you all right?" But Gary already pulled out his phone.

Sally thought about that. *Was* she all right? When was the last time she had been *all* right? How many years? How many times since the voices in her head, since the pictures in her dreams?

And now she had one more, a baritone voice, a lonely voice, a voice lost in lost causes.

A Voice of the City.

"Something's coming," she said to the dashboard.
Something's here, the voice in her head corrected.
"Airport?" Gary asked, starting the car.
"Airport," Sally answered. "Let's get this over with."

Chapter Eight

Doctor Dumas lay in wait for Sanders when the colonel came in the next day. Sanders felt both exhilaration and the weight of ages at seeing the thin, bald man. Answers would be forthcoming, answers to guide decisions. Sanders only hoped he wouldn't regret those decisions.

"Yes, doctor, what do you have for me?" he asked as he took his mail and daily orders from Goodknight.

Dumas gripped a vinyl portfolio to his chest. "I've gone through the bio-chemical analysis, sir, and the results of the MEG we took on Major Street. That and a review of her recent mission video and past medical entries bring me to rather distressing conclusions."

"Oh, good," Sanders said. "Distressing. That's just what I needed first thing in the morning." He looked meaningfully at Goodknight.

"Your coffee's on your desk, sir."

Dumas waggled his portfolio. "Sir, these findings--"

"In my office, doctor." The colonel took off for his door, leaving Dumas to decide if he would follow.

He did. Sanders dropped his mail on the blotter and crashed down into his chair. "Have a seat." He took up the ceramic mug of coffee before him and ventured a tentative sip. How did Goodknight manage it? The stuff was as hot as if she'd just poured it.

"First of all, colonel, I want you to know I have only the deepest respect for this office and what you're trying to accomplish--"

"First of all, doctor, I don't care for a bunch of bullshit on my time. Just tell me what I need to know and I'll be the judge of all other things and sundry, if you don't mind."

"Oh." The doctor seemed adequately chastened. He sat down in the seat Street had vacated the day before.

"How long have you been with us?" the colonel asked. "Eight months? Ten?"

"I've been with the program for a year and a half." Dumas mustered a measure of his usual stick-up-the-ass composure. "It's all right. I don't expect you'd keep track of every doctor for just one patient. You have dozens of agents under your supervision. But do understand that I'm not some resident straight out of med school. I came here after a stint as chief of neurology at Walter Reed."

"I'm aware of your qualifications. You wouldn't be here if you weren't at once trusted, expert, and circumspect." Sanders felt a little chastened himself for not realizing the doctor's length of service. They had gone through a barrel of medical staff since Street took on the cat and her original physician had gone off to prison. Dumas's tenure was a godsend. "Please, doctor, tell me about my agent."

A little over a mile away, in a squatter, less grandiose building than the great black brick of NSA headquarters, Childress dropped two boxes on the table where Ponce and Grace huddled. The room in which they gathered didn't offer much to look at, just three cheap desks and a long, foldable worktable. Surrounding the table, a plethora of broken-down swivel chairs looked as if the NSA had raided a Goodwill store.

"Breakfast," Childress said. "Don't say I never got you fuckers nothin'."

Grace and Ponce had been hunched over a laptop. Now Ponce redirected his attention to the boxes, peeling up the lid of the nearest. "Did you get any of those cake doughnuts? The old-fashioned kind, not the fluffy kind?"

"I got doughnuts. Be glad they ain't used. What we got, Top? Anything yet?"

"Plenty, maybe." Grace watched the laptop screen. It flickered with video. "Ponce here has the eyes of an eagle, or the imagination of a ten-year-old."

"It's not imagination." Ponce snagged an apple-cinnamon filled roll with Dutch apple topping. "Upper left quadrant. Right when she punches the skinny guy in the throat. It's right there."

"I'm not seeing anything."

Ponce spoke with his mouth full, waving Grace away from the computer. "Just gimme. I'll go through frame by frame. You'll see."

Childress grinned. "Damn, top, you got m'boy's dandruff up. That's what you get for callin' all-nighters."

Grace leaned back in his rickety chair and stretched. "It's dander, not dandruff."

"You had a close look at Ponce lately?"

Grace rubbed his eyes. "What did you find?"

Childress gave up trying to raise the morale -- or whatever -- of his fellow agents. He stalked to one of the desks and slumped into its much more substantial, if still bargain basement, chair. "Got goose eggs. Her house ain't got nothin' but house. Nothin' there to say why she'd go all MX Johnson on the FBI. All I can figure is, when she was in the ISS, all her other team members were FBI except the one CIA puke. All them FBI retards either went with the bad guy or gave up in the pinch, so maybe the major was holdin' a grudge."

"No," Grace said with finality.

Childress spread his hands. "What can I say, top? I don't buy that shit myself. She even has a picture of her and her team on a bookcase, so there's that."

"There has to be something, something that shows that she *didn't* do it rather than did." Grace seemed to chew his teeth. He stood suddenly and started to pace.

"I figure maybe the trigger was more recent," Childress said. "Maybe with that Batman SOB. I mean, she didn't start comin' down all crazy till after that, right?"

Grace continued to pace. He rubbed the back of his neck. His uniform had a tired look, the creases long erased. And Ponce had lost both his tie and his suit jacket somewhere along the night. Only Childress gave off a look of fresh professionalism. Childress had standards.

"Hey. Boss." Childress rapped on the desktop. "You hearin' me? 'Cause I need you requestin' a field team in Indianapolis, that dirt pile excuse for a town. We need to look more into this Black Superdude guy and see if he's got voodoo mind control shit all over the captain, yeah?"

"Major," Grace corrected without looking.

"Okay, major. Can we get a team on the ground, or not?"

"Sure. I'll get somebody on that soon as I see the colonel."

"Somebody." Childress tightened up. He hated it when the sergeants got muddled. "Do I get to know who these mystery men are?"

"I'll call you."

"You will? I'll wait with bated breath for that one, boss. 'Cause I don't need no rookies, no geezers, and no second-chancers sniffin' the dirt out there in India-noplace. You saw what a wreck that fucker made of *us*."

"I said I'd call you."

"Okay..."

Ponce cut that uncomfortable conversation short. He snapped his fingers repeatedly and gestured for Grace to approach.

Oh well, Childress thought, and lifted himself from his chair to see what the latest pipe dream was.

"See? Right there." Ponce stabbed one meaty finger at the laptop screen. He pointed at two blurry circles, or maybe spheres, smudging the upper left corner of the frozen video image.

"So?" Childress ventured.

Ponce tapped the circles repeatedly. "What *are* those things? The FBI has flying marbles to play with?"

"Don't know," Childress said. "Maybe you should isolate that quadrant and enlarge and enhance the image so's we can read assholes and serial numbers and shit like that."

Ponce gave him a dirty look.

"Just bein' a nuisance, man. Gotta keep in practice."

Grace pointed at the screen. "I can't take that to Sanders. If we knew what they were... I mean, somebody could've kicked over some golf balls."

"Not golf balls," Ponce objected, and dropped his hand to the trackpad. "Golf balls don't show non-ballistic motion."

He tapped a few menu commands and the video reverted to normal speed. Childress and Grace watched as the "golf balls" swung more or less through an arc. On one occasion, though, the one ball visible seemed to halt, reverse direction, and regain its original path with a sudden, intelligent course correction.

"What was that?" Grace asked.

"That's what I've been pointing out," Ponce said. "Looks to me like a drone of some kind."

"Yeah, well, that's cool an' shit," Childress said. "Y'all keep it up. A few dozen years and you can convince the colonel Martians made her do it. Me, I got last week's paperwork to do."

"She didn't do it," Grace insisted.

"Really, top? 'Cause we're lookin' at her doin' it right the fuck now."

"I've known her years longer than you. I know she would never--"

Childress gestured to cut him off, then headed for the door. "That's great, top. That's loyalty. But ain't none of us others known her that long. So I, for one, gonna do the police work. If it shows my boss is a cop killer, then I got no prob takin' her ass down."

And he was gone, dramatic exit achieved.

What, Childress asked himself as he strolled down the hallway of that quiet, crappy building, was up with that crew? Top had them far and wide, even out to California, scratching around for proof of innocence. What kind of sense did that make? Major Street got herself caught dead to rights on video. It was her and no mistake. Now, maybe if the entire video were faked, some uber-Hollywood computer graphics stunt or some bullshit like that, but that simply wasn't the case. Grace and Ponce watched genuine FBI files, certified untampered.

So why did Childress ask for boots in Indianapolis? Why bother, given the givens? He managed only two responses. One: he was a sap. Two: Black Batman. A brother with impossible weapons and an impossible jet might also manage impossible video. Why? Childress had no clue.

But he knew he'd find out if he got half a chance.

Barring that, he'd put the cuffs on Street himself.

Dumas scooted to the edge of his chair and laid his portfolio on the colonel's desk. "I was tasked to discover evidence of the guilt or innocence of Major Street regarding the incidents in Ohio and Pennsylvania. My findings in that regard are inconclusive. That is, I found no chemical markers to indicate she lied about her innocence, also no forensic indications of physical exertion on the level necessary during the time frame I was given."

"So you're saying she's in the clear," Sanders tried to clarify.

"I'm saying my findings are inconclusive. Chemical analysis for exertion -- for past exertion -- is not terribly dependable. Also, though I measured a number of stress indicators during her MEG, I can't isolate if they were from lying about her involvement in yesterday's attacks."

"Doctor, she was, for all intents and purposes, under arrest during your tests. That might have added some stress to her day."

"I'm inclined to concur. Also, I found no unusual record from the implant download. It keeps a record of neural exchanges for up to forty-eight hours. Major Street's output was within the normal range except during a three-minute time frame outside the target period."

Sanders gave the doctor a level stare.

"It was nothing." Dumas waved the colonel's concern away. "An altercation at a fast-food restaurant."

"So, once again, you're clearing her."

"No, sir." An impatient tone entered the doctor's voice. "Unless Major Street has great reserves of calm that she can draw upon while killing multiple government agents, she could not have been responsible for the attacks the other day. Her cat, on the other hand--"

"Her *cat?*"

"It showed great distress during its MEG." He put up a hand. "I know, sir, it's a cat. But it also showed greatly elevated chemical markers for stress during the time interval you assigned to me. There were also significant increases in neural throughput recorded by its implant."

Sanders took a taste of coffee. He had seen this coming. He had hoped the eggheads would dismiss his suspicion. That wasn't happening. "Doctor, we aren't investigating if the cat attacked those FBI field offices. There was no cat on those videos."

"I don't know if that's strictly so."

The colonel, pointedly, looked at his watch.

Dumas opened his portfolio and spread several papers in front of him. "You've heard of proprioception?"

Sanders shook his head while rubbing his eyes with the heels of his palms.

The doctor grimaced. "You see, that's the problem. You've managed her as personnel, how to use her, control her, get her paid, officer efficiency reports, that sort of thing. She should have been monitored medically this whole time. From what I can gather, her first physician is locked up for crimes against humanity and her platoon of subsequent doctors didn't do much more than mark time until their replacements came through. There's never been a long-term study of this patient. Put simply, you, colonel, have a mental patient on your hands and you don't know how to deal with her."

Sanders twirled a finger to nudge the man back on track. "You were talking about property exceptions."

"Proprioception. It's the neurological concept of knowing one's place in space and time, knowing where your body is and that it is, in fact, your body. And there are other neurological concepts of self involved here. Just think, sir. How do you know that your hand is yours, that it's resting on your desktop? If you place your hand behind your back, how do you know it's still there? How do you command a body part you can't see? How can you move around in a pitch black room? Your brain keeps a concept of who and where you are. It's a fragile thing, entirely intrinsic to the operation of your synapses. It can be fooled, disrupted, and your sense of space and self altered. Do you understand me, sir?"

Sanders thought so, though the subject was outside his pay grade. He fought an urge to check his watch.

"Well, complicate that concept in the case of Major Street. Thanks to her implant, she's in two places at once, or one place or the other depending on which brain is most powerfully represented. Her concept of self is not one of being human, but one of being a morphologically complex … changeling. She can control the cat, that is, see, hear, smell, or feel through the cat, and still be entirely herself. But it works both ways. The cat can experience the major's senses, too. Woman and animal's senses of self and embodiment are less fundamental to their individual minds and more a sliding scale between them. And it isn't just communication. Major Street can *become* the cat and the cat can *become* her, or any mix of those two extremes."

This was getting a little out there. Sanders took a sip from his coffee and started shuffling his mail. "This depth of symbiosis has never been mentioned before."

"Actually, it's been catalogued over and over, just no one's put it together." The doctor slid a highlighted log across the desk. "After the initial implant but before Street became an approved enhanced operative, her Internal Security Service superior reported her 'sleepwalking' naked through her house, led by the cat. She was naming things, as if the cat were using her to become familiar with its surroundings."

Sanders didn't touch the paper. He had heard that story. He had thought it apocryphal, the kind of thing agents invented because it yielded lots of juice.

Dumas slid another paper toward him, part of a medical report. "Later, during training to help her command the neural link, Major Street participated in a weapons fire exercise. She was assigned to shoot paper targets with her standard-issue sidearm, in which she is rated 'expert.' During the firing exercise, she became distracted by the light from a laser pointer. She deviated from her assigned targets to shoot the light. The light was held by an evaluator. Imagine if it had been a random ten-year-old kid."

"Doctor, these were anomalies from early implantation. Before calibration."

"All of Major Street's calibrations aimed to *clarify* and *strengthen* the neural link. There has never been an expressed need to firewall her from the cat."

"Firewall her? That would be counterproductive."

The doctor sighed. His face worked into a stiff mask, as if setting himself to a necessary but unpleasant task. Sanders knew that face. His dad had used it decades earlier to explain to an obstinate kid the concept of losing a hand to fireworks.

Dumas slid another document across the table. It was a photograph with penned annotations. Sanders recognized Street and that Voice of the City character.

"Here is Major Street trying very hard to kick a man's head in. You'll notice his head actually made contact with the car. Why he's alive is anyone's guess." Dumas slid across a graph. "This is the record for that moment from Street's implant download. It shows the cat more in charge than her."

He slid another, similar, graph across. "I took the liberty during her diagnostic to switch on live recording." He tapped the paper with an index finger. "This was twenty minutes ago."

Barbara Eglemann was a bundle of nerves. First, that attack two nights before, complete with men gunned down in their sleep, a terrorist standoff outside the doors, and an engineering impossibility she had yet to explain to her boss. Then the CID boys had shown up, forcing back the press of local law enforcement to make the mess an internal Army felony investigation. Now the stakes had upped again with the arrival of the NSA. How many more bundles of letters would invade her world before they drove her off the deep end of sanity?

And the damned sun hadn't even come up.

She'd met the agents at the front gate. They wore rumpled suits, like they had just fallen off the airplane. That was okay. Who cared what they looked like? Eglemann herself had just thrown on sweats and a Hulk Smash! t-shirt, so who was she to judge? Hell, she had noticed when already at the gate that the shirt was on wrong-side-out.

Originally, there had been two of them. One, the black guy, had split off with a CID operative to check out video files or something. Anyway, neither NSA agent got close to the trans-universal generator itself. CID-controlled troops had taped off and guarded the dark, brooding building. Eglemann had told the agents all she knew of the events of two nights earlier, but that hadn't been much. She had spent the incident barricaded in the generator room, after all. Her experience of that night was limited to computer readouts, broken-open electronic panels, and the sound of gunfire outside her doors.

But the NSA wasn't satisfied with ignorance. She led the remaining agent down the long hallway of a one-story office complex half a block from the generator, temporary offices for the project administrators. Eglemann had tired of answering the inane and repetitive questions of policemen. If he wanted more, he could speak to her boss, whom she had called ahead to roust out of bed.

They stopped at a door with a Post-it identifier at eye level. Eglemann grinned sheepishly and indicated the note and its cousins on every door up the hall. "This is really sudden, the move. That's all we have for nameplates."

The agent wasn't impressed with that fun fact, so Eglemann knocked on the door. "Doctor Rodriguez? It's Barbara with that man."

"Come in," she heard, and led the man into the office.

Inside crowded a folding table, boxes and boxes, and cables leading from a laptop on the table to a router box and uninterruptible power supply on the floor. The ten-foot-by-ten-foot tableau stood under a single overhead light.

Directly under the light and behind the table, Doctor Rodriguez sat in a camp chair, her hands full of documents from the box in front of her. She looked a little crazed, or perhaps a lot befuddled, as if the messy puzzle around her defied unraveling. And, God damn it, she looked gorgeous. Five o'clock in the morning and she looked like an anchorwoman on Fox News. The injustice of the thing!

Her boss wore an expensively simple blue dress that seemed molded to her using CGI. Even as she sat in the low, slumping camp chair the dress showed nary a wrinkle beyond a smooth line at her lap. She was a heartstopper in that dress or not, a kind of lost-in-the-wilderness Weatherlady Barbie that men would tune in to just to see her wave at the map. The seat's lack of height only emphasized her lost little girl look. But that was okay. Doctor Rodriguez usually looked that way. Her obsessive-compulsive nightmare of a life demanded she not leave the house without looking just … so. She may have radiated beauty enough to make pudgy Barbara Eglemann self-conscious, but the woman needed gallons of help.

"I'm sorry," the boss said in that tone that turned strong men to melted butter. "I'm stymied by what to do here…"

"Sorry, Doc." Eglemann sidled around the table, kicking boxes aside, and took the papers from her boss's hands. "It's a mess. We're all coping. What are you wanting here, today's reports? I'll dig those out while you deal with these guys."

"I had everything arranged on my desk."

"Yes, doctor, and your desk is behind yellow tape and about twenty armed guards."

She was something, plain enough. Slim, athletic build with coffee-colored skin and big, watery eyes. Her long, black hair fell like an overactive waterfall. The gene pool was monstrously unfair.

Eglemann dragged the box off the table and squatted over its documents. She gave Doctor Rodriguez a pointed look and a tip of the chin toward the agent.

On cue, the lovely genius darling turned toward the man, her hands, emptied of papers, still poised in the air.

"And you are…"

The tall, Hispanic Adonis stepped forward and held out a hand. "Agent Tejada, NSA."

She shook his hand with surprising firmness for such a dithery thing.

"I apologize for the confusion," the executive director of the National Inter-universal Transmission Initiative said in that lost voice she fell into in unfamiliar situations. Soon enough she would find her bearings and the magic would fizzle for the visitor. "We had an incident."

"Yes," Agent Tejada said. "I understand. That's why I'm here. Your engineer--"

"I'm Doctor Sinfonee Rodriguez. I'm here to cooperate with your investigation in every way possible."

Well, maybe not *every* way, Eglemann thought as she sorted papers. There was no way in hell the doc could get them into the generator facility...

"Good to hear it," Tejada said. "I need access to your generator facility, where the incident took place."

"Oh!" Doctor Rodriguez stood, her hands still up like she didn't want to get them dirty. "We can't get into the facility now. The Criminal Investigations Division-- Is that who they are, Barbara?"

"Yes, Doc."

"They've locked us out."

"I really need to get in," the agent said. "There's been another incident out east and I want to see if any of it's connected."

Doctor Rodriguez seemed to forget her befuddlement. She crossed her arms over her elegant dress and eyed Tejada as if he'd made farting sounds. "Interesting. How do you plan to do that? Are you a post doctorate in high energy astrophysics or one of the new graduate students in N-space geomatics?"

"Uhh..." Tejada responded.

"Are you planning to map the gravitational sinks around the generator chamber and calculate their intensities and deformations to correlate the coordinates of space-time events?"

"Actually, ma'am, I was just going to look around."

Doctor Rodriguez didn't notice the formality. "You're going to look around." She scrunched up her face but couldn't wrap that concept around her brain. "What is it you plan to see? I mean, it's just a room."

"I'm a glorified cop, ma'am," Tejada said. "You'd be surprised what I can find by just looking around."

"Oh. Yes, I would be. But it makes no difference. The CID..."

"I'll take care of the CID," Agent Tejada said. "I just need one of you to lead me through the facility."

Eglemann wanted to see that. She'd tangled with the CID enough in the last few days, she would gladly have paid good money--

And twenty minutes later they were inside the building with the keys in their hands and a polite CID investigator admonishing them to stay clear of marked-off surfaces. Eglemann was there with the doc. Tejada stayed with them while the second agent, named DeBoy, returned long enough to march off again, putting eyes on every nook and cranny in the generator facility except, apparently, the generator room.

Eglemann pressed her palm to the reader and swung open one of the huge double doors.

"I'm surprised it opens so easily," Tejada said as he stepped through into the theater. "It's huge."

"It swings on spring assists with hydraulic boosts at the hinges, or something like that," the doc said. "Barbara's an engineer. She could explain it better."

"Actually, no," Eglemann said. "I'm a nuclear engineer, not a civil one."

The generator room echoed. Someone had left all the lights on even though the equipment was off and the staff restricted from entering. The government. No respect for taxpayers' dollars. The focusing platform surrounded by attenuation pylons stood as it had on the night of the incident except for the yellow tape stretched around its perimeter. Nothing had been moved. The equipment stood in standby where necessary, plugs pulled where possible. Other than that, they lacked only people to set the stage exactly as it had been that frightening night. Well, people plus a reality-warping bridge to another world.

"That's the machine," Tejada said, speaking more to himself than to anyone.

The doc, as she usually did, failed to catch that subtlety. "That isn't, in fact, the whole machine. It's the focusing platform with energy attenuators, but the whole machine includes all of these control consoles, servers, and drives plus the two nuclear reactors housed three miles from here in their own facility."

"And this is where the wormhole or whatever came through."

"The trans-universal event is most definitely *not* a wormhole," Doctor Rodriguez began as if someone had called unobtainium an element on the periodic table. "A wormhole, or Einstein-Rosen bridge--"

Eglemann reached out and squeezed her boss's elbow. "Doctor Rodriguez, I think we can dispense with the physics lesson. Agent Tejada here isn't looking for all that. He just wants to know about the incident."

"Yeah," Tejada said, still walking slowly toward the platform. "Like, how did one of those events as you call them happen here if the machine doesn't work and had no power connections?"

"That's something we haven't been able to solve," Eglemann volunteered. "One assumption at this point, and we really hate assumptions around here, is that the event originated somewhere else and just coincidentally landed on our platform."

"Or," Tejada suggested, wagging a finger at Eglemann, "somebody has the wherewithal to focus and direct these things to wherever they want, and they wanted to come here specifically."

"That's another idea, yes," Eglemann nodded, "but--"

"--why, if that's the case, was the lightning post so sketchy?" Tejada finished for her.

"Exactly." Eglemann was impressed. It must have showed somehow.

"Please," Doctor Rodriguez said, "let's not call it a lightning post. There is no lightning involved."

Tejada gave her a wry grin and a wink. "If you have power and control enough to direct something like this trans-universe whatzit, then why don't you have power to do it up real pretty instead of that sputtering, DIY show the other night?" He stopped just short of the yellow tape bordering the platform's ceramic footing. He put his hands on his hips and scanned the massive stage all the way to its fifty-foot-high parabola.

"There are a lot of technical reasons why that might be so," the doc said. She stood beside him in her clotheshorse perfect dress and twiddled her fingers behind her back. For the first time, Eglemann noticed that the woman hadn't brought her stress ball along. Maybe it was lost in all those boxes of hers. "Some theorize that it isn't possible to actually create a trans-universal event, you instead hijack one that's going your way. They criss-cross space-time through the multiverse, an intricate webbing holding the universes together. There are hundreds going through us right now, just not in sufficient focus to affect us. Maybe the platform area is a void and it was difficult to focus an event in that area."

"Then you guys wasted a lot of cash putting it there, wouldn't you think?" Tejada didn't even look at her.

His comment flustered Rodriguez. "Well, I suppose-- But, no. I don't particularly agree with that theory…"

"Here's a theory for you." Tejada took both of them into his gaze. "How about the event thing didn't form too well because the guy in charge didn't care if it did."

"No." Eglemann hated when laymen tried to think all sciency. "It would cost us 4.3 million bucks to turn on that device in front of you and take a trip to wherever. You don't expend that level of resources for a joke. You do it for a purpose."

"And he achieved his. He distracted you guys from the real thing."

Eglemann opened her mouth, then closed it. She had expected to argue how ridiculous that was. But was it?

"Is this the only trans-universal whatever thing around here?" Tejada asked Rodriguez.

She looked up at him with those big, watery eyes. She looked like a deer in front of a lion, but she often looked that way, even when her brain ticked like clockwork. "There are three that we know of," she said after a second. "One is in Wyoming."

"That would be Marshal Hostetter's device. As far as we know, it isn't involved here."

"Yes. Then there's this unit, which isn't yet operational. And there's the bag."

"The bag? What's that?"

Eglemann was getting a bad feeling. "The bag is a collection of quantum phase generators Hostetter brought with him when he came to our world. Arranged properly, they can define events of multiple levels, from something to communicate across universal barriers to full-blown extra-universal travel conduits."

"But the bag is secured in the labs," the doc assured Tejada.

"Really. Can I have a look?"

The doc stared at him. She seemed to think he had grown horns. "Why?"

"Frankly, doctor, I wonder if the bag is as secure as you think it is."

"It's locked up."

"I'm just checking all avenues of investigation. It's what us glorified cops do."

"It's locked up. Isn't it locked up, Barbara?"

"Yes, doc."

"So it's secure?" Tejada asked.

"Yes. It's locked up."

Uh-oh, the doc was caught in a loop. Eglemann squeezed her elbow again. "Doctor Rodriguez. Why don't we show the silly NSA agent what we mean by 'locked up.' It should put his troubled mind at ease."

"Of course," Rodriguez said. Eglemann usually had no trouble nudging her from her episodes. "It's right this way."

So they crossed back to the huge doors. Tejada touched his ear and spoke. "D, meet us back at the generator room entrance. We're going to the labs." Cool. No wire leading to a battery pack or anything.

They exited the room, locked the doors, then traveled along the wall to the left. Before they turned into the corridor curving alongside the generator room, Agent DeBoy fast-walked up to them from the other side of the building.

"Nothing," he said to Tejada without preamble. "What's the deal here?"

"I don't know," the other agent said, "maybe a surprise."

He was certainly right about that. Both agents lifted their eyebrows when the doc led them into a locked room at the outside curve of the wall. Across that compartment stood a big, steel, bank vault door. They opened their eyes a little wider when Rodriguez's handprint and eye scan opened that foot-thick barrier to reveal another steel door beyond. The security paranoia put grins on their faces, but only for as long as Rodriguez fooled with the ten-digit passcode that popped open that door.

As soon as the seal released, smoke burst from the room beyond.

"Whoa!" Tejada darted forward, grabbed the doc around the waist, and lifted her away from the doorway. She gasped, dropped her ring of keys, and fell into the other agent's arms. Eglemann bent double, coughing the sudden blast of smoke from her lungs. Her eyes watered. Her nose felt gritty. From their own fits of coughing, she imagined the others were no more comfortable.

The space beyond that security door was *hot*. It must have been ninety degrees in there. The ceiling writhed with black smoke over a stink of char. Tiny safes lined the walls like safety deposit boxes, the black smoke belching from one particular safe three-quarters way down the leftside wall.

"Let me guess," DeBoy said after a coughing fit. "The furnace room's right next door and you neglected to pay for fire alarms."

"I'm not liking this." Eglemann wiped her face of sudden sweat.

Doctor Rodriguez, breathing hard in the heat, pointed toward the safe spewing the acrid smoke. "That's where we store the quantum phase generators."

"Great." Tejada scooped up the keys.

"That's my responsibility," Rodriguez said. She shook herself free of Tejada's hold. "The keys for these safes belong in no one else's hands." Did she not understand the situation?

"Nevertheless, I think you'd better stay here," Tejada said from the doorway.

"This is not the procedure--"

"Sinfonee, for Christ's sake, the damned safe is on *fire*," Eglemann called and backed toward the exit. "Leave the man alone."

The director made fretting sounds, but stepped back toward DeBoy. Tejada thanked her quietly, then carefully entered the room.

Tejada waved a hand over the smoking safe. "It's hot, but not terribly so. How do we explain that?"

Eglemann thought. She wiped her stinging eyes. "Umm, maybe it's a slow burn, without much fuel. We don't store much that's flammable in here..."

"The bag," Doctor Rodriguez said. "Possibly the leather bag caught fire. The closed room would trap any heat, which might have accumulated over the last several hours."

Tejada glanced around. "You've got a vent here, and sprinklers."

"The vent is designed to close in case of fire, to choke off available oxygen." The doc sounded like an undergrad lecturer. "The sprinkler system, I don't know."

"Lots of bullets flying last night," Eglemann called. "Maybe something got hit."

Tejada pointed at the lock on the safe. "I just don't want a surprise hitting me when I open that door." He coughed.

"If anything surprising was going to happen, it would have done so already," the doc said, and coughed daintily into her hands. "Opening the door would have fed a fire starved of oxygen and caused a possibly catastrophic backburn. Opening the safe should pose no problems. Theoretically."

Tejada gave her a look.

"I can't explain why the fire's still burning," Rodriguez admitted. "If it started last night, it should have been starved a long while ago."

"Well, shit," Tejada said, then inserted the key into its lock, and turned it. He reached for the little handle in the door, but jerked his fingers back before they touched it. He peeled off his suit jacket, rolled it onto his hand, and went at the handle again.

A jerk, and the room filled with orange light, a faint crackling, and a surge of static charge.

Inside the open compartment, a leather bag, or what was left of its smoking hide, had pressed itself against the upper left of the box. Projecting from it like a jet exhaust was a thick, brilliant, orange beam that wavered as if alive. It had burned through the lower right wall of the box to who knew where. It was probably on its way to the apocryphal China.

"What's that, a ray gun?" DeBoy asked.

"No," the doc answered, struggling to see into the chamber. "It's a Category 2 trans-universal event!"

"No, it isn't," Tejada said as he filled the doorway. "It's a Trojan Horse."

Sanders pulled the two graphs from the jumble of papers Dumas presented and laid them side by side. So one was from Street two days ago and the other was only twenty minutes old. The peaks and valleys of the readouts did not match exactly, but easily fell within a common range marked in ink. He didn't know what the graph meant, but he was sure the meaning was bad.

"Sir," the doctor said, his tone carefully modulated, "your most highly-trained and deadly covert agent has lost control. She's under the influence of a single-minded, angry, agitated alpha predator. And she may not even know it."

"She's under the cat's control? The *cat?* Doctor, my dog can handle a cat, and he's just a big ol' sweetie."

Dumas's lips tightened to a razor line. He shifted in his chair before speaking. "Sir, your dog is a domesticated creature that bears little resemblance to his wolf ancestors. A cat is essentially a wild animal, a predator no less, that lives in limited and tenuous symbiosis with man. Given little provocation, it will attack you. It will *eat* you, sir. Can you say that of your dog?"

So, not a cat person.

Sanders swept the papers back toward he doctor. "Is she guilty?" he asked.

Dumas spread his hands and leaned back into his chair. "I can't say, sir. If she killed those men, she may not even know it. She may have been an unconscious drone piloted by the cat. Only your signals analysts can answer that question. My point is, does it even matter? You've a compromised agent and she may be violent. If you hadn't put me on this assignment, who knows when we would have found this out."

"What do you suggest, doctor?" Sanders recalled Case Specific.

Dumas seemed to think for a moment, tapping one finger against his chin. Surely he had entered that office with a definite suggestion in mind. Maybe his thoughts lay not on a course of action, but on how to broach it at that moment.

"I think," he finally said, "that we can short-circuit this problem by removing the implant. That should get the cat out of Major Street's head. But I understand such a process is delicate, that there could be psychological, even neurological, consequences."

"You have what you need to remove the implant right downstairs?"

"Yes, but not to deal with the aftermath. She'll need the best counseling we can arrange." He sat up straight. "I want to remove the implant and submit Major Street to psychiatric therapy through Walter Reed."

Sanders frowned. He turned his chair to face the wall of Special Forces prints. "That'll finish her," he mused. "She'll never again be a steady asset. You could be ending her career."

"Better than ending her life, or, for that matter, anyone else's."

Sanders wheeled back around. "Do you have data, and I mean hard data, doctor, to support that last statement? Because, if you don't, I'll look upon the muddying of my officer's honor with great disdain. Am I understood?" He delivered the statement in a quiet, controlled tone, but the vague threat had weight, and he meant to carry it out.

The doctor shied away. "Well, no. I can't say what is likely to happen. I've a data point of one, and that's never good for making assumptions. I apologize. But," and he gathered himself enough to lean toward the colonel, "I believe I can make a more definite prognosis after examining the cat's brain matter to see what the implant may have left behind." He sat up straight. "In any event, I stand by my assertion that Major Street is compromised by the very nature of her medical status. I believe her to be dangerous through no fault of her own, and I believe it would be a mistake not to act on the facts."

"Fair enough. Now I have a question, and answer carefully. Is she a threat *now*?" Was she a threat at all?

"She's secure, but the longer she remains in that observation room, the sooner I'm obligated to apprise my staff and beef up security."

"You're drifting back toward slander, doctor."

But Dumas didn't cower this time. When steeled, he could jut his jaw with the best of them.

Sanders pivoted his chair so that he once more stared at his back wall. "I'll get back to you on this matter."

"Sir, I'm not sure this can wait--"

"I said I'd get back to you. Stand ready to remove the implant at short notice, but you are not to do anything at all regarding Major Street without direct orders from me. Is that understood?"

"Yes, sir. Quite."

"Thank you. We'll make a final decision soon. Dismissed."

Sanders waited for the door to close before turning his chair. The doctor had left the files on his desk. He scowled at them. Dumas had shown him an unexpected perspective. Maybe it didn't matter if Street was innocent or guilty. Maybe she was dangerous either way. Sanders could choose between standing by his officer and taking what came, or removing her from the field for the safety of everyone. Intuition told him to ignore the data, that Street could yet give more to her country. After all, she had served three years with that cat in her head and had done so with distinction. Sanders's gut told him she'd serve many more years with honor. But could he afford intuition? He had told her he needed more than faith to give her leeway. Dumas had given him data to do the opposite.

He sat there a long time, fiddling with the papers. He shuffled them into different orders, dog-eared their pages, rolled them in his hands, then flattened them back out. He didn't read them. He didn't even look at them. All the information he needed boiled in his mind.

He hated what he had to do.

He tapped a button on his phone unit. "Goodknight?"

"Yes, sir."

"Call a meeting of all team leaders investigating Major Street. I want them in my office in thirty minutes, including Doctor Dumas. Tell them to bring solutions."

"Sir, Agent Tejada's team is in California at the Lawrence-Livermore facility and Agent Childress is at Reagan seeing off a field team en route to Indianapolis."

"Video conference Tejada in and alert Childress to join us ASAP on his return."

"Yes, sir."

Sanders broke the connection. He sagged at his desk. Well, he had half an hour. In that time, the signals analysis crew could find something. Grace and his men might make a discovery. Dumas might change his mind. Maybe, Sanders thought, something would turn up.

His telephone buzzed.

"Yes?"

"Sir, pick up line two. Agent Tejada. He says it's something big."

Chapter Nine

Eight men and women had invaded the colonel's small office. Goodknight pressed close to the door, perhaps to keep out of the way. She clutched a tablet against her chest. Signals Analysis, Electronic Forensics, and Geotracking crowded close to the once-again outward-facing computer monitor. Sergeant First Class Grace stood behind them, his arms crossed over his wrinkled uniform blouse and his eyes red from lack of sleep. Ponce stood beside him, his rumpled suit like the pick from curbside on trash day. The doctor isolated himself at the corner of Sanders's desk. His jaw jutted and worked as if he sucked at something stuck in his teeth. He hadn't said a word since the haphazard meeting began. If not for the equally silent field controllers rooted like twin statues against the office front wall, his muteness might have seemed odd.

"Right now, we're unsure what to do with the thing." Tejada said from the monitor. Leaning close to the camera, he raised his voice to be heard over a loud crackle of static. His high-definition image showed worry lines and frustration. His eyes flicked now and then to someone or something off-screen. "The thing is wedged into a difficult spot, hard to get at without getting yourself tied up in the energy beam. We could use a little help, if you know what I mean."

Sanders spoke from behind the brace of men and women. "Hostetter's on the way. I suppose his role may be more than that of consultant, considering."

"Well, he does control the only working attenuation device in this universe, sir. We need his expertise to handle this thing safely."

"We'll hurry him along." Sanders nodded to Goodknight, who left the room.

"Sooner would be better than later," Tejada said. "The science types here figure something's communicating through the event, otherwise there would be no reason to leave it running and risk discovery. That said, they don't know why the event is so large if just for communication. They also don't know what'll happen if we try to shut it down."

"Do they know what will happen if we don't?" Sanders believed he knew the answer to that one.

"No, sir."

A bustle had ensued on the other end of the call. The picture lurched, then a new face pressed close where Tejada's had been.

"Doctor Rodriguez," Sanders said.

"We must be careful of what we do with this event," the scientist said without acknowledging his greeting. "The field diameter is less than twenty centimeters, not large enough for anything of great size to come through. Either the visitor is an insect or maybe a mouse--"

"Or any number of entirely unknown threats, doctor--"

"--or it isn't a visitor at all. Possibly a communications conduit, hailing channels open."

"--or someone's talking to someone else and we don't want them doing so."

"It isn't necessary that every incident be looked upon with military suspicion, Colonel Sanders."

Sanders gripped his hands behind his back. He had to be careful. He couldn't fault Rodriguez for not taking a hint. She often missed social cues. And all the others were watching. "Doctor Rodriguez, fifteen of my men -- your guards -- are dead. Another several were co-opted by an unknown force. I have an officer here behaving in disturbingly uncharacteristic ways. I think I'm entitled to a little military suspicion."

She showed no reaction. "We're assembling tools here to read telemetry from the event. We may be able to determine its purpose and origin given sufficient time."

Sanders heard Tejada in the background, coaxing Rodríguez to give up the tablet. He also heard a quickly cut off snigger there in his own office, so he gave up on the reasoned approach. "Very good, you do your measurements. Have results by the time Hostetter arrives. Please clear the line for Agent Tejada."

She showed no sign of giving up the screen, but two hands reached into the frame and, with some awkwardness, hauled the scientist out of sight. Probably Eglemann, that godsend.

Tejada reappeared on the monitor. "Sorry, sir. Some of us are a little agitated right now."

"Agent Tejada, do you have any feeling that this and our situation with Major Street may be related?"

Tejada, ever grounded, frowned at the prospect of making wild guesses. "I don't know, sir. I'm not the egghead here. To tell the truth, I'm feeling out of my depth. But I will say this. The coincidences seem to be piling up. Look what Agent Ponce found."

"My thought exactly. Stay with it, son. Call when you have more. We'll do the same."

"Yes, sir. Tejada out."

The monitor went blue. The NSA seal faded in while everyone backed away from the desk to give the colonel some room.

Sanders reached across for his mouse. He clicked the button visible on the screen that maximized Agent DeBoy's window. "You heard all that, son?"

DeBoy nodded from within his window. "Got it, sir. I agree with Agent Tejada's assessment. Too many coincidences, too many demonstrations of how all this *could* work together. Did you have a chance to see the video I sent you?"

"Yes. I'm showing it to the team in a moment. What would you like to say on the matter?"

DeBoy leaned on an elbow and tugged at one of his ears. "It's beyond strange, sir. Cisneros, the perpetrator, had a clean record, but he had a problem speaking clear English. Two weeks ago he was ordered to English As a Second Language classes by his CO. And did you notice in the video that his eyes were closed? Just like the guys at the generator facility. I'd recommend anybody who came in contact with this thing be sequestered for the duration of the investigation, sir. But," and he stared straight into the camera, "I don't see how the major could be affected from two thousand miles away."

"Thank you," the colonel said, and reached again for his mouse. "We'll get back to you as soon as warranted. Sanders out." He emptied the monitor of DeBoy's image and called up another, a freeze-frame from a security camera showing an open room full of men in combat gear.

"One more piece of the puzzle, everyone," the colonel said as he leaned over the desk. "This is video from the guardhouse at Lawrence-Livermore the night of the incident. Agent DeBoy has trimmed it to just the pertinent moments. It'll take just a few seconds of your time." He pressed a button, and the video came to life.

An indeterminable number of men wandered in and out of the camera frame. Some were weighed down by body armor, helmets, and assault rifles while others had freed themselves of all but their base ACUs. Some looked stony-faced, others jocular, most tired. A gaggle of four men crowded the arms room door, the bottom half of which was closed to prevent unauthorized access.

A man, Cisneros, appeared in the doorway far to the back of the room. He wore only boxers and a tank top. Sanders squinted to see what DeBoy and the officer of the guard had referred to, but he couldn't see without pausing the video if Cisneros's eyes were open or closed. The man walked up to one of the armored guards, passed a moment of conversation, then took the assault rifle the soldier offered him.

Sanders wished the video came with decent sound. He got only the turbulence of many voices at once, plus the rattle and clank of equipment. Why had that dumbass surrendered his weapon? Probably out of familiarity. He had likely known Cisneros for months.

Cisneros returned to the bunkroom door and turned toward the men in the foreground.

"You!" he shouted into the room. "Stand witness to the ineffectuality of your existence! You believe yourselves kings in your world, the wonder of all things, and yet you are ignorant of all that ranges around you!" The soldiers stopped their milling about and stared at him. One man alone, the sergeant of the guard, moved in Cisneros's direction. "Behold!" the underwear-clad soldier proclaimed. "The herald of your undoing comes before you as a storm!" Then he turned into the back room and gunfire sounded, peaking out the sound pickup.

The video returned to the first frame, paused.

"Yep," somebody said. "That's a guy who doesn't speak English."

Sanders leaned against his desk and folded his arms. "Well, ladies and gentlemen, you now have a sense of the gravity of our situation. We're the National Security Agency, for pity's sake. We don't like fumbling in the dark and we don't like getting played for fools. Please tell me you've something, even a piece of the whole, that will help this all make sense. Agent Stunig."

The signals analyst cleared her throat and tucked an errant few strands of blonde hair behind one ear. "You asked us to check FBI security video of the Street incidents for authenticity and for tampering. We can report that we have a high degree of confidence in those sources. The chance that anyone inside or outside the FBI falsified those files is remote."

"As we supposed."

Stunig continued. "The authenticity of the video, however, doesn't speak to the guilt or innocence of Major Street. Sergeant Grace has discovered anomalies that made us somewhat skeptical of her involvement."

"Grace?"

"Yes, sir." Grace seemed to have been waiting for his chance. "My team identified some odd spherical objects in one of the video segments. They apparently fly in non-ballistic patterns, like orbiting drones. They looked awfully suspicious, sir."

"It's difficult to see," Stunig added. "The objects move at a high rate of speed and are therefore unclear in the recordings. Also, they're elevated largely out of view of the cameras. We referenced our technology databases and found no working technology that could operate in that manner, sir."

From Grace's stealthy grin and the way the analyst shifted her tablet, Sanders smelled a "But" in there.

"No *working* technology, sir, but we found reference to devices…" She held out her tablet after tapping a few buttons. "…that fit our observations." Her screen showed a wireframe drawing of a ball with three round openings in its lower hemisphere. "It's a Russian drone, sir. Uses microbursts of air for stability, orientation, and propulsion. It's a camera housing accompanied by a wifi transmitter, according to CIA."

"I don't understand," Sanders complained. "Why am I looking at that thing and would you please put your tablet down?"

"It's the best we could manage in the short time allowed." She drew back her tablet.

"You told me the drones don't work."

"We've high confidence in that conclusion, sir."

99

Sanders came close to regretting he had called the meeting. "So you're telling me that Major Street is a Russian spy equipped with inoperable ball-shaped drone cameras for no apparent reason?"

"We've made no claims in that direction, sir."

"But, there is another explanation," the Electronics Forensics man said. He was a big man, nearly as wide as he was tall, with sharp gray eyes set deep in his balding head. "My team examined the metrics of those videos. We compared objects and people against a bevy of data points."

"And you told me earlier," the colonel said, his tone tired, "that your facial recognition routines positively identified the woman on screen as Fiona Street."

"Yes, we did, but with an acceptable seven percent error allowance. But that was only one measure. We also calculated Major Street's apparent height in the videos against the height of objects seen in the shots. We sent men to take careful measurements of everything from table heights to that of light switches, countertops, even defects in wallpaper. And we compared those measurements to Major Street's identified biometrics." The man spread his palms. "It's our professional opinion that the woman in the video is not Major Street. She's three centimeters too tall."

The colonel stared at him. So did everyone else.

"Give or take a centimeter," the man said, and made a phlegmatic sound in his throat.

"You are kidding me," Sanders managed.

"I don't think so," Grace said, and pointed a lazy finger at the signals analyst, Stunig. "Go ahead, tell him about the grayscale mapping."

Sanders gave Grace a cutting look. He seemed to be enjoying himself. Sanders wouldn't have been surprised if the sergeant had held his own meeting earlier.

"We did a software grayscale map of a frame of video," the analyst said. Her tablet came up again, but held to her chest. "Of the moment she looked full into the camera, just before shooting the mechanism." There she was, the colonel's prize agent, full-face and aiming her pistol at the camera.

"Grayscale map," Sanders murmured. "Measure of blacks and whites in an image to figure out contours, water flows, soil compositions…"

"More or less." The woman lowered her tablet. "But its uses are more varied. We mapped the lightness and darkness of the woman's skin surfaces. The subject's face is several levels lighter than her hand and neck." Stunig's tablet came up again, but only a few inches. She put it back down. "We think she's wearing makeup."

The colonel thought he must be dense. "Don't most women wear makeup?"

Stunig looked around at all the men in the room, then back at the colonel. "Not so much. Especially in military service. Even less so among field operatives."

"But that misses the point, if you'll excuse me, sir." Grace seemed to hold his arms crossed with a will, the effort of a man who wanted to talk, but was careful of superiors.

"Go ahead, Sergeant Grace."

"Major Street has an unusually pale complexion," the sergeant said. "Not a lot of women are that fair. Anyone impersonating her…"

"Might need makeup to do so." Sanders nodded at that. "So, are we in agreement? The woman in the video is not Major Street? Geotracking?"

The man seemed like a baby to Sanders, round-faced, smooth-chinned, and wearing stylish narrow glasses. "Stating what we all might have guessed," he said, "Major Street's phone came nowhere near the FBI offices in question. We generally don't activate tracking in her implant. Too much of a chance that someone else might use it to find her."

"What about other entities on our radar?" Sanders pointed at Stunig's tablet. "The woman on those videos may be impersonating one of our own. Why? She's killed and wounded several federal agents. Why? Have you any unusual tracking information that might identify her?"

"We're efforting that," the Geotracking man said.

"Effort it faster. It's been thirty-four hours already."

The Geotracking man straightened. "Sir, between us, CIA, INS, and local enforcement, we've registered 23,000 illegal border crossings just yesterday and today--"

Sanders waved that off. "I know, I know. I need information, soonest." He glanced around the room. "Anybody else? Field?"

One of the two dark-suited statues at the back of the office turned its sunglasses on the colonel. "Her house, negative. Roadside interviews check out. We're putting a team in Indianapolis."

"So, also nothing." Sanders narrowed his eyes at Dumas. "Doctor?"

Dumas wore a frown so deep his end of the desk seemed darker. "I've nothing to add to my earlier assessment. Regardless of her guilt or innocence in this matter, Major Street should be contained."

That forced a crack into Grace's demeanor. "What's that mean?" he asked, glancing from Dumas to Sanders. "Why should her innocence not matter?"

As he answered, the colonel kept his eyes on Dumas. "The doctor believes Major Street to be a threat on a continuing basis."

Grace stared at the doctor as if at a dangerous animal. "Major Street is a highly decorated officer with an impeccable record."

"Major Street is a mess." The doctor searched all the eyes around him. "I'm not saying she's a dishonorable officer. I'm saying she's a sick one. I've recommended to Colonel Sanders that her implant be removed. It was a crime to have put it in her in the first place."

Sanders watched his people, casting for their reactions. Except for Grace, he found none. They all knew of Street's special status, they just didn't care one way or the other. Street was one of thirty-eight agents, each leading a field team of still more excellent agents. Without a personal connection as with Grace, the section chiefs had no stake in the future of any one operative.

That saddened Sanders, but he knew it was best. If operatives were any more than numbers, then it would prove impossible to send them on their missions. Some of those missions could end them.

"All right." The colonel maneuvered to behind his desk. "Except for the field checks in Indianapolis and along Major Street's travel route, redirect assets to discover who our imposter is. I'll schedule another meeting for tomorrow morning. Bring all progress."

Grace stepped to the front of the desk. "Sir, I can vouch--"

"I'm sure you will, sergeant, but not today." Sanders dropped into his seat, a broad hint to end the meeting. "Dismissed."

The section chiefs filed out of the room, the doctor last among them. Grace remained at the desk for several seconds while the colonel pointedly ignored him. Finally, he, too, exited the office. What else could he do?

What can any of us do? the colonel thought. Sometimes, choice was a luxury.

Fiona paced the floor of the observation room, wringing her hands long past when they hurt. She hadn't slept much the night before, mostly angry tossing and turning, then up and stalking the perimeter again. At least they'd tossed her some ACUs to replace her grody sweats. They fit badly, but they always did, and she had greater concerns.

She tried the door almost every circuit, but knew she would find it locked. And as she walked, so did Oz, skulking the baseboard like a tiger prowls its cage at the zoo.

She had nothing to worry about, Fiona told herself, yet she worried. She had nothing to fear, yet she feared.

The murder of federal agents. You didn't walk away from stuff like that. But she hadn't done it, right? She hadn't even been in the area. Oh well, yes, in the cities, sure, but just driving through. Just stopping, for only a minute, to rest her eyes or grab a sandwich. A chance to stretch the legs.

She hadn't gone to the FBI and she hadn't committed mayhem against them. Twice. She hadn't done it. She was *sure* she hadn't done it.

Wasn't she?

Oz didn't care. Oz wanted out.

"Right," Fiona said into the air. "And if it weren't for you, we wouldn't be here in the first place."

If they had just flown back with the guys…

The door latch clicked. She ceased her rambling and faced the exit. Oz bolted from the wall and crouched at her feet. She felt him down there, pushed against her. They hadn't provided boots with the uniform.

Sanders entered, Shotgun Mouse behind him in a crisp gray suit different from the one before. So, a whole day had passed.

The door behind them shut, then clicked as someone locked it.

"I've news," the colonel said, holding his hands at his waist. His tone hinted that the news was bad.

"I didn't do it, sir."

"We know."

"You can check my cell phone location. I wasn't anywhere near--"

"Weren't you listening? I said, we know. Also, don't pull that phone crap on me, or I'll have you locked up on principle."

"Yes, sir." He was right, of course. No operative worth their pay grade would carry a cell phone into a mission. No, you'd duct tape that puppy to the frame of a moving semi-truck and catch up to it later. See, boss, I wasn't anywhere near the crime, no way, no how. Check the GPS record on my phone! Oh well, her denial had been worth a try.

"So, yes, you're in the clear," the colonel said. "That's the good news. Someone's impersonating you. Once we got through that, the puzzle kind of fell away. Not a very thoughtful ruse, this one." He looked around the room, landing his eyes for a moment on each of the plain, middle-grade hotel fixtures. Yes, there was nothing to see there.

Try living in it, Fiona thought.

"As close as we can figure, the culprit is a Major Raisa Kudashova of the GRU. Tough character. Spetsnaz before the General Staff recruited her for the nasty stuff. We got that from computer disambiguation of her image on those videos. I've put everything I have on it and sent the data up the line to the full agency." His eyes landed on her once more.

"Umm, that's good to hear, sir." Then why was she still standing there locked in that damned room with a gray-suited thug at the door watching her like … like a mouse?

"Another issue came up." The colonel stepped close. His eyes locked on Fiona's and would not surrender her. "Your doctor gave you a detailed neurological exam."

"Yes, sir." Here it came.

"Major … have you experienced anything strange since you took on the cat?"

"Sir?"

"Have you experienced blackouts? Fuzzy thinking? Lost time? Sleep-walking?"

Oh, boy. "Sir, I was in complete control of the neural connection the entire length of my trip, sir."

"Hmm. But that doesn't answer my question, does it?"

No, it didn't.

"You realize, don't you, that I can't sanction an agent who may be prone to manipulation?"

"Yes, sir, I understand."

"And if it's possible the cat may have influence over you rather than the other way around…"

Okay, that was enough. "Yes, sir, I can see where that might be a problem. But, sir, respectfully, shouldn't you guys have thought about that before you went digging at my brains?"

The colonel wasn't fazed. "That might have been wise, except we weren't the ones who did it."

No, they weren't. *They* had sent her OpCon to the Internal Security Service. *They* had shoved her kicking and screaming into the arms of the damned, misbegotten ISS. When she complained, *they* hadn't even given her a hearing.

"You've had a hard turn," Sanders continued. He drew his gaze from hers and began a seemingly casual stroll about the room. Fiona didn't watch him. She let Oz do it. "You fell victim to a demagogue, a lawyer to boot, who wanted his own personal secret police force. When the government refused him the agents he wanted, he put the cat in your head as a force multiplier. He did that to you, major, a kind of institutionalized, scientific rape." He wound up in front of her again. "Don't you want to be done with it? Don't you want to be normal again?"

No! "Sir, I was never normal."

He stared into her eyes, then nodded once. "Huh. Well, you will be soon."

What had he seen in her eyes?

"I'm giving the doctor permission to remove your implant."

"I don't want brain surgery. I've had my fill of brain surgery."

"I'm sure. After this last, you won't have brain surgery ever again." He turned away, then nodded to Shotgun Mouse, who knocked on the door.

The door swung open and the colonel stood in its frame, his back to Fiona. He turned slightly, enough that she caught one unsure eye. "I'm sorry, major. We do the best we can."

Then he was gone, Shotgun Mouse pulling the door closed behind them.

Fiona listened to the finality of the lock.

She stood there, cold to her bones.

There had been something in his words, something frightening, and sad.

He had promised her a threat. He had promised to sever the tie between woman and cat. He had threatened to make her normal.

What did he call normal?

And what, in all that, had he promised to Oz?

The man climbing from the Suburban struck Tejada as rugged, trim, and comfortable in his skin, an odd string of characteristics for a geezer of sixty years old. He wore loose jeans, a plaid shirt, a worn leather bomber jacket, and what looked like Caterpillar boots. Rounding out his Marlboro Man appearance was a cowboy hat of brushed felt over a craggy face dominated by a heavy moustache. The man was a living cliché.

Doctor Rodriguez didn't seem to mind. She was all wide eyes and sighing breath for the guy. That had to be expected, Tejada thought, seeing as he was her boyfriend. Strange woman, that one. Tejada had been briefed, but that didn't make things any less awkward. Autism spectrum, high functioning, with moderate obsessive-compulsive tendencies and an off-the-chart genius IQ rating. She wasn't one of the staff astrophysicists. She made up whole new sciences of her own.

And this woman, looking fine in a simple blue dress, who had difficulty carrying on a normal conversation, had a mountain man twice her age on a string? How did that even happen?

The man in question stepped up to them as the truck pulled away. He hadn't brought much, just an overnight bag in one hand and a six-foot walking stick in the other. At first blush, that is, in the first half second you saw the thing, the stick came across as nothing special. Then you noticed the stuff at its head. The top of the thing looked like a ten-year-old had nailed a bunch of dumpster-dived electronics to it, including an old cell phone keypad. Odd.

"Well, then," the man said, his voice like gravel in a wooden bowl. Then he dropped his bag and leaned into Rodríguez's waiting arms. He hugged her, a great, enveloping, one-armed embrace complete with kisses landed on her hair, forehead, and cheeks. He held her apart after a moment and looked into her big, brown eyes.

"Now, ma'am, if you don't mind, I think I'd care to kiss you proper." His moustache crooked up at the ends as he spoke.

Rodríguez's smile shone like noon sunlight off a white sand beach. She went up on tiptoes to meet his lips.

She really leaned into it, as did her overaged beau. Tejada noted that nearly all of Rodríguez pressed to the man except her hands, which just sort of gently flailed at her sides. Tejada turned away, directing his gaze up the street as if something interesting went on there. Good thing he had brown skin, or somebody might have noticed his reddened cheeks.

Real love between those two, as in Romeo and Juliet love, or Maria and Tony. Of course, that shit had ended badly…

When they finally came up for air, the cowboy reluctantly released his lady and stuck out a hand to Tejada.

"Clayton Hostetter," he said.

Tejada gave the hand one businesslike pump. For an old man, the guy had a grip. "Agent Tejada, NSA. Sorry to drag you out here at such short notice."

"I was already on my way, young man. They called me day before last."

Rodríguez watched the cowboy as if he were the sun and she a flower. Tejada felt an insulin attack coming on.

"Alrighty," Hostetter said, sticking out an elbow for his girl to rest a hand in. "Where's this here lightnin' post that's givin' you so much trouble?"

Rodriguez didn't correct *his* 'lightning post' fail.

Machinery and cables blocked the doorway to the safe room. The crap in the threshold looked like a couple of theater spotlights, a laptop, and a cluster of satellite TV dishes roped to a bulky electric generator and stuffed onto a garden cart. The cables and associated power lines stretched away from that aggregation and far down the hall. Eglemann and six white-coated flunkies crowded the machines while a response team of guards in full combat gear waited, edgy, behind them. The air was oppressive with heat, static, and a strong stench of ozone.

DeBoy hung close to Eglemann and nudged her elbow when he saw the others approaching.

Engelmann yelled as she hustled through the cramped corridor to her boss. "We rigged up the N-space sensors to the lab configuration like you asked." She was drenched in sweat and her lab coat carried a dusting of soot. "We have an origin, an eight-group coordinate we've not seen before."

"Anything coming through?" Tejada asked DeBoy.

Eglemann answered for him by spreading her arms and herding the group out of earshot of the scientists and the guards. "We're picking up strong Theta and Delta waves," she said after looking right and left so as not to be overheard. "I mean, it wouldn't bother me otherwise, but those are the frequencies of brain emissions associated with sleep and suggestion, and they're shooting out of that event like water through a firehose."

"Oh, my." Rodríguez squeezed Hostetter's arm. "Amplification?"

"Four orders of magnitude above brain normal," Eglemann said. "Not enough to be a problem beyond the building, but I'm a little worried about the people here in this vault."

"Okay," Tejada broke in, "I'm not liking the sound of this. What do we have here, a radiation problem?"

Eglemann stood open-mouthed, as if she didn't know how to answer the question.

"Theta and Delta waves are electro-magnetic in nature, like radio waves," Rodríguez filled in. "Normally, they shouldn't be a problem for humans, but the amplification isn't something we see in nature. This radiation could be physically harmful close to the source, or, theoretically--"

"Too great an exposure to EM radiation at these frequencies could cause depression and make people vulnerable to suggestion," Eglemann interrupted. "I had wave generators brought in and jury-rigged to act as a kind of wave cancelling speaker system, but I don't know how effective it is, if at all."

"We'll have to rotate people outta here," DeBoy said.

"No, we won't." Hostetter stepped through the group toward the door. "You folks got all you want from this thing?"

"I'd really like to send a probe through to monitor--"

Eglemann cut off Rodríguez. "Yes, we're *done* with it."

Rodríguez looked insulted. "I don't think--"

Eglemann put up a hand. She glanced around to double-check that none of the staff could hear, then leaned in toward her director. "It possibly affected our guards the other night. It may affect us, if we aren't careful. Plus…" Again, she glanced around. "…the readings show more than radiation coming through. We're picking up trace amounts of mass. I've half convinced my staff that it's just error bar stuff, but something solid or almost solid is leaking through from that event. It's a dangerous, alien incursion that does not have our best interests at heart. If it *has* a heart. It has to be cut."

That was about the way to put it, Tejada imagined. He had a cousin with autism. You had to be direct.

"I suppose," Rodriguez said, but Tejada could see that she didn't suppose at all. Still, she wasn't a dummy. She leaned on Eglemann for everything not covered by a couple of PhDs. "Since we have the address, we can send a probe in our own time. Assuming we can get the generator to work."

"Then I'm gonna cut the rope on this," Hostetter said, and gently removed the scientist's hand from his arm.

"Clear the theater!" DeBoy called, and gestured for the soldiers to herd the white coats out.

Hostetter weaved through the departing scientists until he stood in the doorway just behind the machinery.

Tejada wanted to watch. He had studied the file on Hostetter. It had read like a comic book. The federal marshal -- from the Old West, no less -- who stopped his former friend from sucking the universe into oblivion. Or had it been several universes? Or all of them? That stick the guy carried helped him with more than walking. An as-yet unidentified entity had gifted it to him.

Hostetter squeezed past the jumble of machines and disappeared beyond the doorway.

Tejada turned to DeBoy and gestured toward the two women. "Keep these back. First hint of trouble, get them clear of the building." He didn't wait for an acknowledgement. He moved forward to get eyes on Hostetter.

The cowboy stood a few feet from the open, shimmering deposit box. The safe washed him in orange light and tossed sparks throughout the chamber. Tejada swore that Hostetter's leather jacket fluttered in the force from that light.

"This could get messy!" Hostetter called back to him. "I hope y'all ain't too partial to this fancy building of your'n."

"This facility cost over three billion dollars!" Tejada shouted over the static and the hum of machinery. His stomach twisted at not knowing what the cowboy meant.

"That's a shame," Hostetter muttered, then took his stick in two hands, aimed it like a spear, and shoved its head into the glowing deposit box.

The box … screamed. The light doubled in intensity, sputtered, and strobed. The static ratcheted up to an atonal squeal, then a warbling screech. Tejada grimaced against that light and sound. He covered his ears and squinted.

Hostetter gripped the stick as if the jaws of some vicious animal had seized the other end. He wrenched it one way, then the other, braced his feet, and pulled. The stick came out of its hole. So did a portion of the wall, which rained onto the floor in metallic chunks of deposit boxes and sprays of drywall. With all that came a boiling pillar of screaming light that lanced out in opposite directions to wreck the ceiling and floor. It was as if the old man wrestled a monstrously thick death ray with the living, spitting anger of a snared snake.

The light fought him. It pivoted violently at the end of his stick, slicing ceiling, floor and walls, raining drywall, light fixtures, tiles and concrete throughout the room. The overhead sprinklers burst on. The fire alarm squealed though it drowned in the wail of the light. Hostetter struggled. Tejada crouched low and wished he could help, but he had no idea what the man was up to.

Then the light contracted to a wire-thin line almost too bright to look at. The sound rose in pitch and decibels until it became a sharpened wire in Tejada's brain.

At that point, the sound snapped. It cut out with a soft *woof!* and the terrible light winked out with it. Tejada found himself in darkness punctuated by floating, blurry, blue afterimages of lines. Absolute silence engulfed his world almost as much as the screaming light had. His nostrils filled with ozone and dust.

Then, normalcy. Dim emergency lights flicked on. A clatter sounded beside Tejada as someone moved the tracking machinery out of the doorway. Doctor Rodriguez edged past him, quick, firm steps taking her to Hostetter's side. She looked at the gash in the wall, at all the gashes in every surface, then at her boyfriend.

"You reoriented the event and attuned its throughput? I didn't know you could do that," she said.

"You people's the ones what taught me." Hostetter grinned.

"I knew your attenuation matrix could do it. I just didn't know *you* could."

"I been practicin'."

She glanced around some more at the wreckage. "Practice some more."

"Better watch it, girl, or I'm gonna hafta kiss you again."

"Maybe later, after we determine the results of this re-attunement."

Tejada wondered how Hostetter had managed to attune to *her*. And vice-versa.

The thing in Kudashova howled. A commotion of horns and screeching tires slipped past razor slices of pain. The woman screamed in the thing's depths, but the woman was nothing. The split was *everything*. The *beheading*. The conduit had collapsed. The nightmare was cleaved from its source.

For a moment, it lost its hold on the woman. For an instant, she woke up. She had just enough time to realize her freedom, to gather a will to act on that knowledge, before she lost the opportunity to circumstances.

Cars bore down on her. She drove in the wrong lane. She threw all her control into turning the wheel, the steering wheel that seemed so far away and foreign, so disconnected from her muscles. She worked the brake and accelerator though her legs seemed not to know her. She wanted to think. She needed to escape the monster buried within her. But more than that, she needed to save her life.

So she lost her one opportunity. By the time she wrenched the car to the shoulder, though she did so within a few seconds, the monster had recovered. She threw open the door in a last wild scrabble to escape. She lurched into the weeds at the edge of the highway. It had her, she knew it did. She felt her soul falling, flailing in blanketing darkness. She stumbled up against the wire fence at the highway's edge. It came up to her waist, sagging as it cut into her thighs. Leaning far forward, she vomited into the grass.

She gasped, a wretched, hopeless sound. Then she was gone.

The thing that was once more Kudashova straightened. The torture that had shown on its face vanished. It wiped a spatter of vomit from its chin.

That had been close. The conduit had collapsed. Someone--

Hostetter. Only Hostetter could have attacked the nightmare so viciously. Those of this world were too weak, too ignorant. They were sheep. Only Hostetter among them could bite like a wolf.

"What in the world is the matter with you?" came from behind.

The thing inside Kudashova turned at the fence. It stared at the skinny woman in the cotton dress with her fists bunched at her hips. The woman yelled, angry. She went on and on about bad driving and calling the po-lice, as if she had suffered some great inconvenience. Was *she* cut off from her universe, trapped amid an enemy that knew only treachery? Had *she* been attacked? The thing grumbled as it trudged back toward the road. Was *her* world a shambles, at the end of its days?

The thing ignored the woman's complaints. While the human threw up its arms and yelled all the louder, the thing climbed back into its car. It turned the vehicle back onto the road, almost striking the shouting woman, which made her cry all the harder. Then the thing settled back into its purpose.

It knew where Hostetter was. It thrilled to leave the host woman, just drop her there in the car and hurtle across vale and mountain to dive upon Hostetter and make him pay. But, the thing thought, it was cut off from the conduit. Did it still have the strength to launch across a continent after its enemy? It could not draw upon the near-limitless power of human fear siphoned from its parent universe. It needed, it thought with bile in its soul, to think … smaller.

It would need a new vehicle. The current car would be reported, the authorities summoned. But first, there was the Street woman. She was the tie to Hostetter. He cared about her. He would come for her, he had said so. But Hostetter apparently had priorities, and Street was not at the top of them.

The thing would change that equation. It would *make* Hostetter come.

Hostetter and Nightmare gonna meet up soon.

Chapter Ten

The thing that was Kudashova pulled off at the exit on State Road 32 and met its second obstacle of the day. That was no ordinary highway exit.

A gate stretched across the pavement and armed policemen patrolled the barrier. One raised a cautioning hand and walked slowly toward the approaching car.

Nightmare raged within Kudashova's skin. It wanted to kill those damnable monkeys, as it would obliterate all their ilk when the moment came. But the moment still stood a long way off and Nightmare needed to hide until then. It tamped its rage down to a smolder and, ashes dry in its soul's throat, slowed the car to a stop.

"I need to get to the NSA," it said when the guard leaned at the driver's side window.

"Ma'am, this here's a restricted exit," the guard said. "Didn't you see the signs?"

The thing noticed a second guard moving around to the other side of the vehicle. "I'm here to see Major Fiona Street of the Special Directorate of the Insertions and Extractions Command."

"I'm sorry, ma'am, but you'll need identification and an appropriate vehicle pass to use this exit."

It could have reached through that window and snapped the guard's neck. It could have murdered them all, but the conduit had closed and the thing felt hollow from weakness. Perhaps it could slip into one of the men, leave Kudashova and hide within one of those other apes. But no, not in this wakened state. Not just then.

It looked around at the guards, at the barrier they manned. It judged them, judged their gate. Too much. It would have to find another way.

It turned to the guard at the window. "I'll be back," it said.

Fiona became more agitated as the day wore on, and as she grew tense, so did Oz. She paced the room, hating its bland walls with their bland landscape prints and the bland motel furniture that passed for government interior decorating. She hated the fact that no one had spoken to her since the colonel's visit. They watched her, the bastards. The red lights on the surveillance cameras never winked off. The dangerous old maids in the front office had her pinned, that was sure.

How long since the colonel's visit? Hours? Minutes?

It never occurred to her to check the clock on her bedside table.

Oz growled as he stalked the perimeter just ahead of his human. He stuck his nose into every corner, every dark place, every niche between bits of furniture. He sought a way to escape his trap. Fiona corrected him often, speaking words she hardly considered. No exit there. That vent was too small for humans. There's no hole out; it's gonna take a plan.

Oz cared nothing for plans. He knew that plans, whatever they were, kept him from acting. Plans were about the future. Even after his time with the human, Oz had no clue what a future was.

Fiona didn't care what Oz knew. You couldn't teach a cat a damned thing if they didn't want to learn it.

Oz froze, aiming himself at the door. Fiona followed his lead.

Fiona knew it was Dumas before he even reached the door. Oz had made him, Shotgun Mouse, and Nurse Rita by sound, smell, and that weird intuition that made him so surreal a presence in Fiona's head. She even knew their moods.

The lock clicked. The intruders filed in, opening the door barely enough for passage. Oz sprayed caustic frustration over Fiona's mind. He found no escape path through those feet.

Shotgun Mouse entered first, then one of his nameless bricks. Doctor Dumbass, Rita, then two more bricks. They expected a fight.

"Sooo," Fiona said. "Good morning, Doctor Dumas?"

The doc hugged his tablet to his chest. "Actually, it's near three-thirty in the afternoon."

"Oh. Well, no windows."

"You have a clock."

"Who pays attention to clocks?"

Conversation wasn't high on Fiona's mind. The bricks spread out. The situation was tactical, not social.

Dogs, Oz sent her.

Damned straight, Fiona thought back.

"Would you secure the cat?" the doctor asked Fiona.

"Why?"

"Just pick him up, it's not a chore."

"Doc, I'm thinking everything looks like a chore just now."

"Pick up the cat, Major Street. It would be better if you did it rather than one of these men."

Rather than comply, Fiona and Oz separated.

Doctor Dumbass waited a beat. "Major. You're being ridiculous. I recognize a tactical quadrascopic spread when I see one."

"Really?" Fiona showed him wide-eyed mystification. "I thought I was just standing here."

"Umm, why don't we just tell her why we're here?" That was Nurse Rita, bless her assassin's heart.

Dumbass seemed to think about that, at least he deepened his frown and clouded his eyes.

"All right," he said, and cleared his throat. "Let me be adamant. Major Street, Colonel Sanders has requested I remove your implant, terminating the link between you and the cat. This is likely temporary pending further research into the possible detrimental effects of the link. You will be escorted to the examination room where the procedure will take place. Afterward, you will be placed on extended medical leave for recovery. You can see this in no way threatens you. Your cooperation is required."

Fiona heard only danger signals. "My cooperation is required only in relation to how much I understand what's happening."

"You have orders, major."

"I have a big load of questions, is what I have." She backed toward the center of the room, as far away from the bricks as she could manage. She hated that this let them surround her. "I haven't noticed any informed consent procedures, doc. I mean, you can't go rooting around in somebody's brain without consent, can you? That's what got your predecessor sent up the river."

"We've been over this in past sessions," the doctor said with a roll of the eyes. "You gave informed consent when you entered into my improved neural enhancement program. You know the risks and you know the procedures--"

"And so I *know* you might lobotomize me, goddammit! Don't bullshit me, doc. I'm not an idiot!" One of the bricks stepped toward her, maybe didn't even realize it. Fiona turned on him in a fury. "Back off, buddy, or you'll be picking those sunglasses out of your corneas!"

"Okay, that's enough," Rita said, her tone tentative.

"That's *what?*" Fiona felt Oz evaluating targets, who to attack and who to avoid. Nurse Rita rode high on the "avoid" list. "That's *what?*"

"I only meant, this is getting real, you know? Let's all back up and remember that we're all friends, okay? We're all friends here."

"We are *not* friends."

And there, proceedings came to a halt. Fiona had no idea what she would do. It wasn't as if she had a right to noncompliance. After all, no one had threatened to attack her. No one had even hinted at dark motives. They wanted to remove her implant. They wanted to make her normal again. Right?

But Oz growled deep in his gut. He smelled dogs. He didn't trust dogs.

"You're right," Doctor Dumbass finally said. "You're absolutely correct. We are not friends. We're colleagues. We are servants of the same power and that power says you're to report to the exam room and have your implant removed." He looked around at the bricks, then tossed his chin toward the door. Getting the message, the dark-suited agents filed out, all but Shotgun Mouse. Everyone gone but him, the doctor, and Nurse Rita, the tension in the room drained to a manageable level. "Now, major. You've spent years obeying the orders of your superior officers. What do you imagine must come next?"

He had her, of course. She was in enough trouble already if the present little episode got back to Sanders. But the doctor waited, watching Fiona with clinical interest, as if she really had more than one action to choose from.

She told herself she was proving him wrong when she forcibly relaxed her fists and made her body language less ready for a fight. None of it worked with Oz, though. He growled and hunkered close to the floor, his ears flattened against his skull.

"Get over here," Fiona said to the cat, unsure what he might make of surrender.

Surrender. Capitulation. Common sense. Oz understood none of that. His world centered on three concepts: run, hide, or kill. Or sometimes combinations.

He growled again, directly at Shotgun Mouse.

"Oz..." Fiona didn't like to beg, but the cat sometimes acquiesced to false shows of subservience. He knew what they were, too. He used them enough to get what he wanted.

This time, he threw his partner a bone. He slinked across the floor, up Fiona's leg, climbed her shirt, and wound up on her shoulder, hissing at everyone.

Doctor Dumbass followed the cat's actions with a glower of distaste. "After you, major."

"Chill," Fiona muttered as she exited the observation room, Nurse Rita ahead of her and Shotgun Mouse behind. "The worst they plan to do is get me out of your head."

Oz wasn't so sure of that. He still smelled dog.

Kudashova had pulled off the road northwest of Fort Meade. She stood away from the vehicle, just short of a stand of weedy trees that masked the base from the highway. Her back to traffic, she waited. The gun bag hung from her shoulders, full of ammo and surprises. She had slung the assault rifle across her chest and gripped her two pistols one in each hand. She had shed the jacket as cumbersome, but the cool autumn breeze did not raise shivers from her body.

The thing inside her listened. It squatted on the NSA's intranet, monitoring the surveillance device on Fiona Street's cat bag. It listened, but with difficulty. Without constant replenishment from the now broken transuniversal conduit, its two points of reference, the intranet and the female host, were about all the creature could handle.

Where was Hostetter? Was he still in that place where the conduit had died? Had he left that place as quickly as he arrived? No matter. The creature knew how to snare its enemy. It knew Hostetter would come for Fiona Street. He would come soon or he would come later, but he would come.

It listened. It waited. It held steady through the debate in the Street woman's room. It waited until she separated from her cat, until the cat entered its own room and Street entered hers. The thing in Kudashova focused on the cat, which the veterinarian, armored in padded gauntlets, had strapped down to a metal table. It was hard to see what went on in there through the poorly placed video camera and the camera on the veterinarian's computer, but the thing knew what must come. It had read the emails, seen the forms, and had monitored the calls between the doctor and the commander. It knew what must come and knew how that would affect the woman Street.

The thing just needed to exacerbate matters.

So it listened. Phone conversations, forms, audio-visual equipment power-ups, cameras, elevator commands, and Lotus Notes. Kudashova stood just short of the trees, head cocked to one side, pistols held a few inches off her thighs. An onlooker might have thought she concentrated on something, perhaps a sound far away and dim. They would not have seen her pounding to get out, screaming for help, desperate for escape from the shell of her self. The thing inside her noticed everything and knew it could never let her go. She was strong. She was determined. She was exactly what it feared.

When all was done, it would walk her in front of a speeding vehicle, then leave her to herself at the instant of impact.

And it let her realize that fate would be hers. So delicious, the despair of the enemy.

She ticked her chin up a fraction. The monster's moment had come. The thing saw its chance through the camera in the veterinarian's examination room. It unzipped the opening to the gun bag enough to release the three drones. They rose past the slit, hovered at head height, then began an orbit around Kudashova's skull. The speed of that orbit increased until the spheres blurred and threw off a ratcheting Doppler *woof!*

Kudashova placed the heels of her boots together and hunched her head deep into her shoulders.

In the next instant, the grass pushed up where her boots had been as if it had never been crushed. The field by the trees stood empty.

Oz saw it, but failed to understand. The vet placed a tray on the table beside him, a shiny tray with a dreaded needle on it. Beside the needle stood a tiny bottle, its label partially visible. "NEM" he saw and didn't read. It was enough to know the needle came. Oz didn't read anyway. He left that odd task to the human. The human read that obscured notation and the partially hidden line beneath: "SODIUM PEN".

"Pentobarbitol," Fiona whispered as she lay back in the hated chair. Doctor Dumbass sat on his stool to her right, Nurse Rita bent over her on the left, and both held the straps to lock down her arms.

The doctor hesitated. "What?"

Fiona knew what that word meant. She knew the words she couldn't see. How could she not in her profession, where death was as commonplace as ledger entries. Nembutal. Sodium Pentobarbitol. A euthanasia drug.

And once Fiona knew the vet's intention, Oz did, and raged.

"What?" the doctor asked again.

Fiona twisted her right arm away from the nearly closed strap. With a growl deep from her diaphragm, she looped that arm around and slammed Dumbass hard against the neck. The doctor went over like a felled tree, his temple and shoulder glancing off the metal frame of the chair.

Fiona rolled into the space the doctor had occupied. As she left the chair, she felt the faintest tug on her backless paper gown where Nurse Rita took a grab at her and missed.

"Major Street!" Rita exclaimed, hurrying around the chair. "What has gotten into you?"

But Fiona had submerged beneath the dark wave that was Oz. She grasped the metal stool where it lay tangled in the moaning doctor's legs and heaved it in Rita's general direction. The nurse dodged. The stool clanged off the rack of ophthalmoscopes and otoscopes and cannoned about, keeping Rita distracted for a few precious fractions of a second.

The door flew open, crashing against the wall. Shotgun Mouse entered, pistol drawn, two men behind him and one in the doorway.

That was a mistake. The room was too small for four men and two women. The crowd put all prey conveniently close at hand. Fiona lashed out at random, punching one man in the face, elbowing another in the chest. She lunged about the cramped room, sweeping the counter clear of its tissue box, laptop computer, scope tip dispensers, soap container, anything that could pass for a missile and keep her opponents focused on defense rather than getting at her.

Someone grabbed her from behind. She stomped his leather dress shoe and head-butted him when he leaned forward. That impact should have rattled her, but Oz was in control and he hadn't felt a thing. Fiona batted the pistol from the mouse's hand. She exchanged rapid-fire punches and defenses with Rita, spun out of reach, groined another brick and pushed him at the nurse.

Any second, and the ladies out front would get involved.

Any second, and the vet would put Oz down.

Fiona broke one nose, put her bare heel hard into someone's cheek, and fell into yet another exchange with Rita. All the while, she grunted, roared, and screamed at her enemies. She wanted very much to beat them down. She wanted very much to kill them.

Her greatest effort lay in avoiding that outcome.

Only two left against her, mouse and nurse. Fiona hooked the fallen stool over the toes of one foot and sailed it sideways into the mouse's face. She scooped up one of the light scopes and hammered its substantial cylindrical handle against the side of his head.

Then Rita was on her, slamming Fiona's skull into an up-thrust knee. Once again, Oz saved his human from a punch-drunk stupor. Through Fiona's eyes, he remained clear, lashing out his human's arms to sweep the other one off her feet. Fiona shook the kick off, grabbed Rita by the hair, and punched her twice in the face.

Fiona staggered. They were all down, even the guy in the doorway. Four agents, one nurse, and the doctor. Her eyes found the collapsed form of Shotgun Mouse. A wave of fury rolled over her, palpable enough to frighten her. "Mouse!" she yelled at the prostrate man. "Cat!" She pointed at herself.

Then, paper gown half torn off, she darted out of the room to get next door.

"And, owing to the special circumstances surrounding the incident at our Lawrence-Livermore facility, I've asked our colleagues at our OAA division to brief us on likely progenitors and outcomes." The Director, National Security gestured toward the man down the conference table, and lowered himself into his seat.

The man stood. He fastened the two buttons of his impeccable tweed suit. He took a moment to admire the view through the floor-to-ceiling windows that made up one wall of the conference room. Then, centered, he looked around at the twelve heavy-hitters at the table. He nudged the tablet before him, waking its screen, then looked up from the notes he had placed there.

And noticed the projectile swooping toward the windows.

The glass shattered inward. *All* the glass, from wall to wall. Men and women dived aside, the lucky ones under the table. The tenor crack of pistol fire. Detonations along the back wall of the conference room. The coffee service and the pastry cart exploded. Everyone went down who didn't have the table as a shield.

A figure fell in through the window. Tucked into a tight ball, it landed on the table, tumbled across, and ended crouched among the executives who had sought the table as protection against gunfire.

The intruder was a woman.

Without aiming, she raised a pistol in each hand and fired continuously to both flanks, sweeping the cowering, then scrambling rabble.

The man who had seen her first, the man whose presentation she had interrupted, lay tumbled onto his back beside her. The pistol spat hot shell casings into his face. He struck out a hand to slap the gun from her grip. He lunged at her, reaching for the other gun, taking a ringing punch to the side of his head. Then the woman discarded her second pistol, which had clicked dry of ammo. She grasped her assailant by his expensive lapels, rolled onto her back, and kicked him over her head and into a roil of jostling bodies.

At least half the conference attendees lay dead or moaning, crumpled to the floor. Blood splattered the walls and slopped onto the floor along with settling drywall dust. The air stank of rotten eggs. Three men rushed the only exit, two guarding the one in front. The Director. The woman brought up an assault rifle slung at her chest and took down one of the guards with a three-round burst. The other two men pushed through the doorway to what they hoped was safety.

The woman reached into the gun bag at her side, snatched out a green cylinder, popped its pin, and flung it after the escapees. The grenade sailed through the crack of the closing door and went off with a flash of chemical flame just before the door drew shut.

The man in rumpled tweed kicked free of his knot of struggling bodies and cursed as he fought to reach past his twisted, tailored jacket for the gun in his shoulder holster. As he did so he noticed something peculiar. Three small spheres circled the room close to the ceiling. Where had those come from?

He finally slipped out the .45 caliber pistol, gripped it two-handed, and sent three rounds at the intruder.

She dodged aside, under the table and out of sight as if she were psychic. The bullets struck the table pedestal and one still, crumpled body.

A metallic clatter as something landed between the man's legs.

"Fuck!" he yelled as the tear gas grenade went off in his face.

Fiona barely managed two steps outside the exam room. She smelled the sharp, sour stench of adrenal sweat, then spied a security lady slipping into view at the head of the corridor, pistol ready in a two-handed grip. Fiona dived for Oz's door. Two rounds zipped past her shoulder and into the frosted glass entry of the lab at the end of the hall. Screams of surprise and terror. The techs in the lab were diving for cover.

It occurred to Fiona that she might have snared a gun from one of the downed staff.

A third bullet ruptured the frame about the door. Fiona threw herself across the corridor, bounced off that wall, and slammed into the vet room door so hard it tore through its latchworks and flew open against a wall.

The vet shrank against the far wall, wide-eyed and muttering about God and salvation.

On her way to the woman, Fiona ripped loose the Velcro stays securing her cat to the stainless steel table. She kept going, baring her teeth. She gripped the cowering vet by the neck, drew back a trembling fist, and struck with every ounce of her strength.

Her open palm slammed into the wall beside the mewling woman's head. The impact reverberated up Fiona's arm.

No, she thought through the dark fog of Oz. She's a civilian. She's only following ord--

KILL!

Fiona picked up the vet one-handed and heaved her into a corner. As the woman crumpled to the floor, Fiona snatched up the first weapon to come to her hand, the hypodermic needle full of death juice. She raised it like an ice pick, stepped toward the vet--

--and caught a movement in her mind's eye. Oz spit at a figure in the doorway, its weapon drawing down on his human.

Fiona spun and threw the needle. It embedded in the security lady's neck with a dull thump and a flower of blood. The woman stiffened, staggered, then went down in the hallway.

Oz leaped from his table and stalked to the crumpled woman. Not dead, that one. Rip its throat out--

"*Help* her!" Fiona roared at the vet, then straddled the body in the hall and took the pistol from its knotted hand.

She aimed the weapon up the corridor toward the reception room and followed it, keeping close to the wall. She felt the visceral grip of Oz, who wanted the bleeding woman dead. He wanted the vet dead, too. He wanted *everyone* dead. But that was a course Fiona wouldn't grant him, submerged in his killer's soul or not. He gave up that desire for the sake of escape and padded ahead of his human to discover what threats awaited them.

A second security lady came into view in the open rectangle at the end of the hall. She held a sub-machine gun. Fiona sent three rounds toward her, more to make her take cover than to kill. She couldn't let that MP5 come into play.

With those three rounds, she was out of bullets.

She flipped open the cylinder to be sure, closed it, tossed the pistol into the air a few inches, and caught it barrel first. Distantly, the barrel burned. She didn't care. She advanced up the hall, holding it like a club.

All this happened in just a few seconds, then Fiona reached the front of the hall. There. The security lady, crouched low behind a file cabinet just at the end of the corridor. Fiona threw the pistol as the woman peeked around her shield. The weapon clanged against the flank of the cabinet and clattered into the office. The lady read the situation and pivoted into the corridor's opening, machine gun ready. Just as Fiona imagined she would.

The woman fired, but the rounds pounded into drywall and ceiling tiles, not their intended target. Oz saw to that. At the moment the lady revealed herself, he sprang and landed square on her face. A terrible blur of flailing claws and yeowling, he forced his victim backwards, stumbling, then onto her side. She lost hold of her gun. As if dear life depended on it, she beat at the animal raking her face.

Fiona straddled her, reached down with both hands, and seized the cat behind both front legs.

"Let. GO!" she ground through clenched teeth.

He complied just enough, for an instant. She yanked him away, tossed him to one side, and took up the fallen security woman's weapon.

There's a third one, she thought. A third one. Where--

The woman beneath her sprang from her near-fetal position, clasping onto Fiona's mangled gown. Fiona swung the machine gun, slapping its metal stock against her assailant's head. The lady went down like a bag of rocks.

Fiona had no time to check her and Oz didn't care to.

The file cabinet beyond Fiona boomed like a trashcan drum. It jumped and rocked under multiple bullet strikes. Fiona threw herself to the floor. She did the geometry of impact and direction and imagined she had the location of the shooter.

Oz took that information and sped between the two nearer desks toward the third gunner against the far wall.

Fiona raised up enough to throw two short bursts over the desks in the general direction of the shooter. Overhead lights exploded. Glass, plastic, and shell casings rained to the floor.

There she was, the other sentinel, at a ready crouch on the far side of that third desk. And she had a goddamned radio in one hand. Fiona saw her through Oz's eyes, from behind a trashcan. He went still, centering her in his sight, then launched at the woman, single-minded, the vision a sensory tunnel red with the thrumming pulse of blood and an eagerness for violence.

120

As Oz charged, Fiona sent another spray of rounds across the room. Through the cat's eyes, she saw the woman turn and swing at him with the gun butt. Fiona felt her own feet dig into carpet, ignoring glass. She rounded the two desks that prevented direct fire and rushed her enemy. She felt the gun butt strike her torso -- no, *Oz's* torso -- felt him flying even as she ran at the security lady. She hurt -- *he* hurt -- but neither cared, the cat's legs flailing for something to latch onto and propel him back toward the fight.

Fiona smelled piss-and-copper hate.

She vaulted the desk, colliding lower legs to torso with the woman. Both went down on the desktop, scattering all manner of office supplies and bric-a-brac. The security lady whanged her gun against Fiona's shoulder. Fiona gasped at the pain, but managed to slap her own weapon into the woman's face.

Oz was on the desk. He swatted at the woman. He was all fang and claw, going for face and neck. She swung an arm at him, sweeping him and an in-out box onto the floor.

Fiona arced back her arm and brought a tight fist hard into the guard's face. The lady's head bounced off the desktop. Fiona struck her again. And again.

She barely put the brakes on a fourth, unnecessary, punch.

For several seconds, she poised there, half on and half off the desktop. Her nostrils flared and she breathed like an engine, her mouth so closed she showed no lips. She stared wide-eyed murder at the bloodied, unconscious woman beside her. Her fist still suspended, cocked to strike again, she made no movement as the guard slowly slid to the floor in a racket of clattering office junk.

If Fiona had moved regarding that woman, it would have been to tear out her throat.

Slowly, by stiff, creaky stages, she lowered her fist to the desktop. She tried to steady her breathing. She tried to fan away the red cloud of murder that had claimed her.

"Jesus."

She stood. She looked around. Three security officers down, beaten and stabbed in the neck. Four field agents down. A doctor. A nurse.

She had almost killed a goddamned veterinarian.

"Jesus, Oz. What have you done?"

But Oz ignored her. He nosed around the exit door, flicking his tail like a whip.

Fiona opened and closed her fist. She opened it again.

Then she bent over the security lady and worked at removing her scrubs.

Chapter Eleven

Goodknight burst into the colonel's office, breathless and waving a post-it in his face.

Sanders sat at his desk, going through his bland, soul-sucking paperwork. "God dammit, sergeant, have you somehow forgotten how to knock?"

"There's a situation." Goodknight's tone was tight with worry.

The colonel didn't say a word; he didn't have to.

"SecNet reports a building incursion. We're under lockdown. Looks like an attempt on the director." Goodknight licked her lips and referred to the post-it trembling in her hand. "Massive destruction. Twenty-eighth floor. A woman. Heavily armed. Notable reflexes."

"Dammit!" The colonel crashed his seat back as he sprang from his chair. "Call Medical. Alert Grace and his team. Are any of them still in the building? I want eyes on Street! *Now*, sergeant!"

Goodknight was out the door before her commander finished speaking.

"Any details on the incursion?" Sanders bellowed as he yanked out his keyboard tray and called up his security feeds.

"The director was in a cross-division meeting regarding the incident at Lawrence-Livermore. All associated department heads were there. People are dead. The cops don't say who or how many." A pause from Goodknight's outer office, then, "I've sent the alert to Major Street's team. No answer from Medical."

Sanders had the feed list up. He punched the button for the exam room as Goodknight reappeared at his door.

Goodknight released a moan of despair. She hadn't seen the wreckage revealed by the exam room camera.

She had seen the colonel's face.

Grace and Ponce were in the Office of Immigration Metrics when Goodknight's text came through. Ponce hunkered over a desk with a pretty numbers analyst while Grace spoke with the section chief for Europe about Russian entry records. His phone buzzed, he glanced at it, and everything the section chief had told him flew from his brain.

"Ponce!" Grace reached automatically for his shoulder holster. But he didn't have one. He never thought to walk into NSA headquarters armed.

Ponce rushed to his side. "Goodknight sent an alert," he said, putting away his own phone.

"Yes. The major. Twenty-eighth floor south."

Both men rushed for the office door, ignoring the confused section chief.

"How's she on the twenty-eighth floor?" Ponce asked. "She's supposed to be in Medical getting her brain sucked."

Grace didn't like it. If the major was on the twenty-eighth floor shooting up the Director of National Security, then what had happened to all those people in sub-basement three? He and Ponce were half way to the south sector of the building, on the twenty-fifth floor. "Come on," he said, and headed for the nearest elevators. "She's our man. We handle this."

"Whoa, whoa, whoa!" Ponce grabbed Grace's arm, but followed along. "You sure about this? I mean, the building cops will lock this joint down. We won't get within a hundred feet of her. And what do we do if we *do* find her? You realize she could kick both our asses and have our heads for hats, don't you?"

"She's our man."

"She's Captain America, sarge. She's *evil* Captain America if she's broken out of Medical. Any chance they let her go on purpose?"

As if in answer, a baritone boom sounded from somewhere above. The floor shuddered. The overhead lights flickered. The banshee scream of a fire alarm sounded.

"Shit!" Ponce spat. "Never mind."

The corridor filled with office workers glancing about in confusion. Grace marched to where a pair of building policemen walked up the hall.

"Into your offices!" the cops directed, gripping their MP5s. "Into your offices and lock the doors. Lockdown procedures are in effect!"

To emphasize their words, the building intercom sounded a tone, then delivered a similar message in calm, almost sleepy tones.

"Officers!" Grace yelled above the fire alarm and the intercom. He whipped out his wallet to show his ID. "SFC Grace, Insertions and Extractions, Special Detail. My partner, Agent Ponce. We may have information bearing on the present situation."

One of the cops, older and wearing sergeant's pips, held up a hand to Grace. "It's all right, sir, we have things under control. Please go to the nearest office--"

"We know the perpetrator and that she's trained to defeat your level of threat. You can't stop her, officer. Maybe we can."

Another explosion punctuated his words. Both officers flinched at the sound and the shudder it sent through the building. Grace did not.

"Are you armed?" the lead officer asked after a hard squint at Grace.

"No, sir."

The officer unsnapped the Beretta from his waist and handed it to Grace. He nodded for his partner to do the same for Ponce. "You follow me," he said.

Grace checked the load of his magazine and hurried after the cops.

Nightmare swelled with ecstasy. No real opposition had risen to confront it. A few policemen, yes, and fewer of the armed men in suits, but those had been gnats to swat from its hide. Most of the humans ran before the creature's advance, screaming, wild-eyed with animal fear. Nightmare lived for these sensations: confusion, mayhem, terror. It breathed them in, and was strengthened.

It kicked open doors and sprayed the rooms with bullets, or kicked open doors and heaved in grenades. The gun bag grew lighter as the assault rifle fed on magazines and ejected them onto the floor. Water sprayed down from the sprinklers, adding to the turmoil of random violence. A mechanical siren screeched. In the back of Kudashova's brain, the creature caught reports of another emergency, the predicted Fiona Street, but the authorities didn't seem to know one attack from the other. Good, good. Heighten the tension. Surely, Hostetter would come.

At the end of the corridor through which the monster stalked, a door opened, the one to the stairs. Machine gun muzzles slipped through the opening.

The thing halted, bracing its feet and pointing its assault rifle. It waited a breath for the armed men to come into sight. It didn't want them forced into retreat, it wanted them dead.

Kudashova, trapped deep, fought to move her legs, to run, to hide, but the nightmare engulfing her laughed at her need. It didn't care if she died rent by bullets. It cared for her not a bit.

Two policemen emerged from the doorway, caught sight of Kudashova, and brought up their weapons to fire.

"Freeze! Put down the--"

Idiots. The thing squeezed Kudashova's finger, filling the corridor with banging sound and hot projectiles. One of the men fell, the other falling back through to the stairs. Others were there, holding the door for him. The thing caught sight of only hands and feet, so it had no sense of numbers or strength.

Not for survival, but to wreak more havoc, Nightmare whipped its host around to crash through the door of the nearest office. There it found partitions, file cabinets, cheap desks, and the thumping and clatter of cowering humans. The thing reached its assault rifle around the corner into the hall and squeezed off a few rounds at the stairs. Then, as the doorjamb to the office splintered from answering gunfire, the creature turned its weapon on the partitions.

The screams accompanying the trembling, quaking, collapsing furniture brought an erotic sigh past Kudashova's lips. As an afterthought, or maybe a plea for sense from its host, the monster slammed shut the office door before once more riddling the room with bullets.

Grace barely touched the wall next to the door. He needn't have worried about attracting unwanted attention from inside, not with the cacophony of weapons fire in there. He heard the screams, too. It was all he could manage to refrain from bursting unprepared into the room.

Ponce crouched ready on the other side of the door, his pistol ready in a two-handed grip. The sprinklers had plastered his suit to his body and the normally tight curls of his hair had loosened to a sodden mophead.

The police sergeant stood before the door, tightly wound.

All right, Grace thought, and clenched his teeth. He hadn't seen the major when she gunned down that cop. He'd hunkered in the stairwell like Ponce, hoping not to catch a round through the wall. Well, he'd see her in a second. Good odds, it would be the last time with both of them living.

He would have to kill her. His wet-behind-the-ears lieutenant. His smart and capable captain. His major, his better. God Almighty…

Soaking, trembling with rage, and wishing he could be anywhere else, Grace nodded to Ponce and poised to charge.

Ponce leaned back and brought his foot against the door with a grunt. The door flew open. The cop followed with a short burst from his MP5. Simultaneously, he charged into the office, Grace and Ponce right behind him and peeling off to either flank.

Nothing. No one. Grace scanned his end of the office, his pistol following his eyes. Shattered cubicle walls, a toppled file cabinet, two bloodied bodies, one male, one female. He shuffled farther into the room to peer around the three bullet-wrecked desks and the one standing partition. Nothing.

"Clear!" he shouted.

"Clear!" he heard Ponce return.

"We're clear!" the cop acknowledged.

None of them relaxed. It was one thing to find no enemy ready to kill you, it was another to not know where she was. Grace scanned the rest of the place, his stomach tightening at the sight of mangled bodies, probably six in all. They'd been hiding. They had fallen in attitudes of cowering or fleeing.

His officer had done this?

The window spanning the outside wall no longer existed, in one piece, anyway. Shards of plate glass dropped from the metal frames and either shattered against the floor or sailed out into the golden evening sky.

"She went out the window?" the cop asked. He didn't believe it. They were twenty-six stories up.

Grace wasn't sure he believed it, either.

Ponce crept up to the lip of the broken window and peeked out, his weapon aimed ahead of him. His inspection encompassed all four edges of the glass-strewn frame, then he backed into the room. "Nobody out there. Nobody climbing the walls or anything. Nobody on the concrete below, not that I can see."

"Then where the hell did she go?" the policeman demanded. He started rechecking the room.

Ponce looked at Grace, who shrugged.

"I don't know," Grace said, glancing around the room. "The door's the only other way out, and our girl can't fly."

"You sure about that?" Ponce looked back at the window.

Parachute? Glide suit? Fucking jetpack? Grace tried to release his tensed muscles. What had she done? What had Fiona Street found in the headquarters of spies that let her walk out a twenty-six-story window and disappear? He wondered, for the first time, about Hostetter...

"We've lost her," the cop was saying into his radio. "She has disappeared and we have no clue--" He stopped, stood straighter, and lowered his gun. When he looked up at Grace, his face showed incredulity. "Eighth floor," he said. "She's engaged a squad eighth floor center."

For a moment, only wind and the patter of sprinklers sounded through the wrecked office.

Then an explosion from somewhere below.

"Fucking hell!" Ponce exclaimed. "What the fucking hell is going on?"

"She's trained for this," Grace answered, though his voice sounded numbed. "She's an expert at infiltration..."

"You think?" Ponce watched Grace as if his sergeant were an idiot. "Was she also trained for terrorizing her own people? For murdering government employees? Go ahead and educate me, top, because maybe you military types have a different way of looking at the mission--"

"You guys know something?" The cop had stopped checking pulses on the bodies scattered through the room. "You want to let me in on the secret? Because I just lost a man to that maniac. You saying she's one of ours?"

Grace didn't want to say any such thing. He wanted to find someone culpable and beat them to a pulp. He tapped the pickup in his ear. "Goodknight," he said to divert the conversation. "You got anything? We've lost her."

He was surprised she answered immediately. "I've security bulletins for eighth floor center and fourth floor center-west," the sergeant came back in his ear. "That's uncomfortably close to our office, top."

Grace heard the tremor in her voice. Goodknight was defenseless. He tried to remember if the colonel had signed out his weapon that day.

With that thought, he recalled why the major had been in Medical. He recalled the order the colonel had issued, the one to separate the woman from the cat. Did the current tantrum through the halls of NSA speak to an urge for payback?

"Coming to you," Grace said, then signaled for Ponce to follow.

Childress had just parked his car in the lot south of the building when the alert came through on his phone. He pulled out the device and read the message with a raised eyebrow.

ATK ON DNS STREET IMPLICATED 28 FLR
RPT ON CONTACT A/AUTH: AF5D3

"The f--" He stiffened at a sudden, distant roll of thunder. He looked up, squinted at the black cube half a mile away, and identified white specks floating away from an upper floor. Paper? Somebody had blown out some windows.

Somehow, none of this surprised Childress. He wondered why. He replaced his phone in his pocket and turned to the shuttle bus several steps distant. "You better wait here," he called to the driver. "A problem at the building. They won't be wantin' approaches."

"Did those windows just blow out? Did a bomb go off over there?"

"You know as much as me," Childress called back as he reopened his car. "But not for long."

He dropped behind the wheel and automatically checked the load on his underslung Beretta. Full fourteen, he thought, and wished he had another few clips.

He chambered a round and started the car.

Not the elevator, Fiona pushed through the dark fog of Oz. All that bullshit in *Die Hard* movies, no, it wouldn't work. The elevator didn't even *have* a hatch leading out through the top.

More presentable in security lady scrubs and white canvas sneakers that were way too loose, Fiona carried a liberated MP5 down the corridor outside Medical. Other doors lined the hall, but none had people behind them. Server rooms, mostly, plus environmental controls and custodial closets. The NSA had been serious about secrecy for its top secret super-agent program. The only door of interest to Fiona faced her at the end of the corridor. The stairs.

They offered the only way out, but a dangerous one. If Security knew about the mess in Medical, they'd have men on the elevator *and* on the stairs. She had to assume they came for her.

Out, she heard from Oz, and he scratched at the door's metal kickplate. The diode on his neck blazed red.

Right, Fiona thought. You want out. That's why all those people are tumbled on the floor behind us, some of them seriously messed up. Because the cat wanted out. And now Fiona wanted out, too. God knew what would happen if she stuck around. Modern day cops had itchy fingers.

She cracked the door to the stairs. Oz darted through, found nothing, and gave her the all-clear.

They bounded up two levels. Too fast, too fast. Fiona wrapped an arm around the handrail to check that headlong charge. She couldn't smother the need to flee any more than she'd stemmed the urge for violence, but she managed to instill a healthy suspicion of threat within the cat's simple drive.

"Check corners," she said, breathing hard. "Check corners. Look up."

Oz checked the corners, but he didn't look up. How often in a lifetime did a cat *ever* look up? But Fiona did, and that's how she saw the flash of an arm three levels above. Oz hadn't even smelled the threat.

She brought up the machine gun and let loose a withering burst that thundered echoes off the walls. It was enough to command respect, but only for a second or two.

Oz burst up the stairs, a blur. Fiona climbed onto and over the handrail, then dangled into the narrow void between flights.

Just as she hung there, the weapons above answered her machine gun's greeting. Single shots close together. Landing, steps, and wall burst from the impacts. At least three men. Standard pistols.

One-handed, the other holding the handrail so she wouldn't plummet five floors to her death, she slung the weapon across her chest and tightened her muscles to spring. She saw the men. Cops, no armor, just blue shirts and dark pants, so not a specific response team. She saw them through Oz's eyes, then saw them as they realized they had more concerns than the shooter downstairs. Oz ran up one man's leg and at his throat. Yelling and panic sounded from the landing.

Fiona jumped to the next handrail up, then pivoted and sprang for the next. She didn't think about it; she didn't marvel at the impossibility, she just jumped. She found herself vaulting the handrail level with the cops, and watched herself enter the fight even as she watched Oz springing from man to man, sowing chaos with raking claws.

Fiona tripped one cop and brought her knee heavily down on his chest, stunning him. She traded punches with a second, but only long enough to line up a blow to his nose that she hoped, after the fact, had not driven his face into his brain. The last cop flailed at Oz, who sprang away as Fiona finished the second policeman. The cop brought up his gun. Fiona brought up hers. For an instant, she realized what she did, but the urge jumped like lightning across her middle brain. She couldn't have stopped; Oz wouldn't let her.

She boomed two rounds at the man. How she had managed to flip from full auto to single-shot, she had no idea. Why she holed the wall a few inches to either side of his head, she couldn't say. But it was enough to freeze him. In his shock, she kicked him hard in the chest. He bounced off the wall and went down like a sack of rocks.

Fiona staggered on the landing, a broken cry falling from her lips. Trembling, she held the machine gun out before her. She stared at it, flexed sweaty fingers against it, then tossed the thing down the stairwell before Oz could countermand her.

She'd almost killed that guy, a cop. She'd almost killed that security woman, and the veterinarian, for God's sake.

Control. She had to claw her way from her terrible, primitive cat brain and establish some form of con--

Weak, Oz said.

"Shut up!" Fiona screamed.

Another blast of weapons fire, this time from below. The handrail sparked and drywall pulverized into the air.

Below, Shotgun Mouse took careful aim, but he couldn't get a good line on her, the stairwell was so narrow.

Fiona slammed through the door at her landing and into a hall drenched by sprinklers. Before the door closed behind her, she heard Shotgun yelling into his pickup.

"--second floor! She's in scrubs! Consider armed--"

The fire door clicked shut.

Chapter Twelve

The lights went out. Goodknight stared at her suddenly blank computer monitor. Her stomach rolled. "SecNet, IC," she said into her phone headset, her tone strained. "SecNet, this is IC." She got dead air as an answer.

As she scrabbled in her desk drawer for a flashlight, the colonel appeared in his office doorway, his own light in hand. His other hand gripped a snub-nosed pistol.

"All power's down," he said. "Not even getting air through the vents."

A crackle of gunfire from somewhere far off, maybe at the stairs.

"Sergeant Goodknight," Sanders said. "Notify all available teams. Do you by any chance have a weapon?"

"No, sir."

"That three-hole punch on your desk. Take it by the door."

"Yes, sir."

Goodknight snatched up the long, heavy bar of a hole punch, the flashlight, and her cell phone. She froze then, let her cell clatter back to the desktop, and tore open her bottom drawer. There, snug in its soft pack, was the emergency radiophone. If her computer was down, and all the lights, and if SecNet failed to answer its calls, a cell phone might be useless. SecNet controlled access to the building's cell tower node. Without that node, the only possible communications outlet was wide-band radio, if that.

While she sneaked to the wall beside the door, checking the phone to remember how it worked, Sanders lowered to a crouch behind her desk. He rested his elbows on the blotter, gun aimed at the door, and waited.

More gunfire, closer.

Holding the hole punch like a club, the flashlight on the floor beside her, Goodknight punched out a text one-handed. ALL AGENTS LTC NEED ASSISTANCE 4 FLR ACKNOWLEDGE. "Sir, I don't know if this message is going anywhere. With SecNet down, the signal dampeners in the building... They'll block our transmission."

"We can only try," Sanders said.

The colonel watched the door. Goodknight kicked off her heels for a more stable stance.

Her phone rang, just about scaring her out of her skin. She switched it to vibrate and tapped the button to answer.

"Yes."

"Grace here. We're reaching the fourth floor. Check targets."

"Roger." She hung up, turned to Sanders, and was startled again by her phone. "Yes."

"Childress. I'm outside. They're evacuating the lower floors and won't let anybody in. Looks like you on your own."

"Understood. Uh, how did you place this call?"

"I'm talkin' to you, ain't I?"

"SecNet's down."

"Oh. Well, you know all those pretty signal-blocking windows they paid the lowest bidder millions of dollars for? They're mostly down here in the street."

"Omigod. What's going on out there?"

"It's fifty shades of all messed up. I don't think our building cops are a match to a trained assassin."

"She's up here."

"Then keep your head down. You ain't gettin' no help from the rest of us."

She hung up. "Grace is on the floor," she whispered to the colonel. "He says watch targets, he doesn't want to get--"

Gunfire thundered in the hall outside. Goodknight dropped her phone. She ducked and flinched at hammer blows to the wall beside her. Her breath shortened. Her nerves burned. She had no spit in her mouth.

The door shuddered. More gunfire. Goodknight thought she might go deaf. Shouts of warning--

"Get down!" Sanders yelled.

Goodknight dropped as a boom went off. Framed pictures fell from the wall and clattered over the floor. Suddenly, Goodknight was soaked. The sprinklers had activated. The fire alarm screeched.

Well, *something* still had power.

"Colonel! Goodknight! You in there?" came through the door.

"That's affirm!" Sanders stood, wiping water from his face.

"We're coming in. Please don't shoot us."

Goodknight regained her feet as the door flew open. The body of a building policeman, having fallen against the door during whatever had transpired in the hall, dropped over the threshold onto its back.

Grace entered the outer office, a Beretta in one hand. Ponce hunched in the doorway with a cop. Both breathed like marathon runners at the finish line.

"Report," the colonel said, and dropped his gun to his side.

"She got away, sir." Grace spat water. "She was definitely on her way here, but didn't like the resistance. Four cops in the corridor, three agents. All KIA, sir."

"Where is she?"

"Can't say. It's dark. Bugged out east, I think. We need to get you out of here. She may come back. She's got a shipload of grenades and I don't know what all."

The colonel took a moment with that. "All right." He nodded to the cop in the hall, the live one, that is.

"That's Sergeant Collier, building police," Grace said. "He's called for an escort."

"Good. As soon as they get here, we find reliable communications. I've had enough of this shit. Time to put our errant major down."

Grace, for the first time in the years Goodknight had known him, opened his arms in helpless surrender. "Down, sir?"

"She's gone over the line. There are lives at stake, some already lost." Sanders glanced from face to face in the uneven flashlight illumination. His eyes glistened. The muscles of his face twitched from tight fury.

My God, Goodknight thought. He's going to have her killed.

"Why the hell is she doing this, Grace?" The colonel's tone was clipped.

Grace's shoulders sagged. "Sir, I don't know. I think she's pissed as hell."

Kudashova crouched at the border of a blasted-out window in an empty office one floor up from Grace, her gun bag emptied and her assault rifle spent of ammunition. She rocked slightly, forward and backward, hugging her knees. She watched and listened to the people in the other office, one of her three camera spheres hovering unnoticed just outside their door. Rain and alarms overlaid the pickup, muddying both sight and hearing, so she only managed bits of the ongoing conversation. She had killed the intranet with a thought, so no input there. She had killed the power, too, to deny her enemies the comfort of light.

Nightmare had damaged those enemies. It needed just to wait for Hostetter's arrival. How could he stay away with his allies burning? How could he stay away with his precious Street hunted? And she *was* hunted. Her own people stalked her. How many men and women had been killed by "her" hand? How many terrorized? Her people wanted her dead. Hostetter wouldn't permit that.

Again, the thing in Kudashova fumed at the despicable Hostetter. It would wreak upon him such vengeance that men would tremble for generations at its memory.

So it waited, crouching. A weapon lay at its feet, a rifle lifted from a dead policeman. Nightmare ignored the gun, fondling for the moment a razor sharp combat knife. With this, it sliced at Kudashova's forearm, thrilling to the pain that casual attack brought her. So delicate, these apes, so soft and coddled. It drew lines across her arm, bubbling up wells of blood until her hide was a slippery, indistinct mess. Then it sensibly, regretfully, ceased that torture. It would need that arm when Hostetter arrived. It would need it to function.

For a little while, at least.

Kudashova, hunkered at the edge of the blown-out window, awaited her enemy's arrival like a raptor atop a cliff. It wouldn't be long. It couldn't be.

The nightmare hungered. It must feed.

What a mess. Bunch of white people with their apple carts upset. Everything was fine when folks followed the rules, and the rules stated without equivocation that monuments were sacrosanct, especially big glass buildings marking power like a dog marks its territory. You want to trash a third world country, knock yourself out. You break one pane of glass in a big-assed monumental dog whiz, everybody goes batshit crazy.

Childress stood at the intersection of Batshit and Crazy and shook his head. Smoke billowed from windows on three levels of NSA headquarters. Glass littered the front drive. Paper fluttered down to the parking lot like confetti. Three firetrucks had hauled up to the building, blaring horns and sirens. Building cops ran around like their hair was aflame, trying without success to impose order on chaos. Childress stood at a brace of three cop cars with the building police captain, a couple of his lieutenants, and MPs from Ft. Meade. He watched in awe as hundreds of people poured from the building like monkeys out of a lion cage.

He had to admit, it was kind of cool. And his boss was responsible? He never would've given her credit.

"That can't be," the captain told his conferees as they leaned over a floorplan that covered the hood of a police car, covered it several pages deep. "We get confirmed sightings first on twenty-eight, then twenty-six, down to the basement, up to fourteen, then four, then two. South outside, center northwest, center, they're all over the place. Nobody can get from twenty-eight south to the frigging basement in two minutes, that's impossible."

"Impossible's sorta her thing," Childress said. "This kinda shit, it's her bread and butter."

"It's impossible," the captain insisted. "There's at least four of them. That's the only way."

"All right," one of the lieutenants said. "Then if that's the case, how do we tackle 'em? If there're four, or three, or five or whatever, where are they and how do we find 'em?"

"Floor to floor," the captain said. "Base security is sending every man they have."

Childress snorted and turned away toward the building main entrance. It barfed evacuees like a drunk barfs bar food. "Jesus H. Christ on a bicycle, how you gonna floor-to-floor that bitch? That building's the size of a fuckin' city. It'll take a goddamned battalion to search that puppy without your cordons leaking."

"We know our jobs, Mister Childress," the captain growled.

"Yeah, except nothin' like this was ever *in* your job." With that, Childress stepped away from the huddle, toward the doors to the building. He didn't go far, he just didn't want to hear any more bullshit from the amateurs.

He watched the evacuees, evacuees from a building that was supposed to be in lockdown. But, what could he or anyone expect? The place was on fire. You couldn't expect thirty thousand people to hunker down in their offices while the place went up in flames, now could you? Only thing, Major Street knew that fun fact as well as anybody. Likely, she'd set the fires to capitalize on that very consideration. The major wasn't a dummy. She knew to ensure an escape route.

So he watched the entrance and every soul that flew from it, scanning for a petite redhead in scrubs, or whatever disguise she had since dragged off a victim. He wouldn't see a thing. NSA headquarters had more than one door, and there were way too many people to watch at just his one. But what else could he do? Childress wasn't the man to lean back and cop a smoke when work needed doing, no sir.

So he concentrated his gaze on the front doors. He had six other agents on six other doors and had alerted the police to his suspicions, but there were tons of evacuees to scan and no guarantee an escape in plain sight was even the major's plan. Childress was sure he wasted his time.

Then she walked right by in front of him.

For a second, it didn't register. Then he snapped his head to seek out the redhead in scrubs who had just passed in front of his eyes, not twenty feet in front of him, dammit. And carrying a black cat.

There she was, her back to him now, hurrying into the parking lot without *seeming* to hurry. The scrubs didn't fit and she hunched her shoulders. From that angle he couldn't see the cat, but he was positive she carried it. And her neck glowed like an air traffic control light.

He tapped the pickup at his ear. "All agents, Childress, front door. I've made her, headed south into the parking lot. Come and get 'er, boys." He started after her. He snapped his fingers at the cops and stabbed a flattened hand toward the woman. They glanced up, looked around, then looked like they'd wetted their collective pants.

Where you going, major? Childress accelerated to a fast walk. He drew his pistol and gripped it in two suddenly sweaty hands. He remembered Black Batman, who couldn't lay a glove on Street. The takedown would need delicacy. He glanced right and left. Cops drew up, some of them working to get out in front of her. Don't be stupid, he thought. Don't let her know you're on to her. Those whispers of superpowers weren't idle talk.

That's what bothered Childress. Agents whispered about the major, as if she were something beyond natural. She was the agency's super-woman, fantastically experienced and capable.

So why had she walked right in front of a bunch of policemen and her own agent? Had she gone stupid in the last several minutes?

My God! Fiona thought. Are you *stupid?*

Sure looked like it. Submerged as she was, she hadn't had much control over the matter. Oz had plunged them into a stream of humanity rushing along a second-floor corridor. They had wormed into the crowd's middle and swarmed along with it for the camouflage of numbers. Oz was in her arms, she hadn't known how, when they burst from a stairwell into the expansive lobby, policemen and firefighters waving the herd along. By the time Fiona realized they headed for the doors, headed straight into the arms of everyone hunting her, they were through the propped-open turnstile and into the lowering sunlight. The driveway was covered in firetrucks and police cars.

Holy shit! She tried to put the brakes on, but Oz saw freedom from those who would kill him, from the needle. He wasn't as clear on the subject of guns. Those usually went for the humans.

So Fiona, trapped, followed his escape. She could only point him in a general direction.

She aimed him toward the official cars grouped in the second row of the parking lot. A vague sense of grabbing a vehicle swam in her brain, almost drowning in the id drive from Oz. And there, yes, three cars with their doors open, suits leaning against metal tops, sunglasses--

No sunglasses! That one, the older guy in the blue suit, no sunglasses, soft build, probably an analyst, or maybe just an accountant. She could take him in one movement and be out of there in two. Assuming the keys were still in the car.

She leaned on Oz's rudder -- if he had his way, they'd continue right through the lot and onto the highway -- and pointed him at the target. Oz saw him, Oz understood, and knew the man must die.

No! Not *die*, you moron! Jeez, we just want a *car!*

"Ma'am, I'll ask you to stop where you are and put down the cat."

Fiona jerked her eyes toward the voice. A cop. Not ten feet away. His gun was drawn, but down. Her fuzzy mind bemoaned that she had missed such an obvious threat, then the predator washed over her again.

"Oh, I don't believe this," Childress complained as the cop tried to talk to her. He picked up his pace and brought up his pistol.

Fiona heaved the cat and ran. Oz sailed through the air toward the cop, legs outstretched and fur standing on end. The policeman put up an arm to defend himself.

"Freeze, goddammit! Police!" somebody else yelled. The sound of gunfire. Projectiles plowing into car tops and windows. Fiona pounded pavement as close to the cars as possible.

Oz landed on the cop's arm, stepped to his head, and launched onto a nearby car. He skidded, retracted claws, caught footing with his pads, and bolted for the next car, and the next, and the next.

Fiona saw two cops rushing between cars to cut her off. She saw them from above as Oz bounded over them. She turned, no thought, just muscle action, and sped between cars two spots short of the cops. She passed behind them. They continued to where she wouldn't be, oblivious. More cops behind her, to left, a police car squealing into the lane she'd enter in an instant. And Oz was at the man, the one with the soft face, no sunglasses, and their hoped-for ride. Oz crouched atop the sedan, staring into the man's eyes, growling.

Fiona came up behind the target and slammed him into the neighboring vehicle, holding him by his lapels. The cops closed in, only feet away.

They won't shoot, they won't shoot, not with a civilian--

Oz was in the car. Push-button start.

Fiona heaved the man in through the driver's door, followed, and forced her shoulder against his ass to shove him through to the passenger's side. Oz jumped from seat to dash to headrests to back seat, spitting.

Someone grabbed Fiona's arm from outside the sedan. She lashed out, crashing a cop backwards into the next parked car. Then she pushed the ignition button, slammed shut her door, and threw the vehicle into reverse.

From the corner of a blasted-out window on the fifth floor, Kudashova flicked her attention from the milling ants of evacuating people to the hint of a disturbance away from the crowd. Something sparked among the sea of vehicles fronting the building. The Street woman. Kudashova flexed her fingers against the handguard of a weapon she had taken off a dead policeman. Her palms left sweat and blood on the dark, molded plastic.

The car barreled out of its parking space, burning rubber. It lurched to a stop before smashing into other vehicles, and roared. Cops opened fire. Childress heard at least half a dozen shots.

"Cease fire!" somebody yelled. "Cease fire, you assholes! She has a hostage!"

Childress skidded to a stop six or so feet off her left front wheel. She looked right at him.

He had a shot. *Fuck* the hostage, he had a shot. He let loose two rounds, shattering the front windshield.

But Street had ducked beneath the dash. Her tires screamed, threw up a rubber stink, and propelled her up the lane.

A cruiser moved to cut her off. Fiona plowed into its left headlight, stomped the accelerator, and turned the wheel, shoving the cop car broadside into the vehicles across the aisle. Metal screeched and snapped. Something jagged bounced up Fiona's hood and over the top, just missing slamming through into the driver's seat. Fiona careened up the lane, unsure how to clear the parking lot. The man beside her kicked his legs. They got in her way, a few times smacking a shoe into her face.

"You! Key!" she bellowed. "Stop kicking like a wuss and give me the key to this car!"

Two policemen rushed into the lane, pistols raised. Fiona jerked the steering wheel right. She didn't look where the car went. Oz, in the back window, did that for her.

She threaded the car through an empty space between a pickup truck and a van. The space beyond was also clear. She barreled through it and skidded left.

The man struggled to a more or less upright position. He breathed hard and fast, gripping his seat and the dash with trembling fingers.

"Gimme the key!" Fiona demanded, and made a hard right at the end of the aisle.

"Please don't kill me," the man whimpered.

"Fine! Key! Now!"

He jammed one hand into his outside jacket pocket and came out with a thick, black fob. Fiona snatched it and tossed it to the floor.

"Please! I did as you said! Please, slow down and let me go!"

Fiona scanned the parking lot, what she could see of it. Blue and red lights in three directions, a hint of skulking figures. Did she have time to let the man out?

NO! KILL!

No! He's just a guy! Just a … guy … who smells of … gun oil?

Fiona snapped her eyes to the man. He smelled of *gun oil!*

DOG!

His hand dived under his jacket. Fiona wrenched the wheel to heave him toward her, then elbowed him in the face. "You're a goddamned agent!"

He fell against the passenger door. Fiona released the wheel to throw open that door. She punched the man once more for good measure, then forced him from the car.

He tumbled out screaming. Fiona felt no bump, so maybe she hadn't run over him. Fuck him anyway. The only agent in the US inventory who didn't wear the goddamned sunglasses!

Dog!

Fiona felt a violent crunch as her sedan ground its driver's side against multiple vehicles. She grappled back to her seat. Amid screaming metal and shattering glass from the window next to her face, she twisted the wheel away from flying steel and plastic.

A cruiser behind her, two of them. The lead cop raced a dozen feet off her bumper, blaring his siren. She scanned forward, Oz behind. She had to get out of that parking lot.

Childress winced at the cry of rending metal. Holstering his pistol, he climbed atop an SUV and pulled out his cell phone. He squinted into the lot, searching for players, for patterns, for anything that could truncate the messy circle jerk around him. Yeah, yeah, the major was a pro, way above a building cop's pay grade. It *should* be hard for them to catch her. Except… None of the last few minutes showed any signs of professionalism. The major didn't seem to execute a plan. Her behavior looked more like panic.

What would cause a pro to pan--

Nothing. But an animal…

He punched the number for the captain of police.

At the moment the captain's phone rang, he had straightened to field yet another self-absorbed idiot in uniform. An oakleaf colonel came at him, entourage in tow, a big senior sergeant practically chewing his ear. Sighing, the captain handed the phone to his lieutenant.

"Captain! Colonel Sanders, Insertions and Extractions." The army officer pushed out his hand. It was soaking wet like his uniform and the gaggle of straphangers around him. "SITREP, if you don't mind."

The captain shook the proffered hand, but he wasn't in the mood for humoring Army officers. "As a matter of fact, I do mind. I apparently have a suicidal nut job of a covert agent zipping around my parking lot like she saw *The Blues Brothers* once too often. One of yours, I understand."

"I'm afraid so. I'm here to--"

"So I'd appreciate it if you folks stood somewhere else with the rest of the evacuees and let my people handle this-- *What?*"

The lieutenant tugged on his sleeve like a two-year-old. He shoved the phone at his boss. It was on speaker.

"--out of your ass and help me cage this bitch! I need your boss and I need every cop and MP in the area, and I need both right the fuck now!"

The colonel gave the big sergeant with him a quick, serious glance.

"Childress, that you?" the captain of police raged. "Why the hell are you on my line?"

"You got one chance to box this chick in. I can see it from here. She's unhinged, and we can put her where we need her! You gonna play ball, or not?"

The captain rumbled deep in his gut. He hated these people. They were convinced they could push around cops, that they were somehow better because of their uniforms -- or their suits. He particularly hated Childress, who thought he was God's gift to heroes or some such shit. But Childress knew the culprit. *They* knew her. The captain wished they'd dry up and die, but... "What you want?" he asked into the phone while glaring at the colonel.

"Keep her runnin' in circles for just one minute. All your foot units north of the main entrance, wall her off north of Rockenbach. I need wheeled units blockin' Rockenbach and Cochrane, and Canine north of Rockenbach. Y'all gettin' this?"

The captain nodded to his lieutenants. They droned on their radios to the men in the parking lot. "Yeah, we're getting it." And he had to admit he approved. Childress aimed to funnel the crazy woman onto the one street,

Canine, and herd her west to where the road ran out. Like spooking deer into a box canyon.

"Officer?" The colonel again. "May I?" He waggled his fingers for the phone.

The captain gave it up, noting the colonel's granite expression. It contrasted with that of the two NCOs. Their eyes widened with suspicion and a faint tinge of fear.

"Childress, Sanders," the colonel said. "Be advised, the target is sanctioned. Several kills, undetermined wounded. She's unstable. Case Specific is in effect."

The big sergeant stepped toward the colonel. "Sir..."

"At ease, Grace. You roger that, Childress? Case Specific is in effect."

A slight pause. Far out in the parking lot, atop some bulky SUV, Childress turned toward them and gaped. "Yeah," he said. "Roger that."

The colonel handed back the cell phone, then turned toward the female sergeant. "Put that out to all teams, Goodknight. In case she breaks out."

The sergeant stared at him, mouth open.

"Goodknight."

"Yes, sir," and she rummaged in her purse.

For the first time, the captain noticed the heavy metal hole punch she gripped in one hand.

"What the--" DeBoy looked up from his phone. He'd been standing idly out of the way while engineers inspected the damaged safe room and the hole through to the floors above it. He turned his eyes back to the phone screen and marveled that extra-universal events in safe boxes were not the most striking occurrence of his day. The message on the phone could not have been clearer.

They'd just put a hit out on Street.

DeBoy glanced to the exit, which swarmed with structural engineers, nuclear engineers, and electrical engineers, all getting in each other's way. "I gotta tell Tejada."

He broke for the door. "Make a hole!" He squeezed through, bounding over the haphazard sprawl of thick cables and conduit, and jogged up the curving hall toward the main doors of the building. He didn't know why he ran. There seemed no way a kill order could affect him. He was in California. The major was on the other side of the Rockies, and then some. But he ran nonetheless and a cold sweat of dread moistened his palms and the back of his neck.

He plunged beyond the front doors. Tejada stood at the curb with Hostetter and the women. The afternoon sun flooded over them. They looked like four old friends shootin' the shit, if shit got shot amid military guards, CID investigators, and grumbling scientists.

"Tejada!" DeBoy drew up to him. They all turned, interested. They didn't know. "Has your phone rung?"

"No." Tejada shook his head. "And it probably never will again." He held up a device he pulled from his pants pocket. It was warped plastic and cracked glass. "Took a hit in that room back there. Didn't even know it till I got out here."

"Sorry about that," Hostetter said, and touched the brim of his cowboy hat. "I'm good for it."

"So's the federal government." Tejada replaced the phone in his pocket. "They'll pay for it."

DeBoy quaked from tension. "Jesus, man! You haven't heard. They put a hit on the major!"

Tejada blinked at him. The engineer Eglemann made a hiccupping sound and threw her fingertips to her mouth. Neither Rodriguez nor the cowboy seemed to grasp what DeBoy meant.

"What're you saying?" Tejada put his hands on his hips. "Who put a hit--?"

"Our own people!" DeBoy cried, and shoved his phone into Tejada's face.

Tejada's eyes focused on the screen. His eyebrows lowered. His lips twisted, showing teeth.

"Case Specific," DeBoy breathed, and suddenly felt a need to bend over and hold his knees. "The contingency plan...."

"What's this here Case Specific?" Hostetter asked, finally getting that something wasn't right.

Tejada took DeBoy's phone. He shoved it out to arm's length as if it stank. "Case Specific. If the major ever went crazy, as in homicidal -- like all the others before her -- they'd order her killed to protect the public."

No sounds but fussing engineers and traffic.

"And who in tarnation would give such an order?" Hostetter asked, his voice rumbling.

"The colonel," DeBoy said. "Something bad must've happened out east."

"Well, I can't cotton a'tall to this," the big cowboy said. He shook off Rodriguez's hold on his arm and backed a few steps away.

"I don't see what any of us can do," Tejada said, tossing out his hands in a show of helplessness. "It's three thousand miles away."

"I figure *I* can do somethin'."

DeBoy got his meaning a hair before the others. He stood and pointed at Hostetter. "Somebody better grab his stick."

"Mister Hostetter, these are orders," Tejada said. He returned DeBoy's phone and dropped his hands to his sides. "I don't know what's happened, but they wouldn't order this lightly."

"Clayton?" Rodriguez reached out to Hostetter. Her face twisted up as if she didn't understand.

"Sorry, Miss Sinfonee, but I gotta go." The cowboy stepped backward into the street.

Tejada and DeBoy were quick, their weapons drawn and zeroed on Hostetter. "Don't," Tejada said.

Hostetter narrowed his eyes, glancing from Tejada, to his lady love, and back to Tejada without moving his head. The fingers on his stick flexed over the keyboard control unit. "Sorry, young feller. I know you doin' your job, and that's right honest of ya. But, see, I owe a friend, and that's honest, too." He turned to face Doctor Rodriguez. "Bye, darlin'."

A pillar of orange light slammed down atop him, spurting static and dancing lightning. It lasted only a second, then vanished.

In its place -- in Hostetter's place -- was a circle of molten asphalt.

Tejada lowered his pistol. DeBoy lowered his.

Eglemann ran her hands through her hair and pursed her lips.

Doctor Rodriguez stared at the molten circle, her face contorted like she'd start bawling any second.

"Fuck," Tejada whispered, and reholstered his weapon. "D, I need your phone again."

Grace gritted his teeth at yet another screaming report of torn steel. A plume of black smoke poured skyward from half a dozen rows deep in the parking lot. The major wouldn't give up. The chase had passed all measures of the ridiculous, but she didn't surrender. Was her brain even on? Did she act on automatic?

Or did she know she'd be shot the second she gave any agent a target?

"Okay, we got her boxed in," Childress said from his perch on the SUV. "Now herd her. All units in the parking lot, she don't want to get close to you. Nudge her toward Canine. I want Canine blocked at Emory, east and south. Force a right there. Keep her on it. Plug up those side streets."

"Colonel Sanders," Grace tried again. He held himself in a vice to keep from getting in his commander's face. "Sir. I think you're making a mistake."

"Are you questioning my orders, sergeant?" The colonel stared out into the parking lot. He spared not a glance for his subordinate.

"No, sir. Just pointing out a flaw in your reasoning. It doesn't have to go further than that."

"Men are dead. That's where it goes. I should've done this years ago."

"If we remove the implant--"

"We *tried* removing the implant. That's why we're here, in this parking lot, with a burning building behind us!"

Grace couldn't argue that point. He wished he could. But he had to protect his girl. He swallowed hard and opened his mouth to protest again.

He hesitated at a hand on his elbow. He looked down to find Goodknight, her face a blank mask. She held his eyes, then pointed surreptitiously toward the west.

Far out on the blue, tree-fuzzed horizon, Grace caught a glimpse of orange light. It winked out after an instant.

Kudashova gasped at the sight of the conduit. It winked far off, miles and miles away. She pulled back her weapon's charging handle. Hostetter came close to her. Hostetter came to die.

Her orbiting spheres gathered around her, increasing velocity within their turns. A vortex of wind stirred Kudashova's hair.

Childress gripped his phone with such intensity it trembled in his hand. "We got her," he called as Street's battered car squealed, throwing sparks and trailing smoke, onto Canine, the main drag out of the parking lot. "This street dead ends at a concrete wall and a chain link fence. She's trapped. All cars, keep those side streets plugged. We want her straight up the line."

Over the last five minutes, his world had been a whirl of sirens, blue and red lights, screeching tires, and wrecks. Now the sound retreated south and west with Street's smoking, mangled sedan and the flashing bloodhound cruisers behind her.

For the first time Childress realized that no agents rode with the cops. This was bad. Those law-and-order types would likely compound their first mistake and give the major a second chance to surrender, which was to give her a chance to grind them into the pavement.

"Hey! Any agents out there, I need a ride!" He shoved the phone into a pocket and scrambled down to the pavement. He bemoaned his fine taste in clothes. Polished leather dress shoes weren't the best gear for mountain-goating slick metal vans.

Once more on the pavement, he looked around for a sign of transportation. Surely, someone had access to a car…

Something caught his attention, a flash to the east, far across the military compound. He stared, squinting, at a column of orange lightning dropping diagonally from the clouds, or at least it looked like lightning, sort of. Childress didn't know what to make of it.

The lightning winked out after a bare moment, leaving no hint it had ever been. Then a company sedan skidded to a halt beside Childress, bringing him back to the moment. He pulled open the front passenger door and fell into the vehicle. "Go! Follow the others! Overtake 'em if you can!"

The sedan sped forward. At the end of the aisle, it executed a smooth but frightening fishtail drift to make the turn without grinding up parked cars. The driver punched the accelerator again.

Grace watched another orange pillar strike the earth closer to headquarters. He tried to keep his face blank as everyone else but Goodknight ducked at the sudden stab of brilliance. No one there had ever seen a lightning post. It would take them a moment to figure it out. Hopefully, the major could use that moment.

His phone buzzed in his pocket. He snatched it out, saw it was from Tejada, and put it back in his pants unanswered.

Childress turned to look at his driver. He didn't recognize the man, likely not on a Sanders team. The guy had paid some dues, though, if that livid knot on the side of his head meant anything.

"We following?" the man asked. Blood dribbled from his lower lip.

"No, man! Overtake! I wanna be first on the scene when she stops that car."

"We gonna kill her, like the colonel said?"

"You got a problem with that?"

"Only if it's too fucking fast."

Another tail-swishing turn, another dig into pavement and burst of speed.

The agent leaned slightly toward Childress, who held onto his seat and the dash. He hadn't had a chance to buckle in. "Where--"

"Right up the lane! Lay it on!" Childress fished out his phone and punched the correct number. His driver rushed at two broadside police cruisers, apparently without concern. Childress wondered, pressing his shoes against the firewall, if they'd smash into those cars before the phone stopped ringing.

He heard the line open. "Dude! Move your cars on Dennis! Move 'em now! I'm coming up on 'em like a missile!"

But they didn't move. They didn't move. They--

"You want I should slow?" the driver asked.

Burning rubber, the cruisers parted. Childress's car roared onto the road beyond and leaned into a hard right. Two police cars streaked past them. Childress saw the sorry-assed, torn-up sedan they pursued.

"There she is! Catch her!"

His driver dug in. The dude drove like freaking NASCAR. He pulled even on the left of the trailing cruiser. He must have been edging past eighty.

They were running out of street, fast.

"Can't make it," the driver said.

"She isn't slowing," Childress complained.

"She'd better."

At the end of the street, a concrete wall separated the dead end from Highway 32. Street's smoking wreck veered left a stone's throw from hammering into that wall. She left the pavement, the car bouncing violently as it jumped the curb. The cruisers followed her in among trees. So did the agent, as much to keep from colliding with police cars as to continue the chase.

Something orange flashed behind and to one side. Childress didn't quite get a look.

Street slalomed through a grassy field until the wall ran out and a chain link fence took over as barrier. She aimed her vehicle at the fence…

"Naw," Childress muttered. "No way."

Street plowed into the fence. A section buckled, tore loose, and whipped around the field like batwings. The lead cruiser skidded to a stop just short of the impact zone. Twisted aluminum posts and cement anchors pounded the police car as if it were a kettle drum.

The agent and the other cop car hit their brakes and plowed up earth. Childress and his driver threw open their doors, drew their weapons, and scrambled out of the vehicle.

Real life isn't like Hollywood. It isn't a done deal, slamming through an eight-foot-tall chain link fence. Much of the chain link ended up under Street's car, snarling the suspension, tying up the wheels. Her wreck had stopped flat.

Street tumbled from the window of her smashed driver's side door. She landed in mud and tangled aluminum, scrabbling to hands and knees. The cat leaped from the car and stalked around her, its tail a bristle brush.

Childress and the agent rushed toward her, pistols up and seeking shots. The cruiser blocked their aim, as did a cop drawing down on the major over his vehicle's hood.

Shoot the bitch! Childress thought. Shoot her before she--

With a baritone hum and a blaze of orange brilliance, a column of light appeared beside Street's car. Grass sizzled, car tires squealed on the neighboring highway, and trashed aluminum vaporized into a caustic, bitter fog. Childress fell to a knee, blinded, shaking his head to clear his vision. Then the pillar vanished, causing the air to rush back into its space with a dull bass pop.

A woman stood next to Childress, drawing an MP5 to her shoulder. Tank top, slacks, short blonde hair. Who was she, an agent? And where the hell had she come from?

Hostetter stood in the center of a circle of scorched earth. He leaned over to take Street's hand and pull her to him. "Grab the cat and hold tight, darlin'. We gotta vamoose."

The major drew into Hostetter's arms and the cat threw itself onto the major.

The blonde woman cut loose with the MP5, a continuous, barrel-melting barrage.

With a second explosion of brilliant light and static discharge, Street and Hostetter disappeared from the world.

The bullets struck through the orange pillar, then empty air, thudding into the grassy berm leading up to the highway. Panicked cars skidded, braked, and smashed into each other.

When Childress looked, the blonde woman was gone.

"Shee-it!" he exclaimed.

Part Two:
Awakening

"Hold on, little girl,
The end is soon to come."

--Evanescence, *Sick*

Chapter Thirteen

Fiona jerked to a half sitting position, suddenly, fiercely conscious. Her fists gripped the linens in tight bunches. Her feet dug against the mattress, ready to propel her in any direction. Then she saw where she was and who sat with her. No, she thought. Safe. She forced her muscles to relax.

"Been out o' it for nigh on three hours," Hostetter said from the easy chair across the room. "I was beginnin' to worry." He took his feet down from where he had rested them on a five-gallon plastic bucket, then dropped the paperback book he'd been reading to the floor. "How you feelin'?"

Fiona slid her gaze around her immediate surroundings. She found wood plank, roughly-finished walls with no insulation layer. She shivered from chill air slipping between the boards. Bare beams stretched overhead, a rough wood floor below. A greasy-glassed oil lantern gave her light to see by. It illuminated Hostetter's chair, its upholstery bursting out in multiple rifts of dirty batting. It showed the bed for a wooden box covered in a thin, cheap mattress that might have been time-machined from a WWII army barracks. The sheets were threadbare and faded, having once, perhaps, been blue.

She looked down. She still wore the security lady scrubs, but they'd been augmented by a heavy leather duster with rabbit fur lining. Beneath the coat, she felt bandages along one flank, over one hand, and compression bandages on one cheek and her neck. She raised one shaking hand to the bandage at her neck.

"Nothin' serious," Hostetter said, "though I been wonderin' why your own folks got on to wantin' you dead. I recognize bullet creases when I see 'em."

"Bullet creases?" Speech burned Fiona's throat. She licked her lips.

"Yeah, I reckon so." Hostetter got up and crossed the room to an old, scarred chest of drawers. He took from its top a water bottle and a ceramic mug and brought them to Fiona. Sitting down heavily on the edge of the bed, he popped the water bottle's lid. "That car you was in got Swiss cheesed, and they tried to do the same to you. That feller Childress was there. He was drawin' down on you when I arrived, and you wasn't even armed."

I'm always armed, Fiona thought. *I'm a weapon.* "Where's Oz?"

"He's around here somewheres." He poured water into the ceramic mug and handed it to Fiona. "You can't feel him?"

Yes, she could feel him, but faintly. Distance muddied their neural connection. Oz crouched somewhere, somewhere outside, but it was dark, and he was far away. And there was someone else...

She drank. "Tell me what's happened. Where is this place?" She sat up straighter and winced at stings from multiple cuts and bruises.

"Well, this here's my place--"

"No it isn't."

"Pardon?"

"I set you up. You have a nice ranch house, and a barn for Porthos."

"Excuse me. I said this was *my* place. Me'n a few pards been workin' on it for nigh on a year now. Cut and nailed the boards, even made the nails ourselves. No electricity, but I got a right good fireplace in the next room. Can't light it, though. Don't want to attract no attention. Anyhow, it feels like home, since I built it with my own hands. I come up here now and again. To think, and be lonely with myself."

God in heaven, the man could build *houses*. "I hope it isn't next to your other place, buddy, because the sheriff's coming in a hot minute."

"Already here, Miss Fiona." When she stiffened, he put out a calming hand. "Don't you worry, we're a long ways off. They won't find us for hours yet. Can you move about? I'll show you." He took the cup and placed it and the bottle on the chest of drawers.

Damned straight she could move about, Fiona thought, tightening her lips to keep from giving the cowboy a talking to. No way would she lie on her back while agents stalked about outside. She slid from the bed and, stiffly, managed a halfway confident hobble to the door, Hostetter hovering like a momma hen. Every muscle in her body felt like rusty gears.

They entered the one other room, which showed the shadowed forms of a spindly card table and two more broken down easy chairs. Fiona wished Oz were with her; he could see in the dark. Just then, through his eyes, she

caught an impression pine trees and underbrush. And that other someone…
They crossed the uneven floorboards and exited through the only entrance
to the house. Fiona negotiated the two wooden steps into a sloped yard of
sparse grass and tall pines. The trees surrounded the house on three sides,
like bodyguards.

Night. The stars above the shadowed pines made Fiona's heart ache.
She'd only seen stars like that on blacked-out ships in the middle of the
ocean. They were uncountable, bold, and sharp.

She tore her eyes from the heavens and pointed them down the bluff on
which Hostetter had built his getaway home. The yard offered her a long
view, with a valley a good hundred feet below, few trees obscuring its starlit
beauty. Scrub grass and a winding stream, and miles and miles of open land
between walls of night-blackened rock. Far out in that valley, just off the
silvered ribbon of a two-lane road, stood Hostetter's house and the nearby
barn.

It hosted a great number of dark trucks and police cars, some flashing
red and blue lights.

Hostetter nudged Fiona. He held out a set of binoculars that he had
somehow picked up on their way out. Fiona took them with a nod.

Among the vehicles in the valley, she easily picked out Childress. How
could she not? The guy was a caricature of the fashion plate policeman,
exactly like that guy on *Barney Miller*, the signature character of the late
Ron Glass. What was that guy's name? Horus? Harris? "I'm in a lot of trouble, Clay."

"I figured that out, Miss Fiona."

"They'll find this place."

"Not for a while, and by then we'll be gone."

Fiona lowered the spyglasses. "They'll come after you, too."

"I reckon they already have." He gestured down toward his house as
evidence.

They stood in silence, watching the show below.

"I gotta know," Hostetter finally began. Fiona knew what came. "What
they after you for?"

"They wanted to kill us."

Hostetter made a rumbling sound deep in his throat.

"No." Fiona handed back the binoculars. "That isn't it. They wanted to
kill Oz. They wanted to remove our neural implants because they thought
they made me unstable. But they planned to kill Oz and take apart his brain.
So we ran. Or he ran. I got dragged along."

"So, umm, do that mean they was right?"

She opened her mouth to deny it, but all that emerged was a strangled
sound. Then, with him having said what jeered in her mind, she lost composure and burst into hacking, ugly sobs. The heat in her cheeks seemed to

boil the tears that streaked them. She felt humiliated before her strong, implacable friend who looked on her as an equal. She shoved her palms across her face to erase the wet evidence of weakness. She tried to will the tears dry. But she couldn't.

The NSA had become her life. Now her life hunted her, wishing her dead. And she wasn't sure they were wrong in that.

"I... I--I--" She felt an arm around her shoulders. She turned into it, into the warm, musky man who held her, and bawled like a baby.

But only for a minute. When those seconds expended themselves, she made one loud, wet sniffle and separated from the cowboy. Oz, as if by magical command, circled about her ankles.

Fiona patted Hostetter's chest, then backed away. "I'm sorry."

"T'ain't nothin' to apologize for. Except for me. Because, Miss Fiona, there's one more thing I have to ask."

"Okay." Fiona steeled herself, wrapping the duster tighter around her. "Shoot."

"Again, I'm plum sorry to ask, but... But, Miss Fiona, did you kill all them people?"

She'd expected anything but that. Had she beaten up her own men? Had she attacked lawmen in the performance of their duty? Had she committed great destruction of property? Killed those people. *Killed* those people? *What* people? "What? No! What are you even talking about?"

"When we stopped at my house down yonder, before the gov'ment men, I was gettin' together some gear with the TV on. They had what you call that breakin' news. They said you done killed like eighteen people, a lot of 'em not even armed--"

"Jesus, Clay! No! As far as I know, I didn't kill anybody! Why the hell are you asking me that? Christ, the love just rains like a spring shower, doesn't it?"

Hostetter put up his hands. "Okay, first off, I believe you. Second, don't use the Lord's name in vain--"

"What?"

"Third, it had to get asked. They got every lawman from Spokane to Savannah lookin' to shoot you on sight. And you said, with the cat--"

"I didn't kill anybody and neither did Oz!" Had she?

"Okay, I believe the boys down at the house might'a heard that. Get ahold o' yourself."

She did. The rage steaming within her couldn't be made an asset, and it confused Oz. He had no honor to defend. "I'm sorry. You're right. No. No, as far as I can tell, I did not kill anyone."

"Well, all right. That'll do. So now we need to figure who did and how that can get you settled with the law. Come on." Hostetter strolled off toward the shack.

Fiona took another look into the valley, then doddered off after him.

"I don't reckon you recall much that's happened," Hostetter called over his shoulder as he re-entered the house. "You was kinda out of it when I rescued you, then passed out altogether hours ago, l think from exhaustion." He returned to the bedroom, but came out again before Fiona was halfway across the outer chamber. He carried a set of leather satchels joined by a long, wide, leather strap. Saddlebags. "Anyhow, it ain't been dark but an hour. Plenty of cover for sneakin' outta here."

"Sneaking? Where are we sneaking to? I guarantee there's no place to hide. They'll be all over everyone you know." Fiona wished he would hold still. He was already outside again and striding around the corner of the house.

"Well now, I got me a confession to make," he called back to her. "I never did tell you folks *every*body I know."

Fiona reached the corner and paused. There was something familiar… Her head felt muddy. She couldn't think straight. "Dude. You withheld information from the NSA? Not cool, Clay. Uncle Sugar will be testy."

He reappeared from behind the house and passed her as he returned to the interior. "Sorry, but I thought it smart to hold somethin' close to m'vest. In case you folks weaseled on me."

"Weaseled? That's hurtful. I never--"

"I never said you did, just that I wanted insurance if you did. It's poker. I kept me a hole card." He exited the house again, this time carrying his stick, a bedroll … and a rifle.

Fiona leaned against the house corner. "That toy of yours won't worry a tac team. It'd be best if you left it behind."

"Nuh-uh." He stopped a few feet past her, on his way to the back again. "This here gun comes from President Theodore Roosevelt himself. He give it to me for service in the Cuba Expedition. I ain't leaving' it to get stole."

"I forget sometimes what a relic you are."

"Miss Fiona, you lay awake at night dreamin' up jibes about just that thing. You comin', or do I save your sorry ass on my lonesome?"

"Depends. Are you finished bouncing back and forth across this bluff? I'm too tired to chase you."

He grunted, then continued on toward the rear. After a moment gathering breath, Fiona followed him.

In the back stood a beautiful brown horse, saddled, bridled, and whatever else you did with horses. It tossed its mane at Fiona.

"Porthos! I should have realized!" Fiona came forward to hug the horse's head. The animal obliged, nuzzling Fiona's entire torso.

"The professor here been ruminatin' on your situation," Hostetter said as he tied and tightened straps on the horse's kit. "He told me it's possible much of the hullabaloo you been through these last few days might be related to what we done a few years ago."

"Umm, the professor?"

"Don't be thick. You know who I'm talkin' about."

Porthos danced his hind legs, and snorted.

"Oh, yeah. Porthos a.k.a. the illustrious Doctor Schumacher of Boehm/Schumacher events fame. Excuse me, I thought all that referring to your horse as a person was just an affectation."

Hostetter stopped for a second to give her a chiding eyeballful, then he went back to his tying, shifting, and arranging. "He *is* a person. He was one o' the leadin' authorities on the lightnin' posts until he got trapped in one without no silver. When he came out, he was a horse. Anybody what goes into a lightnin' post without silver, they don't come out right." He gave Fiona a sidewise glance. The look in his eye showed pain. "Anyhow, he says you helpin' me save my world, it might've drawn attention you don't want."

"But you said Boehm was taken care of. He and all his avatars were locked away in the bleed, or whatever."

Hostetter patted Porthos's rump and shoved the rifle into a leather sheath near the front of the saddle. "Well, if you recall, I also told you that Boehm had a boss. Now, maybe that boss is pissed at y'all." He slapped the stick into a second sheath.

Fiona leaned against the base of Porthos's neck. She heard the faint thrum of his heart through his massive chest. "This just gets better and better. How does Porthos know…"

"'Cause I shut down a lightnin' post this mornin'. It was hidden inside that facility of your'n in California. And somethin' was comin' through it, somethin' alive."

The way he said that chilled Fiona. She craned her neck to see his face in the dark, but he kept the same tired expression that usually marked his features.

"Okay," he said, and crouched slightly. He interlaced his fingers and held his hands before him at knee height. "Climb up."

"Uhh… What exactly…?"

"You ain't gonna walk where we goin'. You wouldn't last twenty minutes. Now, up. Put your foot in my hands and me an' Porthos'll do the rest."

"Dude. I know nothing about driving a horse."

"You don't drive him, you just sit on him. He's smarter'n you, he knows what to do."

"Hostetter--"

"Put your shoe in the hand, by Jiminy. We ain't got all night."

153

Fiona, grimacing, did as ordered. She didn't want to. Petting Porthos's neck was one thing, scaling that broad, too-tall ribcage was another. There was more than one reason she didn't own so much as a Pekingese for a pet.

As soon as she placed her weight in his hands, Hostetter boosted her up and onto the horse. Fiona never knew how she got atop the animal instead of taking a header over the saddle. It might have had something to do with Oz watching below, and it may have been due to Porthos's sudden dance as Fiona landed atop him. But she found herself in the saddle, first clutching and squealing like a ten-year-old girl in a bat cave, then stable and holding the horn, a long, long way off the ground.

"Alrighty then," Hostetter said. "You good?"

"Uhh--"

"That's great." He handed up Oz. How he had lain hands on the cat, Fiona couldn't imagine. Actually, she could. She trusted Hostetter, so Oz would. Usually. "Now we got us a couple hours overland, so get comfortable and I'll lead."

"Well. Okay." She didn't know how else to respond.

Porthos whickered and fluttered an ear.

"Yeah, I know," Hostetter said, "but she's *our* tenderfoot."

He took the reins and started away from the house.

Hostetter's idea of "a couple hours" didn't line up with Fiona's. They had taken off a few hours after sunset. By the wee hours of the morning, they still traversed the rough land of the Wyoming foothills, seeming to go nowhere. Hostetter kept them mainly to pine growths and coulees of red rock, pausing for long, cautious minutes before attempting to cross roads. He spoke seldom, and usually to the horse.

Fiona didn't fuss about the time. They covered miles in those hours. She couldn't have managed it on foot. As it was, she found herself dozing often in the saddle. Porthos took more responsibility for keeping her on his back than she did.

She started to full wakefulness. Hostetter was shaking her by the knee.

"We gotta wait," he whispered. "You best cover that glowin' thing on your neck."

Fiona slapped a hand to her diode. She watched Hostetter through Oz's eyes. He was a shadow to hers. "What? Why do we have to wait?"

"We gotta cross that there road ahead, but two police cars are sittin' there. I reckon they'll move on, but we gotta wait."

Fiona directed her enhanced vision outward. Yes, two state troopers parked nose-to-nose on one side of a two-lane road. One side. So not a serious roadblock. Maybe they weren't even in on the hunt. The two cops stood just off the pavement, one leaning against the fender of his car. Though the cruisers stood a good two hundred meters off, Fiona could almost hear their quiet, comfortable conversation.

"So," Hostetter said, "you want me to help you down? It might be a spell."

"Will I have to get back up later?"

"Imagine so."

"Then, if it's okay with Porthos, I think I'll stay where I am."

"Hmm. You ain't gettin' sore? Most would be, if'n they ain't rode no horse before."

"I'm fine." But she wasn't, really. Fiona had been doing the splits for hours. First had come cramps as she straddled that saddle, then chafing, then finally she hardly felt anything from her waist down. She couldn't say if that was a good thing or bad, but it was certainly less irritating.

She diverted her thoughts from her over-stretched muscles and took in her surroundings. Pretty much the same as the last time she'd looked. Trees, brush, and more trees, plus great dark spurs of rocky uplands jutting out into the waving grass like ships capsized on the sea. It was beautiful, that land, but harsh, like the man who lived in it.

Hostetter cleared his throat. "Miss Fiona, can I tell you somethin'?"

"Sure, Clay. Anytime."

"Well, I'm hopin' that invitation stays open, 'cause what I got to say ain't good, not a'tall."

Fiona tightened her lips. She tired of bad news.

"You see, I shoulda told you earlier, but I was too ashamed. But you gotta know. I got no right--"

"Just say it, buddy."

She heard him swallow. She smelled sweat, the piquant, peppery sweat of someone else's embarrassment.

"You see, when I came for you, we had to get outta there quick. They was about to shoot you. So I didn't get as good a grip on you as I would've otherwise."

Fiona didn't see what this had to do with anything. Knowing Hostetter, he sidled up to apologizing for inadvertently grabbing a tit.

"So, when we was in the lightnin' post, I kinda, well, definitely, lost touch with you. But only for a second! You whipped away from me, but I reached right out and grabbed your hand and brought you back to me."

"Uh, okay. Thanks. I think."

"That ain't the thing. You see, the way it works, don't nothin' come through a lightnin' post right less'n it carries special silver." He opened his jacket. Fiona caught a glint from his marshal's badge, his old marshal's badge that meant nothing in her world. "You're protected by my silver if I hold to you tight, but that don't happen if I lose you."

"Uh-huh… Oh! Well, don't worry about it. As you can see, I'm my usual, unadulterated self."

"You sure you ain't got no … changes? No extra fingers or not enough toes?"

Just to be sure, Fiona wiggled her toes in her too-large shoes. "Nope, just normal, everyday Miss Fiona here, partner." Her heart strained at the mournful look in his eyes. "Really, Clay. I'm fine."

"Don't nothin' come through the lightnin' post right."

"Sure it does. Didn't you tell me once that a helicopter went through unaffected? It was a great miracle."

"Yes'm, it was."

"Well, so am I. Besides, you only lost me for a sec. Probably surprised the lightning post gods so that they couldn't think straight to turn me into a frog. "

"I hope so. But you'd tell me if anything … unnatural happens?"

"If I grow a tail, you'll be the first to know. After Oz, that is."

He didn't laugh at the joke. His moustache drooped in deep -- and apparently imaginary -- sorrow.

Fiona tossed her chin toward the distance. "The cops. They're taking off. Must have been a coffee break."

Hostetter watched the men saunter to their cars and pull out in opposite directions.

"How about we get going?" Fiona suggested.

"No. We'll wait. Can't be too careful."

Yes, true. But Fiona wasn't sure she could stay on Porthos for another five hours. She'd night jumped into hot zones, trekked across defended desert borders, even snaked her way into jungle compounds through the escape hatches of submarines, but, Lord in Heaven, riding a horse was tough business.

Hostetter lingered five minutes in the shadows before clicking his tongue and guiding Porthos forward.

As it turned out, their destination waited a short distance beyond the road. Out of sight and hearing from the pavement, a tiny house nestled in the cleft of two intersecting walls of rock. Low-roofed, sagging, with a decrepit one-car garage glommed onto its side, the place looked abandoned but for a few telltale points. A rust-eaten Jeep CJ stood outside the garage, resting its oversized tires on crinkly grass rather than a paved driveway. It and the house lay in deep shadow in a copse of spindly pines, one window of the building framing a yellow, wavering light.

Hostetter led Porthos to the front door and tucked the reins onto the saddle horn. He reached up and dragged Fiona off, supporting her while she figured out if she still had legs. Oz jumped from her arms to the grass and skulked to the house's foundation.

"You want I should carry you?" Hostetter asked.

"I'm a big girl. I can--" One leg buckled. Fiona dug her fingers into Hostetter's leather jacket to keep from hitting the ground. "Would you mind?"

Hostetter scooped her into his arms and marched the few steps to the house entrance. He kicked the door twice, and waited.

Scuffling from within. The rattling slide of a bolt. The door opened with a creak and an ancient man stood in its frame.

"Well," he said. "It's about time."

"Can I come in or not, you old coot? 'Cause I ain't what I used to be and this here girl is heavy."

"Hey!" Fiona protested, but not too strongly. Hostetter *was* a geezer, after all. It bothered her to strain his tired old muscles.

The other old man turned back into the house, crooking a finger at them. Hostetter ducked through the shorter-than-usual doorway and clomped into the one room, which glowed in the warmth of an oil lamp. He took Fiona to a ratty La-Z-Boy and lowered her gently onto its sprung seat.

"I got tea on for y'all who go for that sorta thing," the ancient said as he doddered to a wood stove in a corner. "If you prefer, I can offer something a might stronger."

"I'll have some stronger," Hostetter said. He glanced around the little room, found one of two wooden chairs at a square table against a wall, and hauled it over. He plopped it down between Fiona and the oil lamp, which stood on a peeling end table and lit an easy chair of bursting upholstery. "I'm hopin' you don't mind. Everybody we know wants to see us dead."

"Not everybody, and not both of you," the old man said with his back turned at the stove. "You still got friends in the world, though they'll need some coaxin'."

Fiona looked from the old man to Hostetter and back. "I'm sorry. I don't know what's going on here."

Hostetter removed his hat and tossed it onto the table by the one remaining chair. "Miss Fiona Street, meet Mister Willie Dern, a long-time resident of these parts."

The old man snorted laughter at that. He turned his craggy face toward Fiona for a second, then back to the stove. "Long-time resident is an understatement, marshal. Young lady, what you want to drink?"

"Umm, I guess I'll have tea." Fiona read the condescension in Hostetter's eyes and the short snigger from the geriatric and added, "Maybe with a little something extra."

They both seemed to like that answer better. Hostetter's moustache curved up and the old man waggled a finger at Fiona as if to call her a naughty girl.

"Willie here's lived in this house longer'n I've been alive," Hostetter said. "He knows a lot about a whole lot. I come to him when I'm stumped for answers."

"Oh." Fiona didn't know what to say to that. She rubbed her legs through the thin scrubs, trying to wake them up. She'd regret it when they did; that's when the pain of saddle rub would perk up and make itself known. "Hey, wait a sec." She cocked her head at Hostetter. "Wasn't Willie Dern the little kid who was with you…"

Both men grinned at her. Dern doddered over with a mug in one hand. "That was another Willie Dern, honey." He handed her the mug and waggled his hand. "And the same Willie Dern. It's complicated."

Okay… "How complicated?"

"Well, that's the $64,000 question, now ain't it?" The old man shuffled to the chair by the lamp. He collapsed into it by slow stages and sighed when he got settled. He remained still for a moment, looking almost dead, then patted the chair's armrests and reached to the floor out of Fiona's sight. He came up with a pint bottle of liquor. "You do the honors, marshal. I don't wanna get up just now."

Hostetter reached far over, took the bottle, and offered its contents to Fiona. She nodded. He dipped a splash into her tea. Sniffing the drink, Fiona thought she caught the whiff of rye whiskey.

"You came here to find information," Willie Dern said. "I'm nothin' if not information. Here it is. Are you ready?" He looked straight at Fiona.

"Yes, sir. I'm ready." What kind of weird shit was this?

"You live in a world of men," Dern began, leaning toward her. "In this world, men live, they scrape through knowin' just what's around 'em, not even sure of that. They do the best they can, then die." He thumped his hollow chest. "I ain't one of them men."

He took the bottle Hostetter offered and tasted from it. He handed it back. "You know there's many worlds. Your machine over there in California was built to bridge the gap between them. The marshal here's from one world, a kind of nineteenth century version of yours, maybe a might off kilter from your point of view. This monster you're huntin' hails from yet another."

"Hold it." Fiona sipped from her tea. It tore at the inside of her mouth. "What monster? And how do you know about the machine? And, what, you're like Hostetter?"

"What monster? The monster that came through at your place in California, the one what killed all them men. How do I know your business? I know many things. And, no, I ain't like the marshal."

Hostetter took a swig from the bottle and gasped at what it got him.

"You see," the old man continued, "there's all kinds of universes. Why, there's even a universe where only shrimp live."

Hostetter visibly shivered at those words. He took another drag from the bottle.

"But," the old man continued after a wry glance at Hostetter, "there's also the space *between* universes, what we call the bleed. It's what your smart folks in the String Theory call the P-Brane, which says a whole lot about them. But, anyway, that's where I live, in the bleed. Not callin' any one world home, I can be in all of 'em at once. I can know everything that was, is and ever will be, if I was ambitious, and maybe a little stupid." He took a sip from the bottle. "Somebody already tried that, the all-knowing god thing. That was the fella what threatened the marshal's world, what almost destroyed that world until the marshal came here and you helped him."

"That would be Boehm, the Dark Man." Fiona sipped her doctored tea. "He and Doctor Schumacher originally discovered the lightning posts between universes. They both went in. Boehm came out crazy and with superpowers. Schumacher came out a horse." She nodded toward the door, beyond which Porthos chewed grass while Oz watched.

"Yep, that's him. I learned from him that knowin' everything is knowin' nothin'. To really know, you gotta specialize." Dern pointed a gnarled finger at Fiona. "I specialize in you, young lady. And the marshal. And what's comin' for you."

Fiona's legs began to sting, tingle, and burn all at the same time. She squeezed her outer thighs to work some circulation. Or something. "Okay. So you know what's going on. Hell, *I* sure don't. I've been locked up in a cage for the last two days. What's this about a monster?"

"You know about Boehm," Dern said. "You know he tried to destroy the whole multiverse but the Marshal stopped him with the weapons you gave him. Well, Boehm had a boss, somethin' that influenced him from a very dark place. Schumacher knows. Boehm used to brag on his evil pard before he deserted Schumacher and went off to be crazy. Well, that monster was right pissed when Boehm got handed his hat with his teeth in the crown."

"So, it went looking for me because I gave Hostetter the guns." The motivation made sense, though it struck Fiona as more than a little petty.

But Willie Dern surprised her with a dismissive flick of his hand. "You? Hell naw. He didn't even know you existed. He came after the marshal, to kill him for what he done to Boehm."

Fiona glanced to Hostetter. He slumped in his chair, absently holding the liquor bottle. His face said nothing.

"The monster wants to kill the marshal, and it used you as bait," Dern said.

"Bait? What do you mean bait? I don't recall being laid in a trap. The only people chasing me are my own."

"The monster has a lady. It's captured her, drivin' her like a plow horse. Now, she ain't exactly guilty and she ain't exactly innocent. You be careful when you deal with her."

What in hell was that supposed to mean? "Would this be a Russian lady, by any chance?"

"Don't know. I don't know from Russian."

Fiona sputtered frustration. "You just said you could--"

"*Specialize,* little lady. *Specialize.* Now, that monster's powerful," Dern said. "It came here and killed your men in California. It *possessed* them and killed them. Then it jumped into your computers and stole information. It jumped into that lady, killed some more people, then set to listenin' to you so it could find the marshal. And when that took too long, it set up a ruckus to frame you for its next round o' murders. All to get the marshal to come help you. It's close, right now it is. It followed your people out here to the marshal's house."

At that, Fiona stopped messing with her legs. Kudashova. So the Russians' assassin had been co-opted by a monster from beyond the universe. Fiona felt suddenly cold, as if a damp draft blew through the room.

"It'll find you," Dern said, nodding assurance. "It knows what your people know and it knows about me. It'll put two an' two together."

"We've walked into a trap?" Fiona's voice caught. She cleared her throat to continue, this time looking at Hostetter. "*I've* led *you* into a trap."

To her amazement, Hostetter grinned.

"I been in more traps than a prize beaver," he said. "This don't feel like one."

"Well, you better start feelin' around some more," Dern said. "And gimme that whiskey. I'm feelin' a might dry."

Hostetter passed the bottle. Dern took a gulp. Fiona downed the last of her tea. The liquid sent fire rushing through her gut, shocking her out of what might have been a pointless bout of self-pity and apology.

"Okay," she said, placing the mug on the floor, "I want to hear about this monster."

Dern nodded. "It's an old monster, maybe one of the oldest, and filled to the rim with hate. Marshal, you know what it is. You learned about it from the Wild Indians. Sinfonee told you about it."

Sinfonee. The other Sinfonee. Hostetter's true love in that other universe. Boehm had murdered her, cut her into bits and fed her to a lava flow, or something like that.

"Yeah." Hostetter repositioned himself in the chair. He leaned forward, elbows on knees. "Okay, it goes like this. There's this other universe. It's made up of the dreams of everybody in this one, their good dreams and their nightmares. That was normal for that there world until a machine your gov'ment built blowed all your fears and night terrors outta proportion. All them bad feelings went into that other world and they thought we was invadin' 'em."

Dern picked up the thread. "This monster's from that world. He's, like, all our terror, all our paranoia, all our monkey-brain lust all rolled into one. Calls himself Nightmare."

"Why?" Fiona asked. "Because it's scary?"

"Because it's true!" Dern took another belt from the bottle. He was well on his way to getting skunked. Thank goodness it was just a pint. "This Nightmare thing, he ain't here to cause trouble just to be ornery. He's here takin' the fight for his world to the enemy, in his estimation. As far as he's concerned, we're the bad guys. We're the ones overrunnin' his universe with the monsters from our primitive brains."

"Okay, wait again." Fiona rubbed her temples. "You said we made a machine to amplify our fears. What's that all about?"

"You have the answer." Dern pointed a trembling finger at her. "It's sittin' unread in your deep, secret files. They built it to cripple the Germans, cripple 'em mentally. As a backup in case the A-bomb didn't work. You got every bit of paper on the Drehd project back in the World War II. You should read more often."

"So this Drehd file is the key to why the monster, this Nightmare, is causing all kinds of trouble. What's the key to cutting Nightmare off at the legs?"

"Well, he ain't *got* no legs, darlin'."

"So to speak."

Dern passed the bottle back to Hostetter. "Well, the thing is, this monster is weak. He was strong while the lightnin' post was open, but the marshal shut it down. By the way, I wouldn't bet against him startin' that thing up again."

Fiona and Hostetter exchanged glances. "Sinfonee," Hostetter said.

"Only if'n he can get to her," Dern said. "Anyhow, the part of the monster on this side of the lightnin' post is just a small part, not good for much but listenin' and possessin' one person at a time. That's how you trap him and get rid of him. Stuck in one person, he's almost human."

"Okay, so how do we trap and get rid of a non-corporeal threat?" Fiona asked.

Dern looked at her, looked at Hostetter, and looked at the floor. "Well, now, I don't rightly know…"

"You said you were a specialist, in me, Hostetter, and this monster. You *said* that. You know this thing's whole life's history and you don't know how to get rid of it?"

"That's a whole 'nother thing. Out of my sphere of influence, so to say. But," and the old man raised an index finger into the air, "you have people who know about this stuff. Them scientists, they know more than they think."

More than they think? What a load of horseshit. "Mister Dern, maybe you're not up to the minute on the news. Those scientists you mention? They're behind a wall of thirty-six agents and God knows how many soldiers and cops, all of whom want to kill me."

Dern waggled both hands at about head height, almost spilling liquor into his lap. "Eh, well, didn't say it'd be easy."

"Didn't say it'd be easy?" Fiona looked at Hostetter. "Is this some kind of joke?"

"Willie here's given you plenty you didn't have before. You got resources to go on further. I call it a win."

"I don't." Fiona scooted forward in her chair, perching at the edge of the seat. She tested her complaining muscles, pressing her toes against the floorboards. "I have to know about this monster. It comes from our subconscious, unless you're bullshitting me, so it's tied to that Drehd project, maybe. Those files are in California with Doctor Rodriguez. I'm in Wyoming. Then there's all the operational data about that woman you mentioned. She's a Russian, named Kudashova. The colonel had analysts on her. But they're in Maryland." She looked up at both men. "Did I mention I'm in Wyoming?"

Hostetter cleared his throat and sat up straighter. "I could get you to both places quick, but I shouldn't. By now they're lookin' for evidence of my stick gettin' used. I'd just be leadin' 'em to us."

"Us?"

"Well, you don't think I'd let you go into this gunfight on your own, do you?"

Oh, how sweet, stupid, and useless. "Clay, I'm not going into 'this gunfight,' as you put it. I can't. I physically can't. I know my people. They'd ventilate me in half a second, probably before I get out of this state."

Hostetter watched her with his tired, hound-dog eyes. "Miss Fiona, I aim to disagree. One thing I know from close observation, from workin' beside you and watchin' you since I come to this world. There ain't no 'can't' in you. What you said just now, you just makin' noise."

Wow. That had been nice, in a gently backhanded kind of way. Too bad it came from a man with profound ignorance of the NSA and how it worked.

'Hmm…" Willie Dern eyed her, then the bottle, and put it down on the table beside the lamp.

He had something to say. Fiona waited. Her senses drank in the pungent medicine stink of alcohol, the whisper of wind in the trees outside, the muttering of the horse, and the skitter of a mouse too far away in the iron-laden dirt to bother with. She waited both in the warm yellow light of the tiny house and the blue dimness of the sprawling foothills terrain. As long as Oz stayed close, that apparent contradiction felt as normal as breathing. She was used to being in two places at once, but she couldn't be on two *coasts* at once.

Finally, because Oz was in her, her patience snapped. "What?"

"I was just gonna remind you of what I said earlier," Dern said, his tone measured. "I was just gonna remind you that you don't have to do everything your own self. You got friends. You just have to finesse 'em."

Great. A pregnant pause for nothing at all. "That's wonderful advice. Just peachy. But I've a better idea. If you're an omniscient super-being, then why don't you get off your ass and pull some of the weight? It would make things oh, so much easier."

"Miss Fiona--" Hostetter started, but Dern shushed him down.

The old man placed both hands on his armrests and cranked himself out of the chair. Hostetter rose, too, and Fiona after a beat. Her legs complained, but not as much as she had thought they might.

"Young lady," Dern said as he shuffled to his front door. "When you're one of them omniscient super-beings, you got to be careful what you do with that power. It's easy to mean good and do bad." He pulled open the door. "Besides, I ain't got to go against this monster myself. I got you for that. And you got others. Some of them others got power way beyond me." He looked at her, and shrugged. He showed no insult, no sense of forbearance. He seemed almost to hide humor. For the first time, Fiona realized how little she could read him. He projected no telling scent, no undercurrent of emotion. He was sight and sound and not much else. "Y'all be careful goin' on your way. Stick to the west up against the bluff till you get to the road. Don't worry about Porthos. He'll wander back here in his own time."

What? Where were they going? Why would Porthos--

Hostetter stepped forward and offered the old man his hand. "Thankee much, Willie. You always was a good, true friend."

"Go get 'em, marshal. And mind you this here firebrand of yours. You might get through this and you might not, but you can do worse for a partner."

The two men shook hands. Fiona watched them, two crazy old coots. No, she corrected herself. There was nothing crazy in Hostetter. He emanated only respect and pride. Pride in his company with Dern, and pride … in her.

She realized both men watched her.

"Well, Miss Fiona," Hostetter said, hat in hand, "maybe we should be gettin' on."

Fiona screwed up her face. She was missing something, or they were. "Getting on where? We've no place to go."

"Why, I believe Willie here just told us where we gotta go."

"Oh? West along the bluff? That's a destination?"

"And to the road," Dern corrected.

"And to the road," Hostetter echoed.

This was nuts. "Hostetter, we need more than that as a plan. We need more than a direction to go, we need some*where*, and a reason to get there."

The old men exchanged glances. Dern deferred to Hostetter with a wave of his hand.

"I don't think you rightly understand," the old cowboy said, stepping up to Fiona. "You see, you live in this here world where everything and everybody got somewhere to be. Y'all always plan. Y'all always figurin' the quickest way to get from this here place to that there place. But it ain't always like that, Miss Fiona. Sometimes, you gotta just go, and see what goin' gets you."

"You sound like a bad movie guru."

"Don't make it any less true, ma'am. And need I remind you, ain't nobody got better reason to be someplace else than me? You heard what Willie said. That thing what killed all them people, it might go back to California. It might go to Sinfonee, since she runs the machine." He shrugged. "But here I am, stuck with you."

Oh, hell. Fiona deflated. She actually felt herself doing it, caving into herself and losing steam. It didn't help that Oz thought Hostetter's words made perfect, everyday sense.

She schlepped up to the door and the old man on its threshold. "Thank you for your help," she said, extending a hand. "I think."

Dern chortled as he shook her hand. "Yes'm. And in a little bit, you'll know."

Out the door. Porthos waited, head up and watching the approaches before the house. Oz mewled around Fiona's feet, impatient to get a move on.

"You need to ride?" Hostetter asked when he came up beside Fiona.

"No. I'm stiff. Walking will do me good."

"Well then." Hostetter took the horse's reins and started off around the western side of the house. Fiona followed. Oz charged well out ahead.

"Y'all be careful," Dern called behind them. "Have fun stormin' the castle." He cackled at his cleverness.

"There's someone up ahead," Fiona whispered, placing a restraining hand on Hostetter's arm. It hadn't been an hour since leaving the house, a slow march over loose rock, cracked clay, and grass as dry and sharp as knives. A road stretched ahead where the bluff turned south. She couldn't see it, but Oz could.

"What is it?" Hostetter asked. "One of them lawmen?"

"No. Car. A rental. Avis."

"How in tarnation--"

"Sticker on the back. There's someone leaning against the hood... We'd better wait, give Oz a chance to really check it out."

"Okay, but if it ain't a policeman, it could be one of them agents. Or it could be that lady Willie mentioned."

Fiona didn't answer. She focused, reading what Oz sent her from hundreds of feet ahead. Around her, pines whispered in the cool breeze. With her own eyes, she saw only their shivering shadows. But mixed into that, like a veil of fog, was a clear, blue image of the car, a Chevy Malibu, and the figure with its back to the stalking cat.

"What you see?" Hostetter asked, his voice barely audible.

Oz skulked alongside the vehicle, sifting out the smells of asphalt, oil, and gasoline, striving to isolate the human from that miasma.

Female. Her short hair shone blonde in the starlight. She muttered something, a song under her breath, while she leaned against the car's front bumper, relaxed. Nothing of the predator sharpened the air around her.

Fiona heard the whisper of metal against leather. Hostetter drawing his rifle from its sheath.

"Are they close? Will they hear if I cock this thing?"

Fiona's answer came as a sigh. She relaxed, for the first time realizing how taut she had grown in the last several seconds. Her neck ached. She rubbed and twisted it. "Don't bother. It's a friend."

They broke cover less than thirty meters from the road. The Malibu sat in front of them, two tires on the shoulder. The woman noticed them and straightened from her lazy lean against the front of the car. She wore a white raincoat buttoned to the collar, slacks, and canvas sneakers.

"Fiona Street," she said, her blonde hair flashing in the meager illumination. "You're later than I figured."

Fiona left Hostetter and the horse to embrace the woman in a sisterly hug. "Sally Reiser, what brings you out west, in the middle of nowhere, in the middle of the night?"

They leaned apart, Sally tapping her temple. "Oh, you know. Voices in my head."

Right. The strange, inexplicable gift of Sally Reiser, consultant to angels and seer of God. Fiona had recruited her into the Nightwatch initiative a few years earlier after an incident in the Middle East. An incident where

Stephan Michael Loy

Sally had kneecapped a terrorist attempt to crash an airplane into the Temple Mount of Jerusalem. Fiona thought the stories about the blonde Jew's gift were all misinterpreted hogwash, but that gift was also accurate, trustworthy. And she had dropped a mountain on a guy, so there was that.

"Okay, so what are the voices telling you today?"

"Told me to come out here and wait in this spot. And some other stuff, but that can wait. Hey, Marshal Hostetter."

Hostetter touched the brim of his hat in welcome. He dropped the reins to do so; he still gripped the rifle in his other hand.

"I understand you're in a bind," Sally said, turning her attention back to Fiona. "Government difficulties. Wanna tell me about it?"

"What? You don't already know?"

"The voices tend to be cryptic. For no good reason." She seemed to add that last for someone else.

"Well, okay, but we'd better clear out. This place is awfully exposed for someone wanted by every law enforcement entity north of Mexico."

Sally leaned back against the car and put her hands in her coat pockets. "Don't worry, Red, we're good. I've been told I'll know if anyone comes along."

Fiona marveled that she didn't doubt that statement. Sally Reiser was hardly consistent in the odd talents that made her an asset, but when she said something was so, it was so.

"I reckon we don't need Porthos no more," Hostetter said as he tied off the reins to the saddle horn.

"Sure don't," Sally said. "At minimum, we'll use the car if we need to go somewhere."

At minimum?

The blonde got comfortable against the car. Her ice blue eyes, glinting in starlight, measured Fiona with steady attention. Another somewhat unnerving quality. Sally wasn't a warm-and-fuzzy. A hard life with hard choices made for a hard woman. You could cut yourself on her flinty demeanor. It matched so well the sharp cut of her jaw and the ice in those eyes. A woman formed from tempered steel.

She had saved the world twice already, twice more than Fiona.

So, while Hostetter petted Porthos's snout and whispered for him to return to Willie, while Oz, at ease, lay atop the ticking hood of the Malibu, Fiona slouched against the side of the car and told Sally everything she knew.

It bothered her how little that was.

Chapter Fourteen

Childress jerked awake. For a moment, he didn't know where he was. Okay, he lay in the back seat of a car, that was obvious, but how had he gotten there? Where *was* the car? Then his cranking mind began supplying information. Wyoming. The cowboy's house. A place that stank of red dust and horseshit. And the dude nudging his shoulder was what, an FBI agent? State police? A local J. Edgar Hoover, judging by the suit.

Childress heaved to a sitting position. "Yeah, man, what?"

"Relay from your office. You didn't answer your phone." The man shoved a radio into the car.

Childress took the radio, and yawned. He rubbed his eyes, turned so his shoes dropped against the sparse grass outside, and leaned forward with his elbows on knees. "Childress. Go."

"Where the hell were you?"

The colonel. "I took a nap. Must've been a heavy one."

"Naps aren't in your job description."

"I've had four hours of sleep in thirty-six hours." He rubbed his face with his free hand. "Can we direct this call to a more 'Don't rag on Childress' direction?"

"Report, agent."

From the lack of a chewing-out, Childress knew the boss was busy grinding teeth. Time to be careful if Momma Childress's little boy wanted to get paid, like, ever again. "We've physical evidence everywhere. They were here. There's medicinals taken from the bathroom. We don't know what kind. Clothes from the bedroom, pantry raided, fridge gone through. The dude's horse is AWOL. If they ran off by horse, they aren't far. But they got onto pavement to hide where they went. We have state police and locals on the watch and the feds checking every bar, restaurant, motel, campsite and outhouse in five counties. We even have rangers on the dirt roads and the ranches in case they're overland. FBI is running down Hostetter's friends and enemies to see if that leads anywhere. We got meteorologists and just plain Joes looking out for orange lights in the sky."

"So she's hurt."

Just like him, worried about his girl. The only thing he registered was the meds. When would he admit they were angling to kill her ass? "Maybe. Maybe they're just being proactive. You got anything for me?"

"We've ruled her out for the murders at headquarters. Security cameras show Kudashova. But she's definitely responsible for sending eight of our people to the hospital."

"Huh. So, you still got the hit out on her?"

"Case Specific is still in effect."

"Yeah, okay. Look, I know you military types have a way of doin' shit, but do you figure that's maybe a little bit extreme? She ain't killed anybody. All she did was go for a walk."

"Childress. She's unbalanced and, as the casualties show, she's almost unstoppable." He sighed. "Hell, I've an expert medical opinion that she might not even be human anymore."

Well. That was harsh.

The colonel went on. "You might as well know that the Director, National Intelligence chewed my ass for an hour this evening. The fact it was an hour and not five minutes means he's giving us a chance. Still, by noon tomorrow he's likely to take this thing out of our hands and turn it over to a, well, 'more objective agency.' Most likely those OAA bastards."

The spooks of spooks. Nobody knew for sure what they did, but it wasn't pretty. "Boss. I don't know if I can find Street and Hostetter. I mean, for all I know, they're sippin' down Mai Tais on some white sands beach in an alternate reality by now." Childress released the send button on the radio. A response was a long time coming. He looked around, tired, his eyes burning. Two state police cars, a crime lab truck, the FBI sedan, and his own rental. The house, the scrappy yard, the barn way to one side, and more stars in the sky than Childress had seen since Afghanistan.

He thought back to that moment off the dead-end street, when Hostetter had roared in on his Old Testament pillar of fire. A woman had been there. She had let loose a mag from an MP5 at the spot where Street clung to her cowboy. Had that been Kudashova? She had been there, then not, a magic trick. Did she have superpowers, too?

Whatever happened to the good ol' days, when all you went up against was a guy with an attitude and a bomb vest?

"You have an agent there," the colonel finally said. "Turn what you have over to him and get back here. We'll confer on what to do next."

Childress refrained from asking why the boss didn't confer with Grace. It was already apparent that the big NCO had made the colonel's shit list. If not quite that, he was seen as too close to the mission, not objective. "You got it. I'll be on the next plane."

With that, Sanders signed off. Childress looked up, found the FBI puke standing there like a statue, and handed him back the radio. The guy stayed right where he was.

"What?" Childress asked.

"We have something," the man said. "Horse tracks."

"Okay, let me get this straight." Sally hadn't moved from her spot beside the car. Fiona leaned against the passenger door. She had been watching Hostetter remove gear from the horse. Guns, stick, saddlebags. Now he took the bridle from Porthos's snout and twisted all that around the saddle horn.

"Off you go, old man," the cowboy said, and gently slapped the animal's rump. Porthos ambled off the way he had come.

Sally finished chewing her thumbnail. "So a monster from another universe came here looking to lock horns with Marshal Hostetter, but it couldn't find him and latched onto you hoping to follow you to our Marlboro Man. It's right now possessing a Russian secret agent and has killed a bushel basket full of cops and spooks. It's tied somehow to a super-secret government project from the 1940s and also to the California project. You need to get to the government files in DC and also Doctor Rodríguez and her files in California, and both pronto in order to figure a way to trap and defeat the alien. Is that about it?"

Fiona nodded. "That and everybody we know wants to kill us."

"Okay, fine." Sally drummed her fingers on the car's metal skin, then pushed off from the vehicle. "So what I don't understand is, why do *you* have to do this thing?"

Fiona straightened from her relaxed slump against the car. "Excuse me?"

"Nobody gave you this mission, Red. Nobody told you to go after extra-universal monsters. The people who might have told you don't even like you much right now. So, again, why are *you* planning to do this? None of it's really your concern."

Fiona watched the little blonde. She bit back an acerbic response. This was Sally Reiser, she reminded herself. This was a woman outside allegiances. She did what she did out of unenlightened self-interest, her constant, unshakable measuring stick for involvement being "What's in it for me?" That and what the voices told her. Fiona had known all about Sally when she recruited the woman. No sense fussing about it.

"You don't understand," Fiona said quietly, slowly. "This thing is my fault, in a way. I brought it here. I made us visible to it." She nodded at Hostetter, who wordlessly shoved saddlebags and weapons into the car's back seat through the open window. "It's come for my friend. It's killed good men and women. I'm the only one who knows."

Sally threw her hands out to her sides. "So? Make a phone call. To the government. They handle this shit. They have people -- and you know some of them -- who live for shit like this. Let them handle it."

Talking to Sally Reiser was like talking to a child. She was such a civilian. "I will, Blondie. I can do that. Cautiously. But they're unlikely to believe me unless I give them data. They're looking to kill me, you know."

"Then let 'em go to hell. Go off and live in a cabin in Saskatchewan or
whatever and let 'em stew in their own soup. What do you owe these people?"

A loud, metallic rap. Fiona might have jumped out of her skin if she
hadn't felt it coming. Oz had puzzled at the slow growing heat from Hostetter, the normally serene cowboy tightening like a spring.

Sally *did* jump when he slapped the doorpost of her car.

"What's she owe?" he repeated. "Ever'thing. People owe people. You
see somethin' wrong, you gotta make it right. If you don't, you ain't more'n
that monster, that Nightmare."

Fiona put up a hand to cut off Sally's reply. "We have power," she said.
"Power is meant to be used. When you have power and let bad things hap-
pen, you know where to place the blame." She leaned forward, peering at
Sally. "Why are we having this conversation?"

A shooting star streaked by overhead.

"I'm not you," Sally groused. "I don't seek danger for the fun of it."

"Really." Fiona let pass the comment about fun. Her last several days
had been nothing like fun. "Then why are you here?"

Sally put her hands in the pockets of her coat. She looked suddenly
small. "I was told to be here."

She didn't want to get involved. She reacted to the prods of her personal
demons, or angels, or whatever they were. Sally Reiser had a life. She had a
man who loved her and a son. As weird as she was, she was also ... normal.

"It's okay," Fiona said. "You don't have to sign on for this. We'll drop
you at your hotel or wherever you're staying. But, could you loan us the
car?"

Sally rolled her eyes. "Oh, shut up. I *am* coming along. I was told to do
that, too."

"Then why--"

"Just tell me you're all in, that you won't drop out in the middle of the
shit."

"We're all in, aren't we, Clay?"

"All in, yes'm."

Sally released a magnificent, shoulder-sagging sigh. "That's great. All
in. Two women, a cat, and a sixty-year-old man against the source of all
nightmares. How do I get myself into this shit?"

"Hey." Fiona waggled a finger at her. "Don't forget. Two women with
superpowers."

"So what am I then?" Hostetter asked with a sniff.

"You're the sidekick," Fiona said, and shoved his arm playfully.

"I ain't no sidekick. I was a US marshal, y'know."

"That's wonderful," Sally said, meaning anything but. "That's, like, helpful or something."

"And I got a stick."

That struck Fiona as funny. She held her laugh to a chortle, though, so as not to upset the old man too much. "All right then, I figure the best course of action is Maryland first to get everything we can on Kudashova, then to Lawrence-Livermore for the poop on our monster friend and his World War II Achilles heel. Better if you drive, Blondie."

Sally looked up into the spangled sky. She seemed not to be there for a moment. Then she brought her eyes down and locked Fiona and Hostetter with her gaze. "No need to drive," she said, and pulled one hand from her coat pocket. She held a cheap cell phone, the kind sold in gas stations and convenience stores in bubble packs. "I was thinking we'd try something faster."

The agents had gone. They'd asked their questions and been rude enough about it, but in the end had been satisfied with Willie's story. They had tracked the horse to his house, all right. Any old dummy could've foreseen that. But tracking a horse wasn't the same as tracking people on it, and those guys hadn't had the woodsman skills of a New York City politician. The fools had missed the footprints scuffed over by hooves and hadn't noticed when the animal's load had eased. Modern folks. They'd lost so much.

So Willie told them the horse just wandered up to his door and he wondered who might own it. Did the lawmen have any idea? And they'd left.

Probably not for long, though. A few hours, and there'd be eyes on the house. But that was a few hours.

He sat in a camp chair in his ramshackle garage, Porthos blocking most of the open doorway. An oil lantern, turned down low, cast the softest of golden light over a dirt floor bordered by years -- no, decades -- of accumulated junk. It was Willie, the horse, the last of the whiskey, and a torn-open package of Double-stuffed Oreos.

And that other presence lurking in the trees beyond the Jeep.

The bald tires, gardening tools, and rusted Jeep parts stood around only as witnesses.

"Well, I wish I could say I was gettin' too old for this," Willie said as he fished a cookie from the bag, "but that would be a lie, wouldn't it, old boy?"

Porthos rocked his head up and down and pawed the ground outside the garage.

"Yep, you know it. Kinda hard to get old when you sit outside o' time. Still, the bones do creak. I can feel mortality around me, like a heavy wool coat."

Porthos snorted.

Willie waved a hand at him and crunched his cookie. "You would say that, now wouldn't you? But I *can't* just be anybody. I gotta be Willie in one way or the other. This is the Willie I drawed for today. You're supposed to be this hotdog scientist. I gotta explain this stuff to you?"

A toss of the mane and a flick of the tail accompanying a mutter and baring of teeth.

Yes, Porthos knew the way things worked, at least as far as anybody did. And what difference did it make, anyway? Willie preferred his present avatar. An old man against evil, like that Gandalf character in those Ring books. Tragic story. Lots of death.

Willie crunched another Oreo between his yellowing teeth and washed it down with a swig of whiskey. Then he placed the bottle on the dirt floor and worked his way out of the chair.

He shivered in a chill breeze and pulled his ragged, quilted, flannel shirt closer around him. He cradled four cookies in one hand.

"Well, old boy, guess we better get this one over with. Hey! Y'all out there! Might as well come on in! I know you there!"

For several seconds, it seemed he yelled for nothing. An owl hooted. The wings of small, sleeping birds fluttered in the trees. Then a shadow appeared at the edge of the door. Porthos gave it a wide-eyed stare.

"It's all right," Willie said. "Ain't nobody gonna hurt you here. Come on in an' be friendly."

The shadow moved. Despite Willie's certainty that dreams could not harm him, he took a step backward, bumping into his chair. Embarrassment rushed over him. This was no way for a super being to behave.

The shadow stepped into the garage, into the field of the dampened lamp. It was accompanied by a number of whisking, white things, sounding like hummingbirds and difficult to see in the dark against the ceiling. The yellow light showed a woman, blonde, dressed in jeans, a dirty cotton top, and a frayed leather jacket. Her features were drawn, as though by disease, or hunger.

"Want a cookie?" Willie offered.

"Where is he?" the woman asked, her tone dead.

"By that I figure you mean the marshal. Yeah, that's right. I won't bother lyin' to you. You ain't one o' these naïve little people. Sure you don't want a cookie?"

"Where is he?"

"I ain't tellin' you. He's far away from here, though. You should understand he's under my protection. You can't have 'im."

The woman took two quick steps toward Willie, causing Porthos to fidget. This time, Willie didn't flinch, even when she shoved a machine gun muzzle to within inches of his face.

"Where is he?"

"Go ahead. Won't get you nowhere. I reckon it might sting, but there's a infinite number of Old Man Willie's out there, and most of 'em didn't get shot by you. I'll just switch to one o' them. In fact, if you do shoot, I already have."

The gun muzzle quivered, she held the weapon so tightly.

"You sure you don't want a cookie? You look like you ain't ate nothin' in days."

The woman lowered her weapon. She drilled her gaze into Willie with such malice he felt only pity under its attention. Pity for her, that she hated so completely. Willie was a Christian, come everything else. He had love enough in his heart for monsters.

As fast as a striking rattler, the blonde smacked the old hand grasping the Oreos, sending the cookies tumbling through the air. Just as quickly, she snatched each one into her free hand before it hit the ground. She turned away, marching to the garage doorway. Willie heard ravenous chomping, then choking sounds, then smacking lips.

"Why do you oppose me?" the thing asked. "I desire only to protect my people."

"Your idea of protection strikes me a might violent. Unnecessarily so. Have you ever considered talkin' to somebody?"

"To the enemy? To murderers?"

"You might be surprised by what they say."

The thing spit onto the dirt floor. "I've no interest in their words. Their deeds speak with filthy eloquence. I've seen their world as they present it, on their terms. They don't deserve life."

Willie shook his head. "I admit, they got their problems. But a good enough bunch o' them mean well. They try hard." He straightened, then stiffened his jaw. "I won't let you do what you aim to do. These here people, they under my protection."

"You cannot stop me," she said from the doorway, Porthos giving her a wild eyeball. "You are powerful, but you are not a god."

"You're right." Willie nodded. "And that ain't no horse, neither."

Porthos reared as the woman turned to look at him.

With as much precision as a genius horse could muster, Doctor Ernst Schumacher kicked Nightmare in the head.

"You did what?" Fiona couldn't believe what Sally had just told her.

"I went to him and asked for his help. He sorta said yes. Sorta."
"Sorta."
"Well, he doesn't talk much. You know, 'I'm Batman' and grunts, that sort of thing."
Fiona's mind was thoroughly blown. "Wait. He says he's Batman?"
"No, no, no. That was creative license."
"I don't savvy," Hostetter pushed into the conversation. "What's the big deal?"
Fiona looked from Sally, to him, and back again. If her night had not been surreal to start with, it had taken that turn in the last few minutes. Hostetter didn't know. He had been comfy in his little house in cowboy land, reading by a fireplace and drinking with his buddies. He had little idea of what Fiona's crew had been through over the last two years. He stood there with his hands in his pockets, looking up into the starry sky as if watching Attenbourgh's *Planet Earth* while Sally watched that same sky with a self-satisfied smirk. Did she realize what she had managed?
"Blondie. The combined intelligence agencies of the United States, and in particular my team, have been trying to snare this guy for years. Last time we found him, he beat up a bunch of cops and all my best agents. And you say you just walked up to him and said pretty-please?"
"Sorta."
"Would you stop saying that?" But then the hairs stiffened on the back of Fiona's neck. Oz, until then a lounge lizard on the hood of the car, scrambled up and laid back his ears.
A whine intruded on the night air.
"Whoa-howdy." Hostetter pointed into the eastern sky. "Somethin' comin'."
Then it was over them, a searing whine and downblast of wind from a black, tailless manta with a fifty-foot wingspan. Oz sprang onto Fiona's shoulder while she ducked low beside the car. Hostetter grabbed his hat, his coat flapping about him. Sally just stood there, looking up at the shape as if at a bird. The aircraft turned slowly over them, then sidled off a few dozen feet to settle onto the road.
"Holy shit!" Fiona thrust one arm into the car, reaching for Hostetter's rifle.
"No," Sally called over the now warbling engine noise. "He's shy about guns."
Fiona retracted her hand, grasping at empty air. It was hard. Oz, with mental warnings of HAWK!, wanted badly for her to use the weapon.
The clack of releasing locks, then a hum of hydraulics as a ramp lowered from the back of the ship. At the top of that ramp, silhouetted against dim red light, stood the guy. He was almost seven feet tall, built like a boulder, and decked out in leather, harnesses, holsters, and that weird bike hel-

met with the slit visor. He made no move to them, just stood there with his hands at his sides. He wore the multi-chambered grenade launcher things at his wrists.

"Come," he said in that booming baritone voice that had probably never uttered a joke. "Law enforcement approaching. Five minutes out to north."

"You guys get aboard," Sally said, and started around the hood of the rental. "I'll get the car."

Fiona wasn't sure she heard right. "The *car?*"

"Hell, yeah. I'm not surrendering my deposit." Sally dropped into the driver's seat and cranked over the engine.

Fiona didn't realize she stood there gape-mouthed until Hostetter tugged on her arm. "Come on," he said. "This here's what you wanted, right?"

"I don't know what *this* even *is*." Fiona held Oz close to her stomach.

"This," Hostetter said, hauling her up the aircraft ramp, "is what goin' gets you."

They passed the stony figure at the top of the ramp. "Howdy, sir," Hostetter said with a touch to the brim of his hat.

"Forward and to the flanks," the man answered.

Next the car lurched up the ramp, headlights making Fiona shield her eyes. When the Malibu squeaked to a stop and the ramp started up, there wasn't much clearance between the vehicle and the aircraft walls.

Fiona, pressed to the port wall, scanned her surroundings. Not much presented as strange; she had ridden in plenty of utilitarian military aircraft. The usual plethora of metal boxes and conduit along the walls and over-head; red, subdued night vision lights; straps above for handholds. Jump seats were bolted port and starboard to the fuselage, five on each wall. Folded up, they provided only a few feet of clearance between them and the car. Also along the side walls, shallow lockers protruded near the rear of the ship. On the right side of the car, several short, narrow slabs of metal hung close to the walls, one after the other. Fiona recognized them as folded-away table surfaces. The farthest to the rear could be dropped down and propped with braces acting as table legs. The others could, too, but the car blocked that space.

Just ahead of the car's front bumper nestled the pilot's space, with two bucket seats and the usual confusion of operational and communication panels, all in a pit a few feet lower than the cargo deck. No wall between cargo and pilot.

The big guy squeezed past Fiona to drop into his pilot's chair while Sally opened the car door to join everyone in the cargo bay. Doing so proved a task. She could barely force her way out the door, which had room to open only a crack.

"Hey, somebody better lock down that vehicle or--" Fiona cut herself off at the sight and sound of floor clamps reaching to grip the four tires. "Never mind."

"Which do you want first?" Sally called over a rise in engine noise. "East coast or west?"

The aircraft canted under Fiona's feet. Oz gripped her arm hard, but without extending his claws. Fiona leaned over the big guy's shoulder to see through the large, curved windscreen. The road was already a hundred feet below.

"East," she said.

The horizon tilted.

"ETA two hours," the brick in the pilot's seat said.

"Bullshit." Fiona watched forest, plains, and mesas whip by beneath them. "You'd have to go supersonic."

"Already have."

She blinked. "Double bullshit. It hardly feels like we're moving."

"Inertial dampers."

"Dude, there's no such thing as inertial dampers."

The guy in the helmet said nothing.

A tap on Fiona's shoulder. Sally crooked a finger at her, coaxing her away from the cockpit and to the wall next to the car. She pulled out a jump seat and motioned Fiona to do the same.

"He's with us," Sally said, "but he has his own way about him. Please don't run him off."

"How did you even get this guy? We've been chasing him down for years, but could never lay hands on him."

"That's probably the problem." Sally pressed back in her jump seat and lifted her tennis shoes to press them against the car door. "I didn't 'lay hands on him.' I just asked. Politely."

"Who the hell is he?"

Sally tossed her head toward the cockpit. "The lady wants to know who you are!" she called.

"I am the Voice of the City."

Sally threw Fiona a goofy grin.

"Wake up!"

Willie slapped the woman again. His arm was getting tired. He'd thrown water in her face and put smelling salts under her nose, but she hadn't revived. He'd been walloping her non-stop for what felt like ten minutes. Her face had begun to bruise.

Finally, she flinched away and brought her arms up to guard.

Good. He'd only have seconds.

"It's still in you!" he bellowed, leaning into her face. "If you want free, go to California! If you don't go to California, there ain't no path to you gettin' it out! You understand? California! The Lawrence--" He stopped. Her face clouded over. The look in her eyes grew diamond hard. Maybe it hadn't been a great idea to hover so close to a monster.

The thing in Kudashova gritted her teeth and pushed him away with both hands. Willie almost left the ground. He staggered backwards, barreling into and over his chair, then against the back wall of the garage. Garden tools fell from their hooks to clatter about his feet. Catching his breath and beating back the pain of impact, he snatched up the nearest weapon, a star-shaped Weed-B-Gon till head.

The monster climbed to its feet.

Porthos backed out of the garage door, muttering.

"We'll stop you," Willie said. "We won't let you do what you done to other worlds. We won't let you kill this universe."

The thing bent over to retrieve its gun. Straightening, it stared hard at Willie. "You won't have any choice."

It closed its eyes. The tiny spheres that had swarmed around it, that had dropped to the dirt when the woman's lights went out, took to the air, turning in orbit around the monster's head and shoulders. Faster they turned, until they gave off a wind.

"Go back to the world you come from!" Willie shouted. "Don't nobody want you here!"

"Wrong. My *people* want me here."

Then, it was gone, flown away like a genie, nothing in its place but a fading tendril of dust devil.

After a minute alone in the dark, Willie dropped the gardening tool. Porthos came back into view through the garage door opening, looking shamefaced, if that were possible for a horse.

"I hope they're a long way from here," Willie breathed. He wiped his brow with a shaking hand.

Porthos bobbed his head and whinnied.

Twenty minutes streaming over the Great Plains took the edge off Fiona's mood. Okay, so the big guy had reentered her affairs. Sally Reiser had accomplished in a few days what the US government had failed at for years. In the end, though, none of that mattered. The big guy had come out on Fiona's side. That had always been the plan.

Actually, she had to admit, he had come out on *Sally's* side. Though it was not entirely clear that the man took orders, if he did they'd come from the skinny blonde.

Fiona gave up second-guessing her strange in-flight host and took up second-guessing her strange in-flight conveyance. Inertial dampers? That was the stuff of science fiction. If they had really jumped to supersonic speed, the G's would have pinned everyone to the back bulkhead. Of course, the mystery man had managed peculiar things. The unworkable aerodynamics of his jet back in Indy, the same jet, according to Sally, that clung to the top of this larger aircraft. Fiona looked up at the overhead hatch. She'd have to take a look sometime to see what that one-man sardine can was like. Then there was the big guy's bullet-stopping technology and all that non-lethal weaponry. The man was a puzzle, and so was his equipment.

While she roamed the perimeter of the cargo compartment, fingering junction boxes and reading digital gauges, Oz prowled the deck, nosing along the vents and electrical conduits. The vents came across as, well, vents. The conduits were strange, giving off none of the low-level EM stimulation that always tickled Oz's whiskers.

On impulse, Fiona unlatched and opened a junction box on the wall. Inside ran a spaghetti jumble of lines. They looked like fiber optics, but pulsed a dish soap blue. She recalled the line from that movie: "It seems to run on some sort of electricity."

"What you doin'?" Hostetter asked. He lounged in a jump seat, his arms tightly folded and his legs stretched out in front of him, crossed at the ankles. He had pulled his hat down to cover his eyes. How he knew Fiona "did" anything was a mystery.

"Just looking around," Fiona said.

"Well, could you stop?"

Fiona bristled. "Excuse me?"

"This feller helped us out. We're on his plane. It ain't polite to snoop."

"I wasn't snooping. I was, you know, looking around."

Hostetter reached up and held aside his hat. He regarded Fiona steadily.

Fiona slid into the jump seat next to him. "Okay, okay. But aren't you the least bit curious? This guy's tech, it's utterly, completely impossible, unless I'm very naïve. Doesn't that amaze you?"

"Miss Fiona, I'm still amazed that jeans have zippers."

Fiona frowned and looked away. Of course Hostetter wouldn't get it. What was an inertia-dampening supersonic jet to someone used to wood fires and pit toilets? It was just one more thing after automobiles, telephones, radio, television, TV dinners, and the refrigerators those dinners went in. "I'm sorry. I just don't know about him. He's got a lot to hide."

Hostetter resettled in his seat, dropping the hat onto his face. "Well, I reckon he ain't the only one."

Fiona's lips tightened. "Hey. What's that supposed to mean?"

"Nothin' much." His tone was almost bored. "But you got a little girl over t'other side o' that car, she hears voices in her head. You think she tells you everything they say? I wouldn't. It would make a body sound crazy. And speakin' of voices an' heads, I doubt you tellin' everything that cat tells *you*."

"Oh, you figure that, do you?"

"I do. I heard what you told Miss Sally. I heard what you told Willie. I noticed both times there weren't no discussion of runnin' off and hidin'."

"I don't hide."

"That's right. You hunt."

Yes. Fiona averted her eyes, staring into the reflective surface of the car door in front of her. Yes. She was glad Hostetter couldn't see her. He had summed up her fears, her doubts, and the reason for her endangerment in two short words. You hunt.

She was not the rational human she should be. Her existence should focus on ideas, on introspection, on safety, shelter, and social interaction. Instead, she hunted.

She was alone as every predator is alone. She hunted. Her life was nothing without prey.

Oz meowed from somewhere out of sight. He swished his tail from beneath the car's exhaust pipe, and licked his paws.

Fiona rose abruptly from her chair. The seat portion snapped back against the wall. Hostetter made no notice. He was studious about it, Fiona thought.

She left him there, the smug bastard. She went forward, tamping down her flush of anger so she wouldn't appear to flounce. She found herself at the cockpit, leaning over her taciturn pilot.

"This bucket have a phone?" she asked.

"All your contacts are likely surveilled," the big brick said, but he reached to the overhead console and pulled down a handset she hadn't noticed.

"That won't apply to this one," Fiona said as she took the handset. "He's special."

"The National Security Agency has extensive signals interception capabilities. Contacting anyone would be a grave tactical error."

And how, Fiona wondered, did Tall, Dark, and Violent know she was tracked by the NSA? Probably Sally. At least she hoped it was Sally.

She backed away several feet, out of range of the pilot and hopefully everyone else. Then she dialed the only other trustworthy predator she knew besides Oz.

Chapter Fifteen

Sergeant Goodknight exited her boss's temporary office on Ft. Meade, narrowing her eyes against the white, piercing sunlight on the concrete street. The place was a drop from the digs at NSA headquarters, but only if you discounted the lack of reliable power, the sopping wet carpets, and the bulging, waterlogged walls of her former workspace. All that taken into account, the warehouse space commandeered from Grace's field office was a sweet-smelling rose.

Soldiers ambled by on the sidewalks, clueless that the spooks had moved into their neighborhood. They couldn't help but know the news of the day before. The building stood on the horizon, holed and blackened, but no one had advertised that the spyworks had moved.

Yes, the spyworks. The NSA didn't have spies, it so blandly told the world. Just signals analysis, that's us. Just a bunch of electronics nerds with their ears clamped to headphones. That was what the world got told.

It was just as well. The world didn't need to know some things. Like the NSA's nonexistent spy network had lost a violent, super-powered operative.

Where have you gotten to, Major Street?

Goodknight put a hand up to shield her eyes from the sun. She looked right and left along the street for the car the agency had granted her. She wondered where it was. With headquarters in its present state of chaos, Goodknight's role as admin assistant to the colonel had given way to courier. After the disappointments of Street and Grace, Colonel Sanders didn't know who else to trust, except maybe Childress, a thousand miles away. Now Goodknight stood in her undress uniform in the blinding sun on the walk, the heat of the day rising around her. Strapped to her left wrist, the briefcase holding the controlled hard drive felt like it would drag her right over, especially combined with the pistol nestled up under that arm.

Goodknight hated guns. That explained why her army career had so far been bounded by office walls.

Where the dickens was that car?

A white sedan pulled to the curb. The driver climbed out and leaned on the top. "Sergeant Goodknight? Sorry I'm late. There was a problem with the dispatch."

Goodknight started up the walkway to the curb, her sensible heels clicking on the concrete. She stopped at the car, opposite the driver, and gave him careful examination. She'd seen that guy before…

"Mister Short."

"Oh, great. So we don't have to muddle through introductions."

"Since when does the CIA run a motor pool?"

The man laid both hands on the car top and shrugged. Balding head, aviator sunglasses, and a gray sport coat over a white, button-down shirt. No tie. He had the cynical smirk of a man too long buried in the politics of secrecy. A dangerous man, Goodknight reminded herself. Richard Short was deep cover. He had been with the major since before this all began, since before -- and while -- she was bound to the cat.

"This is a special occasion," Mister Short said. "You needed a ride, and I'm the guy to give it to you. Or you could walk…"

"I could scream."

Short raised his eyebrows and widened his mouth as if shocked. "After all we've been through together? And me being so nice with the car and all?"

"Where's the regular driver?" She avoided asking "What have you done with him?"

"He looked a little tired, so I suggested he take a nap. A short one, just to get his wind back. I mean, really, with all the action around here lately… You know we have a pool going at Langley? About what your cover story will be."

"You've got two seconds. Then I call for assistance." Goodknight edged her free hand toward her jacket. Damned uniform and the need for circumspection. How would she unbutton it to get to the gun?

"Don't do that," Short said, his tone suddenly serious. "I'm extending you a professional courtesy since we know each other. No forcible kidnapping. But if you keep on doing what you're doing, I will shoot you, or maybe slug you silly."

She gave up on the gun, for the moment. If she really needed it, the car would provide a shield. "What do you want?"

"To give you a ride. Somebody wants to talk to you."

Somebody. Could he mean--

"Yeah, you got it in one. She would've come up to your desk with coffee and croissants, but that might've caused a commotion."

"You realize she's a disavowed agent and a wanted criminal?"

"Goodknight, you wound me. You should know by now that I know everything." He grinned at her.

Goodknight's blood went cold at that grin. It was reptilian. A group of three soldiers in ACUs strolled up the sidewalk toward her. She gave them a sidewise inspection.

Short leaned across the car. "Look, I'm here because a friend needed my help. Not having many friends, that means something to me. Don't eye those grunts. I wouldn't want to kill a whole slew of American heroes. I promise I won't hurt you. Nobody else will, either, not while you're with me. She just wants to talk." He held up a bunch of random fingers. "Scout's honor."

"Mister Short, you're a lot of things, but not a boy scout."

He threw up both hands as if to surrender. "Correct. The better for you to do as I say and get in the car. You never know what a scoundrel like me might do."

She thought about the approaching soldiers, the shield of the car, and getting out her pistol. She also thought about how little she knew of combat and how she had only managed a minor qualification with the gun. Short was an ass, untrustworthy, and a barroom brawler of a CIA operative. And far more experienced than she.

But, in her short association with him, he had never lied to her.

And he knew where Major Street was. Without this opportunity, how many days or weeks would the major stay hidden?

She reached for the door latch. "Okay, but I'm taking out my gun. For insurance. Don't shoot me."

Short climbed back into the car as Goodknight lowered herself into the front passenger seat. "That really isn't necessary. Makes it seem like you've watched too many movies."

"I don't trust you."

He shrugged and keyed the ignition. "Why should *you* be any different?"

He took her off-post, not far, just into town and to a cheap chain motel. There he exited the car and hurried around to hold the door for her. She couldn't guess if the gentlemanly routine was real, a joke, or a means to ensure she didn't escape. Then, a hand planted firmly at the small of her back, he led her a few doors down and shoved her over the threshold of a room he opened up.

The room was dim from pulled blinds. Inside were four figures, three Goodknight knew personally, one by his file. Street, seated at a table. Hostetter, slouched on the near bed. Reiser lying on her back on the other. The Voice of the City stood like a wall behind Street.

"Have a seat," Short said. He had neatly removed the gun from her grip and maneuvered her to the small round table where Major Street sat with her fingers intertwined. Short pushed Goodknight by the shoulders into the chair.

"Hey," the major said, adding one of her radiant smiles. She sat there in scrubs and a heavy, winter, leather coat.

Goodknight tried to work some spit into her mouth. "You should know that I'm carrying a sealed, trackable hard drive that they'll miss soon. Also, Mister Short waylaid an agency driver who'll sound the alarm any minute."

"Sure," the major said. "And you rode in on a low-jacked motor pool car. It's okay. We'll just be a sec."

Goodknight looked over Street's shoulder at the Voice, his arms crossed and his visor-shielded face scowling. She took in Hostetter, sitting with drooping mustache and eyebrows, twiddling his thumbs. He looked strange in ordinary dress. She had only ever seen him in full cowboy costume. "What do you want?" she said to the major.

"Your help."

"You're a fugitive."

"I am, and there's no good reason for it."

"You put a lot of people in the hospital."

The major winced. "Okay, so maybe there is a reason. But they were gonna kill Oz."

That gave Goodknight pause. But of course she had known. She had run the papers through her station. She just hadn't realized what they meant. Still, did that excuse--

Street darted her hands out, laying her palms open before Goodknight. "I won't lie to you. We've known each other too long for that. The colonel had reason for what he planned to do. He couldn't trust me, not when Oz could take control. He wanted the implant out of me to prevent exactly what happened. Is the doctor all right? He hit his head pretty hard."

"He's all right. They all are."

"Sally says they're pinning a bunch of murders--"

"We know you didn't do that. Kudashova did."

Street seemed taken aback. She glanced over to Sally.

"Don't look at me," the woman said without sitting up. "I just know what I'm told."

"You're all fugitives," Goodknight said. "You'll likely all be redacted if things get any worse. All but you." She tossed her chin at the Voice of the City. "They don't even know you're here."

"That's the thing." Street drew her hands back. For the first time, Goodknight wondered where Oz was.

"We've got to clear things up," the major said. "There's a way bigger problem at hand. This Kudashova. She's got something in her, something from … somewhere else. And it doesn't mean us a bit of good."

Okay. This was taking a stranger path than Goodknight had expected. "Something in her. She's a Russian assassin. What she's got in her is a mission objective."

"No, no, it isn't like that." The major screwed up her face until her forehead lined with multiple furrows. "We've got intel you don't have. It involves the incident at Lawrence-Livermore."

"Really? Well, *I've* got intel *you* don't have." Goodknight sounded braver than she felt. She wondered exactly where Short stood behind her, but didn't dare look. "It's like this, Major Street. Nurse Rita's in the hospital recovering from a coma. You put her out for an hour. The doctor needed ten stitches in his skull. We've got an agent down with trauma to her throat, two agents down with head injuries, and three cops down, one with a broken septum that came close to piercing his brain."

If anything, the major's face contorted even more. Goodknight thought Street might break out crying. "You said they were all right."

"They will be, or so the doctors say. But you don't get a pass on behavior like that. Then there's this rogue Russian assassin running around killing like, a dozen people, I've lost count, all to frame you. And Marshal Hostetter abets your escape, and … and…" She looked at her former boss helplessly. "It's a God damned mess, ma'am."

Street said nothing. No one else spoke. The traffic outside seemed to roar through the room.

"Okay," the major finally said. "Okay. Obviously, there's a lot unsaid. A lot of holes. Let's fill them in."

"What? What do you mean?"

"I need your help, Goodknight. There's a ton of bad mojo going down and I can't do anything about it without you in my corner. But neither of us knows the whole of the problem. You tell me what you know and I'll tell you what I know."

"Are you kidding? You're a targeted rogue agent. I could go to prison if I help you."

"If you don't help her," the marshal said suddenly, "ain't no worries of prison gonna matter. This here world's been invaded, little lady. If the monster gets what it wants, all o' us'll go straight into hell."

Goodknight stared at him. She wanted to tell him off, to point out that she wasn't his "little lady" and comic book nonsense didn't wash with her. But, of course, she sat watching a man out of time, and from another universe. "You, umm, meant that figuratively, right?"

It was Hostetter's turn to stare.

"No, he did not," the major said for him. "Look, let me start. And you know the kinds of things we've been through, so you know that every word I tell you is the truth."

Street took a deep breath and fell forward into a detailed account of what she knew. Her delivery showed a quality of pedantic pacing, as if she had long considered what she would say. There was no deception that Goodknight could detect, just a keen need to be intelligible and complete.

The major told of the confrontation in the doctor's office when she realized the fate intended for Oz, when the cat had stormed over her to gain his escape. She went through every pained detail of their run through the building and their flight in the parking lot, taking a breather after Hostetter's timely rescue. The cowboy broke in to explain how he had transported Street to his known house in Wyoming, then had packed her up to the cabin on the bluff, Porthos his conspirator. The major finished with their encounters with Willie Dern and Sally Reiser, and the ride east in the Voice of the City's magic airplane.

"And I want to emphasize," Street said, wagging a finger at Goodknight, "at no point was I ever subsumed or taken over or replaced by Oz. Even when we broke out of medical I directed him. I let him in the driver's seat, yes, but I was in the co-pilot's slot. The colonel's fears are understandable, but ungrounded."

Well, that was bullshit. Goodknight knew about Childress's observations. Fiona Street the professional spy had not been present in the headquarters parking lot.

"You know, Sergeant Grace stood up for you," Goodknight said. "He never thought you were guilty of that FBI thing and he argued against the Case Specific order--"

"What's Case Specific?"

Goodknight blinked. She didn't know? How could she not know? *Everybody* knew. "That's the sanction they disseminated on you."

Street took a beat to absorb that. "You mean to tell me there's been a death order in my file and *it was unit SOP?*"

"For the last three years."

Street sat there opening and closing her mouth. After a moment, she closed her eyes and shook her head. "Christ," she murmured. "The love is just boiling over."

"Yes." Goodknight peered from face to face. "But it isn't too late for you, not if you turn yourselves in. The colonel's got a handle on Kudashova. Just this morning, the State Department paid a visit to the Director of National Security because the Russian ambassador paid *them* a visit. It seems the Russians have belatedly reported a rogue agent. She killed her own handlers and disappeared with a bunch of weaponry and some secret gear they didn't want to mention. They admitted she was here to frame you for violent, unstable behavior. That way, maybe we'd shut down the enhanced agent program. So the colonel knows you're in the clear for all that, he just wants to get the cat problem solved."

"Solved." The major gritted her teeth before going on. She seemed to listen to something, or smell something bad. "With the colonel wanting my implant and Oz on a platter, it seems the Russkies are getting what they want."

"Come in, major. Your life isn't worth this spy-versus-spy crap."

"But Oz's is." Street narrowed her emerald eyes. She took a deep, slow breath. "This is why I brought you here. We need a few things. Everything you've got on Kudashova. Also, everything you've got on the Drehd project."

"The Drehd project? I don't understand. That was, what, seventy years ago. And a failure."

"It might be the key to hog-tyin' that monster in the Russian lady," Hostetter said.

"The Drehd project may have started this whole inter-universal nightmare," Street added. "It's real, Goodknight. It's just now affecting us, just at the edges, but it's been going on for decades."

"It almost took my world," Hostetter said. "I can swear to one world it truly did destroy."

Goodknight searched Street's face. Was she serious? "And that's all. That's all you need."

"It would be nice if I could get the colonel's ear. To get straight with him for Oz's sake. And to get his help, as well."

Goodknight thought about it. All the major wanted were top secret files with data on active personnel, the loss of which would jeopardize a major intelligence initiative. Right. That was all. "Okay. If you just want the files. And word to the colonel. But it'll take some finagling. Those files are controlled."

Street frowned, but only slightly. Goodknight knew the implant gave her weird insights. She also noticed the hot glow of red at the major's neck. What had Street heard that human ears could not?

Street looked beyond Goodknight, and nodded. Short stepped close to Goodknight's back and handed her a cheap flip phone. "Take it," Street said. "It's untraceable. Call when you have everything set up."

Goodknight wrapped her fingers around the phone. "That's it? You're letting me go?"

"We've worked together a long time," the major said. "I think I know you well enough."

Goodknight didn't know what to say. The major trusted her.

"Okay, get up," Short said from behind. "You can take the car back, but don't bother sending the authorities to this motel. We won't be here."

Goodknight rose from her chair. All eyes followed her. Short had her by the arm and was pulling her toward the door.

"How do I know you're on the up-and-up?" Goodknight asked Street as the door opened.

"I know I can trust you," Street said. "You know you can do the same with me."

Then Short pulled Goodknight out into the sun and closed the door behind them. "There's the car," he said, nodding toward the sedan. "I imagine they're already looking for you, so pull over right when you're asked. Don't wave your hands around too much. It could be unhealthy. People are trigger happy these days."

"What's going on here?" Goodknight asked. "I mean, *really* going on."

"What's going on is that somebody's playing the whole intelligence network for dunces and your old boss intends to do something about it. What's going on is that she needs you to rise above your orders and do what's right. You think you could do that, sarge?"

Goodknight stuck out her chin to him. Short was a bully. She wouldn't give him an inch.

"Yeah." Short sneered, then turned away and sauntered down the sidewalk away from Goodknight, the door, and the car. "See you around, kid. And it'll be me seeing you first, especially if you rat out your friends. Count on it."

Goodknight stood on the sidewalk for several seconds, taking in what had happened. It struck her strange, like a bad TV crime drama, but it had really happened. Fiona Street had asked her to commit espionage against the United States, then had let her go without so much as an idle threat. Well, from her, anyway. What was to keep her from calling in the authorities right then and there? They'd even given her a phone.

On impulse, she reached for the doorknob to the room. She'd confront the major more directly, find out exactly what she was up to, find out why it involved all those other people. Especially Short. He was obnoxious, he tended to live off the CIA's leash, but he was a patriot, as far as Goodknight figured. Of course, who knew with those spook types? They had strange ideas of patriotism.

She twisted the doorknob, expecting to find it locked. It wasn't. She threw open the door.

The room stood empty.

She peeked in, then stepped over the threshold. The chairs at the table had been scooted back. The covers on the beds were mussed. There was no other exit.

Where the hell had they gotten to?

"That sure as hell didn't work." Fiona removed her goggles and widened her eyes to clear the haze of afterimages. She looked around the aircraft interior to find all the others doing the same. Except the Voice of the City, who seemed unfazed by anything.

Hostetter held his goggles at arm's length, squinting at them. "So, explain again about this here directed hollowgrammy thing?"

"That's holography," Sally said, pinching the bridge of her nose. "And it would just make your head explode."

The Voice of the City made no comment. Standing loose-limbed by the driver's door of the Malibu, he remained as impassive as a stone.

So, Fiona thought, adding up the weirdness. We're on a cloaked aircraft hovering soundlessly over a Ft. Meade motel, remote-controlling holograms of ourselves like puppets. She might have decided the impossibilities were getting ridiculous, but that time had come and gone.

"We'll wait a few minutes in case she betrays us," the Voice said. "Then we retrieve the cameras and audio equipment."

"And Oz," Fiona added. He hid under a bed down there, her reader of Goodknight's intentions.

"What you think she'll do?" Hostetter asked as if reading Fiona's mind.

"Oh, she is *so* going to turn us in," Sally answered though the question wasn't directed at her. "Did you see that girl? She thought we were ax murderers."

Fiona placed the goggles on the deck and rubbed the back of her neck. "Goodknight's a straight player, worth every nickel of her Army pay. She won't commit espionage against her government, not for any entreaty of friendship or trust. So yeah, I'm counting on her turning us in."

Hostetter and Sally had gathered close around her. "I ain't sure how that helps our cause," Hostetter said.

"Observe." Fiona picked up the phone on the seat beside her. She punched one button and put the pickup to her mouth.

"Yo," came from the phone.

"Short, did you plant the bug?"

"What am I, an unpaid intern? Of course I did. She won't find it for hours."

"Good. Then it's on to phase two."

"Way ahead of you. I got a few senators to wave howdy to, then there's an F-22 waiting for me at the airfield."

"You sure you can convince the senators?"

"I don't have to convince, just suggest. They know we have the recordings, and the pictures. The bribery will be implied."

"That could be trouble for you."

"When am I *not* in trouble? Don't worry, Street. I'll get this done. You just make sure it's worth it. Oh, and don't worry about the sweet little scientist. I'll guard dog her for the sheriff, no prob."

He hung up.

Fiona sagged, her head almost between her knees. She hadn't slept in … how long?

"I ain't sure I trust that varmint," Hostetter said under his breath.

"He's all right," Fiona said.

"He as crooked as a dog's hind leg."

"Okay, I'll bite." Sally sat down beside Fiona, taking the space the phone had once claimed. "What the hell was that all about? The stuff about bugs?"

Fiona dropped the phone into Sally's lap. "I had Short plant a listening and tracking device on Goodknight. She'll go back to Sanders, report out to him, and he'll have her or somebody round up the files we want, for protection. That'll give us a location. From there we go in, liberate the files, and beat feet to the next phase of the plan."

"Oh. And what is the next phase of the plan?"

Fiona issued a humorless laugh. "Beats the hell out of me. I mean, Short's off to the California facility where he'll get the ball going on starting up the machine and also plant holographic camera/projectors in the sensitive areas. But what we do with all that, I can't say." She looked around at everyone, her gaze landing last on the Voice of the City. "I'm open to suggestions."

The man just stood there. He might as well have been a mannequin. A big, wide, stack-of-bricks mannequin.

"Alrighty then," Fiona said. "So we pick up Oz and the tech gear, mosey on over to Sanders's temp headquarters, and listen in on the soaps. That'll tell us what we do next."

"What do we do if that little girl calls?" Hostetter asked. "What if she sets up a powwow with your boss, like you asked?"

"Then we go, but at a time of our choosing. After Short gets everything set up. After we know where the files are." She glanced between Sally and Hostetter as they exchanged unsure looks. "We need to talk to Sanders," Fiona insisted. "We need his help. If I get a face-to-face, I can convince him of the real threat."

"Unless he blows our brains out from a distance." Sally jammed her hands into her coat pockets. "You noticed the part where this is all a trap, right?"

"Sanders won't kill us. Goodknight, when she reports, will tell him our story about Kudashova and the Drehd project. He'll want answers before he does anything drastic."

"But he *will* do something drastic?" Sally's tone had acquired a serrated edge. Her eyes had turned steely. "I have a little boy, Red. He prefers his mom *without* a hole in her head."

Fiona sat up straight with an effort. She felt the weight of risk and their fears. "There will be no holes in anybody's heads." She turned her eyes long on the Voice. "I think that little miracle is your department."

Chapter Sixteen

The thing inside Kudashova boiled with frustration. It had lost Hostetter. It had lost the woman Street. And now the enemy showed new, powerful allies. Nightmare had wanted to kill something, to exorcise its rage at failure so it could once more think clearly, and plan. But it couldn't have killed the old man. That was impossible in so many ways. That one had not been an old man, not truly. And Nightmare was weak, cut off from itself. In its handicapped state, it could not fight a ghost.

It had settled for a human female, had snatched her as she walked to work from the mass transit stop. Nightmare had felt almost erotic glee at dragging the creature into that alley and stabbing her repeatedly with Kudashova's combat knife after stripping her of her uniform.

Her uniform. That had been the one mitigation that had narrowed Nightmare's choice of victim. Nightmare needed the uniform to infiltrate its enemy. True, it might have been cleaner to jump from Kudashova to the fresher, more appropriate victim, but that hadn't occurred to the beast until after the stabbing was well progressed.

Nightmare had a problem with anger.

So, after switching out her stinking clothes for the uniform, after stuffing the naked, gore-soaked carcass down a manhole, Nightmare had joined the humans walking onto the facility. No one had checked for identification. The guards at the gate had seen uniforms and had ignored what the uniforms covered.

These humans would be easy to destroy.

Now the thing in Kudashova entered the right building at the right time, the destination and schedule gleaned from its earlier invasion of the NSA intranet. It couldn't manage that connection anymore, not without the listening device on the Street woman's cat bag, a listening device far away and connected to a network Nightmare itself had crippled.

No matter. The information had been clear, and recent. Without a location for Street, without a location for Hostetter, the thing in Kudashova would reacquire its enemy the only way it knew how. By shadowing a secondary target.

The monster stopped at a particular door. A paper note identified its occupant. Nightmare knocked, trying to hide its excitement. When the door opened, the monster flinched, arresting just in time its urge to pounce, to lay hands on the human before it, to capture her and make her bait.

"Yes?" the woman asked.

"Doctor Sinfonee Rodriguez?"

"Yes."

Nightmare glanced past the woman, scanning the tiny office stacked with boxes and mounds of paper. "I've been sent to assist."

The woman looked puzzled. "Assist at what?"

There was something wrong with this human. She seemed less focused, but also sharply alert, a paradox. She seemed devoid of suspicion, unaware but imbued with power, like a deep, black lake. Nightmare could reach out, could grasp the woman's slim neck and crush it, and the human would never, even in death, imagine what cruelty acted upon her. She would just die. That was no fun.

But maybe it could have the desired effect. Maybe if Nightmare twisted that head from that neck, Hostetter would come. He'd come to mourn this person. He would.

Kudashova's fingers flinched to act. Blood rushed in her ears.

From behind the human, stepping into view from an unseen part of the office, a balding man in sunglasses looked Kudashova up and down. "Yeah," he said. "Assist at what?"

The monster drew back inside its human shell. It didn't know that man. It wasn't sure it could take him. He had the bold look of a predator in the cut of his face, in the confidence of his stance. "I don't know. They said to assist."

"Oh!" the woman said, jumping a little where she stood. "I guess with the calculations. Tell me, umm, Specialist fourth class Menefee, are you trained in theoretical N-space coordinate conversion?"

"No. I'm just a uniform."

The man in the sunglasses sneered. "I guess they sent her to carry your shit."

The woman blinked at this. She seemed to be translating. "I suppose you're right, Mister Short. She's here to carry my shit. Well, come in Specialist. There's lots of shit to carry. We're moving back to the facility today."

Nightmare wanted to kill. It *needed* to kill.

The beast stepped into the office.

"She what?"

"Yes, sir. She asked me to get files for her. Classified files. But there seemed to be a reason. She was concerned about a toehold situation involving the Lawrence-Livermore facility."

"She asked you to commit espionage, sergeant. Over a seventy-year-old file? What the hell?"

"Something's going on, sir. All due respect, but maybe we've been too caught up in this Kudashova thing to see the real scale of events. Maybe the major has something."

"Are you sure you spoke to the major?"

"Sir?"

"There's a devious, paranoid, manipulative cat to consider. Which one was in control?"

"I-- I don't know, sir."

A long silence. Fiona waited, leaning over the Voice of the City's shoulder while he operated the communications gear from his pilot's seat. She squeezed the headrest of his chair. Squeezed and released, squeezed and released.

"All right. Gather up those files. Have the ones at Lawrence-Livermore sent by rapid, secure transport. Bring them here and put them under lock, there in the vault. I'll put two agents on the door. No, three of them. If Street wants those files and Street is controlled by an alien force, then we'll do what we can to keep them out of her hands."

"Yes, sir. What about the motel?"

"She's long gone from there, but I'll get Childress on it. And Good-knight, when you secure those files, report back. We'll see what to do with that phone she handed you."

"Yes, sir."

"Dismissed."

Fiona tapped the headrest. "Okay, buddy, keep the feed going, but latch onto that secondary carrier signal. It'll trace her movements. I want to know where those files wind up, and when."

"He just said--"

"Always good to confirm. Blondie! Hostetter! Time to put some heads together!"

Tejada leaned back to unkink his spine. The pistol slung under his left arm dug into his side at the farthest extent of his stretch. "Sounds fishy to me," he said. "All this to-do about securing the facility and all of a sudden you have a go to test fire the machine?"

"It isn't all that," Eglemann said, her tone flat. She paid bare attention to him. She seemed absorbed in the control panel before her, checking and re-checking its functions against readouts on the tablet nesting in the crook of one arm. "I suppose the powers that be think there's nothing to be gained from sitting idle. I mean, the machine was threatened, maybe, but it wasn't the cause of all that excitement. It was the target. And how better to resume secure operations than with a bunch of NSA and a contingent of soldiers milling around like gnats at a sweaty horse? Why, I even hear they sent CIA with the codes from the Senate."

Tejada turned away from Eglemann. He stared across the chamber to the so-called machine, the transference platform with energy attenuators, as Doctor Rodriguez had so often informed him. A broken toy, he thought. A multi-billion-dollar broken toy no one had gotten to work even once. Why all the fuss about it now?

"You sure all the repairs are good?" he asked. "That last incident with the lightning post didn't do serious damage?"

"Oh, it certainly did, or rather Hostetter did when he closed off the event. But we know our jobs, Agent Tejada. Everything's good and tidy."

Tejada grinned and looked over his shoulder at her. "So I'm being a big nuisance."

"You didn't hear me say it."

"Sorry, doc. I'm just feeling like a fifth wheel here."

"Don't call me doc. I'm an engineer. I work for a living. And you *are* a fifth wheel."

Tejada added a laugh to the grin. "Okay, loud and clear. I'll go talk to the CID, see if they have anything but the time of day. Want I should bring you anything?"

"Tea would be nice. Maybe a burrito."

"Tea. And a burrito."

"Bean, yes." Eglemann looked up from her readouts for the first time. "Don't worry, I'm good for it."

"Yeah, I bet you are. I'll wander back, Miss Eglemann. With tea and a burrito."

Tejada headed across the machine room, toward the big double doors. He had no clear mission in mind so he showed no hurry to get to wherever he might end up. The CID guys were as restless as he. They'd done their investigation and wanted dearly to go on to other work. They just needed somebody with enough embroidery on their shoulders to clear them for departure. He'd get nothing of use out of them.

Tejada felt much as they did. Nothing more had happened since the trans-universal event and Hostetter running off for Maryland. Tejada suspected that Sanders kept his agents on station just in case the cowboy came home. Hostetter had left his girlfriend in the lurch. She was the only active link to draw the marshal and Street. Maybe. Tejada had the sneaking suspicion the whole fight had moved far east.

He paused at the door. A soldier guided an overloaded two-wheel dolly through the opening. The plastic crates stacked on its bed revealed circuit boards and hard drives, change-outs for the computer banks lining the chamber's walls. The soldier kept one hand against the crates to prevent their jumping off the dolly as she trundled them over the slightly raised steel lip of the threshold.

Tejada gave the soldier a second glance. She didn't give him even one. He'd seen her before. Was it important? His mind told him he should remember that face.

Well, okay. She was a good looking lady. Maybe that's all it was. Or maybe he'd seen her around the facility going about her daily grind. That was probably it.

But he wasn't convinced. Something about her seemed important.

He watched as she crossed the chamber, headed straight for Egelmann. Nothing came to mind, nothing but that vague sense of alert.

He'd check the bulletins as soon as he cleared the facility. Something told him not to let on that he suspected the woman in any way. Recognition and surveillance could go both ways.

Outside, he drew out his phone, and cursed under his breath. He'd forgotten his phone was toast. He hadn't had a chance to get another. Glancing around from the steps, he caught sight of DeBoy under a tree near the sidewalk, conferring with one of the CID men. "D!" he called, and waited while his partner excused himself.

"What's up?" DeBoy asked as soon as he joined Tejada.

"Got your phone? Check the bulletins. See if we have a blonde chick, pretty, kind of square jawed…"

"Like this?" DeBoy had taken out his phone at its mention. He turned the screen to Tejada. The picture filling the phone's face dominated the first item on the daily bulletin. "It's that Russian, the one who impersonated the major."

The hairs on Tejada's neck straightened. That was her. That was the woman in the Army uniform. The assassin was inside the building, inside the most sensitive facility on Earth.

"Call the colonel," he said, his words furred through a suddenly dry mouth. "We have us a situation."

Fiona lay on her back on the rear seat of Sally's rented car. The engine drone of the Voice of the City's weird-assed science fiction jet had fallen silent. She listened, and in that silence found nothing but the muffled sound of traffic and the murmur of conversation between Sally and Hostetter. The big brick who owned the aircraft had put it down in the cleared stretch of a power tower easement north of Ft. Meade, its cloaking mechanism hiding the plane from casual eyesight. He'd deployed what he called perimeter drones and set the ship's engines to standby so that the jet could jump skyward in seconds. Black Batman himself sat like a watchful pit bull in his pilot's chair, staring through the expansive front windscreen. They were as secure as they could be without also perching atop some lonely, inaccessible mountain or floating in the middle of the sea, so Fiona had opted for sleep.

But opting for rest and getting it were not in any way the same. She lay awake, her eyes directed at the car's cream-colored headliner. She held one arm thrown across her forehead and brooded. How long had it been, she wondered? It seemed as though she had laughed and sung Irish songs with her men just a few short days ago, yet here she lay, exhausted, aching, wanted by her government, and she didn't even know what day it was.

She tried to figure that one out. A small thing, knowing the day, knowing how much time had passed in her misfortune. Let's see, she thought, it shouldn't be a chore. The Irish pub, when all had been well, when she had celebrated her promotion with her close-at-hand co-workers. That had been Tuesday -- no, Friday. The live music was Tuesdays, but there hadn't been any band. She recalled that the place had been dead for Friday night. A good night, that. A light-hearted moment with Grace clucking over her half-drunk, giggly-girl goofiness like a mother hen over a newly-hatched chick.

She closed her eyes, hard. Mind wandering. That stuff was minutiae. Huh. Her life was minutiae. She didn't *have* a life, did she? She had work and she had feeding the cat.

She felt a push of petulance from somewhere in the aircraft, from one of the jump seats bungeed down by Sally for His Majesty the Great and Powerful Oz. He lay on the jump seat as Fiona lay in the car, on his back with his belly exposed to the breath of air conditioning. Okay, so she hadn't exposed *her* belly just yet, but still... Which of them had claimed that position first? Did the cat copy her, or did she copy the cat?

Because she didn't know, she groaned, then turned onto her side.

Friday. Then leaving by car from the airport the next day, then two days of travel... But that was where she lost the thread. When the colonel had stuffed her into that glorified cell, she had thought she'd be there for just a few hours. But the hours had dragged on. She had grown impatient, then anxious, then a need to escape had subsumed her surface consciousness. She had stopped paying attention to the time shown on the wall clock. She had no idea how many circuits that hour hand had made around the clock face.

But make it a day, no, two. Then the escape and waking up at Hostetter's cabin in the middle of the night. The jet, the corralling of Goodknight and the deals with Short, and the waiting.

Had it really been a week? Six days at the least? And she hadn't slept, had hardly eaten, during most of it.

At that realization, her stomach growled. Oz laid his ears back and sent her a whiff of disapproval. It smelled like sodden fur.

Okay, so he hadn't cared for the energy bars from the Voice's aircraft stash, or the beef jerky or cheese sandwiches from Hostetter's saddlebags. Maybe he'd like it better in the loving arms of Doctor Dumbass and the veterinarian?

A stink of urine, thick with ammonia, flooded her tired mind.

Just once, Fiona thought as she shuddered on the seat and blew out through her nose, just once, an off switch would be nice.

She sat up. Who was she kidding? She wouldn't catch any sleep. Once upon a time, with a death mark on her head, a monster out to destroy her world, and a runaway government science project helping him get his wish, she could have curled up and slept at a moment's offering of slack time. Not anymore. Not since Oz had entered her head. He hunted, intent on killing the enemy that threatened him. And because he hunted, she did, too.

So, what was the hunt? Where did it stand? She knew the location of the Drehd files. Sanders had locked them up in his interim headquarters, in a room that passed for a secure vault, behind a steel-barred gate, a touch pad lock, and three armed guards plus every other agent working in the building. They guarded papers in a box and the NSA's encrypted computer files as downloaded to a locked hard drive. She'd need to draw Sanders off to have a chance at that vault. She'd have to get him away from the building along with a fair portion of his men. Then she'd have to get through the guards without causing casualties. The vault was no problem, just concrete and steel, but the files…

It would take days, maybe even weeks, to scan through those papers. The Drehd file filled a reinforced evidence box capable of holding ten reams of paper. The associated hard drive would corrupt before giving up secrets to unauthorized users. Fiona prepared, at terrible risk, to steal that information, yet she had no clear idea how to get at it when it came to her.

But she had to get to that data. Within those files lay the secret of a looming inter-universal war, of how it began and, hopefully, how it would stop. If only she could tackle that mystery with the colonel's blessing and his help.

Unlikely. He'd have her shot as soon as she showed her face.

Except that she wouldn't give him the chance, and, boy, wouldn't that piss him off.

She turned her head to find Sally and Hostetter watching her. She'd already known, or Oz had. They were uneasy. Fiona knew this as a stale taste and a kind of static charge in the air. Her people suffered a lack of surety if not flagging commitment. For though neither knew why they entered this fight, they didn't have in them an inclination to quit.

Sally was there so long as her interior voices dictated. Fiona couldn't guess what to do with her, though. Sally was like the original atom bomb, hair raising in her potential for power, but you weren't quite sure if she'd work out as planned. Hostetter was there through bonds of friendship and because the monster loose in Kudashova had sought to ruin his world, had killed the world of another, alternate Sinfonee Rodriguez, and had murdered that woman, Hostetter's love, through proxy. Hostetter was in the fight for keeps.

Of the three, only Fiona balanced on less than a solid commitment. Sally obeyed God. Hostetter obeyed vengeance. Fiona obeyed … the hunt? Oz? Something as abstract as duty?

How would that sense of duty survive going against her own people to grab the files her hunt demanded? When the time came, when the fight commenced, would she have to cede her share of it to Oz?

She raked fingers through her tangled red hair. How long had it been since she showered? Brushed her teeth?

She imagined she'd give almost anything for a washcloth and something substantial to eat. But she wasn't about to whine to her partners; they endured as much as she.

Fiona scooted across the bench seat and inched open the door on the opposite side of the car from Sally and Hostetter. She squeezed through the opening and climbed onto the deck, looking around for Oz. She found him splayed on a jump seat past the Malibu's rear bumper. He tried to look dead to the world, but he wasn't fooling anybody. Well, he wasn't fooling her. She gave him a snap of her chin toward the front of the aircraft, then went to visit the Voice.

He wasn't idle in his pilot's chair. He fiddled with knobs and switches, some of which Fiona had mapped as his communications array.

"Any word back from Goodknight?" she asked.

"Since you asked twenty minutes ago? No."

Oh. A little snark. So maybe he wasn't a robot.

The jet had no true co-pilot's seat, just a padded chair beyond a center console. The station had no controls of its own. The seat didn't swivel, tilt, or do anything else a crewmember might expect. It did sport a heavy headphone set hanging from one armrest, that for seat-to-seat conversation if the cockpit became noisy during flight. Fiona wondered when that might ever be necessary. The cabin had been whisper quiet ever since she climbed aboard in Wyoming.

As she skirted the Malibu's bumper to lower herself into that chair, she wondered who the seat was designed for: rescued damsels or prisoners.

"So," she said as she worked her body into a more-or-less comfortable position in the chair. Definitely, prisoners. "I was thinking. I know the motivation for everybody on this bird, except you."

"You should sleep. If you're exhausted when the call comes, you won't do anyone any good."

197

"I'm a big girl. You don't have to worry about me. But I, on the other hand, worry about you." Oz balanced on the slope of the Malibu's hood, eyeing the Voice with narrowed glassy eyes.

"You don't know how to evaluate me. I'm foreign to you, my motives hidden, my abilities unknown, my loyalties not yet clear. This bothers you." The brick showed no emotion, no concern for any suspicions from Fiona. He was just a guy turning knobs.

"I prefer to know who I'm working with," Fiona said.

"Learn to accept disappointment."

"Ha and ha. I need better than that."

The knob turning stopped. His hand remained poised over the next control surface, his fingers loose and still. He turned his face toward Fiona's in one click of a movement, a gesture for himself, not her. After all, what could she tell from his face, hidden as it was behind his helmet and visor?

"I am the Voice of the City," he said. He might as well have said "I could go for some peanut butter just now."

He continued, "You must ask yourself how the city would respond to attack from another dimension."

Huh?

"Would it cower? Would it panic? Or would it go forth to protect itself? Go forth even to other lands so that its own city limits might be spared the scourge of war."

Fiona blinked at that. She didn't know how to respond. It wasn't the content that stymied her; that was straightforward enough. It was the delivery. Scourge of war? Really? Was he twelve? Or recently evicted from his parents' basement?

"So, umm, not here for Sally?"

"She brought me here. Anyone true and honorable could have."

"Really. So you would have come right along if I had asked you politely a year ago?"

"The Voice of the City does not trust the government."

The Voice of the… It sounded as though he referred to something other than himself. "Well, Batman, I won't take offense. You aren't the only one."

"You aren't the government."

That surprised her for all of a second. She was a major in the US Army, an agent of the NSA. She couldn't get more government than that.

Except she was also hounded by her employer, could expect to be shot dead if he ever got a bead on her. And she proposed to steal from him.

Great.

"Okay." She slapped her palms onto the armrests and rose from the chair. "You're a wonderful conversationalist, Voice, but I guess I'd better get on that all-important taking a nap thing. We should do this again. Over tea, you know, and strychnine."

He didn't respond. He showed no indication he noticed she was leaving. He was a mystery she'd have to figure out.

Hostetter waited for her up on deck. He offered a hand to help her out of the well of the cockpit. She took it and pulled herself to him. He smelled of leather and wood fires, no staleness to him. So maybe the others hadn't been without showers as long as she.

"Thought we had a discussion about this," he said.

"About what?" Fiona noticed Sally beyond him, her arms crossed tightly over her chest.

Hostetter started toward the rear of the cabin. "About leavin' our host alone."

"I wasn't bothering him," Fiona said with a put-upon huff. "I was just getting to know him better."

"Sound travels in this here crate," Hostetter said, and flopped down in the farthest jump seat from the front of the ship.

Yes, Fiona thought. It did. She became acutely aware of the big brick in the pilot's chair. Oz puzzled over him. He wasn't what he seemed...

Fiona headed toward the back and Hostetter, but jerked to a halt when Sally grabbed her arm. The blonde's diamond hard blue eyes drilled into Fiona's, the woman's angular face looking flinty sharp.

"Yes?" Fiona asked, drawing the word out.

"You need to sleep." Sally's tone was that of an NCO giving orders.

"Look, Blondie. I'll take care of myself, if you don't mind, and for dessert I'll even take care of y--"

"Sleep."

Only a split second passed. In that time, Fiona felt Oz go blank. She heard his body thud against the car and begin a sandy-sounding slide off the hood.

Then her eyes lost focus and she heard, felt and saw nothing else.

When Childress entered the colonel's office, Grace was just leaving. They met in the anteroom in front of Goodknight's desk, Childress raising an eyebrow in question, Grace with his jaw set.

"S'up, top," Childress said, fastening the center button of his suit jacket in anticipation of his audience with the boss.

"Have you found her yet?" Grace edged those words like a carving knife. So, who was the dude mad at? Childress was only doing his job.

Which Grace had been found derelict in. "No, I ain't found her. From what I hear, she found us."

Grace heaved his uniformed, bemedaled chest. If anything, the sharp line of his mouth tightened.

"Look, top. I know it's bad. Your favorite officer and all that. But we got orders, she had orders, and she disobeyed hers. There's a way to this shit. If there weren't, we'd be nothin' but super-secret gun-totin' thugs."

"Just remember who *she* is," he said in a voice that ground his teeth. "Remember who she is and what she's done. She saved this country a few years back. She's saved a good many people kidnapped, imprisoned, or trapped behind hostiles. She's saved us all from threats the public never even knew about--"

"Yeah, well, that's great, man, just beautiful, y'know? But all that happened before I came to work. The biggest thing she's done lately is put a lot of agents in the hospital and try to burn down our headquarters."

"That wasn't her. That was Kudashova."

"That was Kudashova who beat up Nurse Rita and the doc and the vet? And those cops and those agents in the parking lot?" Suddenly, Childress felt tired of it all. He felt old. He slapped the sergeant's arm like any good ol' boy might, then whipped around him toward the colonel's door. "Don't worry," he lied, "I won't do nothin' to Street that she don't ask for. We're the good guys, right?"

Childress didn't mind lying to Grace. The big sergeant had always had a soft spot for the major. But when he looked back to grin his no-hard-feelings grin, he caught Goodknight's troubled eye and his confidence turned to poison.

When he entered the colonel's domain, everything he saw took a darker, dirtier edge.

Sanders didn't even need to look up. He sat behind his desk, fingers intertwined on the blotter, watching Childress come through the door like a priest watching Jesus come to crucifixion. Childress had been in the air all morning. What the hell had gone wrong now?

"Agent Childress. Have a seat." The colonel nodded to the chair in front of the desk, probably the one Grace had just vacated.

Childress took the seat. "You needed to see me, sir."

"Yes. There've been new developments." The colonel launched into a short, clipped recitation of bullet-pointed facts. He'd been preparing them for hours. It told in his careful delivery. The major had scooped up Goodknight off the street. The major had tried to get Goodknight to conduct espionage against the United States. She had suborned Hostetter, the God lady Reiser, and that big black dude from Chicago and Indy to her cause, a crazy plan to stop an imagined invasion from another dimension. She had also redirected or suborned CIA assets, further gaining the attention of the Director, National Intelligence and the President. She was expecting a call from Goodknight that would set up a meeting between the major and the colonel.

"She's clearly unbalanced, probably under the influence of the cat. Her medical staff, including Doctor Dumas, believes she might even have experienced some sort of massive collapsing cascade of her neural capabilities, that she might be experiencing paranoid delusional episodes."

He stopped then. It was clear he expected a response from the audience.

"Wow." Childress reset himself in his chair. "Of course, there is that little tidbit of a fact that we *did* experience an invasion from wherever. At the Lawrence-Livermore facility. You were there, sir."

"That was contained. Mister Hostetter closed off the last vestige of that attack long before Street's escape from NSA medical. She seems to think the attack is ongoing, that the Russian agent sent to discredit her is possessed by a monster intent on destroying the world."

"Well, when you put it that way... I mean, most Russian agents got chomps to maybe destroy a bus or a school building, but the world? A bit out of their pay grade, I'd say."

The colonel looked down at his hands, which had a death grip on each other. Childress watched, fascinated, while the old guy relaxed each finger and laid his palms on the table.

"I've authorized you as the interim commander of your team," he said.

"Yes, sir. What about Grace?"

"He's being reassigned."

"Yes, sir."

"You'll send Ponce to link up with Tejada. He can use all the help we can give him. They've identified Kudashova on the facility grounds. She's impersonating an Army specialist. I've ordered them to monitor, not arrest, until we find out what she's up to. For operational clarity, give Tejada overall temporary control."

"Umm, I thought you said--"

"You're the commander, but I have something for you to do before you join your team in California. A special mission."

Aww, shit.

"I want you to requisition a shooter from Pentagon special operations. Agency immaterial. Army, Navy, Marines, CIA, just get the best man you can call here in the next several hours. Specify expert at extreme angles and night fire. You have priority over all missions, including active operations."

Shee-it!

"We're going to have that meeting with Street. I want to know what she's up to and see for myself if she's gone off the reservation. We have a surprise for her should she give us any trouble, which she likely will. That's where you come in."

"Me and the shooter, sir?"

"Yes. Since she has the Voice of the City on her side and knows about Case Specific, it's unlikely she'll show up without defenses. The Voice of the City has technology that can deplete the energy from spent rounds. He can also destroy ordnance within a weapon."

And, here we go.

"Agent Childress, I want you, at the specified time, to take your shooter into the Old Headquarters building. I want you to sight to the fifteenth floor breach of OPS2B. I will be there and so will Street. We expect you will be beyond the range of either of the Voice of the City's weaponry-disabling technologies."

And at that they were only guessing…

"I want you to link into my commo." The colonel tightened his fists. "I want you to apprise us of target acquisition on an ongoing basis. The angles will be tight, and limited." His knuckles whitened. "When I speak the words 'there is nothing more to be said,'" and he forced open his hands and rubbed his fingertips on the blotter, "I want you to direct your asset to apply final sighting parameters, then shoot Major Street in the head."

Even expected, the words raised Childress's hackles. The message was expected. The mission was expected. The words, though, were off. No "terminate with extreme prejudice," no "eliminate the target." Shoot Major Street in the head. Shoot her in the head. Shoot her.

"Do you anticipate any difficulty carrying out your orders?" Colonel Sanders asked. He looked ready to blow a rod.

Childress sat up taller in his chair. He gave the matter the grim moment of consideration it merited. Then he straightened his watchband on his wrist.

"No, sir," he said. "I got no problem at all."

Chapter Seventeen

Fiona started awake, almost striking her head against the back of the front passenger seat. She grabbed the seat in both hands instead, and shook her head for clarity.

Fiona's stomach lurched and her vision swam, multiple images careering before her mind's eye. The inside of the car. Outside the car near the back bumper. And that other image, the white hand from the white woman, a cold hand from dreams, not of the world. The hand had reached out, almost grasping, cool and unfeeling as ice. That image had come from Oz.

"The *fuck*?"

The back passenger door opened. Sally leaned in, a smirk on her face. "It's been six hours," she said without preamble. "We've been busy while you slept. Come on out for dinner."

"The *fuck*?"

As Fiona climbed stiffly from the car, something in her made Sally retreat.

Oz growled like a mountain lion.

"What the fuck did you do to me?" Fiona demanded. She fell back against the car, blinked, rubbed her eyes. It was like waking up after anesthesia. She focused her eyes on Sally in front of her, on Hostetter further back in the plane, leaning over a fold-out table close to the aircraft wall. She brought her eyes back to Sally and her face grew hot.

"I didn't do anything," Sally said, her tone even. After her first few steps away from Fiona, she had spread her feet to a steady, challenging stance. Her face held a quality of dangerous strength, like fresh-quarried stone, sharp at the edges. "I was told to tell you to sleep, to believe it was possible. So I did."

Fiona wrenched herself away from the car. Blood stormed in her ears. "You do *not* get into my head. *Never.* I've enough people-- And some of them aren't even people-- The point is--"

"I don't have super powers," Sally said. "I'm just a poor Jewish kid from Indianapolis. I wasn't altered by the US government to be an unstoppable fighting and spying machine."

"You just slipped me a psychic Mickey!"

"I just stood there and said the words." Sally frowned, looked away from Fiona, then brought her gaze back again. "You're a weapon. I'm just a tool. I do what I'm told and sometimes things work out."

Fiona stepped back toward the car. She reached clawed fingers into her hair and took two fistfuls tightly in hand. She wanted to rip out her hair. She wanted to rip out *something*, anyway. Hair, the glass from that sideview mirror, Sally's goddamned heart…

"Don't be such a baby," she heard, and realized it came from Hostetter. "She said she needed to do it and I backed her up. You needed sleep. You got some. Don't caterwauler, say thankee."

Fiona realized in that moment that Hostetter was right, and that she really was grateful. She'd suffered an initial shock, yes, but she felt stronger than she'd felt in days. The anger … that was Oz.

Oz lurked under the car. Oz crept, muscles tense as rappelling lines, toward Sally.

Fiona straightened, cocked her head toward the car, and slammed him down hard. "No!" she growled. "You will *not!*"

When the cat slunk away from his prey and Fiona drew her gaze back to Sally, the blonde looked nonplussed.

"Uh, will not what?"

"You will *never,* as long as you live, jump into my brain again. Your god or angel or figment or whatever, if he wants a piece of me, he can ask pretty-please or take a flying fuck off a high overpass. My head is *mine*, you understand that? Do you both understand that?" She drew her eyes from Sally to Hostetter. Her fingers twitched in anticipation that either of them would say "No."

"Umm, we understand," Sally said, abashed.

Fiona snapped her narrowed gaze to Hostetter. "You! Cowboy!"

"Alright, alright. I reckon I get the message."

"Good, goddammit." Fiona turned, took a few steps along the flank of the Malibu, then leaned one hand against its sleek, cool flank. "Now what in hell did I miss?"

"Chow," Hostetter called. "We got pizza and some of them hot dogs. And raisins."

"There's a strip mall a short walk away," Sally clarified. "I went on a run to Little Caesar's and a dollar store."

"You left the ship? We aren't five miles from Sanders!"

"Nobody's looking for a blonde chick. At least, not as hard as they're looking for a tall cowboy and a redhead with a cat."

"You needed sleep and we all need chow," Hostetter yelled. "We won't be much good otherwise. Come on back and get your share."

Fiona continued along the car until she came to Hostetter and his table. The old man leaned over a wrinkled spread of maps and photographs, stuff off of Google Earth. As far as Fiona could tell, all the images were of Sanders's new headquarters, where the files on Kudashova and the Drehd project were held. The papers were marked up in pencil, black Sharpie, and white fine-line marker.

Alongside the documents sprawled two pizza boxes, several empty hot dog wrappers, and two dogs still snug in their papers. Hostetter ignored the food. He bent over a shallow can that he just then twisted the pull top from. "Here," he said to Sally, handing her the can. "It probably won't fool him, but it's best you feed the little varmint. That way, he might not kill you in your sleep."

Sally took the can. Fiona lifted the pizza box lid and took a triangle of sausage, bread, and cheese from the half-empty container. It was still warm.

She bit it, chewed, and directed a raised eyebrow at Sally.

"We knew exactly when you'd wake up," the blonde said as she bent to place the can on the deck. "Come on, kitty. Kitty, kitty, kitty."

Fiona swallowed. "Take your hand away from that can or Kitty-kitty-kitty's gonna shred it to the bone. He's pissed at you, Blondie. You farted full-force on a predator's self-possession."

"It couldn't be helped." Sally rose, frowning. "We needed you rested and at your best. I didn't think it would affect the cat."

"Farted with beans and liver." Fiona tore into the pizza again. "Anybody think to score some Cokes?"

Hostetter, sifting through his pictures, nudged a Styrofoam cooler with his boot.

As Fiona dived for a Diet Coke, Oz dove into the can of cat food. He growled as he ate, and Fiona's nostrils and taste buds drowned in fetid Braunschweiger. That was as close as she characterized it, anyway. She didn't dare ask what meal Oz consumed.

She forced down the pizza as if swallowing roadkill.

"What's that shit?" she gasped at Hostetter, then took a great swig of sweetened carbonated water in the hope of drowning the liverwurst in her mind.

Hostetter glanced up from his work. He flagged a few sheets of images at Fiona. "Plans."

Fiona chewed. The sensation of sausage and two-day-old liver made her eyes water. "Plans for what?"

Hostetter laid a large-format printout before her. He smoothed its multiple wrinkles with the side of one hand. "This here's where the colonel put the files we want. We can see a way in, but it'll mean a heap o' property damage. Could be a lot of casualties, too, if we run into too many agents."

"How you planning to get to the files?"

"Accordin' to the bug, they're here." Hostetter tapped one finger against the image. "They got their vault in the middle of the building. Lots of walls between it and us. Smart boys, there. But they ain't expectin' a raid from the roof."

Fiona had thought of that. "They have cameras and motion sensors on the roof. You wouldn't be able to tear the tarpaper before they've a dozen agents with guns in your face."

"If we was climbin' up there to maybe cut through, yeah. But we're thinkin' somethin' a little more ornery."

Fiona took another swig of the Coke. Thank God, Oz had finished his meal. It would still be several minutes before the taste washed from her mouth. "Okay. A little, umm, more ornery?"

"We plan to blast a hole through the roof," Sally offered.

Fiona stared at her.

"With a missile or two," Hostetter elaborated. "The Voice here's got high explosive missiles on his areoplane. Shoot a couple in there, let down a rope and a net, tie up the boxes, lift 'em out faster'n you can sing Dixie."

"Uhh…" Fiona didn't know what to say. They watched her, so she clearly had to say something. "It's bold… Also suicidal."

Hostetter watched her without expression. "How'd'ya figure?"

"Well, a few people cutting through the roof would only attract the security for the building. A jet shooting missiles into the place will attract the attention of the whole damned post. A lot of guys with guns around there, all on edge since the headquarters got shot up. Is the Batplane here bullet proof?"

"Not accordin' to the Voice, but the ship'll be cloaked. Nobody'll know where the shot came from. By the time they suss it out, we'll be long gone."

"Besides," Sally said, "You'll have everyone's attention focused somewhere else."

"We'll do it durin' the meetin'," Hostetter added.

"The meeting. But we've no idea when that is."

"Make sure it's at night," the cowboy said. "Better for concealment."

Fiona thought about it. She didn't like their plan. It gave off a whiff of comic book heroics. Those sorts of things worked well on pulp paper, not so much in real life. Then again, the scheme had a simpleminded merit. Given a judicious helping of luck... "So, who came up with this Barnum & Bailey miracle? Batman didn't have a hand in it, did he?"

"Only so much as we asked for advice," Hostetter said.

"Hostetter and I worked out the bulk of it," Sally said.

Fiona gave her a skeptical look. "So you're a tactician now, Blondie? I thought you were just a poor Jewish kid from Indianapolis."

"I've been around the block."

"Hmm. So which of you two goes down to the vault? Batman's gotta fly the plane."

"I go," Sally said, and raised her chin. "All I do is tie up the package and ride the line down and up. Hostetter has a better handle on working the winch."

"Him?" Fiona jerked a thumb at Hostetter. "He's from the wild west. Electricity is magic to him."

"I'll be okay," Hostetter drawled.

"What if something goes wrong?" Fiona held Sally's gaze. "What if an agent opens the door and finds you in there trying to steal his shit?"

"There are ... contingencies," Sally said. She craned her neck to look forward, toward the cockpit. "Look, we welcome your expertise to finesse the plan, but it'll work. We're pretty sure. Besides, I can't be in danger." She turned back to Fiona and showed her a face-splitting, atomic smile. "I'm on a mission from God."

"You two are certifiable." Fiona leaned over the table to take a look at Hostetter's notes. "Let me see how you screwed this up."

But Sally intercepted her with a gentle but insistent hand to her shoulder. "Not just yet," she said. "You have another appointment."

Just then, Sally's raincoat warbled. She reached into one pocket and retrieved a cheap flip phone. "It's him," she said when she opened the shell. She handed the phone to Fiona.

"I don't get this," the Eglemann woman said. "These aren't the figures we agreed on at our last operational meeting. This whole section here is scratched out, and I've not vetted the insertion."

"Is there a problem, ma'am?" Nightmare asked, pushing as much un-concern as possible into the host's voice. There had better *not* be a problem. A problem could result in truncated plans, in a secondary scenario of ordinary mass murder. Nightmare didn't just want murder. Nightmare wanted terror.

Eglemann, juggling a tablet, three-ring binder, and the clipboard Nightmare had handed her, glowered at the figures scribbled in the margins and the circles and arrows highlighting affected sections of the operational plan. She flipped pages, a stylus between her teeth, read more, and flipped pages back. Technicians hurried around her, test firing consoles and arranging attenuators at the base of the machine. They intended soon to energize their device, to open a conduit to another world.

When Nightmare first realized their intention, it had felt at first threatened, then confused, then ecstatic. The humans made plans to open Nightmare's universe. They hoped to discover the secrets of their hidden enemy. But Nightmare had known they could do no such thing. Their geometry was wrong. They were lucky to make any connection at all, much less the one they intended. These people were incompetent at inter-universal travel.

Then Nightmare discovered why. It had walked its host into the Rodriguez woman's office, had read the white board turned black with calculations. A few of those equations had been incorrect. They weren't anymore.

"I don't know," Eglemann muttered. "She *is* the genius, after all. And these changes won't require more than slight adjustments to the transference platform geometry and the energy attenuators. I guess we can make it work."

"Would you like to verify with Doctor Rodriguez? She's quite busy at the nuclear reactor station right now, but I could message her and set up a meeting…" At which to kill the both of them after the satisfaction of torture.

"Hmm? Oh, no, that isn't necessary. Why do you figure…"

"Security, ma'am." But the Eglemann human didn't care about security. She was sure of her own judgment above that of a uniformed authority.

The engineer made a burbling sound between her lips. "Security my ass. Nobody else on this planet could have made these changes. Yep, as good as fingerprints. Doctor Rodriguez has the super-genius math all tied up around here."

"In that case, ma'am, I'll need you to sign receipt of materials here, here, and … here."

Nightmare collected the receipt, suffered Eglemann's friendly smile, and marched from the chamber. Part of the monster had ached for the engineer to balk. If she had questioned the document annotations, Nightmare's scheme would have lain bare. A great orgy of death would have followed, which might have gone a long way toward raising the beast from its funk of failure. But that would have been self-serving. Better that the humans succeed, or at least perceive success on their part. Then they would re-open the conduit. Nightmare could unite with its greater, more powerful presence on the other side. With the change of a few numbers and a nudge toward careless vanity, it had cleared the way for untold power to flood the human world.

To flood, and destroy.

Suddenly, Hostetter didn't matter all that much, though Nightmare yearned to see him burn with his world.

Perhaps that could yet be arranged.

Sanders waited in ACUs, his arms crossed tightly over his chest. He stood within the black, mangled wreck of an exploded conference room. Most of the rubbish had been pitched out the gaping hole of what once had been floor-to-ceiling windows. The floor stood empty but for a few plastic and aluminum crumbs of the wreckage.

And the one shrouded object centered on the floor. Large as a trash can on a city street corner, silent, and unassuming except for its singular presence, the device waited as the colonel did, but more anonymously beneath its heavy, black, muslin cover. Sanders hoped obviousness would disguise it, that Street, alert for deception, would not suspect the trap flagged for her attention. He hoped, but if she couldn't be fooled, he had plenty of distractions.

The colonel stood facing the long hole to the outside world that had once been the conference room's window. Kudashova had entered there, blasting into a meeting between the Director, National Security and his various department heads. The space was thirty feet wide and twenty feet deep, presenting a suitable space for either negotiation or combat. Its twenty-eighth story location prevented much in the way of options. Both he and Street would be forced to follow through on their meeting. Once engaged, neither could go anywhere else with ease.

"Final check," Sanders said into his comms pickup. "Sound off by numbers."

"Team Alpha, ready."

"Team Bravo, ready.

"Team Charlie, ready."

"Childress. Ready as I'll ever be."

Sanders sighed at that. Well, the man was still dependable. He would do fine from across the way at his sniper's perch.

Three teams and Childress. Sanders wished he had brought more, but he wanted this in the family, so he had brought nearly every agent within his reach but left the purely military out of the loop. He wondered if that had been smart. Sunset diminished into the even, undistinguished gray before nightfall, the most difficult hour for Street and snipers alike to see. But when full dark finally descended on the land, Street's night vision would outshine any starlight scope or thermal optics. The takedown had to be fast.

He glanced at his watch. One minute to time. She was military. She was professional. She would not be late. If anything, she had arrived already. She'd been scoping out the setup, looking for traps. Looking for traps from other professionals who knew how to hide their presence.

When he put away his watch, there she was. A shadowed manta form blocked half the window opening and Fiona Street dropped to the floor as nimbly as, well, a cat. She straightened, hands relaxed at her flanks, dressed in what looked like seventies-era fatigues and combat boots. They were the airy, tentlike fatigues of the Vietnam war, the blouse loose, not tucked in.

Several weapons could wait beneath that shirt.

"I'm unarmed," she said, as if reading his mind.

"I'm not," Sanders said, then spoke into his sub-vocal comms. "Come on in. Show her the money."

Black-garbed, armored agents swarmed into the room, spreading out left and right along the interior wall. Each held a squad assault weapon trained on Street, a deadly enough automatic rifle but supported by pistols in hip holsters and bayonets in hip sheaths. Street reacted not at all. She watched Sanders and Sanders watched her.

"So," he said when the point had been made, "what's with the historical costuming?"

"Army surplus store. I didn't want to meet you in smelly scrubs and I doubted you'd let me into my house." She spread her hands, slowly, without threat, and dropped them back to her side. "Best I could do on short notice."

"Hmm. I guess it would be pointless to say you violate the uniform of the day."

"I think it would be a side issue, yes, sir."

Sanders squinted. He hadn't seen the cat jump from her. Little bastard must have dropped unseen. It could be anywhere. It could still be on the ship hovering there in the window, but Sanders doubted that. Tactically inefficient.

"Where's your little friend?" he asked.

"He's around. Don't worry, sir. I've got him under control."

"Well, now, major, that's the $64,000 question, isn't it?"

"Actually, sir, no. I didn't come here to argue my control over Oz. That should be apparent."

"Well, hate to ruin your day, but that's hardly the case. But, please, go ahead. This is your conference. Do speak." He waved an encouraging hand at her.

"She's too far in," he heard through his pickup. Childress. "Herd her back toward the window."

"Gladly," Street was saying. She pointed in a wide arc at all the troops. "But I said I was unarmed. You said we could talk. Those guns are saying something else."

"Those guns are keeping you honest."

"Those guns are making me nervous."

"If those guns go away, you have every advantage, major. I know your capabilities."

"You also know that I keep my word. I won't do anything if you don't. I came here to talk."

Well, maybe she had or maybe she hadn't. But lowering the guns might help with Childress's problem…

"Colonel, they're useless anyway. I came in the Voice of the City's magic one-man plane, the one that can stop bullets in mid-flight."

Sanders drummed his fingers against his sleeve.

"Or I could use the other function, the one that explodes powder in the rounds."

"You don't have to threaten. That won't get us off to a good start." Sanders nodded first left, then right. "Sling arms."

Each man relinquished his aim on the major, safed his weapon, and slung it from one shoulder. The gesture was made, but the weapons were readily available.

"If you like," Sanders said, "you could retreat without harm. It would be tactically problematic, placing you with your back to a precipice, but you've got your little ship there, so what do you care."

"Thank you, sir. I appreciate the consideration." And she backed slowly toward the opening in the wall.

"Acquired," Sanders heard through his pickup.

"Now. There was something you wanted to say." Sanders, as casually as he could, eased around to his right. Street, as expected, reacted by moving to *her* right, keeping the distance between them. This, Sanders estimated, would make things easier for the shooter, moving her more solidly into his field of vision.

"We've had some … disagreements lately," Street began.

"Belay the Oprah monologue, major. I'm a busy man."

"There's more going on than you realize, sir."

"Goodknight mentioned some harebrained business about imminent invasion from another world."

"Yes, sir. Kudashova's caught up in it. Hostetter is. The Lawrence-Livermore facility. An alien has crossed from its world to ours and it doesn't have our interests at heart."

They crossed back and forth on the floor, Sanders herding her to the far left of the former window, her edging back to stay close to her ship. It was a dance and both of them knew it. Hopefully, only Sanders understood the reasoning behind the steps. "Go on," he said. "I think you're probably delusional, as does your doctor--" He halted a moment while Street snorted, then wrinkled her nose as if she smelled something foul. "--but I promised you a hearing. Convince me."

Street made her attempt.

Shooter and spotter huddled close. The Marine sniper hunched in a chair, his M40 special purpose rifle resting with its stock atop a foam rubber pad the crew had brought for that purpose. The sharpshooter leaned against a desk they had dragged to the window, the window they'd punched out hours ago with the colonel's okay. The spotter balanced slightly above and to the side of his teammate, squinting through his scope. He also wore a radio headset across his softcap.

"She's moving out of sight again," the spotter whispered to Childress. "Get them to move her back right."

Childress knew by then that "get her right" for the shooters meant "get her left" for the colonel. He whispered that into the mic arm poised before his mouth.

"I have scope on the secondary target," the sniper said. The cat. "You want us to track?"

"Forget the secondary," Childress said. Kill the primary, the secondary dies by default. That, or it thrashes about on the floor like its guts were ripped from its body. What a fucked up situation. "Primary's a bigger target."

"At this short range, they're both a gimme," the sniper sent back.

"Forget the secondary."

"Wilco."

Childress thought for a moment. "On second thought, don't track the secondary, but give me its position."

"Far edge of the floor, right where the window opens into space." The shooter drew in and released a mighty breath. "If I didn't know any better, I'd say it was looking at us."

Yeah, right. Over 250 meters? Through twilight? Not a chance. Right?

Wrong. Oz caught a faint glint of light off the forward lens of the sniper scope. Having caught it, he stared.

"So you're telling me," Sanders said, "that a seventy-five-year-old failed science experiment shot down in WW II, which fell into the Pacific near the Solomons into thousands of feet of water, somehow, rather than being destroyed when its plane exploded, rather than being smashed on impact with the sea, rather than being crushed in the depths of the ocean..." He paused and took a theatrical breath that he almost certainly needed. "You're telling me that this device miraculously turned itself on and has been radiating disturbing dream frequencies over the world without a viable power source. And this device has intensified the natural paranoia of human beings and projected that paranoia into another universe, which thinks we're attacking it with our nightmares. Is that about the gist of it, major?"

Okay, when he put it that way... "Yes, sir. As far as I can tell. I won't know for sure without looking at the papers."

"Which you asked Sergeant Goodknight to kindly fetch for you."

"Umm, yes, sir." Dammit. He wasn't buying in. But he had to. Fiona didn't relish going against the government to stop Kudashova's monster. She needed to convince him, for her sake as well as the hunt-- er, mission. But how could she do that with Oz pestering her about window reflections? He picked that moment of all others to suddenly notice windows?

"You put me in a difficult situation, major. Your doctor suspects you're suffering a cascading mental collapse. The same happened to every other person saddled with that implant of yours. You're spouting astounding stories for which you have no evidence. At the same time, you try to subvert NSA and CIA personnel. Yes, we know about Mister Short. We've got him under surveillance at the Lawrence-Livermore facility. Sewer rat like that, he's up to something. For you. You do know he bribed the requisite senators to activate the machine?"

"Yes, sir. We need the machine to send the monster back where it came from. We figure the means to do that is hidden in the Drehd files. Hopefully, Doctor Rodriguez and Chief Engineer Eglemann can get the machine working by the time we find what we need."

"I'm smelling a lot of 'if' in that plan. Also, a strong whiff of you're somewhat out of the loop."

"Sir?"

"Yes. The machine is already running. They solved the math earlier today, thanks to, of all people, the Russian agent Kudashova."

"Kudashova? She's in California?" But, of course she was. She -- it -- sought Hostetter. Having lost him, it would attempt to reacquire. Sinfonee was the obvious roost from which to await its prey.

"Yes. We've got her under surveillance, too. We might not have let her clumsy trick with the math go through, but it checks according to Eglemann. So we've got her, Short, and you, major. This whole thing's about wrapped up, except for your other three conspirators. But, we'll find them. It would be good to recall who you worked for..."

Worked. Past tense. Time to manage an exit.

At that moment, the night lit up. Some of the agents flinched. Sanders barely flicked his eyes in the direction of the flare. Then the boom hit, fluttering the black cover on Sanders's mysterious whatever-it-was.

"And now," he crowed, raising his hands like a preacher after sinners, "I needn't even ask where your co-conspirators are!"

"Shit!" The sniper jerked his eye from the scope.

"Shake it off, man!" the spotter snapped. "Blink it out!"

"Shit, that was bright. Went right up the glass, man!"

"We gotta scrub the mission?"

Childress stepped in to squash that before it ran. "There is no scrubbin' this mission."

"I can't see, man!"

"Blink it off, son, but get the fuck back on that gun!"

"Shit!"

Sally hardly breathed during her near-freefall descent. She didn't fear dropping to her death, not with the winch whining and the seat harness securing her to the line, but smacking the edge of the roof's ragged hole looped through her mind in high definition. She didn't really think *that* would happen, either. She trusted her weird Batmanesque benefactor and her angels hadn't warned her to duck.

She made the floor of the vault so quickly she almost landed on her ass. "I'm in!" she called over her link once her feet stopped skittering for purchase. Then she disconnected the carabiner holding her to the line and spread out the jouncing net with her shoes.

"Hostetter, pay out some slack." That helped. At least the net stopped jerking like a live thing.

It took only an instant to locate the Drehd files. The vault was small, not much bigger than a walk-in closet. Maybe ten feet by eight, three walls lined with heavy metal shelves, the fourth empty except for the ordinary steel-faced door. The Drehd files were a cardboard box on the floor, pushed over against one of the shelving units like the red-headed step-cousin from the wrong side of the tracks. Sally stooped at the box, but hesitated before picking it up.

First things first. She reached into a pouch at her waist (Batman had granted her a utility belt!) and drew out the four skinny, cigar-like cylinders the Voice had pressed upon her. She distributed them as instructed, pressing buttons hidden in the black tubes and balancing the devices on end in an arc clear of the door's swing area.

A steadying tripod folded out at the bottom of each and a green light winked at its cap.

Okay, so that's James Bond.

That chore completed, Sally grabbed the box and schlepped it onto the center of the net.

"Almost there," she whispered, then removed the work gloves that had protected her hands from the thin winch line. She read the serial number written on her palm in indelible ink. "Now for the drive."

"Better hurry up," came Hostetter's tinny voice.

Sirens. Screeching tires. Naturally, everybody in the neighborhood knew about the explosion. They just couldn't know what had caused it. Fantastic that a jet hovered above a building surrounded by police and nobody knew it was there.

Sally took a penlight from her Batgirl belt and shone it against the plastic and metal bricks laid out in rows on the shelves. These were the secure hard drives Fiona had described. She needed only one, the one showing the serial number written on her hand. First one, the serial number failed to match. Second, no match, third, no match.

Yelling beyond the door. People running up and down the hall outside. They were closing in on the source of the blast.

Sally directed the light to the next hard drive. Then she looked back toward the door, then to the net. "Hostetter, is there a weight limit on that winch rig?" Clamping the penlight between her teeth, she shoveled hard drives into her arms.

"And you see nothing wrong in this?" The colonel gestured out the window in the direction of the explosion. Why wasn't he more upset? "You compound several felonies with yet another. This time stealing classified material."

There wasn't much she could say. He'd already written her off and every word he spoke was true. "Sorry, sir."

"Well, then," Sanders said with a heavy sigh. "I suppose there is nothing more to be said."

Oz hissed. He dived into the dark shadows at the edge of the room.

Fiona ducked. She didn't know why.

Something punched into the wall at the far end of the room. Thunder followed the impact almost immediately. The agents along the wall scattered from the impact area.

"Jesus!" Fiona cried. Even as the name left her mouth, she had done the analysis, had done the geometry, and had plugged it into Oz's observations. She flung herself sideways, away from the wall with the crater.

Another boom, and the floor just beyond where she had crouched threw tile and concrete across the room.

"Motherfucker!" Fiona glared at the colonel, who still stood unconcerned near his cloth-covered whatever-it-was. "You planned to shoot me all along! God *damn* you!"

"It's duty, major. You'd do the same."

"God dammit!"

The agents scrambled to unsling their rifles. Some of them reached for pistols. They wouldn't do any good. The jet hovering outside the building broadcast its electro-magnetic bullet-stopping whatiz. But there were a dozen agents and one of her. Fiona dove a hand into the cargo pocket of her fatigues and yanked out the detonator Batman had given her. She pressed the plunger at the top with her thumb.

Every gun in the room exploded, the powder within its ammo vibrating to critical and cooking off with dramatic effect. Rifles went off in the faces of their owners, sending them down screaming. More rifles blasted metal, plastic, and fiberglass into the armored torsos of their carriers, mostly throwing dazed agents against walls. But every pistol cooked off as well, each one strapped to a man's hip. All the agents went down with leg or pelvic injuries. Only Sanders stood. He spoke, but not to Fiona.

"Alpha, Bravo, converge." He flicked his own detonator into one palm. He must have been hiding it up his sleeve. "Two can play that, major. As I said, I know your--"

Oz darted out of the shadows and ran up the colonel's ACUs. Yeowling like a lunatic, he struck at Sanders's neck and face. The detonator dropped, clattering on the floor.

While Oz raked the colonel, Fiona rushed the nearest downed agent. She kicked him across the face for safety, then snatched the bayonet from his sheath. Then, with no clear thought why she did so, she turned her attention on her boss.

Oz sprang away as Fiona charged in. She hammered Sanders's throat with a stiffened forearm, then stretched a leg behind his staggering form to send him heavily onto his back.

Fiona forced a knee onto his chest. She tried to pound his face with the handle end of her captured bayonet, but Sanders deflected every blow and heaved her off so that she rolled onto her side.

They lay side by side, punching, kicking, blocking blows, then Sanders snatched a combat knife from his boot.

Sally dumped a load of hard drives into the net.

"What's takin' so long?" Hostetter asked over the feed.

"Don't bother me. I'm working," she mouthed around the penlight. She had another load of drives in her arms when she heard the latch rattling on the door. "The jig is up," she said. "They're coming."

"Get outta there. Right now."

"One more load."

"One more load of what?"

"What the fuck? You missed *twice*?" Childress couldn't believe it. These guys were supposed to be experts.

"I don't get it," the sniper said, readjusting after chambering a new round.

"It's like she was psychic," the spotter added, then turned a suspicious squint to Childress. "There something you didn't tell us, sir?"

"Fuck it! Re-engage!" Childress snatched his pistol from its holster and moved toward the office door.

"She's alerted to us. Unlikely she'll allow a subsequent acquisition," the spotter complained.

"Re-fucking-engage! She shows her face, you drill it! *Comprendo?*"

"Affirmative," the sniper said.

Childress stormed through the office door, up the hall to the exit stairs, and down the stairs for the outside. All the way, he cussed like a handcuffed gangbanger on Saturday night.

The door flew open, crashing against a shelving unit. A man stood silhouetted in the doorway, two more behind him. Sally froze, half turned to dump her armload of drives into the net. She grimaced around her penlight.

"Heh, heh. Hi, guys."

The lights on the cylinders she'd placed around the doorway went from green to red. A volley of snapping sounds as the agents reached for weapons. Blazing, jagged lines of light flew from the cylinders on the floor, hitting the men in their faces, their chests, their legs.

The men stiffened, jittered, then fell to the floor like dead weights.

Two more men entered the frame of the door. Another burst of lightning. Those men joined their comrades.

Sally blinked. She waited for more agents, but none arrived. After a few seconds, she shrugged, then relieved herself of the drives and started closing the net.

Fiona barely avoided a wide, downward swing of the colonel's knife. She danced to her feet, her own blade gripped close to her ribs, point aimed at Sanders. She held her left arm cocked forward to block his weapon if it came to that.

The colonel, too, had regained his feet. His stance mirrored hers. Each dodged sideways to gain a flank advantage on the other. Great. LTC Allen Sanders, who hadn't known action in years, was still up on his knife fighting technique. What else could go wrong?

An instant's warning from Oz was all she got. Fiona jerked far back at the waist, almost losing her footing. Something whipped past her, almost skimming the protective vest she wore beneath her fatigue blouse. The flying object clattered across the floor. Another God damned bayonet.

So, she not only fought the colonel, but all the agents sprawled bleeding on the floor.

Sanders advanced with a lightning forward slash, following that with a reverse thrust that snagged the billowing material of Fiona's blouse. She sidestepped, then countered with a forward thrust to back him off. She knew she fought at a disadvantage, quadrascopic sight be damned. The colonel wanted to kill her, but she didn't share his commitment. She had to find an exit, but she didn't know how with that sniper at the window.

Thrust, slash, this time at her neck. A hot wetness welled there. He had broken the skin, or worse. Fiona could drop him cold, but dead. She didn't want that. He had done nothing wrong. She could surrender. Would that make a difference? Would he simply put her on her knees, wrists handcuffed at her back, then draw the knife deeply across her neck? Then no one would answer the threat from Kudashova's monster.

Growling, she thrust, then slashed up and down at opposing diagonals, rewarded with a hiss of breath as the colonel took a cut on his forearm. But he didn't retreat. He came on, plunging his blade at her midsection with the power and speed of a human pile driver.

What was he doing? His attack was reckless. It left him open. She could have driven her blade home more than once.

Then she realized his thinking. He doubted her intent to fully commit and had pressed her toward the window. But not for the sniper. He withdrew before setting her up for the bullet, scooping something off the floor with his guard hand.

The detonator.

"What is that?" Fiona asked as she circled away from exposure to the sniper.

"Overkill," Sanders said between heavy, taxed breaths. He held up the device and pressed its trigger.

A white light stabbed from within Fiona's brain. It swept over her, blinded her, and brought her down.

Chapter Eighteen

Sally's light went out. She found herself in almost total darkness, her surroundings lit only by thin starlight from the hole above. That seemed odd. She turned toward where the door had been, the door she couldn't see anymore. All the lights out there were dead, too.

"Hey, Hostetter, something's not quite--" She glanced up through the hole to the hovering bulk of the jet. She couldn't see Hostetter's face looking down. Where had he gone? Why had-- "Oh, crap! Hostetter, I can see you. I can *see* the *ship*!"

"EMP DETECTED. COMPENSATING."

The calm female voice spoke over a honking klaxon as the lights in the jet went from white, to off, to stuttering, to red. Hostetter didn't know what to do. He couldn't leave Miss Sally but he couldn't see the Voice past the crowding bulk of the car. What was going on? Why had the ship suddenly lost its grace in flight? What in tarnation was an EMP?

He held onto an overhead stanchion of the precariously heaving ship and tried to keep his feet from going airborne. For the latest uncountable time, he was glad of the safety line cinched to his waist. "Voice!" he yelled. "What the hell--?"

He jerked his attention to something else, sparks against the overhead, a junction box cover shattering. Something red hot creased his wrist. "Sweet baby Jesus! Ricochets! Some varmint's shootin' at us!"

He twisted in place and peered through the open hatch. Nothing to see but air and rooftop. The ship rotated, then reversed its turn, back and forth over a forty-degree turn. She was unstable. They were gonna crash.

God damned aeroplanes! If the good Lord had wanted man to--

A bullet whanged the overhead between his hands.

"By Jiminy, that's enough!" He released his hold, immediately tumbled onto his side, and grabbed the metal deck grating to keep from rolling out of the ship. Yes, the safety would prevent a fall, but he didn't relish hanging like a piñata for any and sundry to take pot shots at. Ensuring he maintained a solid grip on the floor, he lurched to a locker a few feet away. Prone on the metal grating, he forced the locker door open with his boot. Out clattered gear he cared nothing about, but he snagged his stick before it flew past him and under the car.

Grasping the stick close to his chest, he took a deep breath, waited for the inevitable tilt of the deck, and let go of the grating. He slid across the deck, banging a thigh on the rear car tire, then braced his boots and flung his free arm out wildly for a handhold.

He halted his skate just before launching off the ramp and into space. "Lordy!" he cried. "Thankee, Jesus!" Then he scuttled on his belly to peek over the edge of the ramp.

The ship had steadied in the moments of his slide, but Hostetter wasn't dumb enough to trust a metal bird that shouldn't fly. He held tight and stayed low.

Soldiers in one of those auto-mobiles, what they called a Hummer. They fired rifles up at the jet. One of them hunched over the Hummer's radio.

Groaning, Hostetter appraised his surroundings. He'd have to stand up. He'd have to stand up at the edge of a deadly fall.

But if he didn't, they'd continue to fire on the ship, maybe bring up bigger, deadlier weapons.

He told himself the safety line would protect him. It wouldn't give him balance nor anchor him to the deck, but it would keep him from plummeting to his death. He told himself that, but his mind wouldn't buy that pig in a poke. His grip tightened on the floor grating.

But Miss Sally was down there. The government probably had men in the building, headed for the vault. She'd be taken or she'd be shot, and what would that say about a cowboy's fear of flying?

So, with one great push and a defiant snarl, Hostetter lumbered to his feet, staggered to the winch secured to the end of the ramp, and held onto it for dear life. Wind blew his hair about. He had no idea where his hat had gone. His jacket billowed about him.

He spied the vehicle below and turned his stick so that the base hovered close to the areoplane ceiling. Then he aimed the other end by sight and slapped the base against an overhead metal box.

A blast of orange energy projected from the stick like hellfire. The shot cratered the street in front of the Hummer. That got the soldiers' attention. Hostetter aimed and slapped the stick again. This time, he cratered the street to one side of the vehicle.

The men got the message. They ran like hell.

Hostetter exploded the vehicle like a bomb.

That should keep them busy.

With a grunt, he heaved the stick as far forward into the ship as he could manage. He hoped it wouldn't just bounce off something and clatter back the way it had come, sailing out through the wide opening. It didn't. It struck the top of the car and tumbled down the front of the vehicle, probably hitting the Voice in the head.

Couldn't worry about that, though. "Miss Sally! You okay?"

No answer.

"Miss Sally. You ready to come back aboard?" He leaned past the edge of the ramp, gripping the winch so hard it hurt. The breach in the building's roof showed a jagged outline, blackness beyond. Hostetter could not see into the vault.

More men skulked on the ground, using the building as cover. "Miss Sally, we need to go now."

A green star winked in the vault, its light building from a point to an even blaze. The chemical wand the Voice had given the girl before she rappelled from the ship. In case communications went out. Green meant ready, good to go.

"Hold tight." Hostetter unlocked the winch and threw the switch to reverse the line and bring Miss Sally up.

Nothing happened.

He cranked back the switch and threw it again.

Nothing.

"Carnsarn it!"

Hostetter, forgetting his fear of crashing aircraft, turned and hurried forward. He braked at the limit of his safety line, half way up the length of the car. "Voice! The winch ain't workin'! I can't get Miss Sally back up!"

The Voice of the City reacted immediately, seeming to levitate out of the pilot's station. Both men banged back along the deck, one on each side of the car. Hostetter hesitated short of the ramp, but the big man in black rushed right to the edge. He hung his head out into the dark, staring down for an instant. He wore no safety line.

He retreated just as quickly, stopping for a moment to grasp Hostetter's arm. "Tell her to hold on tight," he said, and continued back to the cockpit.

"Alrighty," Hostetter said. Licking dry lips, he crept back toward the winch, ensuring a solid anchor at every step he managed. "How'm I supposed to do that?"

Hostetter had sunk to his knees, holding tightly to the winch, by the time he reached the edge of the ramp and looked down toward the hole in the roof. Just as he leaned over the edge, the ship's engines screamed, the deck jumped, and both building and earth dropped away.

Sally had been standing atop the netted box and clattering hard drives, just as the Voice had instructed her. She glanced toward the door, wide open and piled with bodies, then up toward the ship again. "Guys? You can take me up now. It doesn't have to be pretty…"

It wasn't. A sudden tug, and the cable to which she clung stretched to the stiffness of a steel bar. Her stomach buried itself in her pelvis. The chemical light flew from her hand and she collapsed onto her ass on the cargo, her legs spread to either side of the winch line. Then wind pressed down on her, whipping her hair and causing her eyes to water. The building dropped away. Up she flew, shot from a cannon, struggling to catch a breath in the downward pressing wind of flight. She clung to the winch cable, terrified. She caught a momentary glimpse of men below, their faces turned upwards, their mouths dark circles. Then the ground arced beneath her, dead streets sliding past her feet with the recklessness of abandon.

Even so, she still gained altitude. When she realized she might be a hundred, then two hundred feet above the post, she gripped the cable tighter and closed her eyes. All that kept her from freefalling death was the carabiner fastened between the winch line and her seat harness. Sally had never climbed a mountain, skydived, or even zip-lined. She thought she might piss her pants, and she didn't have a change of clothes.

A hitch in her throat that might have been a laugh in calmer circumstances. What a thought, that she didn't have a change.

She forced her eyes back open, peered around, and gaped.

No light shone for miles. A scourge of black ink had fallen over Ft. Meade. That empty landscape slid beneath her, ominous in its inexplicability, then the ground rushed up to her, first the black canopies of trees, then the night blue expanse of a grassy meadow. "I don't wanna crash, I don't wanna crash, I don't wanna *crash*!"

Maybe ten feet from the grass, her descent halted. She and her cargo bobbed, then lowered gently onto the ground. Sally fell slowly down the heap of hard drives, landing on her back in the grass. Wind whipped her from the plane's downward thrusting fanjets.

After a moment of realizing she wasn't dead, she also realized she had to do something or the jet would hover above her forever. Trembling muscles brought her to her knees beside the netted cargo. She worked the carabiner securing her to the cable, released the rope, and rolled away from the hard drives and the box. For a while, she managed nothing else beyond an uncontrolled shudder from spilling adrenalin. She forced her breathing to something approaching normal, then waited for her heart to realize it could not, in fact, escape through her chest.

When she felt human, or an approximation of it, she rose shakily onto one elbow.

The jet had sidled off to one side, as far as the length of paid-out cable allowed. It settled primly to the fluttering grass. Hostetter bounded from the plane as soon as it touched ground. He was over to Sally in seconds, cradling her, then helping her to her feet.

"You all right?" he asked, running his hands over her to check for broken limbs. Sally found that funny. The conservative gentleman cowboy who wouldn't picnic with a girl without a chaperone, and he pawed her like a gangbanger boyfriend on a date.

She realized he needed her to answer. She licked her lips, opened her mouth, and couldn't remember the question. "Hi. Cowboy. I went for a ride."

Hostetter sputtered through his moustache. "Let's get you to the ship. Maybe the walk'll shake some sense in you."

He half-guided her, half-dragged her to the plane. When they got there, he lowered her to the ramp and jogged back for the contents of the net. A shadow fell across Sally and she looked up to find the mountainous form of the Voice of the City. He gripped a set of bolt cutters the size of Arkansas.

"What went wrong?" she asked.

"EMP. Electro-magnetic pulse. It blew out every electronic circuit within its reach."

"Long reach. I saw from where I was swinging."

"Sorry about that."

"No prob. I see your jet didn't go down. So maybe it runs on fairy dust?"

"It's hardened against EMP."

"But not the winch."

"It's from ACE Hardware."

"Bought it on clearance, eh?"

"Special for this mission."

Hostetter clambered up the ramp with a cardboard box in his arms. He dropped it behind the car and jogged back out to the netting.

The Voice went to one knee by the winch and used the bolt cutters to sever the cable. "If you're recovered, you should help the marshal with the rest of the cargo. We must leave. Immediately."

"What's the rush, I mean, besides guys wanting to shoot at us?" Sally got experimentally to her feet.

"The EMP. It could not bring us down because the ship is hardened."

"You said that."

"The satellite ship carrying Major Street is not so heavily protected."

That took a moment to sink in. "Holy crap! You mean she's out there crashed somewhere?"

"Or she no longer has its support. Either way, it's trouble for her."

Sally barely heard the last of his words. She ran for the hard drives they'd risked so much to steal.

Oz yeowled like the tortured dead. He staggered along the baseboard of some hallway, sometimes falling flat on the carpet and panting before he rose again. He seemed to have no direction, just a solemnly weighty need to move, to escape, but from what, who could tell? He gave off an impression of defeat, but not the simple defeat of the beaten. He radiated the stink of the beaten *down*. Oz, in his manner, his aimless stumble, and the forlorn timbre of his cries, told the world, if it cared to listen, of abuse, of molestation, of burning alive.

He apparently saw nothing of the physical world through which he dragged. He certainly failed to notice the man, who stooped and lifted him by the scruff of his neck as easily as snaring a couch pillow.

"Well. I've seen you in better shape," the man said, and tucked the cat into the crook of his arm.

Oz lamented with such sorrow it might have driven killers to tears.

The man showed no reaction at all.

Childress had almost crossed the massive NSA welcome center to OPS2B before the lights went out. All the lights, even the emergency power that lit the exit signs. Though two-story windows fronted the building, he could hardly see a thing. The penlight he took from his suit jacket pocket proved as useless as a dowel rod. His phone proved dead, so he couldn't reach its flashlight function. What the hell had happened?

He jumped at a sudden rending crash that thundered through the building. A portion of the ceiling caved in, pouring black debris into the cavernous space. Childress was nowhere near the collapse. He didn't even taste dust on his lips.

Still, he approached the scene. What else could he do? He had no idea what had brought about the mess, but someone could be in there. Someone could be hurt. So he inched forward with uncharacteristic caution, afraid at every moment that he could fall through a pit opened in the floor, get brained by a chunk of falling debris, or suffer any number of other tragedies reserved for selfless dumbasses.

For Childress was selfless, a real hero type. And Childress was a dumbass of highest dumbassery credentials. Why else would he have shown up for work on that day of all days? Should've called in sick.

He halted his advance. Did he hear someone talking? He couldn't make it out, but it came from the center of the ragged field of destroyed ceiling.

Screwing up his face to focus his hearing, he oriented on the noise and stumbled after it.

Several times he almost fell. Several times his thin-soled dress shoes lowered onto something jagged. Each time, he repositioned his footfalls, continuing toward the sound with awkward lurches. He detected a jittering red light when almost to the source of the voice, and it definitely was a voice. He could make out the words without effort.

"Primary system bus non-op," he heard. The voice was female with a soft British accent. "Shunting to secondary system. Secondary system at thirty percent. Parallel routing through battery conduit bus. Testing. Testing."

What the hell?

He had climbed on top of the pile by then. He took a moment to comprehend what he found. The thick darkness, the dust in his eyes, and the black coloration of the object campaigned to confound his senses. The debris scattered across the thing broke up its lines, confusing him even further. But Childress suspected what lay before him -- what he partially stood on.

It was the jet Major Street had arrived in, the Manta craft of the Black Batman.

Get *up*, Fiona scolded herself. Get the fuck up, for heaven's sake.

"I didn't want to do that," she heard from somewhere a few feet away. "Far too invasive a response. Right now, half the post is electronically dead, and part of the town outside the gates. Traffic on the freeways has come to a screeching halt." Fiona shook her head. She tried to remember where her arms and legs were. "We had to quietly divert air traffic before we got permission to deploy the device," that voice went on. Sanders. The voice belonged to Sanders, also the soft press of boots on concrete. "But it was worth it. I wasn't about to allow yet another of your spectacular and bloody-minded hair-raising escapes."

Fiona tried to do something, to find her limbs and order them to action. But every thought came trip-wired with white flares in her head. Her vision consisted of purple and yellow dots. Her sense of smell had become scorched pennies and an eye-watering stink of overripe strawberries. What the hell had he done to her?

She felt a presence next to her, the heat of breathing on her cheek. "This was my bet for a, well, dirty medical procedure. You had your chance at a school solution job, but you gave that up when you went rogue. But this EMP, I imagine it did the job. Your implant was never hardened against such an attack. Prototype shortcoming, and all that."

She could see him then, sort of ... a little. She could see herself. She balanced on all fours, her arms flinching as if fed electric shocks. "You've been fixed, major. There's nothing left but the *coup de gras.*"

He meant to kill her. He meant to do it himself. Come on, come on, you stupid, dipshit redhead. Get your fucking ass in gear!

She tried to raise her head. It lolled and she drooled. Men surrounded her. Others tended to wounded. The colonel squatted next to her. He gripped his combat knife, reverse hold.

The better to drill it into her brain.

"I'm sorry it came to this," he said, and she knew he meant it. "I had high hopes for you."

Fiona burst to one side, toward the window, she hoped. She collided with bodies, couldn't force past them.

"Hold her, dammit. I've had enough--"

Her fingers fell on somebody's weapon. Muscle memory kicked in. She jerked the trigger.

A long burst of automatic fire sprayed her with drywall dust and concrete shards. The bodies jerked away. She shambled ... somewhere. She felt a breeze against her arms. Her face felt numb. Her head ached so *much.*

"She's gonna jump!"

Yes. Into the Baby Manta. It was programmed to catch her. She didn't need to see it. She just needed to jump, to fall. Anyone could fall.

She felt weightless, air rushing about her. Her vision cleared in that instant, or rather her brain's capacity to interpret what she saw, what she heard, what she felt.

She fell. She would smash into concrete in less than fifteen stories. And the Manta was nowhere around.

"Test positive. Download from host accepted. Stand clear of airframe."

The structure under Childress vibrated. A whine rose to a scream. "Shit!" He leaped aside into the dark.

"Goodbye." The ship lumbered upward, throwing off cement blocks, mangled rebar, and dust.

Childress landed against jutting sheets of soundboard. At least he thought it was soundboard, because it broke under his weight and didn't stab him through. He threw his arms over his head to ward off anything heavy headed for it.

The jet disappeared through the hole it had made in the ceiling. It wobbled like a drunk, but a drunk on a mission.

"Acquired!" the sniper yelled.

"She's toast, man. Let it go."

"I got it!"

Not a classic shot. He had to follow the falling target with his sights, rising up from his chair to do so. Unsteady. The kind of mission he would normally abort. But he wasn't behind enemy lines on this one. There was no threat of retaliation if he missed. And, dammit, she'd made him miss twice.

He took the shot.

"Hoo-rah! And the quarterback is sacked!"

The Manta met her three stories above the ground, one floor above the shattered roof of the welcome center. As programmed, it read her attitude and trajectory, flipped over to line up with her, and caught her like a glove catches a baseball. It closed its iris, rolled back upright, and fired its engines to get back to its mothership. It tried to read its passenger's vitals and send those ahead, but its bio-monitor had shorted out.

Blood and microcircuits really don't mix.

Chapter Nineteen

"Tarnation! We only needed the one, Miss Sally!"

They had just humped the last of the hard drives to the ship. For lack of a better place to store them, Sally had popped the Malibu's trunk. The twenty-six drives didn't stuff the trunk, but they nearly covered its carpeted floor. Sally lowered her last armload in among the others. "It was quicker than reading serial numbers. The boss failed to mention that the place was wall-to-wall with the things."

"Well, I reckon we now got to go through the bunch and find the one we want." Hostetter leaned against the lip of the trunk. He neither looked nor sounded enthusiastic. "Then, some time or other, we gotta take the others back."

Sally, about to impress on him the need to go after Street, just blinked. "You did not just say that. Did you?"

"This here's gov'ment property, young lady."

"Look alive," the Voice called from his cockpit. "I've the satellite ship on approach. The major may be aboard."

"*May* be aboard?" Sally glanced toward the hatch in the overhead. It was right above the car, centered.

"I'm reading malfunctions in the bio-monitor as well as several operational systems. It's functioning at thirty percent."

"Where is it?" Sally rushed down the ramp. When her shoes touched grass, she turned in place, searching the sky.

"Out of the northwest," the Voice called back. "1.6 kilometers. It's matte black. You won't see it."

"I see it! It's throwing off sparks like the Fourth of July!"

Hostetter came up beside her. He followed her gaze, then shook his head. "This ain't good." He took Sally by the arm and nudged her toward the ship. "Get aboard. It ain't safe."

"We're sitting in a tree-lined meadow, dude. Nobody can see us."

"No, but they can see *that*." He nodded toward the limping, sparking aircraft and pushed her more insistently toward the mothership. Sally didn't argue. If the colonel had the wherewithal, he would follow the craft to its roost. He wanted all of them, not just Street.

"Raise the ramp and gun them engines," Hostetter called forward as they hurried back aboard. "Soon's that thing ties up, we gotta vamoose."

The engines built up a keening whine that settled into the almost subliminal hum of fan blades at speed. A rattling sound rose above the engines, a racket like hail on a tin roof. Then a few thuds, one hard slam that reverberated through the hull, and the dock status at the overhead hatch went from red to yellow.

Hostetter, while Sally stared at the hatch, struggled onto the hood of the car, bent double. They had done the same when Street climbed up to launch in the Manta. Though everyone had assured Sally they were being careful, she knew she'd never see her damage deposit again.

"Bad seal," the Voice said, and rose from the cockpit to join Hostetter at the driver's side of the car. "Let's get her out of there, then we'll eject the satellite and trigger its destruct."

"I got it," Hostetter said, hunched under the hatch. He turned the double latches holding the hatch in place and let the door fall open. Sparks rained down over his arms, fluttering to the Malibu's skin like red-hot snow. Hostetter cursed under his breath. "The iris on the ship, it ain't open."

"Press the emergency release," the Voice said. "That black blister to your left."

A second later, Sally heard a metal-scraping-metal squeal from the iris. Street dropped feet-first onto Hostetter, dead weight. The cowboy almost fell off the Malibu, but replanted his boots and leaned into the disgorged body. Limp arms, limp legs... Then Sally noticed the blood greasing Hostetter's jacket.

She backed away, crashing against the ship wall and rattling some of the jump seats.

Hostetter lost all footing and slid off the car like a hiker off icy rocks. The Voice grabbed one of his arms and took a fistful of the major, halting their tumble enough to mitigate injury.

Injury. Street had already covered that particular. "Omigod," Sally keened. "She's dead."

"She ain't dead." Hostetter dragged the limp woman across the car and transferred her into his arms. "Need somewhere to put her."

The Voice already clambered around the car. He clanged down the table on which they'd stared at aerial images, then dropped another, smaller table that scraped beside the first. The second table barely had room to drop; it almost scratched the car's back fender. Hostetter rearranged the major so he could lay her onto her back on the extended table surface. The Voice helped, catching her by the shoulders and lowering her head with infinite care. The tables weren't long enough. Her legs hung mostly in thin air.

"Omigod, omigod." Sally threw her hands to her face and turned away from the sight. She hurried away what little distance she could, coming up short against the secondary cockpit station.

"She ain't dead," Hostetter called up to her.

But she was. How could she be otherwise? All that blood, her white face *smeared* with blood...

"GSW to shoulder, tearing her left deltoid," the Voice said in his deep, calm tone. "Looks to be the result of a .50 caliber, probably steel-jacketed round. Sniper rifle."

"How you figure all that?"

"Tore through the muscle, but no spalling, no fragmentation. Clean tear. The size of the round's just a guess. Pulse is thready." A pulse! "Open that locker. No, *that* one. Pass me that oxygen unit."

She had a pulse, but she was shot. A face flashed into Sally's mind's eye. A handsome face, a strong, dark face with intelligent, kind eyes. Gary's face. Gary was Sally's love, her only and greatest aside from her son. Gary had been shot in the gut. Twice. And Sally had suffered through the terror that he might die. She didn't want to do that again. She pressed her hands against her ears. She didn't want that again.

You promised! she screamed at the voices in her head. You said they'd all be okay!

They are *okay.*

She's shot, you fucking dumbass!

Yes. But she's okay.

No! None of that bullshit "cradled in the arms of God" shit! You said--
I say a lot of things. And all of them are true.
Please, don't kill her. Please. I helped her into this. I made it possible. Please, I don't want to be the cause-- Don't kill her. Don't kill her, *please!*
Don't worry, don't worry. You don't know the effort expended keeping her alive. She has a part to play still. And so do you.
I can fix her. If I believe enough, I can put my hands on her and--
No, you can't.
WHY?
Because the five of you need more than that.
The five-- The … what?

Sally darted back toward the grisly scene. The Voice had gotten scissors from somewhere and was busy cutting off the major's shirt. Hostetter had gathered an array of medical supplies from some locker, or cubby, or rat hole of some kind. One-handed, he arranged them on the Malibu's top. His other hand held an oxygen mask to Street's horribly bloodied face.

"Has anybody seen Oz?" Sally threw into the tense scene.

"She may be going into cardiac shock," the Voice said with infinite dispassion. "Elevate her legs. She's not pumping blood efficiently."

"Elevate 'em how?" Hostetter's tone was rocky with anger and fear. His words trembled from his lips. "This here table ain't long enough--"

"Improvise." The Voice held a syringe in a cellophane package in the free hand that didn't monitor Street's pulse. Between his teeth he clamped another packaged syringe, a long-assed needle like you might use on elephants.

Hostetter cannoned around, looking for something, anything, to hold up the major's legs.

"Have you seen Oz?" Sally asked, hating the mewling sound of her voice.

Hostetter gripped the latch for the Malibu's rear door. His eyes glanced between the door and the table. He swung the door open so hard it thudded against a jump seat. It still opened only a crack, but wide enough to lift the major's legs through the opening and rest her ankles on the sill of the rolled-down window.

"Hostetter--" Sally began.

"What!" he roared.

Tell him never mind.

"Never mind."

Hostetter didn't seem to hear her. He struggled out of his jacket, the major's legs still propped in the door window, and rolled the garment into a thick wad. He placed the jacket under the major's ankles.

Go to the ramp.

The Voice shoved the needle of the smaller syringe into Street's neck and evacuated its contents. He threw that needle to the deck and spat the gigantic one into his hand.

Go now. You don't want to watch that.

The Voice tore open the packet holding that great sword of a medical instrument. He jiggled the syringe free of its packaging, which landed across the major's face.

Sally backed away. She didn't want to see it, she really didn't. But she couldn't look away. She couldn't close her wide-open eyes.

The Voice stabbed the needle into Street's chest.

That got Sally moving. She jerked away, crawling and falling over the cockpit chairs, around the front of the car and down its far flank away from the mutilation of her boss. "Omigod," she repeated, unable to stop. "Omigod, omigod, omigod!"

It's all right.

"It's *not* all right. It is most fucking definitely not all right!"

Breathe.

She halted her frantic stumble around the cabin, ending at the rear quarter panel away from Street's miserable body. She tried to sink her fingernails into the curves of the car, but she only smeared the metal with sweat.

"She needs an IV," the Voice said to Hostetter. "That drawer above you. Higher. Yes."

Go to the ramp.

Like a puppet jerked by a spastic master, Sally trudged to the right side of the ramp.

That button, the red one at eye level. Press it.

"Why?"

Am I in the habit of explaining myself? Press it.

Sally pressed the button.

A thumping sound followed by a hydraulic whine. The ramp started down.

The two men hesitated in whatever they were doing to Street. Hostetter squinted at Sally. The Voice pointed his enigmatic visor her way.

"What the tarnation you up to?" Hostetter called.

The ramp lowered, a slow revelation. A man stood outside, just beyond the dropping door. A big man, dressed in jeans, heavy shoes, a plain white polo shirt. He wore a rumpled raincoat. In one elbow of the coat huddled a black, furry ball.

"Sergeant Grace." Sally felt both defeat and relief.

Grace mounted the ramp, headed straight toward Sally. His sharp blue eyes glanced about the cabin as if seeking out threats. He opened his mouth to say something. It had been something serious by his expression, but he caught sight of Street, and his features wrenched in pain.

He shoved the ball of fur into Sally's hands and hurried to the operating table.

Sally slumped against the Malibu's back bumper. The ball in her arms trembled. She held it close, and petted it.

"They're right behind me," Grace was saying. "They tracked your damaged bird. Lift off now, or there'll be a problem."

"Miss Street--" the Voice began.

"I've got her. Hostetter and I have her. Go."

"Her condition is serious."

"I'm a special ops Army sergeant-first-class. I'm cross-trained in battle-field medical procedures. *Go.*"

Sally didn't hear or see if the Voice actually went. She hugged Oz and sobbed into his fur.

Colonel Sanders stood at the precipice of the conference room, a chill breeze fluttering the ample folds of his ACUs. His men were busy behind him, helping the wounded. He ignored them. His new in-ear receiver-transmitter was up and working, the Faraday bag he had carried it in somewhere on the floor behind him. All he wanted just then was data. The jet had taken off, according to Childress, limping into the eastern sky. Had it scooped up Street before she struck the ground? If it had, would that make any difference? The sniper was positive he'd hit his target. But where *was* Street? Where was the cat? Both were notoriously hard to kill.

Half of Charlie team pursued the jet. They reported it may have gone down. They had a location and were closing in with caution. Another thread that would soon be tied up.

Except that Sanders knew Street. He refused to count her out until he saw her lifeless corpse.

"I'm sorry," he said to the breeze. "It could never have come to anything but this."

"Sir?" an NCO asked as he hurried by. His men had come to Bravo team's assistance. Not a man in Bravo would walk anytime soon.

"Nothing." Sanders waved him away. "Just thinking."

But not for long. He had started the wheel rolling, so he had no choice but to help it crush all those in its path. "Childress," he called into his comms unit. "I need transportation. Work some up. I need to get to a working telephone so I can call our boys in California."

What came back was harsh, and not just from static. "And I need a goddamned winning Powerball. Shit, colonel, there ain't nothing moving or flying anywhere in a three-mile radius, and no way to call anything in."

"Then start walking, young man, until you find something that suits. A helicopter would be nice." The frequency stayed quiet for a long several seconds. Sanders gave the kid that long to bluster to himself. He opened the feed again. "Say the words, Childress."

The words came back. "Yes fucking sir."

Well, not exactly the words desired, but Sanders could live with them, under the circumstances.

A flash in the distance, within the circle of dark. It wasn't a light, but fire, or an explosion. After a moment, the boom shook the building.

Something streaked off toward the west.

Grace found Sally in a vault of self-isolation more effective than any prison cell. She sat curled up at the driver's rear wheel of the car, her chin to her knees, the cat cocooned within the curve of her body. She rocked slightly, forward and backward, and stared at nothing. Grace had heard and felt the thundering *chunk!* when the smaller plane ejected. He had heard the faraway explosion as it self-destructed. He had felt the vibration of engines through the deck and the sway of the plane as it lifted from its clearing. He had felt the rattle as the ship went supersonic. He had heard all that and felt all that while he fought to keep his major from dying. Now he was done, or had done all he could. He had backed away from his work, leaving Hostetter hunched over Fiona Street's corpselike form. He had not gone forward to the Voice of the City. He didn't know where he stood with either man. He knew where he stood with Sally.

Groaning, he lowered himself to the deck across from her. He could have taken a jump seat, but he didn't wish to hang above the woman.

"She's stable," he said. When Sally showed no sign of hearing, he tried again. "It isn't as bad as it looks."

This time, her eyes darted up to meet his gaze. Those were cold eyes, eyes behind a wall. She continued rocking.

"She won't be using that arm for a while. And I hope your friend is going to a hospital, or she may not use it ever again. But she'll live."

Sally's eyes turned away from him. She stared through a wall.

"What the hell were you guys thinking?" Grace didn't care if she took offense. He wanted to know. The response she gave him put him off balance.

She laughed.

Hers was a cynical, choking laugh that sputtered to nothing in a few awkward seconds, but it was a laugh. She got the joke, whatever it was. Or it got her.

"Thinking," she said, her tone dreamy. "I wish I had the luxury."

"I don't get you."

"You wouldn't." For a moment, it seemed she had finished talking, opting to return to her thousand-mile stare. Then she snapped her eyes back to his. "You make decisions. Everything you do, you do from choice. Either you know why you act or you trust the ones who direct you. You have a purpose. You might even have goals. I get squat in all those departments."

"Sally, everybody chooses. You chose to help the major. You did that."

"I didn't choose, I was told. I didn't know why and I still don't. And I was lied to." Her head snapped a bit to one side and she jutted her jaw. "I *was*, goddamnit, and don't say I wasn't!"

Grace decided not to respond to that. He hadn't contradicted her unless the conversation had gotten beyond him. And he had seen that wild stare and hardened face before. She spoke to somebody else.

Well, part of the time.

"Sure, I know," she said through her teeth, glaring at him. "Nobody said anything, Sally Reiser. Nobody said a goddamned thing. You're just hearing things, little girl. You're just full of crazy talk."

Grace had seen crazy many times. This *was* crazy. Or maybe simply crazed? "Sally, if we had thought--"

"Don't feed me that bullshit!" Her head jerked again. "*Any* of it!"

Grace waited, watching her. After several tense moments, her shoulders sagged and her head drooped back to her knees.

"None of this is your fault," he said.

She made no response.

"What you need to know is that she would have been here anyway, even if you hadn't helped. That's the way she is. She would have been here, alone except for that cat in your arms. Maybe Hostetter, maybe even me. Because that's the way *we* are. But, Sally, without you, it might have ended differently. Without you, the Voice of the City wouldn't be here. All his medical gear wouldn't be here, and who carries a setup like that, anyway? Without you, Fiona Street might be dead."

She turned to him, the wall between them dissolving. So many lines wrecked that woman's face just then. They drew down the curve of her mouth and cut furrows across her brow and cheeks. She showed, for the first time, a tortured heart. "That's the thing," she said, her voice throaty, hitching. "It wasn't me. It never is. And he doesn't care if you live or die, if anyone lives or dies. He just wants me to serve."

Her file said she talks to God, that he shows her visions and tells her things. Her file said she prevented the destruction of a major American city, that she helped expose and prevent nuclear terrorism. It said she prevented a Middle-Eastern war. It also said she could be paranoid-delusional, schizophrenic, mad. But the major trusted her. Grace gave his officer high marks in trust.

But things had changed in just a few days.

"Sally, I'm sorry, but I have to ask." He licked his lips. No way would she take this well. "The voice that directs you, is it this monster thing, or..."

"Or what? God? The monster or God?" She snorted and curled her lip. "What's the difference?" Then she turned her gaze back to the wall.

"Coming up on a landing," the Voice of the City called from up front.

Grace frowned. He climbed to his feet.

"Is she brain damaged?" Sally asked.

"What?" The question caught Grace unawares. "Why would you ask that?"

She opened her arms and lowered her knees. The cat dug deeper into her lap, hiding its head and mewling. "He's lost. Something's been taken from him."

Grace frowned. He reached down and petted the shivering ball of fur. "We can't tell anything here, but the EMP probably burned out their implants. It would seem like a part of them suddenly died. Violently." He waved away Sally's intensified look of concern. "It would *seem* that way. Hopefully, the-- It's temporary."

She made no response except to curl back into herself. After a moment, Grace left her. He squeezed along the space between car and hull to approach the cockpit.

Beyond the expansive windscreen of the jet, the white and red lights of a city sparkled like stars. They drifted lazily away to the left as the Voice of the City turned his craft.

"Where are we?" Grace asked.

The man in the driver's seat didn't even look at him.

"You can trust me," Grace said. "I've been with the major for years."

"So was the government that put her on that table."

Grace sighed. "Fair enough. But tell me you're on approach for a hospital."

"All right. We're on approach for a hospital."

Grace mentally kicked himself for not seeing that coming. Without asking for permission he wouldn't get, he climbed across the front of the Malibu and down into the cockpit to the co-pilot's chair. He slumped into that seat, struck immediately that it could not be what he had taken it for. No one could fly from that seat. It accessed no controls. It wasn't even comfortable.

"Where are we?" came a soft voice near the Malibu's nose. Grace twisted around to see Sally standing behind the pilot, stroking the curled-up cat.

"Indianapolis," the Voice of the City said.

"Where? I don't recognize..."

"Interim headquarters. The medical facilities are much more extensive than we have here. We'll land in less than a minute. A response team is standing by."

Well, *some*body got something out of him.

The streetlights flattened out as the ship lowered on VTOL fanjets. Grace continued to be impressed. The medical station aboard, supersonic flight that had crossed the eastern states in less than forty minutes, and now he landed in a populated area with no concern of being observed. The Voice of the City was a curiosity within a mystery, wrapped in an enigma.

Down the jet settled, down to acres of empty parking lot barely lit by sparsely situated streetlamps. Then, when Grace estimated they must bump against pavement, the ship continued to sink. A black band of concrete and earth rose up from the bottom edge of the windscreen, replacing the street-lights and parking lot. The lighting went from dim night to subdued red. Grace sat up straighter as he realized they had dropped below ground level into an underground hangar.

The ship came to rest on a steel plate pad in a vast underground struc-ture. Rust-toned steel pillars arrayed into the red-dark distance, each at least thirty feet in height. Grace leaned forward and peered up past the top edge of the windscreen. Yes, leviathan doors rolled closed overhead. The parking lot had slid away to admit the aircraft to its nest.

"Cool," Sally said. "The Batcave."

The Voice of the City slapped a button. The ramp at the rear of the air-craft whined. "There'll be a cart outside. Get the files to it, then follow the cart."

He boosted out of his pilot's seat and squeezed past Sally toward the rear of the ship. Grace climbed from the well of the cockpit to see what the man had going.

The ramp dropped. Just beyond it waited a robot two-shelf cart with a flashing red light atop what looked like an antenna. Beside the cart, a com-pact forklift raised its platform, which held a stainless steel tray close to seven feet long and three wide. The forklift trundled aboard as soon as the ramp locked down, whining straight to the major's impromptu sickbed.

"You! If you care about her!" the Voice of the City shouted toward Grace. "Take her legs! Marshal Hostetter, take her by the armpits!"

Grace got to the Malibu's back door. He gently maneuvered the major's legs through the window space, letting Hostetter's jacket fall to the deck. He found it awkward as hell, but he managed to keep hold of Street's calves and slam shut the car door. By the time he steadied his hold on her legs, Hostet-ter had her under the arms and was lifting her clear of the table.

Someone -- Hostetter, undoubtedly -- had covered the major's bared torso with a towel.

236

"Soldier!" the Voice called from just behind the forklift. He had a remote control in his hands. "Kick out the lower support for the table. You too, Hostetter. Lay her onto the robot platform."

Three solid clangs and the table no longer existed. It was just metal thumping against the hull. Grace and Hostetter shuffled toward the forklift, then hefted the major onto the stainless tray. Two straps curled against one side of the platform. Grace ran one across Street's knees, the other across her torso. He fastened both into snaps on the other side.

"Stand back," the Voice ordered. Grace and Hostetter took a few steps away and the forklift backed out of the ship. Clear of the ramp, it pivoted, then sped off across the steel-grate landscape, the Voice of the City following.

Grace stood on the ramp, watching the forklift depart. Nothing out there but a low, blank-walled concrete bunker that disappeared into the dark in two directions. It seemed huge, the size of a strip mall. Even so, the empty cavern dwarfed it. The Voice of the City might have constructed a vast underground secret base, but he hadn't put funds into interior decoration.

Hostetter stood beside Grace, looking older than his outdoorsy sixty years. His shirt, jeans, and hands showed black with dried blood. Those same hands trembled.

"Umm, somebody…" Sally ventured. She looked from the retreating forklift, to the robot cart, to the ship interior, then to the men. "Somebody should, I don't know, load up this cart with stuff. Like he said."

Grace didn't know what "stuff" she referred to, and didn't care. He squinted at her. She still held the cat. She had the distant, empty-eyed look of combat shock.

"It's just, we did it all for the files," Sally soldiered on. "If we don't retrieve them…"

"Take that shit and shovel it in a hole," Hostetter rumbled. With long, stalker's strides, he took off after the forklift.

Grace followed as if from reflex. He halted after a dozen steps and backtracked to Sally, lonely on the ramp. He closed his hands on her shoulders and looked deeply into her stunned eyes. "The files can wait," he said. "Let's go see to our friend."

He maneuvered her after Hostetter as if she were the cart she so worried about.

The bunker was a model of thrift, especially when it came to lighting. Grace directed Sally from pool of light to pool of light, the dense shadow between illumination stretching thirty feet. They followed Hostetter, who followed the faint track or sound of the forklift, as far as Grace could tell.

He couldn't see the machine, though. It had gone on ahead and entirely out of sight.

The secret headquarters for the Voice of the City couldn't be called a maze, but he did go in for short corridors with multiple feeders, some barely wide enough for a big-shouldered man, some as wide as boulevards. The passages seemed to go on for miles of overlapping spaghetti courses, not a sign anywhere to orient an occupant. And why not? There would normally be only one occupant, the structure's presumed designer.

They wound up in a twenty-by-thirty gray room that might have been featureless but for the window stretching from knees to ceiling and the width of the wall opposite the door. Hostetter stood at the window, leaning against it with apparent concentration, both hands splayed on the glass.

Beyond the window spread a bright room crazy with monitors and white machines, some free-rolling, some extending from robot arms in the walls and ceiling. Those machines focused on the forklift with its stainless steel tray and the motionless naked woman upon it. Robots hovered over her, scanned the length and width of her, injected, touched, and swabbed her. The Voice of the City rushed at the fringes, snapping on switches and buttons in the walls.

"It looks bad," Sally said.

Grace said nothing. It *was* bad, but why confirm the obvious?

Hostetter's fingers gripped the glass, making squelching sounds.

The Voice of the City exited the lighted room without so much as a glance at his machines' point of focus. He came through a door that opened in the rightside wall.

"What is this?" Grace asked.

"I don't answer to you," the Voice said. He drew up to Grace with the threat of a predator. "I wonder if you should be detained. I've no idea where you stand in all this."

Grace refused to back away from the hulking pile of brick. "I've known the major for years. You've known her for hours. I trust her with my life and my honor and she trusts me with hers. There's no question of my loyalty to her. There's every question of yours."

"You are a government agent. Your government wants her dead."

"Then I suppose it'll be displeased with me. You can decide now to trust me the same as she does, or we can go at it now to see who stands. It's up to you."

"I would not fight you within sight of that woman, who has given so much just to be betrayed. But I would drag you kicking to detention and gladly watch you rot."

"Voice." That was Sally, barely audible as she stared through the window. "What is this?"

The change was dramatic, as if a dog had been heeled by a pull on his chain. The Voice backed off, turning away from Grace. He faced Sally instead, and his tone was almost genteel. "This is my trauma center. These machines and their accompanying mainframe are programmed to alleviate the most serious of combat injuries." He shrugged. "I often am damaged in my line of work."

"So, you can be hurt," Grace jabbed.

The brick stiffened.

"Don't press your luck," Sally said to the glass. "The Voice here isn't all wrong. For all we know, you're leading the colonel here as we speak."

"I'm not." Grace took on a more humble tone. "The colonel's wrong about Major Street, or at least I think so. I was caught in the middle. I had to choose a side. So I did."

"Taking a big risk regarding your job," Sally said, "not to mention that retirement pension."

"Man does not live by pensions alone."

Sally tilted her face up to see the Voice's visor. "Leave him be," she said. "We'll continue as if he's a true friend and here to help."

"Thank you," Grace said.

"If he proves our trust mistaken, kill him."

"Again, thanks," Grace said with a touch of acid.

The Voice responded with a curt nod. "What about the files?" he asked. "You didn't take care of them as instructed."

"Higher priorities," Grace said.

The Voice separated from Sally. He paced across the room in a wide arc, ending at the door they had all entered through. "There is no higher priority. The major risked all to obtain those files. They must be searched for battle intelligence. Within those files lies the weakness of the monster and the salvation of our world. Let us see to that all-important duty."

Hostetter leaned away from the glass just enough to slam his fists against the window. Sally jumped. Grace was surprised the window didn't shatter.

"Hostetter?" Sally asked.

"I ain't goin' nowhere. Y'all play with files all you want."

"There's nothing you can do for her," the Voice said. "The machines will do all that can be done."

Hostetter raised his fists again. Grace thought he might strike the glass a second time. Instead, he opened his hands, flexed his fingers, then planted them against the window again. His previous handprints had left pink smears of blood.

"Look at her," the cowboy said as if gravel rolled in his mouth. "She's violated, beaten, naked. Ain't no soul like hers should be treated so wrong. Somebody gotta stay here."

"The machines--" the Voice insisted.

"Not for the carnsarned machines! For *her!* Because she deserves respect, and a hand to hold if she needs it!"

Nobody said anything to that. Hostetter stared through the glass and rumbled.

After a moment, the Voice stopped staring at the cowboy's back. He turned, stiffly, and left the room, headed the way they had come from the ship. Grace took one long look at the unconscious, helpless major, then patted Sally's shoulder and took off after the Voice.

They were *all* right. But Grace couldn't stand around and worry.

He'd rather have a job while he did that.

Chapter Twenty

"The hard drives weren't difficult to crack," the Voice of the City said. He stood at the front of yet another gray room. To Sally, they all were burdened with the same blank, somber mood.

"You've been at it for forty hours," Grace said. He sat in a plastic office chair like Sally. He crossed one ankle over one knee and crossed his arms over his chest. Grace had been tightly wound for the last two days. He'd barely spoken a word to anyone.

"Forty hours, but for twenty-six drives," the Voice explained. "It took more time to feed the paper files into the optical character analyzer. Government security codes are shit."

Grace waved a hand, giving him that one. "So, what did your computers come up with?"

The Voice waved a black remote at the back wall of the room. Sally saw nothing to wave the remote at, but the wall behind the Voice suddenly brightened with images and text.

This had been the theme for the last few days. At every turn the Voice showed technological resources straight out of comic books, no explanation of how he could have amassed such power. He harbored a server farm to rival Google's, stocks of food, weapons, and crime-fighting tools that would cause survivalists and police forces alike to salivate from envy. He was Bruce Wayne with unlimited funds and absurd anonymity for a buyer of such strange equipment. He was Professor X with a supersonic attack jet docked beneath his school in a wealthy New York enclave. He was that guy in the Fantastic Four with gigantic, time-and-dimension-bending toys that he built from scratch on government grants. He was everything a boy could want that didn't make any sense.

And now he lectured them in a blank room with only two chairs and images broadcasting from nowhere. Sally had stopped being surprised.

What would Hostetter think of it all? It was one thing for impossible tech to irritate the major and the sergeant, but how would all that fantasy sci-fi stuff hit a man of the nineteenth century? Maybe it didn't hit him at all. Magic was magic, after all.

"The data structuring worm and analysis application--" The Voice flicked a laser pointer onto the wall graphics.

"Let's just call it the Bat-computer," Sally said. She tried to push a smile at him, but the last few days had been hard.

The Voice pointed his visor at her, and nodded. "The, umm, Bat-computer has ordered all the pertinent files into a linear progression with hyperlinked solutions where applicable. Also, if you note here…" He pointed to several projected icons shunted to one side. "…we have access to a number of files we weren't looking for, thanks to Miss Reiser's overly enthusiastic capture at the NSA vault. All of it comes down to this. Give me the next image, please."

The projection swam and reformed. It displayed several documents, some in scratchy handwriting and some from barely legible typewriter ribbons. Centered in the projection was a black-and-white picture of a rock.

"In 1937, at the site of the Mt. Rushmore memorial, then in progress, workmen dug a strange mineral deposit out of the mountain. It was radioactive, hyper-dense, and exhibited signs of instability in our space-time framework."

"Instability?" Sally asked.

"As in, it acted weird," Grace explained. "I've heard of this one from Hostetter. The rock is an extrusion from a pressurized zone between universes. He called it a Keystone."

"I verified these documents with Marshal Hostetter," the Voice said. "What you say is correct. The Keystone, as it came to be called, was retrieved by Doctor Emil Drehd, a physicist from the University of Chicago on loan to the National Bureau of Standards. Owing to a dramatic and believed apocryphal meeting Doctor Drehd had with at least two, umm, time travelers, the government classified the substance and brought it, a few years later, into the framework of the Manhattan Project. This Keystone is an artifact of immense power. When coupled with other exotic materials liberated from Germany during World War II, the Keystone could be the heart of weapons of uncharted explosive power. These attributes, however, weren't known until deep in the war, after the United States had committed to construction of an atomic bomb."

Grace raised a finger to interrupt. "One second. In our records, Hostetter said the Keystone was destroyed. It was used as a focusing agent for an atomic explosion that defeated a monster attacking the eighteen contiguous universes. He said there was only one Keystone."

"There is never just one Keystone, or just one of anything, most likely. The N-space dynamics of quantum physics states that there are infinite universes, that everything that can happen, has happened. If one Keystone could exist, then several, perhaps millions, could as well. Hostetter used the Keystone from his universe. The one referenced here and shown in this photograph originated in our universe." The Voice stood still a moment to see if anyone would comment further, then turned back to his wall.

"Doctor Drehd surmised that the Keystone and its sister stones might have uses beyond that of bombs. In 1942, he got a green light for his Drehd Machine project, a device of psychological warfare on regional scales. The Drehd Machine would, if successful, inflict large populations with extraordinarily high doses of Theta and Delta waves, inducing depression, paranoia, fear, and despondency. The United States may have been able to incapacitate the Japanese without destroying two of their cities. With the population and defense forces collapsed in fits of melancholy, American troops could have just walked into Japan. But, this didn't happen. In 1943, one of three test units for the Drehd project... Give me the next screen. ...was loaded onto a purpose-built aircraft to be moved to the Solomon Islands."

The Drehd Machine -- Sally had to do mental transposition to get the name right in her head -- seemed about the size of a Hummer. Not one of those military trucks, but the big, honking Hummer 2 of gas-guzzling infamy. Beyond that, it looked something like an old radio, the ones families gathered around in the olden days to hear Little Orphan Annie or The Shadow.

"The plane was shot down near Tarawa, here, with a loss of all hands. It's unclear, but the machine may have been operational at the time. They may have been testing subsystems in preparation for their operational test."

"So it's true," Sally said. "We turned on a nightmare machine and tucked it away at the bottom of the ocean?"

"It isn't clear when or even if the device was operational. The subsystem tests were at minimal power, if they happened at all. Also, it's unlikely the machine could have survived being shot out of the sky. For that reason and because the government decided on an atomic bomb approach over all others, the United States terminated the Drehd project. Next screen, please."

"Who's turning these slides? Grace asked. "Do you have a staff down here?"

"It's just me. The software listens."

"You don't have to say please to software."

"I do. Here. We have detailed plans for the Drehd Machine. Doctor Drehd and his staff, realizing the possibility of debilitating radiation from their device, also designed countermeasure devices that were always in use during live tests. These devices projected counter-frequencies to the Theta and Delta frequencies broadcast by the machine, kind of a noise-canceling solution."

"Eglemann at Lawrence-Livermore jury-rigged something similar during that incursion a few days ago," Grace said.

"And we have her report. It was on one of the extraneous drives liberated by Miss Reiser. Using both Drehd's and Engineer Eglemann's specifications, I'm in the process of printing the components for a workable set of these countermeasures."

"Why?" Sally thought she was missing something. "We don't need to defend against a machine at the bottom of the Pacific."

"Actually, we may want to. If Major Street and Marshal Hostetter are correct, that missing machine is the root of all our problems. To counter it is to, at least temporarily, alleviate the problem. Also… Next screen, please. The radiation projected from the Drehd Machine is similar to that released by the entity reported in the last spontaneous event at Lawrence-Livermore."

The Voice stopped. He palmed his laser pointer and held his hands behind his back. He let those last words sink in.

"We have a weapon against the monster," Sally said.

"Will it kill him?" Grace asked, leaning forward in his chair.

"No way to say," the Voice answered. "It isn't even built yet, and there is no means by which to test it."

"But you think it'll work," Sally said. She felt electrified. Her fingers danced on her knees. They couldn't hold still.

"I do." The Voice cocked his visor. "I don't know to what extent."

For the first time since the major fell from the Manta into Hostetter's arms, Sally felt hope in her breast.

Told you so, her inner voice teased.

A few robots puttered about the major's bed, occasionally checking their patient's pulse, breathing, and temperature. The surgeon machine, the anesthesia drone, and the pharmacological platform all stood against the back wall of the medical facility, their charging jacks plugged into green-lighted receptacles. Quiet reigned in that white room, quiet and a simulacrum of comfort.

The bed was vinyl-sheathed memory foam, the sheets linen, the blankets velvety microfiber. The lights had dimmed since the operation, the better to aid in the patient's rest.

Hostetter had dragged in a cheap plastic chair. He had placed it beside the bed and lowered his long frame into it. He'd hardly left that spot for almost two days.

He held Street's hand, his own still covered in flaking blood and dirt.

"I came here to help," he murmured, more to himself than to the woman at his side. "Truth be told, I came here specific'ly to help you. Then that thing, it followed me. I reckon I should've stayed where I was." He sighed, a world of regret in the gesture. "I know I done bad. I could've kept the monster intent on me, on my world. Instead, I brought it to your'n. And Sinfonee. She died." He quieted. He licked his lips. "She died. The monster killed her just to get to me. And now, because of me, she might be in danger again."

He rubbed his free hand across his eyes. Wet filth smeared his face once he took his hand away. "When I was a kid, I didn't have no worries. All I needed was to shoot good enough to eat, work hard enough to keep my horse shod. When I look back on them times, they don't seem like they really happened. I put the worries of a town, then a territory, then a whole super-territory onto my shoulders. Mind you, that last weren't no earthly domain. Territory 87 Dogpatch by 4 it's called, a spread of lightnin' post coordinates that I ain't yet forgot."

With his free hand, he tapped his forehead. "Still got it, right up here. Guess I need to, what with all them fancy gadgets your folks attached to my stick dead as fence rails. I ain't got no destinations I can reach with my stick but what I got stored in my head. But I reckon I got more responsibility here, with you, than in all the multiverse I can reach." He squeezed the major's hand. "I done lost somebody I cared about. Won her back. I ain't about to lose you. Don't imagine there is another you in all God's creation."

The major's hand squeezed his.

Hostetter sat up straighter. He turned his gaze to the small white fingers buried in his. Had he imagined it?

As he watched, the hand rolled over. Its palm pressed against his and the fingers laced through his, and the hand squeezed his.

He dragged his gaze to the major's face. She grinned shakily at him, red-eyed and pallid.

"You look like shit," she said in a voice scratchy from disuse.

A robot attendant wheeled up and popped the latex nipple at the end of its feeder arm into her mouth. It squirted a slow stream of what looked like water and Miss Fiona lapped it up.

"What the hell is that?" she asked when the robot decided she had enough.

"That there's the Voice of the City and his magic." Hostetter breathed hard. He wasn't sure he could continue without his voice trembling. "You was shot. You're in his secret base in Indianapolis. That machine there is kinda a nurse."

Street rolled her attention away from the retreating machine and focused on Hostetter. Her eyes held no strength. Darkness ringed them, and the sockets around them showed too prominently, the skin stretched like rice paper. "Okay," she said. "That was no nurse. Who puts a secret base in Indianapolis? And you still look like shit."

Hostetter's bushy moustache curved up at the ends. "Look who's talkin'."

"Seriously, Clay. You can do better. All you have is your health." Her speech plodded. She was one too long in the desert. She licked her lips. The robot with the suckling arm zipped back over to offer her a nipple. She gave it a warning glare. "I'm not in diapers."

"Actually…"

Her eyes widened, giving her the look of a badly carved jack o' lantern. "Really?"

The robot insisted she take a sip. It snaked the nippled end of its arm back and forth, trying to press it to her mouth.

"Go away!" the major complained, but breathed out the words in a hollow whisper. The machine apparently did not hear, and she soon surrendered to the inevitable.

"Miss Fiona." Hostetter hung his head. He knew his face reddened, but he had to confess his sins. He hoped the lady didn't hate him afterward. "Miss Fiona, I got me a piece to say."

"Okay. Could you break that machine for me?"

"It's about when you got shot, and we had to stop the bleedin', and, like, get you stitched up."

"Last I remember was the colonel scrambling my brain. Oh my God! Where's Oz?"

"He's fine, Miss Fiona, but I got to tell you something. It's a might … indelicate."

"What? Did you force me to drink whiskey and stick a rawhide bit in my mouth?"

"No, ma'am. But we had to get to your shoulder wound and later, the robots, they operated…"

"Out with it, Clay. Do I still have both my legs?"

"Yes'm."

"Does Oz?"

"I guess I kinda saw you, you know, nekkid."

Hostetter's face and neck blazed. He forced a sidewise glance at the major.

She didn't show shock. Maybe her face couldn't do that just yet. But she watched him with eyes that wobbled a little.

"Saw me in the buff, eh?"

"Yes'm."

"Without a stitch, in all my glory."

"Yes'm."

"Hmm. So what did you think?"

"Miss Fiona!"

"Don't Miss Fiona me, you old letch. You're the one ogling young ladies while they're unconscious on operating tables getting their insides put back together." She tried to grin, but the effort escaped her. She seemed to sink deeper into her bed. "Well, you owe me dinner. And flowers. Though I'd put on a show right now for a goddamned glass of water."

"You ain't mad?"

Her brows drew together and she looked away. "Forget it, Clay. I sometimes forget about you and where you're from. Now, get me water. Please. And get me Oz."

Hostetter scraped back his chair. He removed his fingers from her grip and patted the back of her hand. "I'll get you both."

"I can't feel him, Clay. There's a dark place where he was."

"You been drugged. Maybe that's why." On impulse, Hostetter bent over and planted a kiss on her temple. "He's all right," he said. "And now that you're back, we all are."

"That's nice," the major said softly, her words indistinct as she fell toward sleep. But she reopened her eyes suddenly, snapping them toward Hostetter. "Did we win? Did we get the files?"

"Sure did, and lots more. You rest. I'll go get that water."

"And Oz."

"And Oz."

Fiona looked like a horror and she knew it. No one looked good in a paper hospital gown. Her shoulder, under a mountain of bandages, felt nonexistent thanks to the Voice's pain medication. The big guy had told her she'd be three weeks in recovery, but she knew she wouldn't be allowed the time. The monster wouldn't wait three weeks. The thing was nothing if not a conscientious worker.

Fiona took in the briefing on what the Drehd files revealed. She collated that with the ongoing activity at the Lawrence-Livermore facility and the mystifying reality of 3-D printing a device described in eighty-year-old schematics.

"So," she said from her wheelchair, the Voice standing like a mountain at her side. "You can print out every component, every little widget and bolt, in their intended materials no less."

"No," the big brick said. He stood with her just off the huge printer platform, its robot nozzles and laser heaters whipping with precision on rails over the active area. Sparks, hums, and screeches sounded from that platform, and heat, heat enough to blister if Fiona got any closer. "I could print the device as depicted in its schematics, but that was a machine from the 1940s. It would be huge. Also, the materials specified would be less than efficient. Plastics and metallurgy were somewhat wanting back then. Also, they hadn't the concept of the microprocessor. My system ingested the plans as laid down in 1943 and updated, improved, and miniaturized them. Whereas the original Theta-Delta jamming device was as big as a small truck, ours will be the size of a lady's purse."

"Wow. You're unbelievably good."

"A large lady's purse."

"Doesn't change that I don't believe you. So who's gonna put all the parts together? You a mechanical engineer, too?"

"No. But the machines are. The system will assemble the device."

"Too bad it takes days. We could use more than a few of these things to spring a proper trap."

"This isn't the only printing facility I have. Three more are active of the six I have on line."

Fiona gave the Voice the hairy eyeball of doubt. "One of these days, son, you're gonna tell me how you do all this."

"I doubt it," the Voice said, and watched her through his creepy red visor.

"That sounds like a challenge. Well, we'll see. Now, how about you take me for a ride. I'd like to see Grace, if I can." She rubbed the elbow of her left arm, the one with the sling and heavily bandaged shoulder.

"As you wish," and the Voice took the handles at the back of the chair.

"So you're a *Princess Bride* fan, too?"

"I don't know any princesses."

"Aww, Voice, I'm hurt. And I've got a rolling throne, too." She fought back a sense of helpless invalidism as he wheeled her from the whirring, sparking room. She could have walked, she was sure of it. Her shoulder was damaged, not her feet. But everyone would throw a fit if she tried. "Hey, Voice. You said you have six of those printers, four active?"

"That's correct."

"Get another one going. I have a plan."

"Would this plan prove as effective as your last, in which you were nearly shot to death and lost your link to the cat?"

"Depends. On if people, not you, are willing to give me a chance."

"You're a dangerous commodity, Major Street."

"Why, thank you, Voice. Like Captain America or Wonder Woman, no doubt."

"I was thinking more like dynamite."

Grace lay on his bed, watching television. There wasn't much else to see in the modest ten-foot-square room. The bed, a table, and a straight-back chair, all made for temporary lodgings, as in hours, not days. The only things not gray in the room were the television, Grace, and the cat.

"Hey, top," Fiona said as the Voice wheeled her into the room.

"Hello, ma'am."

"Will you be needing me further, Major Street?" the Voice asked as he released her chair. "I still have repairs to complete on the airframe."

"I'm good, I'm good. Sergeant Grace can take care of me. And you really ought to give that jet a name, buddy."

"For the last time, I'm not calling it the Batplane."

"I get that, but there are other possibilities. Like the Quinjet, or the Phantom Cruiser, that sort of thing."

"Another few cultural references, major?"

"Bye, Voice."

"Until later."

He pulled the door to when he left.

"Can you believe that guy?" Fiona, one-handed, maneuvered her chair close enough to reach the bed and pet Oz. The cat remained curled up, non-responsive. Fiona felt nothing of him in her head. That emptiness made her feel lost. "That Voice, he's definitely a visiting alien. He knows less about the world than Hostetter."

Grace waved a hand at the television and its droning talking heads went silent. "I've figured out pretty much where we are. An abandoned mall near the outskirts of the city, Eastgate Mall, I think it's called."

"Oh, yeah, I remember the place. My parents used to drag me there when I was a kid. Went dead in the early nineties, a discount place nobody seemed to want. It's covered now by a fairly extensive solar farm, I think."

"That's how I narrowed it down. The Voice draws power from that solar farm. There aren't that many in town. I wonder if he owns at least part of the solar cells or is he tapping in illegally."

"He doesn't seem like the type to do anything illegal. I mean, besides pounding people's faces."

Oz lay like a catatonic lump. He didn't purr. He didn't react at all to Fiona's touch.

"How're you doing?" Grace asked.

"The arm's coming along. The Voice has great drugs."

"That isn't what I meant, ma'am."

Fiona slumped in her chair with great care, careful not to move the shoulder. She listened to the white noise in her head, the hole in her mind where Oz should have been. Shock, maybe. Drugs. Those were her best hopes. But she knew the truth, that Colonel Sanders had scoured the cat, the enhancements, the power from her brain. She wanted to say she was lost. She wanted to say she felt empty inside. But she chose to say something entirely different. "Why are you still, after all that's happened, calling me ma'am? Do you really think I have rank anymore?"

"Habit, I guess. And that is also not what I meant."

"I'm fine, top. I was a person before I became a person and a cat. I can deal."

"You know, with the implant destroyed and you sans superpowers, the colonel may decide you aren't worth hunting."

"Yeah, I thought of that. But I crippled eight of his men and stole a bunch of classified files. They don't give a pass on that sort of thing."

"They could, with incentive."

"The only incentive we get is saving the world for their sorry asses. Again. I've a few thoughts on that."

"As a general, I assume. You won't be on the line in your condition."

"Why, top, what has the Army always taught you about assuming?"

She scratched Oz behind the ears. He just stared, glassy-eyed, at the gray wall. "What about you?" she asked, not wanting to see Grace's face. "This wasn't your fight. Still isn't. You could be sitting pretty. They could give you the team."

"That ship's definitely sailed. I think I was on my way to the proverbial radar station in Alaska."

"I'm sorry. I didn't mean for any of this to happen."

"Nobody did. But we do what we can with the tools thrown our way."

Tears welled up in Fiona's eyes. She tensed to hold them back. "If you bugged out now, you might be able to salvage something."

"I'm right where I need to be," Grace said.

Fiona could master her tears no longer. They tracked down her freckled cheeks.

"So, what's this plan of yours?" Grace asked.

Fiona sniffed. "Well, it isn't a whole plan. Maybe more of a side plan to the main plan that doesn't yet exist."

"I can't wait to hear."

Fiona wiped the heel of her good hand across her cheeks. "You know the Voice is printing devices to jam the monster's nightmare frequencies."

"Yes, ma'am. We all decided that was best. While you were out."

"I asked him to print an extra. I want to send that one to the Pacific, as close to the Solomons as we can manage. We can figure out the ideal naval battle group when we get the chance."

"I don't see how--"

"Routing documents, top. We both know how to bullshit that stuff. We get the device to an attack submarine, one close to where the Drehd Machine went down."

Grace stared at her for a moment, then scooted Oz out of his way and sat up straighter in bed. "You want to jam the signals coming from the Drehd device?"

"It's the root of all evil, after all. Maybe jamming those frequencies will weaken the monster when we go for him."

Grace looked into the distance, through the gray wall. "There's nothing to say that would happen."

"Nothing to say it won't." Fiona said.

"You can't be sure the jamming device will reach its destination."

"I want to try."

"No guarantee you can get anyone to hook it up to a ship, or operate it once it's hooked up."

"Can you be a tiny bit more supportive?"

He looked at her. "I think you're right. We should try. But we'll need to seriously grease the wheels."

"We can have the Voice make the thing really simple to use, I mean iPhone simple. I mean, press the big red button simple. And we can make sure it only *plugs* into sonar, that it doesn't need hard-wiring."

"Sonar." He smiled. "You've really been thinking about this."

"Only for the last five minutes."

"You'll need something more than good machine design. You've got to get the thing on station."

Fiona frowned. They both knew where that thought would lead.

Grace brought it into the light. "You've got to talk to the colonel."

Chapter Twenty-one

Childress slammed through the front door of the guard station with the attitude of a man looking for a fight. His eyes were rimmed in red, his suit four days old and still marred with dirt from that damned batship and the mess it had made. It was one thing for Black Batman to put Childress down on the pavement. It was another to mess up the suit. The suit was the man, goddammit, and the man was looking like he lived under a bridge.

"Show me where he is!" he called to no one in particular. The half dozen soldiers in tactical gear looked up at him with suspicion. After the events of the last week, these weren't men to suffer strangeness lightly.

Ponce and DeBoy moved to intercept their new boss. Childress thought about scuffing them up right then and there. Bastards looked like they'd just showered, shaved, and gotten dressed for the prom, their suits were so crisp.

"Tejada's grilling him back in the holding room," Ponce said. "It's right back here." He led the way across the common room.

"Tell me who the hell's in charge that the bastard was allowed to run loose so long." Childress was right on Ponce's heels. Maybe the guy moved faster because of it.

"It wasn't a mistake," DeBoy said from Childress's side. "At first, he was just another agent, this time from the CIA. Joint's crawling with them. CID, FBI, Army Intelligence, you name it. Then we got a message that he was in on whatever you had out east. We were told to hold tight, observe, don't arrest. It wasn't until yesterday that the colonel had us scoop him up."

"What's he been up to all that time? Three days, is it? And what about the Russian? She's still runnin' loose?"

"We didn't get orders to grab her."

"Shee-it! Is this a cluster-fuck, or what?"

Ponce reached a door near the far end of the room. He pulled it open, but turned, blocking the entry. "We just work here, *amigo*. You're the one with the higher pay grade. Tell *us* what's supposed to make sense."

Childress almost collided with him. "What makes sense is we should've greased the both of 'em the second they showed their faces. That would've saved a whole bunch of trouble."

"Like the major?" DeBoy asked, his tone blank.

Childress tried to count to ten, but made it only to four. "Yeah, you dumb fuck, like the major. Except the major turned out fuckin' hard to kill and zeroed out half our roster while we tried. And, no, we aren't exactly sure she's dead. With that bitch, I want a body on hand. Now, where the fuck is this CIA prick? I feel like sharing some feelings right now."

"This way," Ponce grumbled, and turned up a narrow hallway beyond the door. Childress and DeBoy followed. Halfway up the hall, they stopped at an unmarked door with a frosted glass window. Ponce pushed the door open and stood aside.

"--stipulates your agency is restricted from activity within US borders." Tejada paced around a metal folding chair holding a balding man. The man seemed unconcerned with the interrogation leveled his way. He slouched in the chair, one hand on a knee, the other held up as he examined a fingernail he might want to chew. "But here you are, meddling in a classified project outside your purview, bribing United States senators to release control of two nuclear reactors."

"Ah, congressmen," the man said. "They get bribed at least ten times a week. I just wanted them to feel needed."

"Mister Short, this isn't a game or ... or some stand-up karaoke or whatever the hell you think it is. Do you realize what kind of trouble you're in?"

"I never do. See, I'm always in trouble, so that's just too much thinking."

"What the fuck is this?" Childress demanded, stepping into the room. "Why the livin' fuck are you standing around having a conversation with this fuck?"

"Trying to find out what he's been up to," Tejada said. He straightened his suit jacket, which about made Childress blow a gasket.

"So you *talk* to the bastard? A spook bastard like this?" Childress was almost to screaming at his man.

"Maybe we should take this outside."

"Hey, if you guys need to get organized, don't mind me," Short said. "I'll just sit here and think about adjustable rate mortgages or something."

Childress elbowed Tejada aside and leaned over the CIA man. "We don't need a minute, shithead. We need to ask you one fucking question. Where're Hostetter, Reiser, and that big black brick with the fancy guns?"

Short put up both hands, a theatrically demure show of surrender. "Don't lean on me, officer. I was here the whole time."

Childress cocked an arm back and punched Short in the face. Short's head snapped back. The front legs of his chair jumped from the floor.

"Jesus, Childress!" Tejada dashed forward, grabbing Short's chair before it fell over.

DeBoy snatched Childress by the collar of his jacket and hurled him away from the prisoner. Ponce caught his boss and held him by the arms.

"What in hell is the matter with you?" Tejada asked.

"Let me the fuck go! I'll get the bastard to talk."

"He's an agent of the federal government!" Tejada yelled back.

Childress struggled. "No, man," Ponce said into his ear. "I don't let you go until you settle the hell down."

"Hey, that almost hurt!" Short complained and tentatively fingered his nose.

Childress tried to shake off Ponce, to no success. "I'm calm already! Let the fuck go!"

"You don't sound calm."

"I'm calm!"

This time when he tried to shake free, Ponce let Childress go.

Childress stepped right up to Short. He bent down to grab a fistful of the man's white, button-down shirt.

"Son, you get the first one free," Short said, his tone even. "But if you plan to take another pop at me, you'd best tie me down first."

The two men's noses almost touched. Childress's face boiled.

"Your buddies stole classified documents pertaining to this facility," Childress spat into the other man's face. "They put out a plan to start up the reactors and set off an event. They're on their way here on a crazy woman's mission. Now where the hell are they right the fuck now?"

Short's answer came in a monotone of poisoned broken glass. "Don't know. Mongo only pawn in game of life."

Childress threw Short away from him. Tejada had to dive for the chair again. "You're on your way to Leavenworth," Childress growled at the CIA man. "Or maybe we'll find out who you've pissed off the most over your career, do a little extraordinary rendition in their favor."

Short straightened his shirt and rearranged himself in his seat. "Ah, whatever. I've been due a little vacation time anyway."

"Mister Short." Tejada pinched the bridge of his nose. "As I was saying earlier, you don't seem to understand--"

"No, son, you're wrong." The CIA man slapped his thighs and rose from his chair. Bold as brass, just like that. "I understand exactly what's going on. I understand you fellas have no clue and that you're hunting down the one person who does. I understand you're keen for a spy-versus-spy adventure when this is way far beyond that shit." Short stepped away from the chair. He circled the room slowly, patting his pockets and taking each man into his gaze. "I understand that I was put here to bodyguard a certain little genius physicist in case a whole lot of things went wrong, and I can't do that with you guys throwing spittle in my face." He stopped in front of DeBoy. "You got a cigarette, buddy? You guys took all mine."

"Grab that SOB," Childress sneered. Ponce and DeBoy took hold of Short and manhandled him back into his chair.

"All right, all right, my shirt's been wrinkled enough today." Back in his seat, Short gave everyone a cheery grin. "Why, I even knew Kudashova was here before you fellas did. Okay, yeah, I didn't tell you, and I really should have. I know that. But, guys, you have no idea how fun it was timing how long you took to catch on."

"You're laughing awful hard, you fucker." Childress leaned against his knees before the man, daring him to try for a punch. "In my experience, laughing boys don't know jack about what's up. What, you thinking Major Fiona Street's gonna storm in here and save the world, including your sorry ass?"

"Well, yeah, that was one of the plans."

Childress feigned surprise. "Really? Well, ain't that something. Well, Short, you have a lot more confidence in the major than I do. 'Cause I don't see her doin' that shit now that she's dead." Okay, so counting a few un-hatched chickens wasn't exactly a lie, just a play on probabilities. "Yep, that's right. We dumped her out a fifteen-story window and shot her on her way down. So you see, umm, *Dick*, that the plan you're depending on could be a little shaky."

Short looked a little shaky himself. The sincerity of Childress's delivery had rattled the smarmy little prick. That was clear in the sudden shiftiness in his eyes, in the tightness of his lips, and in the long come around for a snap-py reply. "Well," he said, "I guess it's good that wasn't the only plan."

"Yeah, bet it wasn't." Short had been busy-bodying around for three damned days, and he had been up to more than shadowing Rodriguez. He wasn't going to talk, though. Why should he? From his point of view, every-thing went peachy. "How long before the reactors come on line?" Childress asked his people.

"They've been on line for thirty-some-odd hours," Tejada answered.

"You know what the fuck I mean."

"If you're referring to the event launch, that's..." Tejada glanced at his watch. "Twenty-seven hours from now."

"Lock this bastard up. No bureaucrat or lawyer gets his feelers on him unless I say so."

"What?" Short said with theatrical concern. "Not even a phone call?"

"Giving you the CIA treatment," Childress replied, then rolled out of the room like thunder, DeBoy and Ponce in his wake. "Go through his shit again. Go through it three times. There's gotta be a hint of what he was up to."

"He wasn't carrying much," DeBoy said. "His motel room came up goose eggs, too."

"You saying you're too stupid to fox a weasel like that?"

"I'm saying that he's a field agent. He knows what the hell he's doing."

Childress turned on DeBoy, got right up in his face. "And *you're* a god-damned field agent, D. And you're NSA. You're the elite Scooby squad of the late great Fiona Street. What the fuck you doin'? Asking for a demo-tion?"

"I'll get right on his effects," DeBoy grumbled.

"Good decision, D. And you, Ponce. I think our little Russian girlfriend has been a tourist long enough. Take maybe a thousand agents and heavily armed troops and toss her in the holding room as soon as Short vacates his chair. I want to see what she looks like in sweat."

"*Cierto, jefe.* I've been nervous with her around. But we still have or-ders from the colonel--"

"Fuck the colonel. I take responsibility. We don't play kid gloves no more with these people."

Mutters of affirmation, though not particularly enthusiastic ones, and the two men left Childress standing in the hall. Noise from the other direction, Short and Tejada in some kind of argument. Jesus H. Christ, beat that SOB down with a Louisville Slugger. That would stop his complaining. But Childress didn't have time for that rat, nor did he have a baseball bat.

What he had was an outstanding problem. Short was in hand and Kudashova was boxed unless she went on another killing spree. But Blackman, Reiser, and the High Plains Drifter were still in play and invisible. Where would they strike? When would they appear? These were Childress's questions.

He rubbed his face with both hands. He needed decent sleep. He needed a shower and a change of clothes. He needed to eat something better than airline food. But no. He slapped himself alert and started back down the hall to the common room.

What he needed was to dig up some answers, and he knew where to start.

Sanders tried to remind himself that the Navy captain sitting in front of him was a superior officer. Not by much, but still.

"I don't understand. To where?" he asked.

The captain thinned her lips just a bit, but otherwise maintained her unruffled, professional demeanor. She took a tablet from her desk. She held it up as if the gesture emphasized her point. "Strike Force 7, via the *USS Abraham Lincoln*, for delivery to one of its task force attack submarines. The package showed up on manifest four hours ago and was delivered by regular packet to the aircraft carrier. I have to say, colonel, that this sort of thing is highly unusual, the kind of shenanigans we'd expect of the CIA."

"I apologize, captain, but I'm at a disadvantage here."

Her face grew still, a clear sign she wasn't buying that kind of talk. "Okay..." She stood, replacing the tablet on her desk. She was a small woman. Sanders towered over her. The window behind her framed her in a mandala of limpid light, the indirect illumination from one of the many interior courtyards of the Pentagon. She stood in that light behind her desk like the queen of England might stand anywhere she pleased. She was a captain, with her own office in the Pentagon, even if it didn't have a Washington, DC view, and she had him by the testicles, and knew it.

"Colonel, I understand. Certainly, I do. I run hundreds of requisitions and equipment deployments through my office every day. I can't be expected to remember every one. But some I do remember, the ones classified secret, inter-agency, and from black box spooks like you. Those have a kind of … bouquet to them. Hard to forget, and, I would imagine, hard to forget setting up in the first place. I'm not asking for much, Colonel Sanders. I just want to know what this package is and what purpose it's to have on one of my boats. Common courtesy. No, *professional* courtesy. Until I know what I've got here, that package stays sequestered in the *Lincoln's* hold. It doesn't go anywhere, not an inch, unless it's to kick it overboard into the drink. I hope that suits you, because it sure suits me."

Properly scolded, Sanders choked back a snide retort. He didn't need inter-service backbiting over something he couldn't even recall. "I'll need to see the invoice, ma'am."

She picked up the tablet, touched its screen a few times, then handed it over to him with a great act of ceremony.

Sanders took the tablet in one hand. In his other he still held his cap, which she had pointedly not invited him to put down. He scanned the fields of official gobbledygook that showed shipping agencies, origin, destination, coded priority, and special handling codes. Yes, the package, whatever it was, had originated from his office. The description read, in typical opaque double-talk, "package, communications and signals analysis, item 1 of 1, restricted sealed." It had been channeled to engineer and sonar, the submarine at discretion of the task force commander. Attachment, power, and usage instructions were attached to the shipping container. Specific tags… Sanders felt his stomach tighten. He handed the tablet back before his fingers sweated all over it. The list of codes under "Specifics: Other" identified Childress's special team, their override priority, and Fiona Street's agent number. One other note stood out from the miasma of black type. Sanders's own classified phone number.

"Sparking any memories?" the captain asked.

"One moment, ma'am." Sanders drew his phone from the interior pocket of his service dress tunic. He clicked on the Messages button and there it was:

> I'm sorry. This has to be done. Grace agrees. Please. Let it on board. They don't have to hook it up. They don't have to turn it on. But it needs to be on board. In case you need it.

Oh, God in Heaven. Sanders screamed inside. Inside his head, he smashed things and threw things. But the captain saw only stern self-possession and a calculating, cooperative demeanor. He hoped.

She was alive. She was alive and she hadn't slowed for a second. He should warn the captain, implore her to contact her aircraft carrier, demand that they root out that … thing Street had sent them and toss it into the ocean. How had she done it? Her clearances were erased, access terminated.

She shouldn't even have throughput to his phone. But she did. She had the Voice of the City with his uncharted tech. And she had Short. Yes, the greasing CIA codes had stood right next to hers.

And she had Grace.

So the colonel had to ask himself: what, again, was Street up to? An invasion from another world. A monster bent on Earth's obliteration. And Short believed her. Reiser and Hostetter believed her. And now Grace, who had always cautioned listening, had gone over to her.

What was that young major doing?

"Yes, ma'am. This is from my office. It's experimental signals analysis equipment." Uhh… "Your task force is uniquely situated to test its applications."

"And what, may I ask, is experimental signals analysis equipment?"

Beats the hell out of me. "I'm sorry, ma'am. That's classified Most Secret, as you can tell by the code in box thirty-seven. Need to Know Only."

"It's on my ship, colonel. That means I need to know."

"With all due respect, ma'am, that isn't the case. You sailors carry highly classified freight all the time, with no knowledge of its workings until your mission specifies otherwise. There will be orders. For now, I respectfully request you permit storage on an appropriate ship as specified and await further clarification."

She stared at him. She might have been looking at a freshly painted wall, a new, pristine covering of a surface previously spattered with blood.

"You're not going to tell me a damned thing, are you?"

"Not when I'm not permitted, ma'am."

She stared at him some more. She was an expert at staring. Sanders wanted out of her sight as soon as possible. "All right, colonel," she finally said. "I'll release your toy, whatever it is. But I don't want you NSA spooks going behind my back again. You want something carried by the United States Navy, we're glad to oblige if you're on the up-and-up. Otherwise, find another country to do your cloak-and-dagger work."

"Yes, ma'am."

"Very good. You may leave now. I'm busy."

So that was it. She was pissed and wanted to brace him up. That was all. Sanders saluted, pivoted, and marched from her presence.

Fiona Street had sent classified freight to a naval task force.

She had stood a good chance of getting it installed and operated without anyone being the wiser.

But she had thought a play ahead, in case a smart captain asked questions.

She had ensured her old boss's cooperation through a combination of zero reaction time, pressure, and a list of destabilizing allegiances.

Sanders felt heat and ice at the same time, a warm pride that his protégé officer had maneuvered him so cleanly, and icy rage that the same was true.

He had set into motion days ago that her clearances be grounded and all data purged to which she had been privy.

Fulfilling that demand was taking far too long.

"Raisa Kudashova, you are under arrest! On your knees, your hands behind your head!"

Nightmare halted in the foyer of the machine facility. It looked around, squinting at the arms-bearing men rushing up from all directions. It calculated. It saw they intended to take the host captive. It made a decision.

The monster spread its arms. The gesture took an effort, for the host screamed inside, pounded inside, resisting as it realized what the next few seconds held. The monster spread its arms. It ignored the harsh shouts for it to kneel, for it to submit. It spread its arms. It spread its fingers. It opened its mouth.

Out of the host roared vengeance fueled by rage.

From the Russian's tunic pockets, three spheres arose. Ponce recognized them as the devices from the briefing days earlier, the devices that supposedly didn't work.

"Cease! Now!" he yelled at the woman. "Put down the spheres! Get on your knees and put your hands--"

The spheres lashed out. Three men went down from head collisions. The spheres returned to Kudashova, flew around her like wasps, then so quickly they left only blurs.

"Fuck! What the hell?" someone yelled.

"Stay frosty!" Ponce shouted, his pistol held before him, never taking his aim from the Russian.

"Fools! Animals! Monsters!" Kudashova sneered, and her voice pierced like the scream of a jet engine, pummeling the men with a hammer's force of sound. "Pray to your deities! Grovel! Wail and gnash your teeth! You are dead! The end of your world is nigh!"

Ponce staggered backward. All of his men stumbled, disoriented, their ears ringing. Ponce, with an effort, caught his retreat. He threw a hand across his face to block the suddenly tornadic wind rushing off the orbiting spheres.

Kudashova stood before him, a warbling figure behind the blur of her spheres. She laughed, and it was no human laugh, but a hitching, hyena cry.

"Down!" he shouted. "Get the fuck down now or we will use deadly force!"

The spheres darted out, headshots, dropping men in rapid succession. Three men, six, in a second.

Ponce didn't need to give the order. Every man standing emptied his clip into the Russian. Bullets sparked off the shield of orbiting spheres, which had retreated to their mistress and struck out again in a patternless hemorrhage of violence and defense. More men went down. Men scattered, crouched, dived for the floor, but continued to fire as Kudashova laughed.

Then, silence.

The spheres were gone. They had flown off. Ponce hadn't seen where. Kudashova stood with her arms held outward, surrounded by unconscious men. Her eyes darted. Her mouth hung open. Blood spread over her uniform shirt. Then the Russian fell over onto her back.

She fell like a cut tree, crashing onto the ungiving terrazzo floor with a sharp crack of spine and skull. The front of her uniform was a shiny greasing of blood.

"Think she'll stay down?" one of the few ambulatory agents asked.

Ponce gave no answer but labored breathing.

Fiona hobbled up to within thirty feet of the jet. It stood by itself in the open cavern beyond the bunker, its ramp down. Except for a couple of LED work lights high up in its overhead, the ship stood in utter darkness in an utterly black chamber. The Voice didn't waste his secretly produced energy.

Grace stood beside her, one hand lightly on the elbow of her good arm. He had reason to stand there ready to support her. She wasn't exactly steady on her feet, even with the cane from the Voice's stash. It was one of those geriatric canes, the kind with four little stabilizing legs flaring out from the bottom. The thing made Fiona feel eighty years old.

"How'd you know he was here?" Grace whispered, and nodded toward the ship. Someone moved around in there. Shadows danced in the work lights, and an occasional crash sounded.

Fiona didn't shrug. That was too much work, and hurt. "He wasn't in his room and he wasn't with anyone else. Where else would he be?"

"I think he's conflicted," Grace said. "He feels he needs to go, but he doesn't want to desert you. That's why I figured you needed to handle it."

Fiona wished someone else could play the babysitter. She needed a babysitter herself. "Okay. I'll talk to him. Don't know what I can say, though…"

"You want I should--"

"No, no. It's best we talk alone. That's how Clay and I are." With that, she doddered forward, taking her time to husband her energy. Thirty feet was a long way.

Somewhere along that trek, Grace turned away and returned to the bunker.

Fiona made it to the ramp before halting to rest. For no apparent reason, her bad shoulder ached beneath its bulbous dressing. Probably because she thought it should. She squinted up into the aircraft, peering around the side of the Malibu, which no one had bothered to remove. The deck of the Manta was littered with junk, the locker doors on the right side swinging freely open. Hostetter leaned heavily against the car, his head hunched and a half-pint bottle of Jack Daniels in one hand. He looked miserable.

"Hiya, cowboy," Fiona said. "Whatcha doin'?"

Hostetter didn't acknowledge her for a good several seconds. Then his head ticked up an inch or two, not enough to reveal his eyes past his hat. He gestured lamely with the bottle. "I brung it. In my saddlebags. Meant it for medicinals. I think I'll use it to numb m'brain."

Fiona took a breath and started her struggle up the ramp. "I was told you were upset. Didn't know you were Trashing-the-Place upset."

Hostetter looked around. He seemed to notice the open lockers and the jumble of fallen gear for the first time. "I'm good for it. I'll clean up." He straightened with a visible effort. "I couldn't recall where my saddlebags got to. They was right in the car, where I left 'em."

Fiona made the deck and continued to the nearest jump seat without stopping. "Mind if I sit down?" she asked, but didn't bother to get an answer. She couldn't believe how much she trembled when she lowered herself to the chair.

They waited in the semi-dark, Fiona breathing heavily, Hostetter staring at his yet unopened bottle. Someone would speak first. Fiona decided it had to be him.

"Your boy in California," he finally said, not looking at her. "That polecat with the slick talk. He done got himself arrested."

"Yeah. I heard that. The Voice has really good monitoring equipment."

"You said he'd take care o' Sinfonee. He can't do that from no cell."

"No, I doubt he can."

Hostetter raised the bottle. It jittered in his tightly clenched hand before he lowered it again with an effort. "You said she'd be safe."

"And I meant it, Clay. And she still is, if you stop and think. I mean, the place is filled with federal agents. My own people--"

Hostetter drew back and heaved the whiskey bottle with all his strength. It deflected off the seal of the ramp opening with a *clack!* then spun off to shatter on concrete.

Sally Reiser stood a few feet from the impact. She whipped her gaze to the splash of liquor and glass, then turned questioning eyes back to the ship.

"Your own people!" Hostetter roared. "Your own people is too durn dumb to see what's in front o' them. That Russian lady's right there, right there with my Sinfonee! And your people worry about trackin' and ropin' *you!*"

"I'm doing my best, Clay. We all are. You know it."

"It ain't near good enough."

Fiona had to concede that. She fiddled with her cane, not wanting to catch the old man's eyes. "What are you gonna do?"

"Sinfonee gotta be protected. I won't let that monster near her."

"Umm, guys…" Sally called. She held out a crumpled sheet of computer paper.

Fiona ignored the blonde. "The monster hasn't bothered her, Clay. Maybe it has no intention to. If it follows form, it's just watching her to get to you."

"Like it watched you to get to me? How many folks did that watchin' kill? It almost killed you." He shook his head, his moustache drooping at a steep angle. "No. I ain't lettin' that thing near my girl. I gotta go, Miss Fiona. I'm sorry, but I gotta."

"I wish you wouldn't. The best chance to stop the monster is here. We need you."

Sally tromped up the ramp. She stopped at the top, looking back and forth between Fiona and the cowboy.

"I know you need me, and that gives me trouble," Hostetter said. "But Sinfonee needs me, too. Ain't nobody there I trust around her."

"That may be a moot point," Sally said. She turned the paper in her hands, not wanting to interfere.

For good reason. Her insertion into that delicate moment filled Fiona with ire. She turned to the blonde, hoping the irritated look on her face was hint enough for Sally to back the hell off.

When Sally didn't respond right away, Fiona issued a put-upon sigh. "Well?"

"There's been a report to the Ft. Meade headquarters." Sally referred to the paper. "Kudashova's dead."

For a second, that statement meant nothing. Sally might have said there was a sale at Macy's. Then Fiona put the two words together. Kudashova. Dead. "Are you sure? It wasn't disinformation?"

"It sounded legit. That Childress guy has Short, and he told the colonel Kudashova was dead. They blew her away in a confrontation of some kind. A lot of casualties."

Kudashova dead? It didn't make sense. All of Fiona's expectations led to her and Kudashova at the end, one-on-one for the fate of the universe, that sort of thing. But she was dead. Did that mean the mission was scrubbed? Was it all done and over with?

"The monster," Hostetter said, his voice a monotone. "The monster's gone."

"It seems that way." Sally nodded. "So, you see, there's no reason for you to run off in a huff, marshal. I mean, not that you're in a huff. I mean, you didn't even hit me with that whiskey bottle, so, yeah, I'm cool. No judging here."

Hostetter seemed to swoon. He collapsed gracelessly into the jump seat three up from Fiona.

A movement at his sprawled boot. Something had darted away from his fall.

"And I guess you can really recuperate now," Sally went on to Fiona. "No fight for you, Major Scrappy Pants." With that, she regained control of her mouth and shut herself up.

Fiona shook her head. Sally faded from her vision. "I ... I don't know. I want to be sure." She peered into the space beneath the car. Yes, something was there. She damned well knew what.

"How can you get any surer?" Sally stepped closer to Fiona. "They shot her full of bullets, boss. Your big fight with the monster is canceled."

Fiona tried to see the corners of that revelation. It was possible. She'd had missions scrubbed because the object of the op had been offed by his own men, or run out of office, or had choked on a chicken bone. Why couldn't the all-powerful monster of the nightmareverse get greased by a bunch of twitchy government employees with guns? Sometimes, the simplest means were the most effective. "No, I want details. Are they still on to fire up the machine?"

Sally looked lost. "I-- I don't know. That wasn't in..."

"Is there video? Security camera images? The colonel likes that stuff. He wants to see, too."

"Umm, I don't know..."

"How successful was Short?"

"Uhh..."

"Well, find out, dammit! This is important!"

At that exclamation, Sally jumped. Her awkwardness at interrupting vanished, replaced by a sharp-lined face holding resentment and confusion.

Fiona felt like a heel. She also felt like punching the woman. "I'm sorry. It's the shoulder. Look, check it out, okay, Blondie? It's important to be sure."

"I'll have the Voice take a look." Sally was ice.

Great, Now Fiona had two of them upset. "I'm sorry," she repeated. "I'm an ass."

Sally didn't dispute that judgment. "I'll go get the answers." She turned down the ramp. "I'm sure we'll have them by the time you hobble to the bunker."

Okay, fine.

Fiona turned back to Hostetter. He sat in his jump seat, mouth open, staring at the side of the car.

"Clay?"

"Yes, Miss Fiona?"

"Is that good news? About Kudashova?"

"Yes, Miss Fiona."

"Okay, so can I hope that you'll stay, at least until we have clarification? I wouldn't want you running off half-cocked, ever. Certainly not for no reason."

"Yes, Miss Fiona."

"Oh, thank goodness. I need you, Clay. I really do. I couldn't do this without your help."

That seemed to trigger something in Hostetter. He looked up, blinked, and focused on Fiona. "I reckon so, Miss Fiona. But I gotta wonder. With the monster gone, what's it you plannin' to do?"

She opened her mouth, then closed it. She gripped her cane, but nothing came to her. With a subdued, mirthless laugh, she shook her head. "Friend, I have no idea."

She called to the cat. It growled at her and slinked away.

"I've no idea what Mister Short was doing," Sinfonee Rodriguez told Childress. She stood behind her desk in her new, cramped office where she couldn't find anything and shuffled her notes into a more discernible order. Though linear time was an old-fashioned notion that failed at the quantum level, she kept it in mind for the upcoming test fire, arranging her papers by necessaries for pre-fire, necessaries for fire, and necessaries for post-fire and the after-action report. She had been in the process of further sub-categorizing her sheaf of papers when the NSA man walked through her door.

Necessaries. That would be language she must have picked up from Clay. She would have to redouble her work on his diction. She'd also have to be careful with hers.

She remembered the man standing before her desk. "Mister Short came with authorization to power up our reactors. What he does otherwise does not concern me."

"Doctor, this Short guy's tight with Major Street. She's a traitor and probably crazy as catnip. She's got your boyfriend tied up in all this. Don't that concern you a little?" This Childress person bothered Sinfonee. He stood too close and he pressured too much. He felt like a light in her eyes. All her life had been noise and light, too much of both, no governing valve. Childress made that input flare, confusing the order she imposed on her world. And why was his suit so filthy? Why was it so rumpled? She could give him the name of a good occupational therapist.

"I'm busy. I have papers." She waved to the multiple piles. "I have to get my papers together. I've a meeting in less than three hours."

"I just told you your boyfriend's in deep with a traitor. That make a dent in your paperwork?"

Sinfonee panicked a little. She felt she might be missing something. What could Clay and Major Street have to do with papers? "Clay and the major are friends. They've been friends for years. I don't see--"

The room tilted, rolled, went suddenly blurry. Sinfonee gasped as something shoved her, *pierced* her, made her too small. She screamed, unable to right her mind against the sudden, warping reality of her senses. The light burned. The noise assaulting her brain grew to a crescendo of discordant detail. Childress said something, but she couldn't make it out. It sounded like gibberish. Then the noise and the light receded. The over-stimulation that had become her lifelong norm became a disorienting starvation of sensation. She felt cold and alone, trapped in a dark box at the bottom of an empty pool.

What was this? What mathematics made this possible?

Then she was in Childress's arms. *Childress's* arms, not Clay's. Not her Clay's. Why was she-- But it wasn't right. She shouldn't be in the loud man's arms. She should be-- But she couldn't feel Childress. He seemed somehow unreal. Only distorted sound and distance seemed real. That, and the other thing, the thing she couldn't name, a cold dread up her back, grasping, searching, enveloping her, so cold it hurt.

She lost touch even with that. It was like getting elbowed aside into a black room. A door closed, a bolt slammed to, and she could see her life but not feel it, not work it, not do the things she needed to do. The room that trapped her was dark and small. The room was a closet.

In a terrible, frightening way, it felt like peace.

"Are you okay?" Childress asked, holding her by her arms. "You sick or something? You keeled over."

"I'm fine," Sinfonee heard herself say, and tried to glance around, to see who had spoken. It hadn't been her, she was sure of it. It had sounded like her, she had felt her lips move and her throat vibrate, but she hadn't said--

"You sure? Maybe I should get you a doctor."

"I'm fine. I ... tripped on something."

"Doctor Rodriguez--"

"Please leave. I need you to leave. I have work to do, papers to arrange. I have a test fire tomorrow."

Childress released her. For an instant, Sinfonee tried to claw him back to her, but she didn't control her hands anymore. She didn't want him to leave. She didn't want to be left alone.

Because she wasn't.

"If you hear a word from Hostetter or any of his furry freak band, you tell me," Childress said.

"I will tell you."

"I'm not playing no games, sister. You tell me the second they contact you, because you won't last a day in the federal pen, and that's a fact."

"I'll tell you. Please leave."

He gave her a look, one she was used to, the one from those who didn't understand, who thought she was different but didn't know why. Then he left.

She cried out for him not to, but he didn't seem to hear.

A knock at the door, tentative, respectful. Fiona took two deep breaths and scrunched her face to wake its tired muscles. The knock repeated. Maybe the person on the other side of the door didn't wish to wake her. That would have been cool if Fiona had been asleep. She was a back person, mostly, and when she didn't sleep on her back, she preferred her left side. Neither of those had a chance of working out. She'd lain in bed for hours -- on her *right* side -- the ache in her shoulder mocking her. They clipped you, it said. You're out of the game, benched, maybe down for the season. Whatever came next, whatever the monster threw at your world, you can't handle it. You're a casualty of war.

Friendly fire.

The knock again.

"All right, I hear you," she called. "Gimme a sec."

Steeling herself, Fiona got her right arm under her and shoved her sorry ass to a sitting position. It took less out of her than she might have thought. She'd been shot in the shoulder, after all, not the heart. Buck up. Get to work. Stop being a pussy.

And... Sit there at the edge of the bed and breathe.

She got up. Whoever was at the door wouldn't wait forever. She took black tactical pants from the floor with her one good hand and maneuvered into them. Thank God for the Voice of the City and his peculiar forethought of a wardrobe department. For reasons Fiona could not hope to grasp, the man had a regular Army Surplus store of black tactical gear for all sizes and occasions.

"You okay in there?"

Sally. Right. "I'm fine. Hold your horses."

The shirt came next. Fiona didn't bother with a t-shirt, just the loose, black, multi-pocketed blouse that fit like a tent and so was easy to climb into. She hardly pained her shoulder, which made the scratchy feel of the blouse worth it. She'd need socks and the boots, but she had already admitted defeat there. She couldn't lace the boots without help. Nor could she work into the arm-and-shoulder brace the Voice had supplied her.

She took another cleansing breath, let it out, and straightened her back. Then she went to the door.

"Five minutes, almost," Sally said as she breezed into the dark room. "That beats yesterday. In a month you might be ready to take on a hamster."

Fiona flipped on the light to illuminate her simple, gray quarters. "Ha and ha, Blondie. You want me to toss you out on your ass?"

"How many minutes will that take?"

Fiona frowned, then went back to sit on the bed. Sally was being a hard case. Did she still hold a grudge for back at the jet?

"Hey," Sally said, "it was a joke."

"Your future in stand-up is doubtful. Why'd you wake me up?"

Sally hesitated a moment, but decided to pretend the subject really was changed. She started in on her infernal pacing, three steps one way, three steps the other. "You said to let you know as soon as the signals came through. The Voice has been monitoring all military channels in the ranges you gave him and his communications stuff is, as you might guess, mind-blowing. He not only got the communiques you wanted, he broke their encryptions without even trying."

"And that's the long-winded way to where exactly?"

She stopped pacing. "The device has reached its destination. We got confirmation it was off-loaded to the submarine and is safely stored."

All right. One more puzzle piece in place.

"Okay? Red? Yay?" Sally folded her arms across her chest.

"Oh, sure. Yay. I forgot on account of my shoulder hurts like hell. Anything from Lawrence-Livermore?"

"They've started up the reactors. They're ready to open a lightning post to the monster's home universe."

A progression of events outside Fiona's control. "What about the rest of it? Kudashova."

"She's dead. Official notification in Childress's report to Sanders. Security video you don't want to watch while eating. A spanking new autopsy report. She's pushing up whole hills of daisies."

Fiona bunched the covers in both hands. The death of Kudashova still felt wrong. What kind of world killer got stopped by a bunch of bullets? Probably the ordinary mortal kind, she decided. "How about Short?"

"Still in custody, held at the post lockup until Childress can transfer him east. But the Voice registers fifteen holo-projector/receivers, so I guess the spook got his chores done. Wanna come down to the command center? We can put on some popcorn and watch some of the bugs."

"I think I might." Fiona threw Sally a sharp glare. "Speaking of which, has anyone fed Oz lately?"

"He's your cat. You feed him."

"I wouldn't know what to feed him. Does the miraculous Voice stock cat food as well as all his other stuff?"

"Like I said, he's your cat. Find out."

Fiona frowned. She felt off, even hunted. Did she really worry over Oz's meals, or did some unseen other eat at her? "I have an uneasy feeling… Can't shake it."

"All right." Sally looked over into a corner of the room. Neither of them had mentioned the thing in that corner. Sally knew damned well Fiona wanted it forgotten. "Will you need me to push your wheelchair?"

Bitch. "That's all right. I can do fine on my feet."

"If you say so."

"I do."

And right after that bold assertion, Fiona had to eat crow. "But, umm, could you help me with the brace?"

"Sure, whatever you need."

Double bitch. "And my boots?"

Chapter Twenty-two

"All right, friends and neighbors, let's go down the line." Eglemann stood behind the big, boxy structure of her primary controller, communications bud in one ear, her mic wand curving until it hovered at her lips. Everything was ready, she knew, but procedure required a thorough check. "Power Base?"

"Power Base, go."

"Throughput?"

"Go."

"Attenuation?"

"Go."

"Signals Acquisition?"

"Go."

She read through the other half dozen checks, receiving a "Go" at each reply. "We are All Go for test twenty-three at the National Inter-universal

Transmission Initiative, trans-universal event 23, level three. Doctor Rodriguez, we are All Go and awaiting your directives."

Doctor Rodriguez stood ahead of the primary controller, her back to Eglemann. She faced the event platform, its attenuators thrumming with electro-magnetic potential. Would this test succeed where all others had failed? Would the modified math finally provide the geometry needed to cross the universal divide? Eglemann had a feeling this time. Her skin tingled with expectation. This time, their efforts would find a reward.

"Throughput up .0013," Doctor Rodriguez said over her pickup. "Attenuator Four angled .2 degrees. Apply."

Eglemann blinked. What the hell? She made changes at the moment of ignition? She peered slowly around, trying not to show the surprise she felt. She saw questions at every station. Most of the engineers stationed about the generator room met her gaze with raised eyebrows.

Eglemann lowered her mic pickup and strolled around the primary controller. She angled to the director's side and stopped almost rubbing lab coat sleeves.

"Umm, Sinfonee, what are you doing?"

"Last minute geometrical correction." The doctor thought nothing of it. She came through loud and clear on the link.

"Sinfonee. You're messing with the vetted geometry. This is hardly the time."

"Don't worry. It's just a fine tuning. I don't want to miss the mark for the twenty-third time."

Eglemann so hoped this wasn't an autistic brain fart. "Doctor Rodriguez, maybe it would be better to leave last minute changes for a future experiment. Here, with the generator active and the power flowing, we can't stop to verify your math--"

"You don't have to." Sinfonee snapped her head to glare at Eglemann. "No one needs to check my math. No one here could. I am the N-space physicist here. You are the engineer. Please return to your station and carry out my directives."

Okay. Autistic brain fart it was. "Very sorry, doctor. I just didn't want us to blow ourselves to kingdom come when we let loose all this power."

"We won't. Carry out my directives."

Eglemann watched her boss for another few seconds, considering whether she should shut down the firing. But the lady was correct on all points. She was the math genius in residence, and Eglemann was merely her loyal vassal. Who helped her match her clothes in the morning. Who helped her make sense of the hundred administrative crises that developed every day. Who helped her count her money.

But still just an employee.

Eglemann turned away from Sinfonee and walked back to her station. She tilted the mic back to her lips and spoke into the link. "Throughput: up .0013. Attenuation: bring Four an additional .2 degrees. Apply."

"Throughput, applying."

"Attenuation, applying."

The increased whine from the throughput apparatus covered the sound of an attenuator rotating ever so slightly.

Eglemann noticed a figure close to her side. That Childress dick, the guy who liked to yell at people.

"There a problem here?" he asked, glowering with his arms crossed. The guy wasn't happy. Maybe he never was. Maybe it was his funky suit.

"Nothing a little organization wouldn't fix," Eglemann said after covering her mic.

The chamber beat like a living heart. The thrum of the generator flowed through Eglemann's bones. The hairs on her arms stood on end. She knew that, in seconds, *every* hair would do so. Nobody bothered to wear hats in the facility. The two dozen operators at the control consoles, the twenty-odd technicians manning the data banks against the curved walls, the security personnel and the federal agents scattered over the floor, all those people had to feel the power building in the room. Vibrations first, then the feeling of a low-level current sparking through you. In a minute, the fingernails would resonate a bit uncomfortably, then color perception would skew toward the red. Sometimes, people hallucinated. Sometimes they saw auras. In seconds, if the math held out, they would see something else entirely.

"All readings nominal within change parameters," the primary controller team reported.

Sinfonee held out her arms to the platform as if to embrace what would form there. It seemed an odd gesture for someone confused by social cues.

"Engage," she said.

Eglemann nodded to the engineer at the primary controller station. Nodding back, he pressed the appropriate button.

A lightning post flashed to life.

Something whipped out of it.

Eglemann screamed.

"What you got?" Grace burst into the room, Sally hurrying to catch up. The command center was dark and gray like every other chamber in the underground lair. It was marked by a single swivel chair before a bank of a dozen large-screen monitors. On the desk below the monitors sat three keyboards and a USB dock loaded with every I/O port imaginable. The Voice hunched in the chair and all the screens were active.

The major stood behind him, one hand on the back of his seat. She leaned slightly forward, either to rest her weight on the chair or to peer more intently at the information flashing before her. One of those holo-VR goggles they'd mentioned hung from her good arm's wrist.

"Chatter out of Lawrence-Livermore," Hostetter said. He leaned over the planning table about six feet behind the Voice's chair. It looked like a kitchen island, except this island was covered with maps, tablets, and a scatter of holo-goggles.

"It got heavy round about the time the machine turned on," Hostetter continued. "Then ever'thing cut out before we worked out the cyphers." He handed both newcomers a set of goggles. "Put 'em on. We're goin' in."

Grace drew up opposite Hostetter and watched the back of the major's head. "Did they get a sniff of you on their lines? Maybe they cut you out."

"Negative," the Voice said. "They could not have detected our taps."

"This is the NSA you're talking about."

"Something's happened," Street said without turning around. "We've got strange stuff coming over social media and some of the news blogs. Voice, I need that link. I need it yesterday."

"Working on it." The big guy played his fingers over two of the keyboards.

Grace frowned. He looked up at Hostetter, who shook his head.

"What's going on?" Sally asked, positioning the goggles onto her forehead.

"Trying to figure that out." The major pointed to one of the screens. "Two A10s scrambling out of Beale. They're headed toward our guys. Get a line on them."

"I have that call," the Voice said.

One of the dozen screens lit with the grimacing face of LTC Sanders. "It's you," he said.

"Yes, sir," the major answered.

"That settles the question. I lose contact with my people in California and you bull into my communications array only a few minutes later? What are you up to, Street?"

"I'm not responsible for whatever's going on," Street said. "I'm calling to help."

"You're wasting your time."

"As are you, sir, if you're running a trace on this call."

"Not planning to stick around, are you? That's all right. I'd be astounded if you did, and a little disappointed."

The Voice held up a finger and Street waved him down. "That isn't it, sir. It's just … well, I have it on good authority that the line can't be traced."

"What the hell do you want?" The colonel's increased concentration on the screen showed he really had been stalling for a trace.

"I think I can help us both out. We're tracking increased traffic on Twitter, confused stuff about a disturbance at the lab. It's coming from passersby, mainly, and employees looking out windows from other agencies. Give it a few minutes, and there'll be video on YouTube. You're being jammed, so you'll probably find out what's up the same time that CNN does. But our comms go through ... unexpected routes. My man Short is your prisoner, correct?"

The colonel stared at her, confirming her statement by resetting his jaw.

"What you don't know is that he set holographic receiver-transmitters all over the trans-universal facility before you took him into custody. I'm linking to them now to get a look inside. Stand by, and I'll pipe a flat image to you."

"What kind of bullshit is this, Street? You sound like a comic book."

The Voice ran his fingers over an array of controls, then nodded to the major.

"Feed coming through in the next few seconds," Street said. "Please, sir, don't cut the line."

The major turned to Grace and the others, and nodded. Grace glanced at Hostetter, who had hung his goggles over his eyes, and at Street, who worked hers one-handed onto her face. Following their lead, he pressed his VR device over his eyes.

"Ready receipt," the Voice of the City said. "Live in three. Two. One."

The view went from black field to high resolution 3D with deep stereo sound. Grace cringed, startled by the realism of what entered his senses. He was inside the generator room of the trans-universal facility, Hostetter at one shoulder, Reiser at the other. The major and the Voice were a little farther ahead, the Voice sitting. On nothing.

"You seeing this?" the major yelled above a roar of growling machinery, static, and animal howls. She wore her black tacticals. Her shoulder brace was gone, but she still held her arm close to her side. "Colonel, you got this?"

A thick, blinding, trans-universal event blasted between the base and parabolic crown of the transference platform. The orange lightning throbbed, seeming to flex itself thicker by small degrees. Out of that light, dark tentacles thrashed, as amorphous as smoke but as violent as sledgehammers. One tentacle streaked over Grace's ducking head to stave in the flank of a control console. To Grace's amazement, the limb flew right through Sally's upper torso to no ill effect.

"Sweet Jesus! Sinfonee!" Hostetter pointed toward the base of the event.

Difficult to see through the glaring electric backlight from the lightning post, a figure stood with arms out, like a preacher calling his flock to prayer. But the figure was no clergyman, but a white-coated woman with dark skin.

Her long, black hair streamed in all directions like a jagged halo. An umbilical of smoke connected her to the crackling fire of the event. She laughed, a sound like a car crash in slow motion.

Hostetter charged toward Sinfonee, but bent almost double after a few steps. He looked as if he had slammed into something solid.

"Clay!" the major called. "Careful! You aren't really here! You're in the Batcave!"

Gunfire. But from where? And where were the shooters, and the technicians and scientists who should have been running the machine? There, cowering behind consoles. At least some of the white-coated technical staff. Grace turned in a quick circle to find soldiers at the big double doors. Childress and a few other agents huddled with them.

"That's it!" Street shouted above the roar of chaos. "Back us out, everyone but me! Transfer me outside the generator room!"

"No! Sinfonee!" Hostetter protested, but the major made a throat-slitting motion to the Voice.

The bizarre scene seemed to explode away, then Grace peered into black until he removed the goggles.

Gray room, computer screens, and two others as wide-eyed and shell shocked as he was.

"What the hell…" he managed to breathe.

"That…" Sally blinked and rubbed her eyes. "That looked bad."

"What *was* that?" Grace demanded. "Are you saying we were looking at Lawrence-Livermore? Real time? That shit was real?"

"I want that confirmed," the colonel snapped from his screen. "What are you trying to pull, Street? Major?"

The major was not with them. She hadn't removed her goggles when they had.

"Someone should do some explaining right the hell now," Sanders warned.

Hostetter, looking tight as a coiled spring, laid his goggles gently on the planning table.

Sally looked at Grace. Grace gave her the raised eyebrows and darting look of a man out of his element.

Just then, Street staggered a step and removed her goggles. She turned immediately to Sanders. "Sir, that was real-time from the machine facility. That was at least a Level Three event that seems to have been hijacked by something on the other side. It's taken Doctor Rodriguez and most of the security force. The soldiers and most of our agents have those tentacles in their backs and are organizing a double-circle cordon around the facility."

"If what you showed me was real."

"Goddammit, it's *real!* I'm not your enemy here!"

Sanders's face receded from the screen a bit. Hostetter, standing a few feet from Grace, was a hunched, dark silhouette as he leaned against the planning table. He seemed to have trouble breathing. "All right," Sanders said, his tone less hostile. "I saw Childress and a few others, no tentacles on them. Wonder why they weren't taken."

"It wants an audience," Sally whispered.

Everyone but Hostetter zeroed in on her.

"It wants an audience." Sally threw strength into her voice. "It doesn't want to destroy us. It wants to *terrify* us while it destroys us. It feeds on terror."

"And you know this … how?" Colonel Sanders showed a renewed measure of hostility.

Grace tore his attention from the blonde, from the colonel, from all of it but Hostetter. "Marshal? You okay?"

Sally's strength faltered. A quaver crept into her voice. "I saw it. I looked into its eyes and it looked into mine. It … *hates* me. It hates me more than *anything*."

Street narrowed her eyes at the blonde. "Sally?"

"It's doubt, and fear, and animal lust and it hates me because I'm none of that."

"Of course you aren't." The colonel's tone was dismissive. "Major--"

"It lives in a world that's barren of me, a world without hope, without warmth, without a chance to live, and it wants nothing to change. It wants nothing to change, nothing to threaten its dark existence. It wants darkness forever."

"Major, get control of your friend there." Sanders had hardened almost to the point at which he'd answered the call. "She's adding nothing to this conversation."

"Its world is dark and full of dreams," Sally said. "Its world is dark and full of dreams."

"Sally." Street said more firmly.

Sally ceased muttering about darkness and dreams. Her eyes flitted about the room as if she'd just then walked through the door.

"What?" she asked.

The major gave her a look that was equal parts irritation and worry, then turned back to Sanders. "Sir, I strongly advise you contact the *Lincoln* task force and direct them to initiate orders regarding the shipment we sent them two days ago. That package--"

"You're in no position to suggest anything, major. You're on even shakier ground to direct the actions of the United States Navy--"

"That device could be crucial, sir. It's a counter-signal to the one Nightmare runs on. If we block the signal--"

"We'll deal with this situation the old-fashioned way. With Tejada on the ground, I can release agents backed by military for surgical strikes on facility hostiles--"

Hostetter blew like an over-pressured engine. With one bellow of rage, he swept all the gear from the planning table. Goggles and papers flew into Grace's face. He threw up his hands for protection.

"*Tarnation!*" the cowboy roared. "Enough of this *talk!* Sinfonee's got that thing in her, and somethin' like a damned rotten puppet string comin' out her back, and all y'all do is count coup!"

Street stared at him, her features sinking into naked exhaustion. The colonel, Reiser's weird behavior, and now Hostetter, the supposedly steady one. She was getting it on all flanks. "Clay--"

"We can see the enemy! We need to hit that bastard in the throat! Stop talkin' bullshit and start loadin' guns!"

"Clay!" Street's admonition was a hellion screech.

That might have been the end of it. Hostetter shut up. But the colonel didn't.

"I'm not overcome with confidence," he said. "You can't even get your ducks in order."

"My ducks are plenty fine, sir. But, if you send in yours, a lot of innocents are gonna get killed."

"You've been on the firing line, major. You know--"

"Ain't none o' us ducks!" Hostetter bellowed.

"You need to shut him up," the colonel said.

Knotting his hands into trembling fists, Hostetter blew through his moustache, shot the major and the monitor evil looks, and stormed around the table toward the exit.

It didn't seem like the wisest thing to do, but Grace slid over to block the cowboy's exit. "Hold on, marshal," he murmured. "Give her a chance."

"I've been on the firing line, yes." Street barely controlled her voice. "I've been on the firing line, and I know what can go wrong. More importantly, and I hope you realize this, the surgical targets you refer to, colonel, are our own men. You're proposing eliminating American soldiers and American agents in a free-for-all on American soil!"

"If they're aiding and abetting that thing out there--"

"Under control of it, colonel. They've no choice in the matter! Set up a cordon, okay, but don't go in there guns blazing."

"Well, how do you expect me to go in? With harsh language and a hearty tsk-tsk?"

"*We* go in, *my* people. The Voice is the king of non-lethal weaponry. We'll go in and take down this monster."

"We'll what?" Sally said, her eyes flaring wide.

"We'll what?" Grace echoed, so utterly struck that he forgot who stood in front of him.

Hostetter heaved him out of his way. Grace stumbled to one side, right into Sally. The cowboy rushed for the door.

"Clay!" the major yelled, then spat out obscenities when he exited the room without looking back. She turned to the Voice of the City. "Prep the jet," she said, and the man rose from his chair.

"No, whoa! Do *not* prep the jet!" Sally put up a hand that stopped the Voice as surely as an "off" switch.

Street cocked her head at that, then pivoted to face the blonde. "What? What did you say?"

"I said, no jet." Sally tossed her goggles onto the planning table, not taking her eyes from Street. "We've made no plans, not even a mission statement, which makes me wonder what good a jet is. Prep the jet for what exactly? I went on that holographic ride to the tenth level of Hell. Didn't you?"

"God damn it, Street, get your crew into some sort of order or this conference--" The colonel said no more. His screen went blank the instant Street leaned past the Voice's chair and pressed a button.

When she returned her attention to Sally, Grace thought he should move between them.

"What the hell are you doing?" Street asked. She took a few steps aside to get a clear view past Grace.

"I don't need to answer that question. You do." Reiser was jaw-jutting aggressive.

"What the fuck is this?" the major asked. "Cold feet? You wanted to know if I was all in. Now *you* try to back out?"

"I'm not backing out of anything. I'm just using my head. Yours may have gotten cracked once too much."

"We've no time for this. There's an incursion into our universe. Monsters waving goddamned tentacles around, people possessed, people we know. Lives threatened--"

"The colonel can handle it. He has the people, he has the resources--"

Grace frowned, giving up keeping between the two women. Whenever he stepped to keep them apart, they moved to defeat that effort. Now they faced each other, inches apart, next to the planning table. The Voice stood like a statue, observing.

"He doesn't have the jamming devices," the major said. "He can't corner a goddamned smoke monster without the jamming devices!"

"Then *give* them to him!"

"By the time we do that, we could use them ourselves! Voice! The jet!"

"No! *Not* the jet!" Sally slapped the table. "Damn it, Red, what is the matter with you? Was Oz the brains of your team?"

"What-- Where is this coming from?"

"Look at you! Look at us! An over-aged cowboy with a broken stick! Me, I'm nothing! You with a busted arm and a short circuit in your brain! The only soldiers we have worth a damn are Sergeant Grace and the Voice, yet you want us to go to war! Against monsters! That's where this comes from! Are you insane?"

"No. Not buying it. I know your record. I know what you've done. You went up against nuclear terrorism without even a can of pepper spray."

"I had a goddamned army behind me!"

"You didn't have an army in Jerusalem."

Sally held up an index finger. "We were up against one guy, Red, one fucking guy!"

"You didn't win because he was one guy. You won because you have access to enormous power. You dropped a mountain on that one guy."

"I couldn't control it! I don't have power, power has me! You cannot, we cannot, count on that power to help us!"

"Why not? Come on, Blondie, we both know you're listening to more voices than mine right now. Why can't we count on your power?"

"Because we have to count on you!"

Abrupt silence. Nothing but the tick and whirr of computers.

"Well then." The major straightened and raised her chin. "Then you know what you have to do. You're on a mission from God, right? God tells you to depend on me, to follow me. And I say we get that jet in gear and go hunt us an other-worldly monster."

"You aren't hunting anything," Sally muttered.

"Is that from God, too? Why am I not--"

Sally reached out and squeezed the major's left shoulder.

Street's face twisted in a grimace of pain. Her left leg buckled, recovered, and she staggered against the planning table. Grace rushed forward and supported her before she hit the floor.

"That's why," Sally said.

Using the table and Sergeant Grace for support, Street worked back to a shaky, sweat-drenched stance. She breathed heavily. Her hands trembled.

"I wish to speak," the Voice of the City said. He had been standing there like a statue, not even his head following the back-and-forth fight.

"Later," the major said between heaves of breath. "I don't need three out of four ganging up on me. It seems only Sergeant Grace is willing to see this through, and he's brand new to the party!"

That was enough. Grace had tried to hold back, had tried to refrain from entering the collapsing building of Fiona Street's alliances, but that was no longer possible. "Sorry, ma'am, but what you just said, it isn't so."

The major froze. For a second, she did nothing, her profile a study in blank neutrality as Grace's statement worked into her mind. Then she turned to him, mouth open, brows drooping, her green eyes darkening from the blow he'd delivered. "You, too?"

"I'm just saying that Sally has a point. We're weak, combat ineffective. We should cede to higher command."

"Top. We've known each other for years. We've worked together for *years*. And you're siding with the Jesus lady you met fifteen minutes ago?"

"I'm not a Jesus lady," Sally protested, folding her arms.

"I'm not siding with anyone," Grace said. "I'm looking at the tactical situation, which is not good on our side."

"Godammit!" the major spat.

"I would like to speak," the Voice of the City said.

But Grace and the women gave him no chance as they broke into a riot of attack and accusation. Grace didn't follow where it started or how it progressed. The fall was like a greased slide to a dark basement. Angered, unwilling to hear what the others said, they yelled at each other, they jabbed, they defended, they bitched.

None of this would have happened if Fiona had taken the plane from Indy.

They wouldn't be in this mess if Fiona hadn't opted for her harebrained escape from NSA headquarters.

If Grace had backed her up more…

If Sally had managed to play on the team rather than throw the game…

If Fiona could think with *her* head rather than what was left of her cat's…

If any of them had the sense of a goose--

"Stop it! Stop it the fuck *now!* Shut the hell up!" Street slashed the air with her one good arm, her hand a white, quivering fist. She grunted at the end of that gesture, her face tightening. Grace and Reiser both fell silent, but the major seemed too pained to carry on.

"I need to speak," the Voice of the City said.

No one stopped him.

"We wish to live our lives in peace. But sometimes monsters deny us that peace. We are forced to fight. Forced. But we cannot prevail. Not on our own."

"Oh, God, I think I'm gonna hurl." Sally groaned, then buried her head on the planning table.

"No, he's right," the major said through gritted teeth. She'd stopped sweating, and had managed to stand upright. "This isn't the time to count our weaknesses. Our weaknesses are controllable. I'm going in. When something needs doing and only you can do it, you go in. I'm going in whether you guys do or not. I might get my ass kicked. I might get killed. But I won't stand around with my one good thumb up my lily-white ass while somebody's dealing out shit on my corner. I'd do better if you were with me. I'd do better if *everyone* was with me. But I don't control that. I only control myself. I'm one person standing up, and where there's one, there ought to be many."

Computer whispers and heavy breathing. All but the Voice leaned on the table.

"We're out-gunned and out-numbered," Grace said into the quiet.

"Then we'll be out-numbered together," Street said.

"We're gonna get killed," Sally grumbled.

"Then we'll get killed together."

The Voice of the City stood away from the others. He had said his piece. He waited to hear theirs.

"Well, shit." Sally grimaced and ran her fingers through her hair. "Voice, get the jet."

One of the three soldiers thudded onto his back. He had that surprised look of somebody who knew he might get shot but hadn't truly believed it in his bones. Equal parts shock and pissed off.

"Mother of God," Ponce muttered. He crossed himself, grabbed the soldier's armor at the shoulder, and dragged him as far out of harm's way as he could, which was only a few feet.

More bullets ripped into the heavy twin doors to the generator room, throwing fletchettes of steel.

Childress ducked, then glanced at the huddled faces. Ponce, D, and the two still-upright soldiers. They all showed a stony anger, frustration for the fix they'd landed in. Monsters in the machine room, plus four security men with goddamned tentacles extending from their backs. The security shambled like zombies but shot like aces, keeping Childress and his group cowering outside the room.

And, yes, they cowered. They couldn't charge in and they couldn't retreat. One of their company had discovered that the hard way when the grunts outside had riddled him full of holes. The guys in the machine room kept the group out and the guys outside the facility kept them in. It was a bitch of a press.

"How's he doin'?" Childress asked of the fallen soldier.

Ponce was on him, ripping open his protective vest and searching for wounds. "Umm, armor took most of the hit, but he's bleeding on the left. Uhh…" Ponce felt around for the man's first aid kit, found it on his web belt, and tore out the packed dressing. "He'll be all right, if we can get medical help. Any chance of that happening, guys?"

"We have to break out of here," one of the soldiers said, breathless. He ran his fingers over his trembling assault rifle as if petting a nervous dog. "Can't go in, not with that thing in there. We have to break the cordon."

"That's cordons," D said, his only calm voice in the huddle. "Cordons plural. And it's suicide. Best thing is to wait, keep our heads down, and hope for outside help."

"Shee-it!" Childress managed to hang the word with infinite frustration and cynicism. "You know what's gonna happen when the cavalry gets organized? They'll roll over this place like a bulldozer and we'll be friendly fired out the ass."

"I can't see Tejada letting that happen," D said. "You maybe, but not Tejada."

"My point is, if we want to get outta here, we do it our own selves."

"You're the boss," D murmured. "Waiting for your astounding brainstorm."

The door splintered again. Childress flinched as debris sliced open one cheek and smeared his face with blood. "Fuck!" He squeezed the grip of his impotent pistol. Three pistols and two rifles among them, and not one of those weapons worth a goddamn.

"What the fuck's going on here?" one of the soldiers demanded, clutching her M26 machine gun to her vest. "What the fuck's in that room and why don't it kill us and get it over with?"

"Despair!" roared from within the machine room, from that cute little sister with the screwed-up head. "Despair!" It boomed again in a voice like breaking glass and shattering bone. "Know that your end is upon you! Know that Nightmare controls your fate!"

"That's your answer," D said, licking his lips. "He wants an audience. We got elected."

"This is fucking ridiculous." The other soldier -- the one petting his rifle as if it were a dog -- twisted his face with rage. "Let's shoot our way out of here and bomb the motherfucker!"

"That's our people," Ponce said as he held the compress to the downed grunt's side.

"Fuck that, they're zombies!" Dogboy's gun hand trembled. He was losing it.

"Peterov, settle down," his partner said in a soothing tone, her larger weapon held steady. "We aren't shooting our own people. Seems to me, if we stay put, they aren't shooting us, either."

"For now," Dogboy said, his weapon rattling in his grip.

"For now," the other guard agreed.

Peterov? What the hell kind of name-- Well, Childress preferred Dogboy. Unable to watch the kid's shakes any longer, he reached out to steady the clattering weapon. "Be frosty, man. This shit ain't done."

"This shit blows," Dogboy complained, but he started to settle down.

"Yeah," Childress said, nodding, "but if it don't blow too much on us, I count that a win."

"Your bar for a win is low as shit," Ponce said. "We'd have to dig a hole to go under it."

He finished wrapping the wound. The poor soldier shivered like a hairless cat in a snowstorm. With one of them down and five huddled so close they were elbows to guts, Childress knew there was no win to have. All words, nothing else.

Rescue couldn't arrive soon enough, and rescue would likely be as bad as the trap.

Shee-it!

Sanders had his back to the video on his computer screen. He rubbed his face with both hands and listened to the disaster with the dead calm of hopelessness.

"Right now," Tejada said from the video, "we've no good options, but are doing our best. Local police, military police, and what men we could muster are surrounding the facility and returning harassing fire. As per your instructions, we haven't yet used deadly force, but it's just a matter of time, sir."

"Wait for reinforcements," Sanders said. The dead tone of his voice distracted him from his purpose. He dropped his hands and thought hard to recall what he wanted to say. "Umm, yes. I've two sniper teams and a Marine recon on the way, but their time on target is thirty minutes. That's still enough just for containment. A Major Browning of 2nd Ranger Battalion will arrive soonest to take overall command."

"Any word on what we're gonna do, sir? I mean, they're our own guys…"

"That remains to be seen." Sanders looked over to Goodknight, who sat in the chair before his desk, her mouth hanging open and her eyes glazed. She was supposed to be writing everything down, but her pen lay inert in loose fingers. The colonel knew just how she felt. "Maintain containment, look for Major Browning, and we'll see what he gives as analysis. Anything else? Anything on the machine, on the people inside?"

"Nothing since the cordons went up, sir. No comms in or out. But the reactors still show throughput, and the energy levels drawn have got to equal something big. Wasn't the machine only rated for level three?"

Right. Beyond that level of energy output, the machine would not contain the event. "Monitor and report any concrete change. Sanders out."

Tejada knew to let it go at that. When Sanders turned back to his desk, the video screen was blue.

"Hell of a day, eh, sergeant?" When Goodknight didn't respond, he reached out and jostled her shoulder.

Her eyes snapped alive, but wide with concern. "What are we going to do, sir? We aren't equipped to fight monsters of smoke. And, sir, our own people."

"We'll handle it," the colonel said, though he had no idea how.

"It's already public. It's trending on Twitter, Facebook has woken up, and some of the local broadcast and cable organizations have reporters on the scene."

"But they've no idea what the real story is."

"No, sir. Do we?"

That was a valid question. Sanders had to admit he didn't like its answer. But one person did have a sense of events. One person who'd recently hung up on him. "Something Street said about jamming the monster's frequency. Goodknight, send a priority communication to the *USS Lincoln* in PACFLT. Tell them to release the sub that got Street's package. Have it break open the orders accompanying the device and follow them to the letter."

Goodknight was already out of her chair and hurrying out the door. "So you've decided to trust the major, sir?"

"I've decided to trust longshots. We don't have any other kind."

They left the command center, the Voice leading through the gray maze of passages.

"The holographic system," Fiona was saying. "Let's make sure that's up, keep informed of what's going on inside. And as long as the links hold out, we can communicate with the men. And guns. Voice, you have any guns down here?"

The big man barely canted his head. "We have many guns."

Every second, he reminded Fiona of that black guy on that Star Trek show playing Schwarzenegger in a Terminator film. "That's good. Guns. Non-lethal and otherwise."

"I hope we have a better plan than comms and guns," Grace said.

"Not so much," Fiona answered. "But it's a two-hour flight, so we've got time."

They turned an, as usual, unmarked generic corner and found Hostetter marching toward them. He wore his duster, had found his hat, and gripped his stick in one white-knuckled hand and his rifle in the other. He looked as grim, as bent on business, as the two Colt revolvers slung at his hips.

Both parties met and halted in the corridor. Hostetter touched the brim of his hat. "Miss Fiona," he said. "Miss Sally."

"Clay." Fiona pointedly stared at his pistols. "What do you think you're up to, buddy?"

"I reckon I need help." The cowboy's tone was stiff. He held back a storm of emotion. "I can't find a way out o' this place."

"The way out's through the plane, Clay. We're launching ASAP, within a half hour."

Hostetter held up his stick. "Don't need no plane. I got my own way, thankee very much."

It took a moment for that to sink in.

"Hold it," Grace said. "You aren't thinking about going to Lawrence-Livermore yourself? Alone?"

"Not exactly. But I ain't goin' with you."

"Not going with us?" Sally looked from face to face. "What's that mean?"

Hostetter directed his words at the Voice, who stood as impassive as a wall. "I'm askin' to be led outta here. I don't have to. I'm just bein' courteous." Again, showing the stick. "I can leave any time I want, but it might make a mess of your home, sir."

"Whoa, whoa, cowboy." Fiona gripped Hostetter's rifle arm. "You can't tackle Nightmare on your own. We've a team here, buddy. We'll take him on together."

The sneer Hostetter directed at her made her release his arm. "This ain't no team. Pardon me sayin' so, Miss Fiona, but all y'all can do is get yourselves killed. And that won't do, not when my Sinfonee's in danger."

"Clay--"

"In danger. *Again*." He shouted that last. His breath came in rough blasts. He took a moment to calm it. "I can't lose her again. You know that. You know what happened last time. I can't abide it. So I gotta go. I gotta handle this my own way."

"Elevator," the Voice said quietly. "Northwest corner of the hangar. I can show you."

"Thankee, sir. Much obliged. Can we go there now, if you don't mind?"

"Clay..." The guy broke Fiona's heart. She knew what he felt. She knew the turmoil tearing him apart. They had both lost loved ones, and to violence, to evil. In the infinite weirdness of the multiverse, Hostetter had found his love again. A second chance.

"You ain't talkin' me out o' this," he told her.

"I'm going with you."

"Miss Fiona--"

"Just to see you off." She watched him, saw gratitude but also impatience in his stern features. Then she pulled her gaze from his and directed her attention to the others. "Umm, guns. Round 'em up and get to the ship."

"You sure about this?" Grace asked. "Medical still has to prep you. We don't need delays."

"There won't be any. I'll see the marshal out, then get to medical to get trussed up, drugged up, and braced in. You'll have my tac gear ready on the plane."

Grace hesitated as if he had more to say, but chose instead a slight, respectful nod. "All right," he said. "Fifteen minutes."

"Yes, Dad."

Grace took Sally's arm and hauled her up the corridor and around a bend to the right. Fiona and Hostetter followed the Voice, who took the corridor straight on.

It was another few minutes and another few turns before they pushed through the doorway into the hangar. The jet stood there as it had for days, the ramp down. The Malibu still blocked much of the view into the aircraft. It had hunched there undisturbed, covered by the excuse that a moment might free up in which to return it to the agency. Truthfully, no one had really wanted that job. The agency would be pissed when they got the Chevy back. The dings in the hood and the cracked windshield would prove embarrassing to explain.

The Voice halted near the plane. He pointed farther on, into a dark corner of the hangar. "There. The elevator comes up in the abandoned mall above us, in a falling-down arcade. Push the button to go up. The code down is One-seven-four-zulu-beta-six."

"Okay," Fiona said. "One-seven-four-zulu-beta-six."

Hostetter was already on his way. Fiona walked fast to catch up. By the time she did, Hostetter had pushed the button beside the narrow elevator and the door was sliding open. Fiona dodged in beside him. There was no up or down button. The elevator car ascended on its own.

Neither Fiona nor Hostetter spoke during the ride.

The doors opened into gray light. Beyond stood dingy walls and an empty floor of chipped tile and raw concrete. Deep and narrow, that hole led to a brighter area that was itself a dim manmade cavern. An old mall, moldering from neglect, Fiona thought as they stepped cautiously from the so-called arcade into the greater space beyond. It had never been much to start with if her childhood memories still served. Her parents had brought her there many a time, unable to afford the prices at the swankier shopping centers in town. Eastgate Mall had been a sprawling neighborhood market filled, when it *was* filled, with Mom-and-Pop fledgling enterprises that were more heart and happy wishes than business models. The same had been true of the place that charged them rent.

Now the mall lay dark and ghostly quiet. The few former shops within range of the dim light were black caves in the walls. A few aisle kiosks hulked in the open with broken glass and peeling plywood counters. Dust covered everything, dust and dead dreams.

"Here," Hostetter said, pointing his stick at a rusted metal door in one wall. The latch had been busted and lay in pieces on the cracked floor. A steel bar lay across the door, held in place by braces bolted into the wall on either side.

Hostetter drew up the bar and lowered it to the ground. He pushed open the door and brilliant light flooded the chamber.

After five or six days underground, Fiona had lost all track of time. The morning sun surprised her.

They stepped out onto an unkempt parking lot, grass and tall Canada thistle pushing open its network of asphalt cracks. Less than a hundred meters beyond the building they exited, a Dollar General convenience store showed its yellow and white cinderblock exterior. Traffic hummed in the near distance, but Fiona saw no cars thanks to the Dollar General and white, scarred cement blocks set as a wall around the mall.

Holding her good hand to shield her eyes, Fiona scanned beyond the obvious, looking for traps and threats by habit. She found only blue sky, a few wheeling grackles, and chill autumn air.

Until she turned south.

"Oh, my God..." Looming higher than the mall and reaching back to the visible distance, thick steel supports held huge panels aloft, each rectangular frame challenging the footprint of most people's houses. The solar farm. "It looks like something from science fiction..."

"Miss Fiona, you just left the underground home of a superman, and you're threatened by a monster from another world, and you're talkin' to a feller from another universe."

"Well. Okay."

Hostetter stepped away from the building and lifted his stick.

"Wait. Clay."

"You ain't talkin' me out o' this," the cowboy said.

"All right." Fiona held up a cautioning hand. "I just want to say something. I want you to remember what Willie Dern told us back in his house. Do you remember? It seems like a thousand years ago."

Hostetter lowered his stick. "That old cuss says a lot of things."

"He said, to me, you don't have to do this alone. You have friends, they just have to be finessed." She licked her lips, saw he still stood there, so went on. "Clay. I don't have to be finessed. I'm with you to the end of it. You know that, don't you?"

"I reckon I do, Miss Fiona."

"Then please, don't do anything foolish."

Hostetter chuckled at that. The sound was so normal, so human. Under all the recent circumstances, it seemed out of place. "You know me, little girl. I can't promise not to be foolish. But I'll promise you this. I ain't chargin' reckless into nothin'. The stakes are too high and my Sinfonee is at risk. No, ma'am. I got my own path in this, one can't none o' you follow."

"I just thought, after all this time, we'd be doing this together."

"And maybe we will, Miss Fiona. Maybe we will. But not right now."

"Does that mean you'll be back?"

"I do hope so, and hopefully with friends."

With that, he raised his stick, thumped it hard on the asphalt, and disappeared into a blazing pillar of orange, coruscating energy.

The lightning post winked out a brief second later. The day was as it had been. Even the grackles still cawed overhead. The only evidence of Hostetter was a molten circle where he had struck the stick.

What had he meant by friends?

Chapter Twenty-three

The firecracker chatter of automatic weapons reverberated over the streets around the trans-universal facility. Tejada rushed along the sidewalk across the street from the grounds, crouched to not present a target. He thanked the good Lord and his own forethought for the wall of civilian cars and HMM-Vs between him and the gunmen holding the machine building. Sixty-odd men, some in combat gear, some in suits, held the facility at against him at all points, not bothering to take cover against a battalion's worth of troops. They stood in full view, lethargic in appearance, violent in action, shooting at anything that moved. Even birds.

What the hell had happened? How had Tejada gone from routine coordination with the agencies swarming the grounds to scurrying from car shield to car shield under fire? He shuffled past a bullet-wrecked Hummer with flat tires and a stink of transmission fluid, glass sprayed over the sidewalk as thickly as candy sprinkles on a kid's cupcake. He passed three soldiers, two with their SAWs aiming over the hood of a Hyundai Sonata, a third a Marine corpsman hunkered over a flinching airman with a bloodied shoulder. Jets roared uselessly overhead, rattling windows and Tejada's bones. The double ring of soldiers and agents firing from the facility hardly noticed the aircraft.

"What the hell," one of the riflemen at the Hyundai said. "It's like they're sleepwalking."

The masonry of the building behind him shattered. Drumbeats of bullets made his car shield jerk.

"Not too asleep," his buddy groused.

The two returned fire, directing their aim well above the heads of their opponents, as ordered.

"I'd like to meet the dumb son of a bitch who told us we couldn't shoot back," the first soldier complained.

Being that selfsame son of a bitch, Tejada moved on. He dodged into the next doorway, where four more soldiers and two local policemen kept tabs on opposing gunmen through the door opening and two shattered windows. A desk had been heaved onto its side, an improvised additional shield in case the walls proved inadequate. Dozens of craters were drilled into the wall opposite the windows and door. Framed pictures littered the floor along with crackling glass, drywall chunks, and random, trampled office knick-knacks. The stairs facing the doorway showed gouged risers with a ripped runner. The newels supported no bannister. It lay splintered over the floor. Tejada gave the men a questioning look.

"They're upstairs," one of the cops volunteered. He paced in a tiny box pattern, keeping well clear of both windows and doorway. "After the last spray of auto-fire, they thought it might be better to move somewhere out of line of sight."

"Thanks," Tejada said, slipping around the desk and up the stairs. He moved quickly, keeping far to one side, out of sight from across the street. Or he tried. He met two men coming down, each so weighted by combat gear they looked inhuman, like giant, camouflaged turtles.

At the top of the stairs, the space spread out into a wide office pool full of cubicles with cloth-covered walls. Much of these had been swept away, thrown onto each other in the extremes of the room. Three desks had been shoved together in the emptied space. Major Browning and his hastily assembled staff bent over the desks, studying hand-drawn maps and aerial printouts. All the men wore ACUs.

Browning, a steely-eyed square-jaw with a carrot red crew cut, looked up. "Agent Tejada, good. Come over, young man."

Tejada filled the hole made for him at the desks. Browning directed his attention to the largest map, a near-comical thing drawn in hurried Sharpie with a flurry of annotations.

"Here, agent, is where I want you and your remaining men." The major pointed at a section of sidewalk across from the facility's front door. A rectangle next to his finger was marked "Lincoln."

"Yes, sir. The gold Navigator. I just passed it five minutes ago."

"Gold? I figured it for kind of puke colored. Anyway, get all your men and put them there. Your approach is along the left of this sidewalk--"

"Sir. Approach?"

The major frowned, but took his finger from the map and straightened. "We're mounting a coordinated assault on the facility in one hour, weapons loose, calling targets, wound shots if possible but deadly force is authorized. This mess has gone on long enough."

"Major, those are our people. They're under the influence--"

"Of a force classified secret -- even from me -- that has taken control of what I've been led to understand is one of the most dangerous facilities on the face of the Earth. That's why we also have close air support from two A10s and one F22 for ceiling security."

"A10s? Tank buster aircraft? What are you expecting, sir? And why would you need a high altitude fighter for a ground terrorist attack?"

"Agent Tejada, this is the United States military. We skimp on nothing. If I were called to secure a nuclear missile silo in enemy hands, it would not reach the level of importance ascribed to this mission."

"My men are in there."

"I realize that. I also realize that we've no idea whether they, too, have been co-opted by the enemy. But don't worry. I'm giving you lead through the front door. You'll have discretion regarding any of your men you might meet."

Yes, for about ten seconds before the following teams go in blazing. "Thank you, sir. So, the specifics?"

The major gave them, quick, clipped, and professional. Tejada left the table in less than a minute.

He met more men coming up the stairs.

The *USS Jimmy Carter* nosed through the dark of the Pacific, searching the water like a bloodhound sniffing the ground. The captain leaned against the coaming between Helm and Command, his arms and back braced tightly against the steel lip of the hatchway. He had to hold tight or tumble across the steeply tilted deck. Still, the uneven steel construction wasn't doing his back any favors.

"Thirty degrees down-bubble," the officer of the deck intoned. "Course zero-four-seven, Depth 1800."

"Trench wall at two-three-seven meters, closing at twenty," Sonar called down. "Recommend correction to plus three degrees."

"Make it so." The captain nodded to his officer of the deck.

"Affirmative." The OOD held to the forward periscope platform in Control, one elbow crooked over one of the railing's support posts. His other hand gripped a comms mic, which he drew to his lips. "Come to zero-five-zero."

"Zero-five-zero, aye," the intercom acknowledged.

"Chief, what you got?" the captain called back toward the Radio Room. He felt the boat turn under his feet.

"VLF still anomalous," the master chief called forward. "We can't get heading or distance, but it's there all right. I have to tell you, sir, this equipment is extraordinary. We're searching frequencies way below our normal capability."

"Suggestions?"

"Maybe a neutral turn at our next pivot. Might be able to assess signal strength."

"Roger. Officer of the Deck, note that. Three-sixty stationary at the next pivot."

"Aye, sir. Remain nose down?"

The captain thought about that. Of course, nose down. The VLF would lose contact if they took its sensors off target. But were they really nose down enough? "Go to forty degrees down bubble, reduce speed to one-quarter."

"Aye, sir." The OOD gave the orders.

The dive chief half turned from his post behind the helmsman. A hint of worry lined his brow. "Taking it awfully close to specs, aren't we, sir?"

"We can handle it, chief." The deck slanted downward toward the bow.

"There comes a point, sir, where we can't fully control descent on a crash dive. And we can't see very well. There are mountains out there, sir."

"It's still a doer, chief." Nonetheless, the captain chewed on the NCO's guarded advice. "Distance to wall?"

"One-four-four meters," Sonar replied promptly. So they were a bit scared, too.

The plane shuddered, knocking Street into the Malibu. "Shit," she muttered, and accepted Grace's hand to steady herself.

"Don't worry. We're almost to Mach two. A little instability is expected." Grace went back to strapping her into her gear, but directed tight-lipped, worried looks her way. That was okay, he thought. A little worry was normal. Four people, one an untried woo-woo mystic of a girl, going up against giant, tentacle-waving monsters too scary for Hollywood. Arrogance would show a great dearth of common sense.

The major held out her bad arm while Grace secured her body armor. He'd jury-rigged something with Velcro, safety pins, and nylon line so that the vest attached under that arm rather than across her shoulder. He'd also plastered Velcro over the armor's front surface. To this he had stuck two pistols, a shock stick, and two 250-round drums to feed her assault rifle, all within reach of her good hand. With the armored-and-armed vest, the rightside hip, thigh, and ankle holsters, and the thigh and waist ammo bandoliers stuffed with shock cylinders, she looked like something out of a '90s action movie. Only the shoulder brace that would strap down over the combat gear ruined that impression. Or maybe not. There was always *Die Hard*.

"So okay," Grace said into the rattle and roar of the ship. He tightened the last of the many straps. "You've got a number of choices in your arsenal. Grab one, use it up, drop it, and pull the next. Each load is non-lethal, according to the Voice. Not the reloads for the M4 though. Red mags are live, the Voice's stuff is blue." He tapped the two bulging packs on her left leg. They counterbalanced all the hardware on her right. "Your signal cancellation units. We put them in a circle around the monster, turn them on, send him back to wherever the hell he came from. That's the plan. It is not to kill our own people."

"Well, top, our own people may try to kill us."

"Bridges when we come to them, ma'am. We'll use every trick we have to keep that from happening. Too bad we don't have the cat."

As the major was prone to do when conversations got tough, she changed the subject. "I weigh at least 500 pounds."

"No, you don't. I'll stay on your left, your exposed side."

"You'll stay wherever you're needed. I don't want a babysitter."

He opened his mouth to say something, thought better of it, and went on fastening her shoulder brace. "We'll shoot you up with the Voice's magic pain killers just before drop. That'll take the edge off--"

"Top."

He sighed and stopped fiddling uselessly with her uniform. "Yes, ma'am."

"I was a damned good field agent before I got Oz."

"Yes, ma'am."

"I'm Airborne, Air Assault, and Special Ops. A little clip of the wing is not gonna slow me down."

Grace froze the look on his face before it got where he knew it was headed. "If you'll excuse the commentary, ma'am, that was a dumbassed claim to make."

"Sergeant Grace--"

"I'll finish, if you don't mind. That was grade-A bullshit. You're wounded. You should be in the rear with several weeks of recovery ahead. But here we are, shooting toward danger like an arrow from the bow, because you have to prove something to the powers that be. You want to show that you aren't the threat they take you for and that's what you'll do if it kills you. If it kills all of us."

"I thought we were done with all this."

"We are." He reached for his own vest and started pulling it on. "But don't pretend this is smart, what we're doing. It isn't."

She cocked her head at him. "Then why are you here?"

Grace's answer was more a mumble than an assertion of purpose. "Because I haven't any better idea." He shrugged on a shoulder holster and pouch vest. "I think I'd hate myself if I could do something in this conflict and didn't. Besides, somebody has to keep you out of trouble. God knows you're no good at it."

"And because it's fun." She whipped up a wide smile. It looked out of place.

"And because it's fun."

Grace slapped pistols, shock sticks, grenades, and the Voice's special toys all over his vest and web belt, then patted his armored chest and sighed. "So. I look cunning?"

"Right out of Armed Forces GQ. Voice! We're ready!"

The major took up the M4 assault rifle laid in the front seat of the Chevy and lumbered down the length of the car to where Sally waited at the back bumper. Grace followed, his own rifle in hand.

"Whose idea was it to take off with this crate still aboard?" Street slapped her elbow along the flank of the Malibu.

"Voice says he wanted it to balance the ship," Sally offered. She leaned against the trunk, arms crossed, staring at the closed ramp. "I think he just forgot it was here."

"I did not forget it was here," the Voice of the City said as he came down the other side of the car. He crossed in front of the others, marching to the lockers over by the retractable table.

"You sure you want to do this?" Sally asked, not looking at anyone. She seemed tiny in her armor. She showed fewer weapons than Grace or the major, just two shock sticks and a small automatic pistol in a hip holster. All of the weapons had come from the Voice, who maintained a sizable armory in his Indianapolis secret base.

"I'm sure I don't want to do this," Street answered. "But I'm sure it has to be done."

The Voice returned with three stainless steel-and-brass gun bracelets, copies to the multi-tube weapons he wore on each wrist. He handed one to each of his partners. "These are loaded with plasticene rounds, oiled clay like in a child's art kit. Same as in most of your firearms. Non-lethal. They'll knock a person down at thirty meters, but will cause no lasting damage, even if aimed at the head."

"Gee." The major turned the device over in her hand. "Thanks, Voice."

The big guy shrugged. "Point of clarification, they might put an eye out."

The bracelet consisted of eight metal cylinders with slightly bulging, sleek sides, open at each end. Grace saw no obvious controls.

"You make a fist…" The Voice demonstrated. "… and activate the weapon with a downward flick of your wrist, like so."

"Like this?" Sally, who had pulled the weapon over her left wrist, snapped her hand downward as the Voice had shown. A sharp report like a softball hitting a bat, and a fat blob of gray appeared on the ramp.

Everyone looked at the splotch of clay.

"Uhh, oops," Sally said.

"Perhaps," the Voice said, his tone diplomatic, "you should wait for the entire briefing, including the part about safeties."

"Sorry."

"Blondie, you're such a dunce sometimes," Street said, grinning.

"I can't help it. Guns and stuff, they aren't my thing. I'm more, you know, metaphysical."

Grace groaned, and wished Hostetter were with them.

"When we hit the dirt," the major said to the blonde, "you stay close to Grace. Climb in his pocket, if you have to."

Sally's expression went from contrite to frosty. "I'm not a defenseless little girl."

"I'm sure you aren't. You aren't trained for this, either. It'll get nasty. Everyone to their skills and, as you said, your skills are more metaphysical, less cracking heads and kicking crotches."

"I've kicked a few crotches in my day."

"And I can't even *count* all the crotches *I've* kicked."

"Can we get off the subject of crotch kicking?" Grace asked.

"The point is, you, Blondie, stay under our wing. I want you in one piece when we need your particular brand of Armageddon, all right?"

Sally gave her a stubborn look.

"I said, all right?"

"Okay. I heard you."

"Thanks. Very important. Now, what's next on the agenda, Voice?"

The Voice of the City inclined his visor at Sally. "I'd like to finish the weapons briefing."

So he did. He went over the safeties for the BBLs, or Bracelet Blob Launchers, as the major decided to call them. The Voice also gave the group pointers on the shock sticks, shock bars, and kinetics-transference ammo for most of the guns they carried. Then it was the communications equipment and the Theta/Delta cancellation devices they had printed off in the secret headquarters. Grace marveled at the extent of weird contraptions, but even more at the fact that the Voice, for the most part, had failed to give them names. What inventor of science-fiction technology fails to christen his creations?

There wasn't much to do after that. They had their gear, they knew their weapons, they had gone over the plan, such as it was. Finally, it was just the waiting.

"How long?" the major called as the Voice headed back toward the cockpit.

"Fifteen minutes," the big man said.

The major leaned against the back of the car, her good arm resting elbow on trunk and her legs crossed at the ankles. Consciously or not, she copied Sally.

"So we'll be on station around three in the PM," Street said. "Maybe an hour to take out the bad guy. Believe me," she said in an aside to Sally, "these things rarely take more than an hour. So. What's everybody doing after?"

Grace knew her intention, and it had nothing to do with him.

Sally turned a blank stare on the major. "You think there'll be an after?"

"Oh, there's always an after. So, what'll you do when you've saved the world? Again. And don't say 'I'm going to Disneyworld,' that's cheating."

Sally moved her gaze back to the ramp. "I've always wanted to see San Francisco, and we'll be right next door."

"Frisco's cool, I can see that. Lots of sights, good restaurants. Me, I prefer a bit more … involvement. I'm going to Vegas!"

"Like to gamble, do you?"

The major snorted. "That has to be a question? Plus, the food is free, lots of places anyway. And I'm sick of pizza, hot dogs, and the Voice's ration bars. Vegas, baby! City of Lights!"

"I thought that was Paris."

"Have you ever *seen* Vegas?"

It went on like that, just the two of them. Grace opened the back door of the Malibu and climbed in. He had an awkward time of it with all the gear ballooning his form, but he had fifteen years in the Army, so he made a way. Once inside, he lay on his side facing the front seats. A few minutes of peace before chaos claimed him, that's all he wanted, he didn't ask for much.

With the expertise of long practice, Grace shut off his brain. No more worry over the course of the next few hours, no questions about his future with the NSA, the Army, or any government service. No more fretting over his wounded, reckless major. He just lay there and stared at the back of the driver's seat.

"Meurrl?"

He looked down. Two green flecks of light winked at him from beneath the driver's seat. He squinted, relaxed, and tapped the carpet below his head. "Hey, boy. Come on out."

292

Oz scooted into the open, then slinked along the seatbacks, his eyes ever on Grace.

"Bad place for a little cat," the soldier said. "It's going to get rough in a few minutes."

Oz sat, and licked a forepaw.

"Yeah, you're all that, huh? Audie Murphy, Sergeant Rock. A regular Vin Diesel of cats, are you?" Grace stuck out his hand, palm down. "Come here, you gadget."

Oz strolled under his hand and received a full-body pet. He purred like a glass-packed muffler.

"Major Street," the Voice of the City called from the cockpit. "Five minutes out. It's time to set up for broadcast."

Grace sighed and scratched Oz beneath the chin. Moment of peace. Over.

Chapter Twenty-four

"Come!" the voice of broken glass thundered. "Come witness a new world unfold into yours! Come see the end of your days, you killers of dreams! Come forth, I give you passage!"

"She gives us what?" Childress wondered, glancing at the others.

"It wants a face-to-face," D said.

Childress blanched. "Fuck no! I don't need no tentacles in me."

"Maybe there won't be tentacles," Ponce suggested. "Maybe it wants us, you know, all ourselves. No fun posturing to drones."

Childress rolled his eyes. He flexed his grip on his pistol. He didn't know how to deal with this particular Big Bad. He wished he'd read more comic books as a kid.

"Perhaps you need incentive," the alien voice cackled.

Immediately, two armed guards outside the building directed their SAWs into the atrium fronting the machine room doors.

"Watch it, watch it, *watch it!*" Ponce warned. He grabbed the downed soldier's vest and wrenched him away from the view of the guards.

The wall and floor just short of the group erupted from gunfire. Flying tile and drywall burst at them like shotgun blasts.

"Shit!"

"Jesus!"

"Fucking hell!"

The guards outside ceased their harassment. They just stood there for a count of five, then directed a fusillade at the ceiling tiles over the cringing bunch.

"Jesus, Childress!" D shouted above the din. "We have to do something."

Tile dust and fluorescent light shards rained down on Childress. All his men hunkered dusted and wild-eyed. What should he do? To do nothing meant taking a mag full of rounds if the boys outside thought to fire again. To do as the nasty lady asked could be worse.

"Hey, sister!" he yelled at the top of his lungs. "How do I know you're on the up-and-up? Referring to that bullshit about passage!"

The chortle she sent him sounded like a tank rolling over gravel. "I am Nightmare. I am powerful beyond your knowing. I am the pure truth of the animal mind."

"Now, see, that's what I mean! So far, you haven't been nothin' but a dick!"

"If being a dick is demonstrating the ultimate beauty of vengeance against the enemy, then I stand proudly accused."

"Yeah, like I said!"

"Still, I grant you and your ape minions leave to join me. No harm will come to you while I have need of your witness."

"Mother of God," Ponce muttered, then crossed himself.

The female soldier widened her eyes and mouthed "What the fuck…" to anybody watching.

Dogboy's lower lip quivered.

D shook his head and rested the slide of his pistol at his brow.

Childress gritted his teeth. "Now that's the kind of bullshit I'm talkin' about! You can see that it isn't the greatest incentive to threaten to kill us when you get an itch, you know what I mean?"

"Point taken." Walls, floor, and ceiling spasmed behind them, over them, even within their huddle. Ponce threw himself over the wounded soldier. An overhead light fixture broke loose and swung down on one cable, cracking across Dogboy's helmet.

"Fuck this!" Dogboy yelled. "Fuck this shit!" He lurched up, slapping the butt of his M4 against his shoulder, and lunged for the outer doors.

"Peterov!" the other soldier called. She rose to stop him, but D was faster, grabbing her belt and jerking her back to the floor and into the group.

Dogboy bellowed guttural obscenities and let loose at full automatic as he charged the men outside. The deafening exchange of gunfire lasted one or two seconds, then Dogboy went down like a toppled gravestone.

The place grew heavy with the rotten egg stink of expended ammunition.

The comparative silence lasted barely a breath, then craters once more punched into the double doors above Childress's head.

"All right, all right!" Childress heaved to his feet, legs shaking, and stumbled several steps beyond safety into the machine room. "You've made your point! You've made your point!"

Doctor Rodriguez waited across the chamber, standing at the edge of the event platform nearly a hundred feet away. She showed no better than a silhouette thanks to the bright, cracking pillar of light behind her. She laughed, and the sound made Childress piss himself a little.

The others followed, the lady soldier first, then D with his pistol, then Ponce, who had taken up the wounded grunt and hauled him, wincing, with one arm over the agent's shoulder. No dummy, Ponce also carried the soldier's M4. Armed, their weapons trained on Rodriguez, Childress doubted they worried anybody. The animal fear and shock on their faces made them seem as harmless as kittens. Nonetheless, four zombie-ized security men lumbered into positions to cover. Three of them wore Army uniforms and the last was one of Childress's own boys, all of them slack-faced and dull-eyed.

Childress fought to control his racing breath. He tried to ignore the hammering thump of his heart. He tried not to be hopeless, or not to let hopelessness show in his manner. Predators, vipers, monsters, they thrived on hopelessness in their prey. He didn't want to look too much like dinner.

"All right," he said, and took a long, deep breath. "All right, we're here, just like you asked. A bunch of dumbasses visiting the queen. What the fuck you got to say?"

That laugh, which had not fully ceased, rose again to hurt the ears. Doctor Rodriguez the Monster Conduit took a step forward and the lightning post behind her widened to fill the available space. "I've nothing to tell you," the beast gloated. "I want to … show you something."

She spread her arms. Her white lab coat billowed as if a wind pressed from behind her. In that instant, something poured out of the flashing orange light. Childress and his people were still a good hundred feet from the platform, too distant to see immediate details. But something rolled out of the event like a yellow-gray mudslide, a tumbling mass of wriggling jelly that seemed to whip thousands of hairs at its surface. Then it broke up, or rather separated into its constituent parts. Jelly didn't pour onto the floor of the facility, but a great, roiling mass of creatures.

Of … shrimp?

Childress's brain dodged around the idea of what he saw. He was a reasonable man, a man of definitive goals and a conservative worldview. Shrimp. Shrimp he could handle. Shimp had a certain concrete feel, even if the idea of them registered as stupid under the circumstances. Feel my power, I give you shrimp, that sort of nonsense.

Except these were shrimp by the thousands, still falling in piles from the guttering lightning post. These were shrimp by the swarm, by the horde. And these were shrimp the size of German shepherds.

They stampeded out of the lightning post, chittering like castanets, four-foot-long antennae waving, searching, a forest of them. The creatures flooded left and right, storming the limit of the round chamber, driving terrified technicians from hiding. They fell over men and women like waves, even over the zombie-ized security personnel. Those who went down did not get up. And all the while the nerve-wracking clatter of the alien creatures beat upon Childress's ears. He couldn't know, there was no way to know, but he knew the sound was a battle cry.

"Good God!" D exclaimed, and glanced with dismay from the tide of giant shrimp to his inadequate service pistol.

Ponce stepped up. He literally put one foot forward, slapped the M4 against his shoulder, and let loose into the shrimp at full automatic. The guttural tattoo from his weapon was a bass counterpoint to the shrimp army's alto clicking. The female soldier joined in a heartbeat after he opened fire, her machine gun a lower boom than Ponce's smaller rifle. Together they sprayed shrimp guts through the chamber by the gallon, the bathtub-load, the swimming pool. The walls ran with the stuff, a pink ichor laced with the hairline impressions of skeletal legs. A briny, sewer-like stink blasted through the chamber.

Childress did nothing. What could he do with a lousy pistol?

But even assault rifles have their limit. At full auto, the two weapons went dry in barely three seconds.

The remainder of the shrimp army -- all several thousand of them -- filled the machine room. The creatures surged to within a few feet of Childress and his people, encircling the group. They waved hundreds of antennae at the humans, clicked deadly-looking mandibles, and reached with spiny legs. Ponce had thrown down the M4 and taken his pistol into his free hand. He hadn't dropped the wounded grunt throughout the useless, violent display. The lady soldier held her machine gun like a club and grimaced at the swarm in terror and disgust.

A boiling tumble from within the mob of creatures, then three humans in ripped and punctured lab coats flew from that horrible storm of crustaceans to land on their faces at Childress's feet. They sobbed. One was hysterical. They struggled onto their hands and knees, trembling.

"I thought you might want company," the monster inside Rodriguez crowed.

Childress helped the nearest technician to her feet. But she wasn't a technician. It was Chief Engineer Eglemann. Not only had her lab coat been violated, but her face and arms were pockmarked with red welts beading blood, scrapes crisscrossing her cheeks and forearms. She looked as though she had fallen into a bin of acupuncture needles. She shook like a mouse under a cat's paw and her eyes had an unfocused look.

"Doctor Rodriguez knows her," the monster rumbled. "It would be good for the doctor to see her die. The others are extras."

"What about the rest?" Childress sneered past a throat dry from fear. "What about all the other technicians?"

Doctor Rodriguez tilted her head as if considering him. "Those of the shrimp world are a warrior caste. When they swarm, they kill. I had to give them something, so sorry."

"Bullshit you're sorry. You did 'em for the fun of it, you lame mother--"

The shrimp skittered in. Their chittering increased. Antennae brushed Childress, brushed Eglemann. Childress heard a disgusted grunt from the soldier somewhere behind him.

Doctor Rodriguez took several steps toward the group, the clacking shrimp parting to give her admission. As she approached, the diameter of the coruscating event widened to take up the emptied space. Childress watched the pillar reach the edge of the containment platform, then extend beyond it.

The lightning post enveloped the parabolic reflector that had capped its height. Then, free of that constraint, it thudded into the ceiling. Concrete, steel, and aluminum roofing exploded away from the lance of fire. The pillar had lost containment and speared into the sky. Childress threw an arm across Eglemann as girders crashed to the floor. The building was coming down around them.

"There is nothing fun in war," the monster roared. The voice it sent through Rodriguez sounded like all the fingernails on all the chalkboards on Earth. "*This* is the response when you attack my people. *This* is what you reap when you murder and debase. This is your due!"

"Well, that's just peachy." Childress let Eglemann shiver against him, but he stood. No way would he cower to that psycho freak of nature. "So this is what you brought, is it? The world attacked by shrimp. Fucking shrimp, man. That's all you brought from your fucked up universe? Did you never see *Forest Gump*?"

Rodriguez grinned, a sickly forcing of her lips that showed no humor. "You ... are mistaken. These warriors..." and the shrimp raised a din of clittering mandibles, "...are not of my world." She turned, Vanna White style, and gestured toward the crackling pillar. "This, however, is."

As Childress watched, a shadow formed in the heart of the event. A deep grumble rolled across the chamber, shaking the floor. Then, as if feeling blindly for support, a scaly leg thumped out of the orange pillar, slapping the floor with its clawed foot. The claws flexed and tore tile from the mangled ground. It was a big leg, a huge one, the muscled, armored leg of a dinosaur.

Then the rest of the creature pushed into the world, and roared.

"*Shee-it!*" Childress's legs turned to jelly and he collapsed to the floor. The others were right there with him, wailing in terror. The stench of piss and sour sweat blasted out from among them, but drowned almost immediately beneath the foul, rotten, dog breath of the beast out of the pillar.

A dragon.

A fucking *dragon*. So freaking huge it couldn't stretch out its long, scaly neck in the confines of the machine room. So gigantic it had to crouch on its four massive legs in order not to bump what was left of the ceiling. It had to tuck its barbed tail, as long as its boxcar-sized body, around its feet for comfort. Its leathery wings tried to flex, but the fifty-foot ceiling was too low for them. They draped, shivering, as if hungry to fly.

A *dragon*.

As Childress gave in to terror, another ghastly lizard head pushed out of the lightning post's orange light.

Tejada had just checked the load of his M4 when the roof exploded away from the trans-universal facility. A deep boom sounded, making him and all his men hunker to the ground, then a gleaming orange pillar of light stabbed into the sky from the middle of the building.

"Holy shit!" one of his men yelled. "Something's gone wrong as hell!"

Tejada licked his lips and took stock of his people. Seven of them, all in suits sans jackets, their torsos sheathed in black armored vests. The vests held three mags of ammo for their M4s. They were as ready for a firefight as any other bunch of guys in shiny Oxfords.

"Form up," he commanded. "They'll send us in within the next few seconds."

"How you know that? The op isn't scheduled for another thirty minutes."

"Just form up. You'll see."

They did, jockeying into an overwatch pattern. Tejada and three men crowded at the edge of the Navigator while the other four braced with their weapons aimed across the street. They would cover Tejada's group as they advanced on the building, then Tejada's people would take positions and cover the other team's move. They'd leapfrog like that all the way into the building, assuming they didn't get cut to pieces.

The moment they took their positions, Major Browning crackled onto the improvised net. "All teams, all teams, flash! Facility containment compromised! Prepare to move in on five count! Acknowledge!"

Reports snapped over the communicator in Tejada's ear. When his turn came, he was terse. "Six, ready."

"On five! One! Two--"

The two dragons stomped restlessly to either side of the pillar of light. The floor shook beneath them. They rubbed shoulders. They growled. They nipped at each other with saber-sized teeth. Their massive heads, the size of small cars, bobbed over Doctor Rodriguez and flicked pointed tongues at the prisoners. The scientist looked up at them lovingly, then down at the humans sprawled at her feet.

"This is your future. You brought horrors to my world, so I bring nightmares to yours."

Childress tried to get it together. He was responsible. If any chance existed to get his people out of there, he was the one to find it. He disentangled himself from Eglemann's grasping arms and worked back to one knee.

"All right." He held up a hand in surrender. "I hear you. You definitely got our attention. What can we do to negotiate?"

Doctor Rodriguez dropped her mad grin in sudden confusion. "What is this 'negotiate'?"

"Everybody's got a thing, you know. You got a grievance. What can we do to make that grievance of yours go away?"

She cocked her head and furrowed her brow. She wasn't getting this line of thought at all. "Why, you die, of course."

Childress waved his hands. "Now, see, that doesn't work for us. How about a counter-offer?"

"You die after long suffering and maddening terror."

So, not one for compromise. "Look, I get that you're pissed, but you have to understand. There's seven billion people out there. Some of them got nukes. There's no scenario in this universe where you and a couple of lizards--" The shrimp set up an ear-bleeding racket of clicks and clacks. "-- and your other buddies even get a toehold on this world."

"Seven billion?" The monster stepped toward him, arms spread wide. The event bulged larger, freaking out the dragons, who flinched out of its way. In the process they smashed several hundred shrimp. "I have endless horrors to send against your seven billion frightened apes. I only need to call, and your worst nightmares will appear before you--"

Exactly at that point, Fiona Street flashed into existence. She stood a little off to the left of Childress, facing the mangled double doors. She looked like a walking armory in black fatigues, her left arm held to her side by a stiff plastic brace. Her legs were nearly hidden within a roil of shrimp until they scattered to leave a circle around her.

"Agent Childress," she said. "I--" Then she blinked, and looked around. "Eww," she muttered, "this shit's thick."

"You!" the monster screamed. "You! Where is he? Is he with you?" The shrimp slashed at Street with their needle-like legs, but the sharp appendages went through her as if she were a gas.

"Street!" Childress growled. "You're *with* this crazy train?"

Street seemed unsure who to address or what to say. She showed a tight-lipped frown as she scanned around the chamber.

"You!" the monster continued. "You and Hostetter! I will hurl nightmares into the ether, to find you, to make you pay. I will find you and teach you the meaning of terror! You will know why you fear the dark! You will not escape me!"

Street's face twisted in irritation. She turned to the monster and her pair of freakish dinosaurs. "Don't put yourself out. I'll be here in a minute." Turning back to Childress, she winked. "Keep your head down." Then she was gone.

A howl of frustration and livid rage blasted through the building. Childress and his fellow humans cringed from the sound and held their ears. This time, it wasn't dragons roaring or shrimp chittering. That nerve-curdling rumble came from Rodriguez.

"Up!" she screamed at the giant lizards. "Find them! Kill them! Kill them all!"

The dragons roared, filling the air with the stink of sun-broiled roadkill and a rain of drool. Then one of them crouched low on its haunches, steeled its muscles, and leaped at the ceiling.

"Five!"

"Go!" Tejada commanded, and he and his three agents darted around the corner of the Navigator and into the open.

The zombie-ized men around the building alerted on them like robot sentries, but hesitated at finding so many targets. Then the streets around the trans-universal facility erupted in a deep, loud, firecracker explosion of gunfire. Men went down on both sides.

The first dragon punched through the facility's roof, shrugging girders and concrete among the men below. It clawed its way onto a perch atop the building, swung its horny head to take in the scene, and bellowed bloody-minded fury.

"Fuck!" somebody yelled over the net.

Major Browning's plan evaporated. The net crashed under a weight of astonished reports and requests for orders. Nearly every advancing gun pivoted upward to take on the huge lizard. Thousands of rounds from hundreds of gunners blasted the dragon to little effect. They were like fly bites on an Ironman athlete. But those targeting the dragon found themselves targeted by the cordon of zombie agents and soldiers. Men in the open went down. Men behind cover had their priorities divided. The attack devolved into a rout webbed by wild bullet tracks.

Tejada had thrown himself to the ground. Two of his three teammates did the same. The third lay behind them on the neatly mown and now violated lawn. He moaned and held his reddening side. What to do? No way could the overwatch team draw up to relieve them, not through that hail of gunfire. Even so, the overwatch still covered Tejada. After momentary shock at the sight of the dragon, they'd returned their attention to picking off smaller, human-shaped threats. But Tejada was still pinned down. The lawn ruptured a few inches from his face. Where the shot had come from, who could tell?

"Get up!" he yelled to his men. They returned him wide-eyed incredulity. "Get up!" he tried again. "We have to rush the wall! They'll pick us off out here!"

Easy to say, difficult to do. Something whizzed past Tejada's cheek. He felt the air disturbed in the bullet's wake. He didn't want to move. He *needed* to move. His mind told him one thing, his body another.

He took two deep breaths, forcing the air in and out in angry snorts. Then, with a savage grunt and expenditure of will, he rolled onto his side, clasped his rifle to his chest, and lunged onto his feet.

The first bullet burned through his upper leg. The second, from the opposite direction, seared the flesh of one shoulder blade. Tejada stumbled a few long strides toward the building wall, then collapsed onto the knee of his uninjured leg.

A dead-faced agent approached him, pistol extended and flashing fire.

Tejada got off a solid gut shot before crashing onto his face in the grass.

Chapter Twenty-five

The *Jimmy Carter* was not happy. Its hull made sounds like cracking trees, over and over, always from different locations. At uneven intervals, a low, arthritic groan shuddered through the ship. Submariners glanced worried eyes about them, fearful the so-far solid ship might implode and kill them all.

"She's just stretching," the captain said with as much calm as he could manage past dry lips. They operated close to their rated depth, never a place a submariner wanted to be.

"Executing neutral turn," the OOD reported. Immediately, the deck twisted and the groans and pops intensified.

"Sonar, call out," the captain said, keeping his tone level.

"Wall at nine-three meters, obstacles at two-zero-zero, two-two degrees down relative."

Obstacles. Mountains. The Solomon Sea was lousy with them. Usually no hazard, but at extreme depths…

"Got a heading," the master chief called from Radio. "It's strong. Come back three degrees."

"Follow his nose, OOD."

"Correcting three degrees port…"

"There! Come back a bit…"

"Coming back. Umm, a bit."

"I *told* you! It's a fucking dragon, I said. So there! You believe me now?" Fiona pointed through the wide windscreen of the jet at the mind-bending scene below. Hollywood couldn't have managed it better. The milling, darting ground figures within smoke and the flashes of a gun battle. The battered building, most of its roof on the surrounding grass, a pillar of electric flame piercing the sky. A neighboring building had somehow caught fire, sending a black tower of smoke into the afternoon air. And atop the trans-universal facility, clutching the exposed upper wall like a bird on a perch, a dragon the size of an airliner spread its leathery wings.

"Uhh…" was all Sally could say.

"This isn't what we bargained for," Grace said through clenched teeth. All of them crowded the passenger area next to the Voice.

"Couldn't agree more," Fiona said, and pushed the looky-loos back from the windscreen. "Ramp," she ordered. "Everybody. Voice, not you. I think there'll be need of air support. Land us down there near the front door, by the numbers."

"Which numbers?"

"The *original* numbers, the ones we came up with for the insertion. Everything else, I'm just making up." She yelled all that as she rushed for the ramp, Grace and Sally behind her. All three halted at the Malibu's back bumper, staring at the still-closed exit a few feet in front of them.

"We're jumping into a hairball short our most powerful man," Grace said.

"I know," Fiona answered.

"Just thought I'd mention it."

"Coming in," the Voice called. "Down in three, two…"

Sally Reiser was no stranger to over-the-top quasi-military bullshit, but the looming operation scared the daylights out of her. As the Voice counted down, she pictured the plan "by the numbers," as Fiona Street had called it.

On three, the jet decloaked. For some reason, invisibility had to go when the weapons deployed, something about power consumption and geometry she didn't care in the least about. The ship pounced to a hover over the front lawn of the machine building, turning so that its ramp faced the entrance. It also fired off smoke grenades and a barrage of hundreds of shocker cylinders similar to those she had used during the vault break-in.

On two, the landing gear deployed and the plane settled toward the grass, scattering men and blasting the ground with the fanjets nested within its wide Manta wings. The Voice threw some switch or other and his anti-gunfire tech took effect. Every firearm within a city block ceased to function. Bullets already flying from their barrels stopped mid-flight and fell to the ground with a thousand tiny thuds and clinks. Chambered rounds failed to go off. The Voice would have instant confirmation that his secret ray beam worked because the radio nets he monitored would go crazy with reports of weapons malfunctions.

On one, he set off the shockers, each one electrocuting any standing body within six feet. This, the smoke, and the disabled weapons made exiting the ship a safer prospect than it might have been otherwise. Their weapons hardened against the anti-gun tech, Grace and Street would have the only working guns so long as the Voice transmitted his magic ray. Sally didn't count her own pistol. She barely knew how to use it.

At zero, the ramp slammed down without hydraulic restraint. Light, noise, and that awful, rotten egg stink of gunfire streamed in. Fiona marched down the ramp, Grace abreast of her, Sally at his heel as the major had instructed her. Smoke blew across their path. Sally couldn't see much of anything. The screech of the Manta's fanjets rose to a higher pitch and the ship levitated, whipping the banks of smoke into colliding cyclones.

Grace and Street carried M4s, his braced against his shoulder, hers tucked under her right arm. They shot at shit, a measured *crack! crack! crack!* and pivoting of their aim. A bunch of shadows materialized from the smoke, men in suits, guns pointed at Sally and her protectors. Grace and Street shot them down. Sally had to remind herself that the falling men weren't dead. They weren't even seriously hurt. The soft ceramic bullets had been designed to knock down and knock out, not to kill.

"How do you know who to shoot?" Sally asked.

"Quiet. I'm working," Grace snapped.

How they selected targets became obvious in seconds. They shot everybody, no time to sort out the players.

Sally thought she might wet herself when the dragon let loose a roar like cracking thunder. She gritted her teeth and repeated under her breath, "It's all right, it's all right. God is my shepherd, God is my shepherd..."

The great beast on the wall spread its awful wings. Silhouetted by the lowering sun, the smoke obscuring it to a dark form, the creature looked like some nightmare vampire bat but for the snakelike neck and head. It roared and crouched, tumbling masonry down from its perch.

The Voice's jet hovered fifty or sixty feet off the ground, facing the big lizard. Four dim flashes winked from beneath the ship's wings. Four vaper trails lanced for a split second toward the monster, then the dragon exploded.

It really did *explode,* four red-orange blossoms of flame that blew away the smoke for a second and made Sally stagger. Sally watched, stunned, as the creature swayed, its wings fluttering, then fell forward off the wall. She felt a grab at her armor, then a violent jerk as Grace snatched her to one side. The bulk of the dragon arced over the lawn to smash into the cars and Hummers littering the street, but one massive hunk of meat, maybe the size of a sofa, crushed the grass where Sally had stood. It made the ground shake.

"Fuck!" she exclaimed and bent over, hands on knees. She breathed foul air in great gulps, tasting sulfur and sweet copper. She thought she might--

"Don't you faint," Grace shouted above the din of fanjets, bellowing men, and explosions where the dragon came down. "I have enough to do! I can't be carrying you on my back!"

He grabbed her vest and dragged her away from the smoking, super-sized slab of meat. They stopped, Sally's back against something hard. She blinked, looked around with darting eyes, and saw they'd landed against the facility wall. The smoke rolled back in, but not before Sally's eyes locked on a half-dozen bodies splayed on the ground around her. These were not the work of the Voice's non-lethal clay bullets. The men fallen around her showed spattered blood, missing limbs, and one -- she gulped -- no longer had a head.

"It's all right, it's all right. God is my shepherd, God is my shepherd..."
He really is. Keep faith, kid, you're doing fine.

"No thanks to you," she growled, then looked up to see Grace giving her the eye.
Move about twenty feet to the left.
Huh?
Now!

This time it was Sally grabbing hold of armor. She latched onto Grace's with one hand, rushed across his front, grabbed Street's web belt on the way by, and grunted from the effort of dragging them with her. If her actions hadn't come as a total surprise, Grace at least might have resisted and she wouldn't have moved him an inch. But sudden action threw him off-balance so he and the major stumbled after her until they slapped against the wall a good deal farther on.

"What are you--" Street started, then the wall at their backs shuddered and bucked. Twenty feet back, where they had stood a moment before, the wall collapsed outward from ceiling to ground, tumbling concrete in an avalanche over the grass. A gaping hole opened and a terror emerged into the filtered sunlight. The ground quaked as the beast strode forth, clawed legs as thick as overpass pylons, a fat gut the size of a Greyhound bus. Its serpentine neck lashed back and forth, searching, searching, its mouth hanging open while its tongue flicked side to side.

The dragon halted with just its tail still in the building. It bellowed into the smoke-laden world. Its wings spread, flexing one leathern span well beyond where Sally pressed against the wall. She could see the wing in perfect detail, the veins coursing through thin skin stretched between long, bony, clawed appendages like fingers.

After a moment as if posing for a picture, the dragon swept its wings down and lunged into the sky. The wind the wings generated knocked Sally and her team to the ground, heaving grass and dirt into their faces. Street was the first to recover, scrambling back up despite her bad arm.

"Voice!" she yelled into her communications pickup. "Dragon! A *second* dragon! Fetch!"

"You'll lose fire suppression support," came back in Sally's ear.

"Slay the dragon, right the fuck now!" Street had tumbled her M4 upside down and attempted to load a new magazine one-handed.

"Wilco," and Sally heard the fanjets whine and the by then familiar, deeper growl of the jet engines gaining power.

"Come on!" Street ordered, and headed at a jog back toward the hole in the wall.

Sally followed, her head tucked deep into her shoulders for fear of the dangers around her. She kept her eyes on the major. The major, even wounded, seemed to fear nothing. Then she noticed something else close by Fiona Street's side, a small, black blur in the grass beneath the smoke.

The cat. Where had it come from?

"Falcon, Falcon, this is Ranger Control. Bogey inbound, vicinity Grid Zero. Clear and hot, splash bogey. Acknowledge."

"Ranger Control, Falcon 1. Weapons hot, bogey acquired, committing."
The pilot of the A10 Thunderbolt close air attack craft jockeyed his plane
for a viable approach to the gray speck on his target acquisition screen.

"Falcon 1, this is Falcon 2. On your left," his wingman called.

"Roger, 2. Locked and hot, going with guns." Of course they were going with guns. The Maverick missiles slung under both aircraft's wings were
kinetic entry bunker busters, not much good against aircr-- "Ranger Control,
Falcon 1. Clarify target. I have two bogies, not one. I say again, two bogies,
over."

"Wanna split 'em?" Falcon 2 came back.

The lead pilot ignored him. No telling what those targets were, and the
last thing they needed was a case of friendly fire.

"Falcon, Ranger Control. Unable to identify either target. Splash both.
Prioritize, uh, biological, over."

Prioritize *what?* "Control, Falcon. I do not understand 'biological.'"
Damn it. They'd have to fly through and get the shots on the second run.
What the hell were those dope-smoking dicks doing down there?

That was how two A10s flew through the track of a giant flying lizard
and a pursuing black craft like a huge manta ray. Falcon 1 squeezed his eyes
shut at the lizard and wrenched them open again, then twisted his craft
through the air to follow.

"Holy God!" Falcon 2 exclaimed.

"What *was* that thing?" Falcon 1 called, tripping over his words.

"That, good buddy, was a dragon."

"There's no such thing as dragons!"

"Okay, then it was a target. You know, a biological?"

A biological. A goddamned *dragon!* "Uh, uh… Coming round left on
its three. Going to speed."

"I'm on ya, boss."

Falcon 1 pushed to over 400 miles per hour, turning back toward the
bogies in a long, wide arc. Before he reacquired visual on the, umm, biological, he dropped his speed to 300, poured on some back thrust, punched
back forward, and landed his nose almost in line with the target. "Smooth
track. Engaging cannon. Guns! Guns! Guns!"

The 30mm auto-cannon mounted in his aircraft nose burped 500 rounds
just ahead of the flying lizard. The black manta craft veered off, but the
dragon flew right through the hurtling stream of bullets. The beast jerked,
folded in its wings, tumbled, and fell toward the ground.

"Target destroyed. Second bogey."

But too soon. "Flash! Flash! Target is not destroyed!"

"What? Where?"

"It-- Shit, lost it. Back to our six. Pulling around to--"

The transmission strangled and went to silence. Falcon 1 glanced over his left shoulder in time to see a fireball and something glance off his canopy and send spider webs of breaking glass cutting into its surface. "Shit!" He glanced around, trying to locate--

A frantic beeping. The proximity indicator.

Falcon 1 slammed forward into his panels. He felt sudden deceleration, then tumbling. Alarms sounded. Attitude readouts spun wildly. The blood in his head seemed to whip back and forth. "Mayday! Mayday!" Something huge, sharp, and curved punched through the windscreen, flexed, and tore the canopy from the ship. "Shit! Ejecting!" Falcon 1 let go of his useless controls and gripped the eject handle beside his chair. For a split second he realized his next act could be suicide. He had no idea where the escape would send him. It could hurl him into the ground as easily as anywhere else. He couldn't see anything and he was blacking out. He pulled the eject handle.

The Voice of the City saw the ejection, saw the chute open, but didn't bother watching the pilot's downward journey. He flicked his attention back to the mangled jet. It burned, losing parts, and crumpled into a rough ball of steel as the dragon battered and twisted its remains. Then, perhaps its fury sated, the beast spread its wings and released the wreck, letting it fall toward the thickly populated earth.

No time to worry about that. The dragon spun in space, hauntingly graceful, then thrust like a missile toward the Manta. The ship might have suffered the same as those fighters, but the Voice kicked in his scramjet along with a touch of the right fanjet, pitching into a downward spiral that foiled interception by the creature.

Corrective spin, level off, station keeping, sensors out. There it came at him from below. The Voice goosed the fanjets, touched the scram for just an instant, and stood the Manta on its nose. The dragon flew at the windscreen like a jump scare in a bad 3D movie. The Voice thumbed weapons control and sent his last two missiles into the monster.

One missile shot by under the dragon's wing. The other connected with a hind leg and blew it neatly off at the hip.

The dragon kept coming. The Voice hit his right-side fanjet to nudge the ship from the creature's path. He felt a tremor of turbulence as ship and reptile failed to intersect.

Left fanjet, hard on the scram, and a tight turn to re-engage. But the sensors had lost their lock. He punched wide scan and found the beast coming up fast from the rear. Scramjet on. The Voice felt the pressure of acceleration even through the inertial dampeners.

Bank right, bank left. The dragon stayed behind him, perhaps leery of exposure to more missiles from the front. The Voice climbed, aiming for clouds, but still the creature pursued, hard to the rear. No weapons back there. The Voice attempted anti-missile chaf. It wouldn't hurt the beast, but maybe the creature would dart aside to once more become a target.

The dragon blasted upward, barreling through the release of chaf. It persisted and gained through the subsequent launch of flares.

Up they climbed. The air thinned. The Manta hadn't been designed for high-altitude flight. It was the Voice of the City, and the city was on the ground. The dragon gained, reaching out its arms and snapping its saber-toothed jaws in the rear-sight monitor. Time to veer off, to take the battle back below, though the beast might jump him on the turn.

Which is why the Voice hesitated, then disregarded that action. Instead, he poured on the scramjet. He checked the tightness of his harness, then reached one hand to his utility belt and drew out an oxygen breather the size of his fist. He slapped that onto his nose and mouth and blew out a breath to lock the seal.

The ship complained. Its engines took on a piercing, soprano whine, the effect of less oxygen than it liked. The Voice glanced repeatedly at the rear-sight monitor. The dragon drew closer, trailing slobber. Finally, it gained to within twenty feet.

The Voice of the City hit the ramp control. The ramp groaned open, the sound soon overwhelmed by the howling release of cabin air. Then it was engines and the ravenous roars of the beast. The monster's gaping mouth filled the rear-sight monitor.

The Voice slid the fingers of his free hand along the control panel. He found the switch for the cargo couplers, and opened them.

The clamps on its wheels released, the Malibu rolled from the plane. Its speed relative to the jet was something like two hundred miles per hour in reverse. Relative to the charging dragon, that speed was much greater. The car slammed right down the jaws of the massive beast. But the Malibu's body was wider than the dragon's head. Two tons of hurtling steel met tissue and bone, however strong.

The car proved a bitter pill to swallow.

Chapter Twenty-six

The monster was *pissed*. Childress had thought the thing insensate with fury when Street appeared, but this was something else again. Childress kept his people huddled close, the civilians as far to the center as he could manage. The shrimp teased their prey, darting in razor-sharp legs to poke or slash at a body. Not enough to cause real harm, but enough to elicit ragged shrieks of terror. Probably for the benefit of their nut job boss. But even the shrimp seemed nervous about the monster. The floor between Rodriguez and the cringing humans emptied of giant crustaceans. All of them crowded the three remaining sides around the prisoners, some skittering over their buddies where they were way too thick to get by on the floor. Childress found no relief in gaining one clear flank. Enough of the bastards swarmed the floor that when they attacked, the direction they came from wouldn't matter.

Worse, the open floor allowed Rodriguez to come closer. She stood no more than ten feet from him, her arms still outstretched, the look on her face one of bloody-minded madness.

"She's here," Rodriguez said. "And if she's here, he is, too." A couple of deep sighs, as sensual -- face it, as orgasmic -- as sighs could get. Those sighs made Childress want to piss himself. Again.

She seemed to recover with a force of will, running her white-eyed gaze over her hostages. "Tell me, are any of you precious to them?"

Uhh… "Why?" Childress preferred to have a hint at what the right answer might be.

"Because, if you are precious to them, I'll save your deaths for last. I'll make your ends worthy of nightmares. They will see your deaths for the rest of their lives, short as that may be, even with their eyes shut tightly against the horror."

Childress tightened his grip on his pistol. He could put Rodriguez down before her crawdad buddies got to him. It would constitute his last act on Earth, sure, but he could take her out with a single shot, he was sure of it. But then, who said that would do any good? Rodriguez was a carrier, a puppet, not the real thing. Would drilling her through the eye socket defeat the big bad? No idea, none at all, but Childress had serious doubts.

"So, are any of you precious?" she asked him.

"No," Childress said, pushing derision into his tone. "We're just a bunch of working stiffs, lady. You kill us forever in front of your enemies and they'll be annoyed our bodies got in the way. So your vicious torture extravaganza might have to wait till some other time. Tell you what, you head on back to the crib and we'll call you when somebody precious comes along."

She frowned and gave him the eyeball. Maybe he'd gone a bit too far?

"No matter," she said in that booming, inhuman voice of broken glass and twisted girders. "I know something of value to them."

She abruptly lowered her arms to her sides and raised her crazy eyes to what little was left of the ceiling. "This Sinfonee they care about, and they must come to me to come to her." She took a long, deep breath and let it seep away. Then she brought her face forward, eyes closed, and stretched her neck as if to clear a crick. "Would you like to see, just a little, how you will die today?"

A rise in the pitch of sobs behind Childress. The muffled drone of Ponce and D calming the hostages, telling them it would be all right. Why do people find that necessary, to lie in the face of the obvious? No way would it be all right. All right had broken down a couple of counties over. At that point, something occurred to Childress, a sure, if gruesome way the hostages could win. A way to send the monster into fits. He looked down at his pistol hand, his mind frozen numb with revelation. He looked at the gun gripped by his fingers. He watched himself thumb back the hammer.

The monster could not take joy in murder if the victims were already dead.

"Hold heading!" the master chief called from the radio shack.

"Holding at two-three-nine," the OOD announced.

"Now. Down."

"Down? *More?*"

"Give it to him, OOD." The captain clutched his railing that much tighter. The deck approached vertical.

"Affirmative. Helm, ease down bubble. Reduce engines to idle…"

"We're diving!" The diving chief snapped the words unnecessarily. The captain felt the drop through his feet, almost losing his body grip on the coaming.

"Engines back! Back half!" he thundered.

"Engines back half, aye!"

"Stay on heading!"

"Heading, aye! Two-three-nine, four-four degrees down bubble, depth 2100."

"Wall at seven-two meters, obstacles at one-five-eight, twelve degrees down relative," Sonar reported, the sailor's voice almost a squeal.

"Sir!" the OOD called. "We can't maintain this attitude for longer than a few minutes!"

Okay, that would have to do. "Master Chief!" the captain called.

"Solid target, sir."

"All right. Let's give the spooks their few minutes of fame. Irradiate the target."

"Irradiating now."

Sirens, smoke, the shouts of men in hand-to-hand combat, and an earth-shaking explosion from somewhere close by. Sally kept close to Grace and Street, terrified something might charge from the confusion of drifting dust. Street bounded over the jagged chunks of wall and twisted girders, braking at the hole where the dragon had come through. She leaned her good shoulder against the cracked building and showed her teeth in a pained wince. She sweated like a dockworker.

"Are you okay?" Sally asked from beside her. "You aren't looking so hot."

"Watch outward," Street said. "With the Voice gone, their weapons are working again. It'll take them a second to figure that out, then we're in trouble." She took two deep breaths, then leaned quickly around the edge of the hole. She glanced into the building, not two seconds, then rested her shoulder again at the wall. "Sinfonee's got it in her, just as we saw earlier. She's maybe ten feet in front of Childress and the others, right through here by maybe twenty meters at one o'clock. Our people are surrounded by giant shrimp."

No matter how much Sally wanted it to, that didn't sound funny.

"Childress isn't looking too good," Street continued. "I think he's about to try something stupid."

How had she gotten all that from a glance? But then, the cat. Sally started searching, wondering where Oz was, then remembered. No. *Not* the cat. Street was only guessing.

"It's gonna be tricky," Street yelled across Sally to Grace. "Whatever you do, avoid shooting our people -- and that includes Sinfonee -- with live ammunition."

"Status on the signal intervention?" Grace asked. He referred to the gambit with the submarine in the Solomons, the submarine they couldn't even know had gone into play.

Street screwed up her face. "No way to know until something happens. If it doesn't come through, it's up to us."

"And if the stuff we carry doesn't have an effect?" Sally asked.

"You're a civilian," Grace answered. He snapped the drum from his rifle and slid in another with red tape on its side. "Let the pros worry about such things."

Which wasn't much of an answer.

"Shit!" Grace shouted. A half dozen men appeared from the smoke, all bringing up weapons to fire. Grace dropped his rifle, which swung loosely at his hips from its lanyard. He snatched out two pistols, one from his vest and another from his thigh, and started shooting two-handed into the men.

The major couldn't help. She had ejected her drum for a fresh one, which she hadn't yet attached to her rifle.

Sally never knew how the pistol got to her hand, but it was out in front, her eyes on the sights, and she jerked the trigger like a maniac. Men went down. More took their place. How many attackers? A lot. But Sally didn't count them.

"Cease fire, cease fire," Grace said, and nudged down Sally's hand with his own. A jumble of men lay in the grass. No more seemed to be coming.

Sally started breathing again. "I shot those men," she said.

Grace tossed his empty pistols into the surrounding rubble. "I doubt it, but you get a gold star for effort."

"Get behind Grace," Street instructed Sally, then finished switching out her magazine. She forced a grin onto her sweaty, ashen face and gave Sally a carefully executed wink. "Trust us," she said. "We used to work for the government."

With that, the major swung wide into the building, her assault rifle leading the way.

No graceful, dramatic entrance. Chunks of wall and ceiling sprawled out beyond the breach, making footing questionable at best. The major kept her weapon trained on the nearest roil of shrimp, or at least Grace tagged them in his head as shrimp. But he'd never seen shrimp the size of German shepherds. He should have stumbled, screamed, and fled; any normal man would have. But Grace had seen too many strange things since science had joined his captain to the cat. All that escaped him were a shudder of revulsion at the wet, gray-pink creatures and an intake of breath at their briny, river-water smell.

That intake of breath was enough to get them noticed. The sea of crustaceans turned as one to face the intruders and all their noisome clacking ceased.

"Hiya, Sinfonee," the major called, but didn't look at the doctor. "Keeping some lowly company, I see."

Doctor Rodriguez jerked at the greeting. She stiffened like a dog on the scent of prey. "The Street woman! Are you here this time, or hiding behind your tricks?"

"It's me, Sinfonee. Don't send any of your buddies to check, or it'll get messy real, *real* fast."

The major had advanced maybe a dozen careful steps into the ruined building. Grace followed to one side, making a clear field of fire. Slowly, so as not to excite the natives, he plucked a handful of shock cylinders from the pouches of his vest. He held the assault rifle in his right hand, pushed tightly into his shoulder, but the shockers occupied his left, their green lights winking. He extended that hand beneath his M4, his wrist steadying its barrel.

The lightning post blazed like a firebox from hell, lighting Rodriguez in sharp relief. But she was the major's problem. Grace slid his gaze over the hostages and saw immediately what Street had meant.

Childress stood, but rather than watching the source of danger, he focused on Eglemann at his feet. His thumb stroked the hammer of his automatic. Grace saw the same concentration in DeBoy, somewhat less so in Ponce, but each man held his pistol cocked and eyed one of the civilians in their clutch. None of them planned to turn their guns on monsters.

"You enter here and issue threats?" Rodriguez's voice boomed over the tortured space. It shook dust from the shattered rafters.

"No, not threats." Street remained calm. "I come to bargain. Like maybe you send those people my way, we clear them out of here, okay?"

"Or what?" the monster asked, derision as thick as molasses.

"Or there's gonna be a blood bath, assuming your friends have blood."

"Where is Hostetter? I want Hostetter!"

"Can't help you there." The major halted within ten paces of Rodriguez. She kept her weapon trained on the shrimp, which clittered and clacked and tensed to jump her. "He decided to sit this one out."

The nearest creatures capered not ten feet from Grace.

"You lie!" The event beyond Rodriguez guttered. Grace couldn't be sure, but it seemed to decrease a few feet in diameter. "Hostetter ruined my plan of conquest! Hostetter prevented my righteous apocalypse! I will strike him down for that effrontery! I will strike him down!"

"Speaking of which, Childress, I want you prone," Street said. "Get on the floor with the others. Get on the floor now."

Childress didn't seem to hear her.

"I am talking to you!" Rodriguez bellowed, and Grace thought his ears might burst.

"Fine," Street said, "then do it directly. Let Sinfonee go."

Rodriguez actually hissed. It was weird. She twisted up her face to loose that reptilian sibilation, then raised outstretched arms.

The lightning post burst outward, tripling its diameter within a single second. It burned only inches behind Rodriguez, only feet from the still-standing Childress.

Rodriguez broke into a drenching sweat.

"You will see the error of mocking a force beyond gods!" she shrieked. "You will see that nightmares are real, that terror can be infinite. You, Fiona Street, will see the true face of all you dismay!"

The words resounded, beating upon Grace like something physical. And, when they finally echoed away…

Nothing happened.

Street, who had dropped half to a crouch in expectation of ... something, rose back to her full height. Rodriguez stared her down in godlike righteousness for a few awkward seconds, then turned to give the crackling pillar a puzzled look.

"I understand," Street said. "Performance anxiety. It gets to the best of us. Ready to negotiate?"

"What have you done?" the monster growled.

More like what had the United States Goddamned Navy done!

"I've offered you a course of action," the major said. "Our people--"

"Murder them all!"

The shrimp, released by their master, surged at the humans in a tide.

Grace flung his handful of shockers and let loose a series of three-round bursts from his rifle. The shockers landed a few feet in front of him and electrocuted a swath of attacking crustaceans. The bolt of static passed over him, the major, and Sally thanks to the markers the Voice had pinned to their vests. The shockers went off again, then a third time, depleting their stored charges. The shrimp stormed over their fricasseed brethren and in from either flank, but the major sprayed that near distance, splattering wriggling bodies by the dozens.

Still they came. Grace hadn't fired a shot yet, and he knew that Street would run dry in seconds. But he had priorities, and the slashing, sword-like legs of the nearest arthropods were not at the top of that list. He snatched out a double handful of shockers and flung them over the near swarm of shrimp. They landed among the hostages, lightning lancing out to take down monsters falling upon the prisoners, but mainly to take down Childress. He fell, clearing line of sight for Grace, who drew up his rifle to thunder rounds into the creatures diving for the hostages.

"I'm out!" he heard.

"Get behind me!"

As the major ducked under Grace's protection, he hammered both near and far swarms of shrimp. Vaguely, he registered a higher-toned repetition of gunshots, the little pistol they had forced upon Sally. Grace gritted his teeth, throwing out rounds, splashing charging bodies at such close range that guts sprayed over him in gruesome showers. He watched, helpless, as three killer shrimp stabbed legs into the soldier at the edge of the hostage huddle. The spears of appendages jabbed right through her armor, right through her arms and neck. The creatures dragged her out of the group and repeatedly lanced her through with their quivering, bloodied legs.

The major reappeared at Grace's side just before his drum ran dry. Her extra ammo drove back the onslaught, but only for an instant. Grace ejected his spent drum, reattached the second, and brought up his weapon for further suppression.

The hostages stirred. DeBoy and Ponce scrambled to their knees, looking disoriented after the shockers. But not too disoriented to throw themselves over the civilians and let loose ineffective fire from their pistols.

A shrimp got past the major, several did. She rotated, firing around her feet, then jerked back to ward off the ever-pressing wall of creatures. A creature slammed into Grace's side, clamping down on his hips. The river stink of it flooded his nostrils and its excited clitter of mandibles deafened his ears. A sharp stab through his ribs, another into his back. A metallic skitter of sharp piercers over the weapons velcroed to Grace's vest.

Grace staggered from the strikes, but hammered his rifle against his assailant. The beast fell from him, clattered about at his feet, and jumped for him again. In the two seconds of respite, Grace snatched out his shock stick and jabbed it into the leaping form. The smell of broiled shrimp flew up his nose, and he thought he might throw up. He jabbed at and electrocuted three more attackers in succession. There were too many of them. A platoon couldn't keep them at bay, much less two gunners short on ammo.

So, as the major's weapon fell silent, he brought up his M4 to hammer back at the enemy. Too many of them, too damn many. Hundreds splattered across the floor, but there were many hundreds left to take their places. Grace's rifle would last another five seconds, then he was down to pistols shock sticks, and a few grenades, and that just wouldn't cut it. They had to retreat, if that proved possible, but that meant leaving the hostages behind to be kebobbed by the bad guys. And that wasn't going to happen.

As if to mock him, a wave of shrimp crashed over Ponce, sending him flailing to the floor.

Explosions. Pieces of shrimp flying through the air. A dark figure dropped from the fifty-foot ceiling. He fell feet first, firing missiles from the bracelets on each wrist--

Oh! Bracelets! Grace shifted his rifle to his left hand and extended his right toward the squirming wall of arthropods. He flicked his wrist several times, turning his arm in an arc across the front of the creatures. He felt puff after puff from the wrist launcher, like blasts of air from a pressure hose, but the ordnance sufficed to dent the monsters' advance.

The Voice of the City, despite the long fall, landed on his feet amid the huddle of hostages. He sprayed all around, his bracelets clearly not loaded with clay. The ichor of shattering monsters fountained about him. He slapped his hands to the belt at his waist and flung out a number of objects that must have been grenades by the way they went off. Rodriguez howled at the intrusion, raking the air with her fingers as if she had claws to kill with.

Grace, his wrist launcher emptied, repositioned his rifle and spent the last of his ammo. Cursing, he unsnapped the weapon from his vest and hurled it as hard as he could into the thickest approach of the next wave of shrimp. He snatched one pistol from its Velcro fastener and took single-shot aims at the attackers. The major did the same. They were absolutely fucked.

The shrimp rolled over them. The pistols did nothing at all. Even if the rounds had been standard, they wouldn't have held off that rushing wall of monsters. The major went down under slashing sword-legs. An instant later, a dozen of the beasts swarmed over Grace. He saw sickly pink, the black of beady eyes, and the sharp points of legs thrusting toward his eyes. The next fraction of a second would be his last, brought down by animals he himself was used to devouring at all-you-can-eat prices.

They bowled him over. He fell, still striking out with his fists. He was done, for sure, but at least on his back he could see it coming.

Chapter Twenty-seven

Grace found it disconcerting that he saw anything else after that. Shrimp drool washed his face. Pointy legs drove at him like spearheads. They slammed against him, but failed to kill him. They couldn't even manage a scratch. Each time a deadly leg lanced at his face, Grace heard a tiny *tink!* like someone tapping on glass with a key. No pressure of impact, no weight of beast against his body. He might as well have been watching his intended death on television.

What in hell--?

He planted his palms against the shattered floor and, grunting against the two sharp pains in his torso, rose to one knee. There was the major. She forced herself up as well. Gray faced, sweating, plastered in guts, she looked as bad as he felt and probably fared far worse. The shrimp continued to pummel him, their strikes so numerous they sounded like hail on tin.

Weird. Three of them jumped on Street, swinging their spears at her. They seemed right there, but she hardly noticed them except to flinch from the sight of those hammering legs. Grace grunted upright, put one hand at his bloody side, and staggered to his officer. He swatted away shrimp as if they were made of paper and helped Street to her feet.

She gave him a questioning, exhausted look. He gave her one back.

Then they turned to Sally.

The blonde stood just out of arm's reach, one fist held against her chest, her head down. In her other hand, her pistol dangled, forgotten. The slide had locked back on empty. The shrimp stormed at her as they did Grace and Street, and she ignored them with no effort at all.

"Blondie?" the major scraped into her throat.

"It's all right," Sally whispered. "God is my shepherd..."

"You." The forgotten Nightmare growled like a lion. Rodriguez focused for once on Sally, shoulders hunched, teeth bared. "You show yourself at last."

"It's all right, it's all right. God is my shepherd."

By unspoken agreement, Grace and Street staggered out from between Sally and the monster.

"It's about time you showed yourself," Sinfonee Rodriguez sneered. "I thought you'd cower forever and let your war be fought by apes."

Sally lifted her head and cocked it toward Nightmare. Her eyes showed interest and a touch of heart, as if she stared at art. "I know nothing of cowardice," she said in a quiet, almost detached tone. "But I think it vital that you endure a defeat by men." She blinked. Her forehead lined. "Excuse me. 'And women,' she wants me to add."

With that, she dropped her pistol, narrowed her lips, and brought her other fist to her chest. She took in a long, almost impossible breath, then pushed it out in one determined blast.

As if plowed by a bulldozer, the shrimp tumbled away from her, away from Grace and the major, rolling over and over and stacking up, tangled in one another. They rolled past the hostages and the Voice of the City, some tumbling uncontrolled into the flickering lightning post to be destroyed. The remainder stacked up beyond the limits of the fight. Jounced and confused, they tried to separate legs and bodies. They might have rallied for another attack, but chance -- or direction -- denied that outcome.

A flash atop the long pile of arthropods. Orange light and the tickle of added static in the air, then a pillar of energy incinerated fifty-odd squirming crustaceans. Another flash, another, and another. Right along the plowed row of monsters, lightning posts winked into existence, twelve in all, vertical and blinding, melting shrimp and blowing out what was left of the ceiling. Figures stepped from those lightning posts, all of them carrying sticks.

Grace held to the major, mostly to stay upright, but also for steadiness in the face of awe. A knight in gleaming armor strode into the world grasping a massive sword and a lance of yellow wood with a barbed iron tip. A bent man in hoary black robes and a pointy wizard's hat thrust shoulder-first from his lightning post, gripping a twisted staff of intricately carved white wood. Beside him appeared a short, round-faced Asian man wearing furs, leather, and a horned helm. A woman stepped among them in a white toga bordered in blue brocade, her staff one of green-patina bronze. Then Hostetter, as gnarled and rustic as ever, stepped among the others with his stick in one hand and his rifle in the other.

Next to Hostetter, what could only be a lizard exited the light. Broad-chested, standing like a man, with a muscled, whipping tail and a frightening display of razor-sharp teeth, the creature dressed in what looked like camouflage fatigues up to its bare chest. The claws that held its iron staff could have sliced a gorilla in half. In contrast, two smaller entities stepped from the next two lightning posts. Grace recognized them from their bulbous heads, lean, almost emaciated bodies, and their gray, leathery skin and huge almond-shaped eyes. They looked like aliens out of Roswell. Each held what looked like a wand, no more than the length of a common ruler. Beside them, a counterpoint in normalcy, a soldier in gray-toned ACUs left his pillar carrying an unfamiliar assault rifle over the weighty kit of armor and ammo. After him, from the remaining pillars, arrived a bald woman in orange robes, then a black-maned woman -- or maybe it was a boy -- who stood barely five feet tall and dressed in flamboyant samurai garb, complete with two scabbarded Japanese swords in her belt.

From the last post stepped Hostetter, gripping his ordinary stick in one hand and cradling an AK74 in the crook of his remaining arm.

But wait. *Two Hostetters?* Grace glanced back and forth between them. Two Hostetters, one in the worn leather duster with the rabbit fur lining, plus the store-bought cowboy hat and Wrangler jeans. The other wore a duster of oil cloth, a sweat-stained cavalry Stetson, and blue cavalry trousers with yellow stripes down the legs. *Two* Hostetters with the same moustache, the same sad face, and the same lanky, comfortable stance. They wore the same double belts for two Colt revolvers. As if for the purpose of driving Grace mad, they both spit onto the floor at the exact same moment.

"You! Nightmare!" the Hostetter with the AK yelled, his tone brooking no dismissal. "You are held in violation of Inter-universal code and are accused of illegal infringement on an extra-normal territory. By the authority of President Theodore Roosevelt, the United States of America, and the Inter-universal Marshal's Service, I command you to return immediately to your home universe or be bound by law!"

This was un-fucking-believable.

Rodriguez gaped, grunted, and gripped her face. "Hostetter!" she wailed with infinite need and emotional agony. "At last, the enemy is mine!"

"Ain't nobody here your enemy less'n you make it so, ya varmint." AK Hostetter reached his stick hand across to his assault rifle and nonchalantly charged the weapon. "Now you got marshals from thirteen territories pissed off as injuns with watered-down liquor. How many seconds you gonna last in a tussle?"

For an answer, Rodriguez screamed. Grace thought his ears might bleed. She screamed so loudly and with such primal energy that she trembled, she quaked, visible a dozen strides away. The woman drooled. She tore at her lab coat and the tailored suit beneath. If she could have managed an ounce of power, she would have turned the Hostetters and all in attendance into a smoking crater. But she didn't do that. She couldn't. The Voice's fancy jamming device kept her power at bay.

Didn't it?

Deep in the Pacific, the *Jimmy Carter* screamed. The sound was one of rending steel, accompanied by the rank stink of fear.

"We're losing her!" the diving chief shouted. "Depth 2120, 2130!"

"Engines back three-quarters! Stay on target!" the captain bellowed. His palms dug painfully into the hatch coaming that supported him. "Prepare to release ballast! On my command, planes to plus twenty!"

Orders and acknowledgements sounded throughout the control room, yelled to be heard above the buckles and cracks of tortured steel.

"Depth 2140! 2150!"

"All back full! Stay on target!" the captain roared.

Commands flew. The boat sagged downward. The captain felt no slackening of its descent. Come on, he thought. Grab some sea…

"Depth 2160! 21--"

"Blow forward ballast! Planes to plus twenty!" That was enough. The captain hoped the spooks back home had gotten what they wanted from their secretive machine.

The boat screeched. It shuddered as if in an earthquake. But the bow came up, then the deck pressed against the captain's shoes.

"Responding," the OOD shouted.

"Depth 2160! Depth 2150!" Relief crept into the diving chief's tone.

"Trimming," the OOD said, his voice hoarse from yelling. "Trimming at all-back full."

The captain relaxed. He took his aching hands from the coaming and pulled his sweat-soaked shirt away from his chest. "All stop. When all stop acknowledges, one-quarter forward and an easy surface. Let's get some air, OOD."

"Aye, sir," and the officer of the deck rattled off the orders that would take the *Jimmy Carter* on a leisurely, actually convalescent, climb to the clear blue air.

What had it been for? the captain asked himself. Then he grunted. He'd never know. But, for the sake of his battered boat, he hoped someone did.

The lightning post quavered. It sparked and hummed more frenetically than before. It threw out tendrils like solar flares.

Then, as if pushing aside a veil of smoke, something black, something hulking, something worthy of the name Nightmare, pushed from that column of coruscating orange and breathed fetid rot into the universe. The creature was roughly human, or at least apelike, with short, bowed legs, a shambling stride, and huge arms with clawed hands. Its hide was hard for the mind to focus on, but it seemed to bristle with spike-like hairs and scales over leathery, rhinoceros-like skin. The head made Grace want to shriek, with its marble eyes on twisting stalks and its innumerable waving tentacles around a beaked mouth.

And the beast was huge. It stooped its head almost to the floor just to contain its bulk within the building. It thrust that horrible head forward, flung back its shoulders, and screamed. It sounded like a car crash, or a rabbit as its neck is wrung, but louder, worse, burning the nerves. That sound was enough to strike down Grace, to collapse the major. They fell onto their sides and bawled like babies.

Clearly, the signal inhibitor the Navy directed against Nightmare had fallen out of play.

"Well, boys," AK Hostetter called. "I reckon the warrant is duly served. Have at 'im!"

As the monster extracted itself entirely from the orange fire, a dozen streams of energy stabbed at it from the marshals' staffs. Most spread their feet in a defiant stance and sent blast after blast to the tentacle-faced horror. The knight and the samurai girl charged the beast, blades slashing. The two Hostetters let loose with their rifles, one with multiple aimed shots, the other on full automatic.

The man in ACUs joined in, pausing after emptying his first magazine to tear a grenade from one of his pouches and heave it high onto the monster. The canister struck the horror where arm met torso, and stuck. A moment later, it glowed orange, then white, broadcasting such heat that Grace felt it on the ground. The nightmare thrashed, maddened by the device. It hammered a clawed paw against the white-hot place on its armpit and released another skin-shivering scream. Meat sizzled, a smell of gamey steak. Then the heat of the grenade burned through, severing muscle, tendon, and bone. An arm near as long as a school bus thudded to the floor, spewing blood and raising a cloud of dust.

The beast seemed not to notice beyond a few rapid grips at its gushing shoulder stump. Its remaining arm swept at the line of firing marshals, scattering them for a desperate moment. It grabbed at a fallen ceiling girder, a twisted hunk of steel eighteen inches thick, and swung it at the human and inhuman tormentors. The girder looked like a toothbrush in that massive paw.

During the tumult, the Voice of the City roused the hostages out of their frozen stupefaction and herded them toward the dragon hole. The

320

group milled about for long seconds, too much in shock to move with purpose. The monster noticed them. It swung its gruesome head their way, roaring black spittle and hot, rancid breath. Its tentacles snatched at two of the technicians, but were beaten back by DeBoy and Childress using bare fists and shouts.

One of the little aliens appeared among them, just showed up as if he'd always been there, and blithely drew his wand across the serpentine thrashing of the threatening tentacles. The appendages bubbled at the line of his gesture, then fell flopping to the floor, severed from their parent body as if with a laser.

That narrow escape galvanized the prisoners. The Voice urged them into organized action, Childress browbeating the technicians toward the major, DeBoy lifting the remaining soldier in a fireman's carry.

They stumbled to where the major and Grace knelt in trembling shock. No one said a word, just collapsed there among the concrete boulders and steel beams, covered in dirt, shrimp guts, and white drywall dust.

A shadow fell over Grace, jerking his senses back to him. Sally stood there, her expression as calm as a Sunday morning.

"Miracles are mainly a matter of good timing," she said. She drew her gaze across the ragged bunch of white-eyed, panting men and women, then crooked her head toward the monster. "Go. Set the trap."

It took a second for Grace to understand. "What? You want us to try and catch *that*?" He dragged his tongue across dry lips. "We thought it would be Kudashova, then Rodriguez. You know, something smaller."

"This was never about something smaller. Your plan is working. Your submarine proved it. The marshals hold the nightmare here. You can finish it off."

"*We* can finish it?" Grace glanced to the major, but she hunkered in place, her eyes a world of exhaustion. His gaze went back to Sally, who stood in an unbreakable moment of tranquility, not a speck of ichor or dust upon her. "Why don't *you* finish it? God! I mean, that's who I'm talking to, isn't it? At least that's what her file says. If you are who you are, you're the frigging almighty, why don't *you* fix this mess?"

Those calm, serene eyes looked down on him. Sally's head tilted in consideration. "These are your nightmares. You must overcome them. My battle…" She turned back toward the monster and the flaring lightning post. "…is elsewhere."

Grace looked away from her in disgust. Here they had brought a superpowered nuke of a girl, and she turns out to be a dud.

"We can't do this." He held his gaze on the Nightmare beast and the dozen marshals battling it. The scene still struck him as surreal, as something terrifying he watched on TV. No, on IMAX. His mind wouldn't let him acknowledge it as close, dangerous fact despite the constant shower of dust and the ricocheting shrapnel of shattered building. To acknowledge it was too big for him. "No, we can't. We need to get these people out of here, evacuate them. Then let the chain of command take over."

"No chain of command will win this fight," the Voice of the City said. He squatted a few inches from Grace, looking fresh for the fight. "We must evacuate these people, yes, but then we need to eject that beast." He turned his visor on Grace. "We have the tools, the military does not. Let's set the trap and see where it leads."

"The trap is bullshit!" Grace gestured toward the monster. Just then, it stood, straightening its back for the first time. Its black octopus head thudded against the remains of the ceiling then tore the structure loose in a fit of screeching metal and tumbling cement. A way cleared, that awful head lifted far beyond the building. Once upright, the creature lashed that tentacle crown back and forth, sending the wreckage of the ceiling flying.

The humans had dropped for the floor, cowering against falling debris. Now they cautiously raised their heads, darting their eyes like … like…

"Mice," the major said. She hadn't said a word since going down under the shrimp. Now she wrestled to her feet, the only one besides Sally with the nerve to be noticed. She was almost a uniform gray, covered in dust stuck to a wash of guts. Only her eyes showed color, a fierce green surrounded by red. "We look like a bunch of frightened mice."

"Don't you think that's for good reason?" Childress spat.

"Yes!" the major groaned. "We've every reason to fear, every reason to hide, to run away. None of us were trained for this, none but maybe her." She tossed her chin at Sally, who still stood placidly among them. "But it's like this, fellas. It's simple as shit. That thing over there has come into our world. It's busted in through our front door. And it has friends behind it. Now which of you hard-assed bastards would run away from a punk in your house?"

Nobody said a word. Street stared into each agent's eyes, daring him.

"The marshals can't hold it forever," Sally said.

"D." The major's tone had taken on steel. Her commands were clipped, compliance expected. "Take that wounded man out of here. Take the technicians with you. Stay with them." She tore a pistol from her vest and another from her thigh, passing them to the agent. "These are packed with non-lethal rounds. Use them on anyone not in their right mind. You got it? Stay with the civilians."

While DeBoy moved to obey, the major turned toward the monster. "Voice. Grace. Childress. You're with me. Top, give Childress one of your devices. Voice, you get one from me. We're going monster hunting."

The marshals massed a number of staff blasts that hit the beast like a brick hits a bar fighter. The thing fell over, landing on one knee, taking out the entire far wall before it regained its balance.

"You know, you people are still wanted criminals," Childress complained as he took the proffered device.

"Is there a point to that comment?" Street slapped a device into the Voice's hand. "Because we're on a schedule."

"Just sayin'."

"Understood. Set 'em up. Voice and I'll take the far picket. You guys plant yours over here. We'll make the center that pile of shrimp guts by that girder over there. See it? He just stepped on it. Make sure you're far enough out to include the lightning post in the kill zone."

"What is this shit?" Childress asked, turning the device over in his hands.

"Don't worry about it," Grace said before the major could respond. "I'll make sure he does all right."

Street trained her eyes on Sally, that center of calm in a storm. "You good, Blondie?"

Sally's eyes barely focused on the major. "God will redeem my soul from the power of the grave."

"Great. I take that as a yes."

Sally gave her a thumb's up.

That was all they needed. DeBoy moved his people. The Voice of the City had already dived into the wreckage around the fight. The major, tired, bloody, drenched in the guts of her enemy, gave Grace a single nod of her head and staggered into clouds of dust, falling ceiling, and harm's way.

Chapter Twenty-eight

It was one thing to pretend at heroism and fortitude, it was another to scurry over falls of concrete, steel, and drywall while nursing a torn-up shoulder. Fiona staggered at the edge of the field of battle, maintaining as much as possible a three-point contact within the debris. She streamed sweat, her disgusting patina of shrimp guts and dust sliding over her skin in sour bubbles. Her shoulder throbbed. She felt wetness beneath her brace, and she knew the source to be more than perspiration. She had to push, to accomplish soonest what she claimed she would do because she didn't have long in the game.

She cringed behind a jagged chunk of drywall as someone tumbled airborne into the wall behind her. The wizard-looking guy, the one with the pointy hat. He had to be seventy years old. Slamming into that wall must have broken every bone in his body. She hesitated, judging her own depleting resources, but diverted to the old man to check if he was okay.

He rubbed his head and moaned against the wall, but already started back to his feet when Fiona arrived at his side.

"That was quite a hit," she called over the riot of crashing, blasting, and roaring. "Maybe you should sit the rest out."

The old man snorted at the suggestion and thrust out his hand as if reaching for something. From nowhere Fiona could discern, his gnarled staff flew through the air to land with a clap in his grip. "We did not come here to 'sit the rest out,' young lady. We have a calling to defend the law and we will do no less than that." He spoke in a deep, tremulous voice with a smooth British accent. She might have been talking to Ian McKellen.

"Can you beat it?" Fiona asked, holding onto the man's arm as he straightened, though he clearly felt no need for assistance.

Another snort, as if she asked a stupid question. "Of course not, but we can hurt it enough that it might leave on its own. Now that would be something. Excuse me, miss, for I'm obligated to kick this thing's arse, or my name is not Merlin."

Merlin?

He stomped back into the battle, where the gigantic, tentacle-headed monster had torn loose a gallery loaded with mangled server cabinets and heaved it onto the Asian guy, the toga woman, and one of the little alien dudes. They combined bursts from their weapons and blew the makeshift blunt instrument to bits, those bits projecting outwards to punch basketball-sized holes through the few remaining walls.

At that point, the machine room was little more than a gladiator pit surrounded by rubble. The monster's upper body showed bright in the afternoon sun, but its lower quarters and the wreckage of the building lay swathed in shadow except around the orange pillar. As Fiona re-focused on her skirt of the kill zone, she experienced a memory of old Sinbad movies, of Ray Harryhouse or whatever his name was and his high-contrast monster scenes in '60s stop motion. This was a monster movie. Watch for tumbling boulders and sword-wielding skeletons.

She closed her eyes for a second and shook her head. She was getting loopy. Her shoulder leaked like a punctured gas can. Not much time before she ran out of fuel.

"Grace set," she heard in her ear. "Childress is just about set."

A black, clawed fist slammed the floor fifteen feet away. Dust flew, rubble shifted, and Fiona stumbled to fall onto her side, the absolute wrong side.

Her damaged shoulder struck a pile of concrete and girders, sending an electric shock of agony to blow out her brain. It nearly succeeded. She saw spots, tasted blood, felt wave after wave of spasming, burning muscle. She lost her ability to breath for a second, opening and closing her mouth like a stunned fish. She could no longer feel her entire left side.

And yet, she gritted her teeth, grasped her bad shoulder protectively with her good hand, and lurched back to her feet. She groaned. She pushed a hot breath between her teeth, and she took one wobbly step toward… Where? What was she trying to do?

"The Voice of the City is set," a basso voice said into her ear.

Yes. That was it. A few dozen strides to that spot beneath the tumbled gallery, in the shadow of the one partially remaining wall. She took another step. Another. With each step and locomotive puff of breath, her head cleared, her legs found stability, and she at least could pretend she found strength. She willed herself forward, faster, scrubbing one hand across her eyes to try and clear the persistent spots. A few more feet, a few more feet, then she could lie down and die.

When Fiona had almost reached her destination, Sinfonee Rodriguez stepped into her path.

"Where are you going?" she asked, her voice deceptively small, lost, so much like the living Sinfonee.

The voice made Fiona hesitate. By the time she broke that spell of surprise and snatched a pistol from its thigh holster, Sinfonee had her by the wrist and neck, grinning like a snake.

"Did you think that I forgot your insults?" She squeezed Fiona at the wrist, forcing her hand to open and let the pistol fall. "Did you think I would waste vengeance on a bloodmatch fought with fist and claw?"

Fiona couldn't have answered if she had a response ready. The iron grip at her neck threatened to cut off her breathing as well as speech.

Sinfonee jerked Fiona's face to within inches of her own. "You mentioned something of performance anxiety. Are you feeling some for yourself just now?" Her eyes showed relaxed self-satisfaction, a frightening expression matched to the grin. It was so un-Sinfonee-like. The otherworldly angel who had snared Hostetter's heart could not have enjoyed the suffering of others.

Sinfonee manhandled Fiona onto a pile of concrete and girders. Forced along like a rag doll, Fiona staggered up the pile until she hung from Sinfonee's clawed grip at least ten feet above the shattered floor. From there, through her reddening, darkened vision, Fiona watched the battle as from a front-row theater seat.

Shrimp ringed the contest, swarming against the invisible barrier that held them out of the melee. The black beast with the tentacle head, one-armed and bleeding puss, swept slabs of concrete at its tormentors. The marshals stumbled about, nearly done out but refusing to fall, still harassing that Nightmare fiend with staff blasts, rifle fire, and the sting of biting blades. Overhead, in the sun, helicopters orbited the octopus head, infuriating the monster with repeated volleys from miniguns. All of it impotent, pointless, ants against anteater.

Fiona saw herself, but it was something out-of-body, strange and impersonal. She saw her body dangling away from the pile of ruination, hanging from her neck, her feet jerking to find ground. She had lost. She was almost dead, and she knew she would be used before her last light went out. What could she do, there at her end, to not burden her friends?

"Cease this rabble!" Sinfonee thundered, her voice shaking dust and pebbles from the last few standing structures. Her monster went still, its fist held high above its head. It ignored the ineffectual brutality of the helicopters.

The marshals, their opponent frozen, gathered themselves and turned toward Sinfonee.

Fiona, feeling the heat of suffocation in her face, slapped at her right leg as if that held a purpose.

Oh, look. There among the broken concrete slabs, not twenty feet away. Oz. He stood atop a ragged chunk of cement, watching Fiona's struggle with serious green eyes. His tail flicked.

"Hostetter!" Sinfonee crowed. "I have yours! You will watch her die!"

The two Hostetters drew together opposite the tableau on the concrete pile. One showed tortured angst on his face. It was too dark for Fiona to tell which one.

"None o' this is necessary," one of the Hostetters said. "All you got to do is go back to where you come from. We won't trail ya. All o' us can win."

"You speak of victory?" Sinfonee shook Fiona like a doll. "You know nothing of what victory is to me."

The marshals all faced Nightmare's skin of slender womanhood. Fiona's slapping hand landed on something she recognized. Yes, recognized. What the hell was it?

"Don't you hurt her," one of the Hostetters begged. "Let her go. She's a friend."

"Why don't you tell us your terms for victory?" the other Hostetter called. Which one… What did it matter?

"My terms?" The laugh beat like drums in Fiona's head. "My terms are simple. You will meet them whether you wish to or not. For I will take this ape female and crush her neck, and you will watch her turn purple in death, thrashing like a snared rabbit for one more breath of air. And when she expires and I've thrown her carcass down, I will rip out the heart of this host you claim to love, to hear her name plaintive on your lips. And when she's pumped her last drop and fallen like garbage, when you've seen all you cherish destroyed before your eyes, when you can know no greater depths of remorse, only then will I crush you into the dirt with my one good fist. That's how we will proceed, Hostetter. Prepare your meager soul."

326

The reptilian marshal snarled. All of them but one Hostetter aimed their staffs at Sinfonee and raised their blades and guns to strike.

Nightmare frowned. "Don't be stupid. Shoot this host down and I'll take another. Perhaps one of you." It turned hateful eyes on the Hostetters. "You two. Step forward."

Unsure what else to do, the two cowboys obeyed, stopping at the base of the rubble pile. AK Hostetter showed a poker face, his stick braced against a slab of fallen ceiling, his assault rifle gripped loosely in the other hand, finger inside the trigger guard. The other Hostetter, Fiona's Hostetter, wore the face of a beaten basset hound, his fingers flexing on stick and rifle.

Nightmare turned Fiona to peer into her eyes.

Fiona, gasping for air she couldn't get, took hold of the thing against her leg and pulled it from its sleeve.

The monster worked Sinfonee into a garish expression of joy. But no joy touched that forced, quivering grin or those dead glass eyes. "I will feel your windpipe crush beneath my fingers."

Feel this first, motherfucker.

Fiona swung the signal cancellation device up and across, banging it hard into Sinfonee's face. She was weak, barely conscious, so she couldn't hurt a self-proclaimed god or even its host by much, but she hit hard enough to startle her enemy, who promptly dropped her like a bag of bees.

Fiona fell. Someone yelled, "Don't shoot her!" Who they referred to, Fiona couldn't tell. She was too busy enduring exploding pain as she landed on her hip against jagged concrete, rolled end-over-end, and came down at last on her infernal damaged shoulder. She tried to scream, but all that emerged was a strangled yelp.

She'd pass out in another few seconds.

But she hadn't dropped the device.

While the Hostetters charged the monster, dragging her off the rubble pile, as the black beast awoke and corded the hawser-like muscles of its arm, Fiona planted the signal canceller and pressed its single button.

"Street! Set!" she gurgled, then fell forward onto her face.

The lightning post flared, roaring like a furnace. Sinfonee screamed. The black beast brought its fist down, but blew away like leaves in the wind before it struck a blow.

The lightning post flickered. It made static-ridden ratcheting sounds like rubbing sheets of corrugated steel. Grace and Childress rushed across the rubble-strewn floor, yelling Fiona's name.

Hostetter -- Fiona's Hostetter -- had dropped his weapons. He held Sinfonee by one elbow, her back to the failing lightning post. "It's done!" he shouted. "Get outta her! Now!" And he thumped the flat of his hand hard against Sinfonee's chest.

Fiona sighed amazement as a cloud of something flew out of the woman, thrown from her by the man who loved her. The cloud, whipping black smoke trails, fell into the lightning post amid a flurry of sparks and crackles.

Fiona saw the last of the monster sucked into the fiery pillar.

She saw the lightning post wink out.

She saw her Hostetter catch his lady as she slumped into his arms.

Then, she saw no more.

Epilogue One

Fiona fought for consciousness in an ebb and flow of dark, hazy images. Hostetter leaning near. The rough feel of his fingers on her cheek. Men in uniform, but the crisp whites of EMTs, not the rumpled camouflage of soldiers. Childress holding one of his arms close to his filthy shirt. "If you're gonna avoid capture, you better do it now," he said to Grace. "He's on his way." The bright pain of sunlight. The jumbled overhead of the Manta jet. Where was Sally's car?

Fiona opened her eyes to harsh, white light. She squeezed them closed again, then squinted through lashes until the light stopped hurting. Above her, fluorescent tubes hummed within white recesses in a white ceiling. She turned her head to the right and found medical monitoring equipment and a Lego-kit-looking robot checking her blood pressure. A flutter of paper. She turned to the left and found a huge white dressing covering her shoulder. Beyond the dressing, Sally sat in a straightback chair, legs crossed. She leafed through a Cosmo magazine. She seemed unconcerned, waiting her turn at the beauty salon, showing only passing interest in the magazine. Sally seemed different from the last time Fiona saw her. She seemed smaller, more flesh and less stone. She was also clean, rested, and wearing new jeans and a Keb' Mo' tee shirt. So, time had marched on after Fiona passed out.

Fiona was developing a habit of waking up in strange places, though this one wasn't exactly strange. The stark décor of the Voice's medical room was depressingly familiar.

"Hey," she croaked.

Sally kept thumbing through the magazine. "Hiya."

Something landed at Fiona's feet. She knew what it was. Oz's little paws kneaded the blankets between Fiona's calves as he settled into a companionable nap,

"Did we win?" Fiona asked.

"Matter of debate." Sally folded the Cosmo and held it in clasped hands. She rotated in her chair and leaned toward Fiona. "It's now five days since our fun trip to the west coast. The news media is still bananas. Oh my, monsters are real, the sort of panic folks like us went through a long time ago. Umm, you've had two operations on your shoulder and one on your larynx. The robot says don't run off at the mouth too much."

Fiona reached up to touch her neck. Yes, a thin bandage stretched under her chin. Why hadn't she felt it earlier?

"You're still fairly well drugged up," Sally continued. "Grace had out-patient surgery, or what passes for it here. He's resting up in his little gray room like the rest of us fugitives from the law. Hostetter was in a dither about who he'd be sitting with, but he finally, after maybe two seconds, settled on Doctor Rodriguez. She has a gray room, too, after you brained her with that signal cancellation box. Those things are heavy, you know. She had a black eye, a bloody lip, and the whole right side of her face was just, I don't know, ugh!" Sally sighed. "Anyway, Hostetter dotes on her and I got stuck with you. Annnd, the Voice shoved my rental car down a dragon's throat. So much for my damage deposit. Does that about cover things?"

Fiona raised up on her right elbow. The robot backed away from her, taking its pressure cuff with it. A new machine approached brandishing the nipple of its feeder arm.

"Don't even think it," Fiona growled, the threat emphasized by her crusted voice.

Oz backed up the warning with a growl, but his heart wasn't really in it.

"No feeding required," Sally said, and the robot backed away. "Really, Red, it's a machine. You gotta know how to talk to these things." She bent over and retrieved a water bottle from the floor. A straw stuck out of its neck opening. She offered the straw to Fiona, who took a generous sip. "That better? Any questions?"

Fiona scooted to more of a sitting position while the robot arranged pillows at her back. "Yeah. Did we win?"

Sally smirked. "Okay, the big bad went back through its lightning post and hasn't been heard from since. The whole trans-universal blah-blah joint was totaled. I mean, it looked like Godzilla kicked the shit out of it, which, I guess, is kind of what happened."

Fiona lay back on the pillows. "You okay?"

Sally shrugged. "Not a scratch on me. I'd rather be home…"

"You should go. See your little boy."

"Oh, I have, Red. I certainly have. But there's this issue of being a fugitive and all. I figured I should get back here till that blows over."

"Hmm." Fiona closed her eyes. She ached. Everywhere. She gave herself a moment, then looked back at Sally. "You know, like you said. Questions. Just not sure you'll answer them."

"No."

"No?"

"Yes, no. That was not me. It wasn't me with the shrimp shields and the other stuff. Oh, I was there, I was home, but I was, I don't know, out on the back patio listening to the doorbell ring while somebody else got the door. Does that make sense?"

"Umm, was that God?"

Sally sat back in her chair. She tapped the magazine against her knees. "To tell the truth, I've no idea. Maybe. Or maybe he farms out this sort of thing. I'm just a tool, maybe a weapon. I don't get told all that much."

"Sip?"

Sally offered the water again. After wetting her throat, Fiona ran her tongue along her dry, chapped lips. "How about those marshals? Was that cool, or what?"

"Yeah. Hostetter rounded up all the flesh-and-blood marshals of the eighteen contiguous universes. At least, all the ones he could find on short notice."

"Eighteen, huh. I counted twelve."

A sly grin crept onto Sally's face. She opened her magazine and lazily turned its pages. "Well, not really. Twelve fleshies, Red. Did you catch what that other Hostetter said? Thirteen marshals. Twelve of them flesh-and-bone, one not so much."

Fiona blinked. "Are you telling me that God is a marshal?"

"I've been asking that question for the last five days, but he won't give me an answer."

"Blondie, sometimes I'm not sure you're all the way there."

"Then you aren't paying very close attention. Speaking of marshals, I got to meet every one of them. Did you know one is Merlin?"

"I believe he introduced himself."

"They all did. When I heard that one guy was Merlin, I expected a whole cast of big names. Kublai Khan, Athena or maybe Hera… Those two alien guys were a hoot. They have the same name, apparently, both called William Shelton. And they were butt naked and didn't think anything of it." She laughed, a quiet, easy release. "The lizard guy, holy cow! I guess he was on our side, but he said over and over that he would kill us all slowly and eat our flesh. The other Hostetter said it was a compliment." She looked up from her magazine and squinted her eyes at a memory. "When we met, he said I was worthy. Then he said 'My fangs in your throat!' and that was a compliment, too. Like, I don't know, I was good enough to eat."

"The other Hostetter…"

Sally huffed. "He's kind of a dick. Not a fan of Jews. Or black people. Or anybody else."

Fiona squirmed. Her bandaged shoulder disapproved of her position. "Umm, did they square things with the authorities, being marshals and all?"

"I guess you missed the part about being fugitives."

That brought Fiona low. It was bad enough laid up with a bullet wound. It was bad enough that she would always be that super spy who got chicken-necked by a hundred-and-ten-pound autistic Barbie. Now she was a criminal after having saved the world, and her people were, too.

"I need to get out of this bed," she grumbled.

"Not for three-to-six weeks, according to the Voice. And when you do, you've a ton of physical therapy scheduled."

"But, that's it? I mean, is it any worse?"

"No more swimsuits for you, girl."

Fiona slumped into her pillows.

"All right, all right." Sally put down the magazine. She leaned over and took the hand on Fiona's damaged side. "Look, maybe swimsuits, okay? Full-body types, at least with sleeves. Or a SCUBA suit."

"You aren't helping."

"Some guys think scars are a turn-on."

"Still not helping."

"Sorry, Red. I'm no good at this. It makes no difference anyway. It isn't like you can go out in public. Your buddies at the NSA would find you out in a hot minute and give you a bullet bouquet."

"Well." Fiona closed her eyes again. "That'll have to change."

For a long time, neither of them spoke. Fiona drifted toward sleep by the time Sally broke the silence. "You know, I was wondering a thing or two myself."

"Huh?" Fiona flinched back to full wakefulness. Her shoulder let her know its displeasure.

"I watched you from across that building, when Sinfonee held you like a broken doll. And I was wondering then and I wonder now, how did you know to go for that device?"

Oz stirred. The soothing vibration of his purrs ceased.

"Excuse me?"

"You went for that signal cancellation device like you had all your wits and you weren't being strangled." Sally rose from the chair. She headed slowly across the room, slapping the magazine against one leg. "I mean, you were red-faced as a beet and gasping for air. But you grabbed that device and brought it up and smacked Sinfonee with it like it was nothing. Are you really that bad-ass?"

Fiona tried to settle back into her pillows. "Yep, I guess. I'm really that bad-ass."

"Really." Sally turned a squint on Oz, then rolled the magazine tightly and heaved it at Fiona's head.

Fiona struck out a hand and caught the flapping projectile without looking.

"Uh-huh." Sally accepted the Cosmo back, grinning widely. "And how do you account for being that good? Clean living and practice?"

"Sip?"

Sally reached down for the water. She brought the straw to Fiona's lips.

"Nobody can know," Fiona said. "If nobody knows, we might have a way back to normal, or some kind of normal. Colonel Sanders knows that my implant was fried. He knows that Oz and I can't commune."

"But you can. You just did."

"Sure, but the colonel doesn't know that. The implants *are* fried. The thing is, I have Oz in my head anyway. The tie is stronger than ever."

"But how? Without your implant, what you're saying is impossible."

"Says the lady who talks with God and moves things with her mind."

"Okay. So there's that."

Fiona frowned. "I don't know what's up. A couple of days ago, back when Hostetter saved us in Maryland, we went into a lightning post." She licked her lips. "Clay said nobody comes out of a lightning post right. Maybe that was it. Maybe." She turned her head and searched for Sally's eyes. "If the colonel gets a whiff that the neural link still works, he won't rest until I'm in the ground. He sees me as unstable, as a national security risk. Right now, not so much. I'm just another washed up agent. But with the rest of it… It would be his job to kill me."

"I can see how that might be awkward." Sally leaned on the edge of the bed. She brought her face close to Fiona's. "So, how long have you known? You've been keeping this from your friends? When they might have depended on it?"

Fiona shook her head. "No. I didn't know, not until the battle, and I wasn't sure then. Maybe Oz was sure, but not me. I only know it's true because I know how he feels right now."

"And how does the wonder cat feel right now?"

Fiona smiled, a tentative, shaky thing. "Confident," she said. "And home."

Epilogue Two

The three government cars crunched over snow to the open steel door at Eastgate Mall. Snow melted down the windshield of Sanders's car, the second in line. The wipers dashed it away with a heavy splash, clearing the view ahead once more. Sanders frowned. She'd altered the arrangements for the meeting. Good girl. He would have, too.

The doors of the first car opened and a full load of men stepped into the cold and took a critical look around. These weren't just any NSA bricks, though they kept to the tradition of dark sunglasses and dark suits unbuttoned at the jacket. Two of the four were Fiona Street's people. DeBoy and Childress stood in identical black overcoats, inspecting the weeds breaking in lines through the snow. They watched the rusted door, the peeling paint on the wall, and the giant, two-legged tables of the solar collectors to the south. Then Childress nodded to Sanders's car.

The colonel exited into the snow, followed by Goodknight. Both wore their Army undress uniforms with dark overcoats open to reveal flashes of ribbons and brass. The driver and shotgun also debarked, flashing not awards, but the visible straps of shoulder holsters across the white shirts of their suits.

The third car released its human cargo, four big men who drifted toward the trunk, plus one balding, frowning doctor clutching an aluminum suitcase. The doctor crunched his shiny Oxfords ahead to the colonel's side. He looked odd in that company. At least Sanders and Goodknight had uniforms to complement the suits of their security detail. The doctor's black trousers met a finely knitted gray sweater under a bulky parka.

"I don't like this." Dumas said, his eyes darting beneath the fading line on his temple where the stitches had been. "She said she'd meet us here, not at some open door to an abandoned mall. Who knows what's through that door?"

"Don't worry, doctor," Sanders said. "You're protected here."

Doors slammed. The bricks in back came forward, each with a submachine gun held ready at his waist. Childress had gone to the open doorway and returned to the colonel with a rumpled sheet of paper sporting a paint-flecked tongue of packing tape. He showed the paper to Sanders.

"What's it say?" Dumas asked, leaning into the colonel's view.

Sanders elbowed him out of his space. "It says to go on in. There's an arcade a short distance to one side. We're to move to the back of it where an elevator door is held open. The elevator only takes five and will accommodate only one round trip." He sighed, glancing around at his people. "Doctor, Goodknight, you're with me. Childress, you and one other man, your choice. The others remain topside with their eyes and ears open."

"Yes, sir." Childress signaled DeBoy.

They met no incident entering the building, nor at the elevator they found in the shop. The ride down seemed to take an age and when the door opened, they found the exit blocked by a huge bag of muscles in a black, form-fitting athletic suit, combat boots, and a strange, visored helmet. His already rocky appearance bulged with weaponry down to the multi-barrel launchers encircling his wrists. The Voice of the City looked the men up and down, frowning disapproval.

"Move, or be moved," Sanders said, nonchalant, when he stepped to within a few inches of the towering vigilante.

The Voice growled deep in his throat. "Follow me," he said.

So they followed him through the cavernous hangar where the black manta aircraft hummed on idling fanjets, its ramp down. The ship was loaded to the overhead with crates of various sizes, all tied down under taut cargo nets.

Sanders and his team followed the Voice into a bunker bordering the hangar, then along a rabbit's warren of gray halls until they came to a white room. Its walls were punctured by electronics jacks, the only other thing in the chamber a medical bed centered on the empty floor. Fiona Street leaned against the bed, rubbing her left shoulder.

"Colonel Sanders," Street said, nodding a businesslike greeting. She spared a smile for Goodknight, flashed and quickly extinguished, then nodded in turn to Childress and DeBoy. She looked small in the bright white room, but well. No damage showed past her plaid flannel shirt and loose jeans despite the sniper bullet she'd taken.

"You're full of the cloak-and-dagger," Sanders said as he drew to just beyond arm's reach. "We couldn't just meet in a restaurant?"

Street scrunched up her face at that. "Well, sir, it's like this. We seem to have a history of snipers, knife fights, and surprise over-the-top weaponry. I thought that might put people off their lunch. Also, my turf, so double win."

"How's the shoulder?"

"Twinges a bit. My medical program says I'll be out of therapy soon, though I might have stiffness for years." She spared a look to her former teammates, offering them a hesitant smile. "I'm sorry about Tejada and Ponce. Messed up, what happened to them."

Childress canted his head toward her. DeBoy did nothing.

"You realize this place is covered by more than my men at the door," Sanders said. "You're a fugitive from the law. You won't get out of here without my say."

Street watched the colonel for a few seconds, then looked askance to the Voice of the City. "Leave us," she said. "You have work to do."

"Are you sure that's wise?" the Voice asked.

"Quite."

He left her alone with the colonel and his people. She hopped onto the bed, legs dangling over one side. "That's what we're here to talk about, sir. I hope we can come to a mutually beneficial understanding."

Sanders clasped his hands in front. "What kind of understanding did you have in mind?"

"Well, first of all, the perceived threat is that interfacing with the cat makes me unbalanced and therefore untrustworthy. It also makes me more than your people can handle. That's why I asked you to bring the doctor and his stuff." She lay back on the bed. "Doctor Dumb-- Dumas, could you check my implant for functionality?"

"We know about your implant," Sanders said. "We fried it with an EMP."

"I just want you to have no doubt, sir. Doubts are hazardous to my health."

Sanders gestured to the doctor, who approached the bed and opened his case on the floor. Inside, a laptop and diagnostic tools nestled in gray foam.

"You still haven't specified a kind of agreement," Sanders went on.

"One where you go your way and I go mine, and there's no hard feelings," Street said.

"Hmmph! That would be a trick. Half my staff is nursing various aches and pains because of you. The credibility of my department has suffered." He shrugged as if tired. "However, I don't relish continued confrontation, especially considering your friends lately."

Doctor Dumas, squatting beside the bed, started his computer and fiddled at Street's neck with a thin screwdriver-like tool.

"I'll resign my commission," Street said, staring at the ceiling. "It's the least you might expect. And I'll not work in any intelligence capacity for as long as you decide."

"That would be the rest of your life," the colonel said. "And no, you don't get the easy way out. You'll get an Other Than Honorable discharge."

Street snapped her eyes to him, lines creasing her forehead.

"Hold still," the doctor warned her.

"Take it or leave it," Sanders said. "I can always go worse."

"And my people?"

"They aren't your people."

"They certainly aren't yours. These are civilians, most of them. And you've hunted them, sir, threatened their lives--"

"As any criminals should be treated."

"They won't work for you, sir. But they will work for me, even if I work for you."

Sanders grimaced. He put his hands in the pockets of his overcoat. "You just proposed you'll have no more association--"

"That's my intent, but you may need us. Did you meet the marshals? Did you talk to them? There's a world of shit out there, sir. You'll need every gun you can get."

"What are you suggesting?"

The doctor opened the tiny door that was the diode covering Street's implant. He ran a cable from his computer to a receptacle that had hidden beneath the door.

"I'll take that discharge, sir. I guess it's only fair. And I'll keep my people together and continue the search for others, reporting to you in any way you like. But my people are free. Sally Reiser, the Voice, and Hostetter are free and clear."

"I could arrange that. I can't touch Hostetter anyway. Some sort of cockamamie inter-universal diplomatic immunity…"

"And Grace."

"Sergeant Grace was insubordinate. He doesn't get a pass on that."

"Sir, he has fifteen years of experience you do not want to lose."

The colonel stared at her. He showed no judgement, no calculation. He refused to give her anything. Finally, he raised an eyebrow. "I'm inclined to discharge him the same as you, but maybe he could be asked to not re-enlist when his term is up."

"I think he'd prefer to make it to retirement."

"So would a lot of NCOs. We'll see how clean he keeps his nose, but this will go down in his next evaluation. Anything else?"

"Short."

"What's short? I don't understand."

Childress offered an explanation. "She means that CIA puke we locked up, the one who spread around the holographic shit so Street could watch the facility, sir."

Sanders groaned. "I thought you had him on a conspiracy charge."

"Well, yeah, that was convenient. But I guess he helped out, when it comes down to it. Without his engagement, we might--"

Street cleared her throat.

"--*she* might not have set up the monster to get sent back to its world. He kind of helped, sir."

"Plus," Street added, "he's the spook of spooks. How long you think the CIA would let you keep him in any event?"

Sanders looked away from everyone, staring off into a corner. Then he drew his hands from his coat pockets and spread his palms in surrender. "Fine. Give the spook the boot. What more do you want, Street? The fillings in my teeth?"

"I'm not exactly making out in this," she replied.

The doctor disconnected from her implant and coiled away his cable.

"What's the verdict, doctor?" Sanders asked. "Are things as expected?"

Dumas closed his case, stood, and returned with his equipment to Sanders's side. "The implant is definitely non-operational. From what I can tell from a visual examination, the circuits may also be fused."

"Is there any chance it can be repaired?"

The doctor shook his head. "No. Totally destroyed. It would have to be replaced."

"What about back-engineering? If the Russians or the Chinese got hold of it--"

"They'd be frustrated by melted circuits. There's nothing they could gain by dissecting Major Street's head."

Street sat up in the bed. "How about the cat? Do you need to see his implant?"

The doctor stared at her, thinking about that. "No," he finally said. "The cat's implant is undoubtedly in the same condition. I think these devices are a non-issue, colonel."

Street gave Sanders a meaningful look.

"So." Sanders rubbed his chin. "You're asking cancellation of the standing kill order, amnesty for your friends, and a continued career path for your former sergeant. In return, you accept discharge and a prohibition against working in our field until the time I call you back into service."

"And I'm no more a threat than any retired or cashiered agent."

"And I can find you at any time should you break the terms of our deal."

"And anyone you send to find me will have a mondo bad day."

Sanders continued rubbing his chin. "What are your thoughts, gentlemen?"

"I say let her go," DeBoy said immediately. "She saved our lives."

"Yeah, there's that," Childress said. He had a hangdog look, like he didn't want to hear the words he spoke. "I say cut her loose. It'd just be a problem to keep her on, what with discipline and shit. And to kill her? Well, she did just save the world, sir."

Sanders looked at him sideways. "It could be argued that all she did was shoot up a barrel full of seafood, that others, in fact, actually saved the world."

"But that would just be political bullshit, sir. This woman, she's a pain in the ass and off the rails as fuck, but she's the real deal. We owe her more than a kick in the teeth."

"Gee, thanks," Street mused.

"It was nothin'," Childress said.

"Doctor?" Sanders asked.

"She needs evaluation," Dumas said. "Her exposure to the implant technology may have damaged her normal cognitive framework. She may suffer anything from depression to paranoid dissociative--"

"As does half our retirement list," the colonel interrupted, "and without super powers, that's manageable." He spread his palms again. "You have a deal, Street. But I will have eyes on you every second."

Street lowered herself from the bed. "Thank you, sir. I'll feel so comforted that you're watching over me. Now, guys, you'll need to leave. The Voice has put a dolly in the elevator. It's loaded down with the hard drives and papers we, umm, borrowed from your vault. Up, out, and minimum safe distance of at least a hundred meters. You can keep the dolly." She made to usher them to the door.

The colonel's brow knitted. "What's this?" he said. "I expected to study this facility--"

Street waved her arms to gently herd them into the hall. "You're welcome to do just that, sir. The Voice won't mind. But in maybe five minutes this place will experience a controlled demolition that will flatten or flash burn anybody wandering its innards. So I wouldn't recommend that course of action."

"But, what--"

"You wouldn't find it interesting, sir. Why, I asked the Voice about this place just the other day. You know what he called it? His secondary base of operations. *Secondary*. Like a parking space you rent downtown versus your garage."

Fiona escorted them back to the elevator. Of the group, only DeBoy and Goodknight offered her goodbyes, Goodknight with a tight hug and a kiss on the cheek. "Since you aren't an officer anymore," she said.

When the elevator door closed and the car started up, Fiona hurried for the Manta. She rushed up the ramp, squeezed along the narrow space left between crates and jump seats, and joined the others at the cockpit area.

"Did they take you seriously about the kablooie procedure?" Sally asked from the passenger seat. She held Oz in her lap, scratching under his chin.

"I hope so," Fiona said, squirming close to Hostetter on what remained clear on the main deck. "Otherwise, we'll have a lot of explaining to do. Everybody settled in?" She grinned at Hostetter, who frowned at her through his bushy moustache. He looked uncomfortable with a woman pressed near him.

"Miss Fiona, this here ain't proper."

"It'll have to stand in for proper, Clay. Shit's packed in this boat so tight, you can't even lower a jump seat."

"But it ain't proper, Miss Fiona. Miss Sinfonee..."

Street snuggled up close to him like a cat hunting for pets. "I won't tell if you don't."

Hostetter looked horrified. He leaned hard against the crates behind him.

"Oh, lighten up, buddy," Fiona purred. "It's just for ten minutes. Then you can have the Voice's prisoner seat after we drop off Blondie."

"Long as you get the dropping off Blondie part right," Sally said. "After all, I don't have a car anymore, not since our hero here shoved it down a dragon's throat."

"You will be compensated," the Voice said, and pressed the button to raise the ramp.

"Will my credit rating be compensated?" Sally petted Oz from head to haunches. He pushed against her hand.

"I have multiple off-shore accounts."

"So where ya going, cowboy?" Fiona asked Hostetter. She leaned against his chest and flared her nostrils to take in his scent.

"Miss Fiona!"

She laughed. He was such a fuddy-duddy.

"Miss Sally, you stop pattin' that cat this minute."

Sally looked up at Hostetter, puzzled. Then she noticed Fiona and figured it out. "Oh! Sorry."

Fiona leaned as far away from Hostetter as she could, which was only a few inches. "Oh boy, I'm sorry, too." She hadn't seen it happening. Her new bond with Oz would take some getting used to. "But where?" she asked the cowboy. "You could've gone off to play with your friends, especially the William Shelton twins. They were cute."

"I reckon I'll go to my Sinfonee. She didn't take what happened too well."

"I can imagine, though I can't really know. What goes on in her head… She's different, Clay. Take care of her."

"I do my best, Miss Fiona."

"Hey, Voice!" Sally released Oz onto the main deck. "Can we get a move on here? I'd like to see my kid before he graduates from high school."

"The bay doors are opening. We will be airborne in moments."

"Airborne." Street laid her head against Hostetter's shirt. He flinched, but settled when she went no further. "Airborne home. To family, to a loved one. What about you, Voice? Who do you go home to?"

"I go to watch over the defenseless and the true. I am the Voice of the City."

"Oh. Okay."

Hostetter, hesitating, lowered a hand to Street's shoulder. He stroked her hair. "You ain't learned nothin', have you? It don't matter who you goin' to--"

"It just matters that you go. See? I listen. It would still be nice to have somebody waiting."

Oz meowed at her feet.

"Oh, okay, but you don't count."

Moments after Sanders left the building with his party, the channel for their in-ear radios came alive.

"Station 1 here, we have movement. Movement in the east parking area."

"Station 2, confirming. You won't believe this, but the parking lot's splitting down the middle. It's opening up. A stretch of seventy meters or better."

"Station 1 and 2," Childress said into his pickup. "You aren't makin' a whole lot of sense. What do you mean--"

A machine whine flowed over the mall, accompanied by the deep grumbling of firing jets. Childress looked up, past the roofline of the mall, and sighed.

A black aircraft shaped like a manta ray rose into the air while the radio stepped on itself to report.

"Black jet--"

"--out of the ground--"

"--closing back up--"

The jet held a hover at probably fifty feet. The colonel watched it. The other agents watched it. Goodknight watched it with a childish grin. Then the ground jolted, causing them all to stagger. Two more tremors, then a long roll of vibrations like mud flowing down a hillside. Dust and smoke issued from the still-open mall door. When anyone looked up, the ship was gone.

"--parking lot--"

"--collapsed a good couple of feet--"

"--like a crater or something--"

"You want me to put a trace on that ship?" Childress asked as he and the colonel got to the second car. "Satellite's overhead, so we can get a vector and follow it to its destination."

The colonel gave him a disappointed sneer. "Is that what you think we can do, Agent Childress? You think we can track that jet?"

"Well, not if we stand around with our hands in our pockets, no, sir."

The colonel actually laughed. It was a small laugh, full of knowledge. He knew who the joke was on. He patted Childress's shoulder. "Son, it's cold out here. Hands in our pockets is a very good idea. In fact, I'll go one better. I'll settle down into my car here and just sit on my hands to warm them up. Why don't you do the same."

They loaded up. By the time the last car pulled onto the road and pointed toward the airport, sirens wailed in the distance, drawing ever closer.

Epilogue Three

A landscape of black, pitted rock rolls beneath a sky choked with stars. Cosmic clouds stretch from horizon to horizon, red suns exploding within, forcing the vaporous particles of creation into sharp coronas of translucent mass. An orange flash tears into the curtain of reality, and roiling black flame, the living smoke, smashes to the ground in thunder, quakes, and an explosion of glassy rock shards. Nightmare screams. It shudders with fury. Its smoky tentacles thrash outward, smiting the earth, the shallow, oily seas, and any living thing. An entire universe cringes from its own heart of terror. The very land attempts to crawl away, the skies to fly apart, rather than touch hatred at its most malignant.

Across the pitch, gouged land, past tar puddle seas breaking on razor rock beaches in blasts of methane flame, beyond forests of gnarled, quivering trees that whisper and curse the souls of them that walk, a palace of azure quartz rises in splendid crackling booms of sweet, growing agony. Starlight refracts and magnifies in the quartz, radiating inward to light the grand halls. And the people come, people of all description, also the people who are not people at all. They mill, excited, wondering what new doom falls over them like a shroud.

Nightmare has fallen, their greatest general, their most heinous despot. Their trusted protector, the soul of murder. Nightmare has fallen, ejected from its noble sojourn into the world of the devils. Will the fiends come for all the World next? Are they done toying with the denizens of the World and now will strike with merciful, violent genocide? Nightmare has fallen. Who will rise?

The White One listens from the Dais of Dreams, centered in the focused starlight of the palace. The White One who sent Nightmare into battle, who has shimmered with regret ever since. The White One lounges below the heads of its people, below the black-uniformed soldiers with faces stretched close to their skulls. Below the innocent princesses in vibrant, satin gowns as fluid as water and as sparkling as flames. Below the heads of unicorns, the men with wings, the cars with fins, and the snakes. But not below the souls forever falling. The White One lounges and listens to fear and panic, and has enough.

It rises. Tight trews meeting boots of soft hemp. A many buttoned blouse of richest, flowing satin embroidered with tiny, swirling figures de-

341

noting the White One's lineage. The flowing cloak with its voluminous hood, now laid back to reveal the angled artistry of that wise, ageless, sexless face, that face that rules in humble subjection, that loves, but knows no joy. That white face, whiter than purity, whiter than the bellies of deep-roving fish. That face with hair shorn close to the scalp, standing straight up from the electrified wisdom blasting from within. All white, from hair to soles, all white but the deep, glacial green of the White One's eyes. Slim, muscled, graceful, strong, confident, demurring, magnificent in androgyny, the White One stands.

"We see now the folly of sending a warrior to fight our war," the cadenced voice intones, its melodies rich with hope, its tone the breast of mother, its words the sorrow of fate. "It was always thus, but no other avenue fell to us, until now."

Until now? Has some redemption been granted? Has some plan or savior come forth of late that might surely save the World from its end? What destiny is this of which the White One speaks? What poor hope to cling to? What shred of courage to fling at the devils beyond?

"All must understand what visions have come to us of late, visions not possible before the fall of Nightmare. See what has transpired in the world of those wicked? See what hope germinates in our care?"

A weapon! A hero! A plague to send outward to those who defile the World!

"It is a simple thing, that when the oppressors learned of their enmity toward us, they sought to make amends."

The shouts for answers cease. The faces turn puzzled, unsure what to say.

"Look upon the vision. A machine was sent to the depths of their world to arrest the disease that afflicts us. And for a moment, the oppressors showed mercy."

What does the White One mean? What does it say? The oppressors, the evil ones, the senders of plagues, for a few moments only, lifted their boot from the neck of their victim? Is that all there is to hold to, the justice of murderers?

"No. There is more to these people beyond the veil. There is more to them than we or they understand. We have seen it; they show mercy. We have also seen that they are strong of spirit but weak of knowledge. I see that they do not know their crimes."

Then show them their crimes! Send their crimes back to them!

"That is foregone. Their horrors reflect upon them even as they descend upon us. But they would cease their bombardment if only we helped them to find the means. Therefore, I go to the land of devils. I go there to learn and to offer my labor."

Labor? The White One will enslave itself to the fiends? Are we then to surrender and allow their basest whims to befall us?

"No. Again, no. We do not cross the veil to surrender. We do not cross to give up what is ours. We go to find allies. We go to find answers. We go … to offer help."

The White One has spoken. The White One raises its hood to cover all its features. Then, as the assembled debate the sanity of the plan, the White One sinks once more to the floor, to listen, and to brood. "The world is dark and full of dreams, dark and full of dreams…"

For it is seen and known, if the people beyond cannot save the World, then they cannot hope to save themselves.

THE END

FIONA STREET and SALLY REISER
will return in
VOICE OF THE CITY

Find other breakneck thrillers by
Stephan Michael Loy
at **smloy.net**